About the author

Francesca O'Hare was born and raised in Manchester, on the Blue side. She set up camp in Ibiza in 2009 and forgot to go home. She has many titles and guises: dream weaver, fairy and Angel worshiper, bonjepreneur, raconteur, to name but a few... but her favourite of all is that of Mamma to Zephyr, Oro and the furry contingency of the circus that have chosen her.

AN INVITATION FROM THE TRUTH FAIRY

Francesca O'Hare

AN INVITATION FROM THE TRUTH FAIRY

Vanguard Press

VANGUARD PAPERBACK

© Copyright 2020
Francesca O'Hare

A CIP catalogue record for this title is
available from the British Library.

ISBN 978 1 784657 18 5

*Vanguard Press is an imprint of
Pegasus Elliot MacKenzie Publishers Ltd.*
www.pegasuspublishers.com

First Published in 2020

**Vanguard Press
Sheraton House Castle Park
Cambridge England**

Printed & Bound in Great Britain

Dedication

Satya, Thank you for the truth and inspiration xx

For

Joel, Jack, Sam, Lucia, Ruby-Lu, Lara, Mac, Zephyr, Ronny, Aurelia, Oliver, Ella, George, Harry, Ava, Roxy and all of the special children in my life — past, present and those yet to reveal themselves. You are Always Loved!

Anna

Anna took the stairs silently, as always. She had learnt every creak of every board and could now tiptoe quickly and expertly down all sixteen stairs without making a sound — as she did this Tuesday morning and every other morning at six o'clock. She skimmed the hall wall to the end door leading to the kitchen, carefully turning the handle and opening the door towards her. Behind the door two big brown eyes and a wagging tail greeted her expectantly and silently — Hugo knew the game and his silence was rewarded with a huge, silent hug. This was their hour. Mum's alarm clock went off at seven o'clock every weekday morning and from that moment Anna and Hugo's silent peace would be shattered and the torrent of horrible words, pushes, kicks and smacks would begin for another day. So Anna buried her face in the long white shaggy fur and wrapped her arms tightly around Hugo's middle as he put his head on her head and she felt that nice feeling inside her tummy that she only ever felt in "their hour".

The problem was, you see, that Anna was bad. She was "born bad" her mum and dad said — many times a day. In her ten years on Earth Anna had not been able to ever figure out what *exactly* made her bad, as most things she did and said got this reaction, but bad she was. Luckily her little sister Lucy had been born a good girl. She was six and shouted and cried a lot and would often pull Anna's hair and pinch her, but that was OK because good girls can do anything! Anna stayed as quiet as possible at home and she tried so hard to be good, but her badness always came out and meant she had to be punished. Hugo was often bad too, Mum and Dad said. Anna didn't think so — although she never said this to them. She didn't say much at all at home but in school her badness *really* came out! She sneered at the teachers, didn't pay any attention in class, was nasty to the other pupils and hated everybody. That's what bad people do. She had one fellow accomplice in her class — Ethan. Together they made fun of the other children, played pranks on the teachers and laughed at the others when they got something wrong or were sad. Apart from Ethan, Anna had no friends — but bad people don't. At home she had Hugo — who at this moment was breaking free from Anna's grasp and heading for the front door…

"Hu…" Anna clasped her hand to her mouth to stop the word coming out — it was far too early for noise! Oh no, what was he doing?!? She followed him to the door to find him sniffing a shiny, golden envelope. It was too early for the postman. She looked closer and read:

TOP SECRET!

Miss Anna Porter, No 1 Burley Avenue, St Aytas Village, Lancashire

Well that was her! It was November, nowhere near her birthday in April and even then, only Nanna Ratcliffe in Canada ever sent her a card and Mum always opened it first to take out the money inside. Top Secret! What did that mean? Secret from who? She didn't know why but she knew Mum and Dad *must not* see this envelope. Ever.

Taking Hugo by the collar, Anna returned to the safety of the cold kitchen. She crouched down on the black and white tiled floor — which had always reminded her of Grandad's old chess board. *He* hadn't really noticed her badness but he had died when she was four so maybe it hadn't been as obvious then. He used to sit her on his knee and explain to her the roles of all the carved wooden game pieces in the endless battle between the black and white armies — the pawns at the front protecting the more intricate back row of figures, castles and knights and of course the King and Queen. On Saturdays he would let her sit — very quietly beside him — while he and Bob from next-door spent hours thinking a lot and moving very little over big glasses of a strong-smelling brown drink. Anna always did the same on her tiled chessboard — planned how to get through each day against the King and Queen.

She didn't need a clock to tell the time in this hour, she knew the value of every minute. It was twenty to seven. Hugo moved to hide her little frame from the doorway as she turned over the golden envelope. The back was sealed with purple wax — just like in those made up stupid fairy tales — with the stamp of a butterfly indented in the wax. She lifted the wax and slid her tiny fingers under the flap, as it opened golden dust burst from the envelope all over her, Hugo and the tiles! Just at that moment…

"MUMMMMYYY!"

Oh no! Lucy was awake!

"Wait, darling, I'm coming." She heard Mum's gruff morning voice through the ceiling. Anna's heart pounded, it was too early! Mum would be furious, Dad would be worse! She ran to the hall and stuffed the envelope in her satchel — they never looked in there — but oh no, the golden dust! Lucy's crying and Mum's footsteps became louder as they reached the top of the stairs. She ran back to the kitchen door to find the dustpan and brush but the dust had disappeared! Every last twinkle was gone. She stood at the door open-mouthed.

"Anna! Stop lurking in the doorway you bad girl and get out of my way." Mum pushed roughly past her with Lucy in her arms. Lucy pulled her tongue at Anna as they passed. Anna retreated silently back upstairs in amazement. Where had the dust gone? What did the card say? What was going on? She would have to wait until she went to school to find out safely…

Ethan

Squatting on the front-garden path, Ethan gently moved the magnifying glass until it caught the ray of bright November sunlight and made a scorching laser beneath the glass. He moved it slowly and carefully across the crazy paving to the line of marching ants, and...

Zap, zap, zap, zap, zap...

"Ahahahahaha!" Ethan's big tummy wobbled and his chubby shoulders shook with laughter at watching the ants dying one by one. He laughed so hard, in fact, that he lost the laser beam. He looked down on the tiny fried specks on the pavement and saw the *strangest* thing. The line of marching ants who had gone before his victims were returning to the scorched remains of their friends and beginning to carry them along with the rest of the army.

"Stupid ants," said Ethan, "they're dead; and so will you be now... ahahahaha."

He manoeuvred the magnifying glass once again, this time to target the rescuers.

"Oi, Fatty, what are you doing?" boomed a man's voice. Ethan froze. Ely! Oh no! What was *he* doing here? Looking up, he saw the familiar short, wide frame filling the gateway at the bottom of the path. Dressed in his usual combat trousers and jacket, Ely was now taking large strides in his big black army boots towards Ethan. He stopped, bent down and grabbed Ethan roughly by the arm which held the magnifying glass — squeezing too hard.

"I *said*: What are you doing, Fatty?" The boom was now only millimetres away from Ethan's face and he could feel the hot smelly breath of his big brother. He didn't look up.

"Looking at the ants," Ethan whispered.

"What did you say, you, fat horrible creature?" Ely sneered now. "Speak up, stupid, I can't hear you."

Ethan's eyes stung with the threat of tears. Oh no, don't cry in front of Ely, he thought.

"Looking at the ants," he repeated in a tiny voice, as Ely's grip tightened.

"LIAR!" screamed Ely, then in a horribly calm voice, "You were *killing* them. I used to do the same thing when I was young. Looks like you may actually be learning something *finally*. Still *too* fat though boy! I'll have to whip you into shape while I'm on leave. Two weeks training for you, scumbag, now where's *my* mother — I'm *starving*... As you were, boy — kill, kill KILL! Ahahahaha..."

And with that he dropped Ethan's arm and marched into the red front door of the "Old

Rectory" — their grand old house in the middle of St. Aytas Village, next to the church and school of the same name. Ethan looked down at the ants and no longer wanted to play. —Mother was always saying she wished he was more like Ely and Ethan had tried to copy his ways, —but it never made him feel happy inside. Ely had been fifteen when Ethan was born and had until then relished being the only child of the by then elderly vicar and his meek wife. Their "miracle baby" in their fifties had not been welcome news to the spoilt army cadet and Ethan had been made to pay for being born every day thereafter. His only respite had come when Ely joined the army at twenty-one, leaving Ethan alone with just their parents and the fear of Ely's visits.

Ethan had vague memories of Daddy before his voice and movement had been taken by the stroke when Ethan was just three. His voice had been very calm and his words kind, —for all in his beloved church and in the village. He stayed mainly in his room upstairs as Mother now was too old and frail to get him into the wheelchair and out into the garden without help. Ethan often wished he was strong enough to carry him down the grand mahogany staircase and into the beautiful country sunshine. He also wished, right now, he could ask Ely to help him to do just that. Mother spoke very little, and always in a very quiet voice. She prayed a lot — Ethan had often heard her praying to the good Lord for help with the child He had given to her "too late" and to understand why He had prevented her good husband from helping through illness. The Church of England had let them stay in the "Old Rectory" even though Daddy could no longer serve as a vicar. The actual vicar and his wife — a teacher at Ethan's school — lived in a cottage at the back of the garden and visited and prayed with Mother and Daddy regularly. They all prayed for guidance with the problem of Ethan. Ethan was a bully.

That's what they said at St Aytas Primary School; Ethan Jude was a bully. He called children horrible names, he intimidated teachers and dinner ladies alike and at times was violent towards other children and the school pets. He was a bully and this seemed to make everybody angry and upset, — including Ethan himself. But he was just trying to be more like Ely — wasn't that what he was supposed to do? He was very confused about the whole thing and no one wanted to explain anything to him. He was ten and apart from Anna — who was apparently as bad and unkind as him — he had no friends. He had so many things that were bad, as Ely had always pointed out, he could only see the faults in others too. Like that ugly monster in his class, Venus — the girl with the hideously deformed face. And Louis, the boy who didn't speak. They were his and Anna's prime targets, they were weak and never fought back, so they deserved it — just like Ethan with Ely. One day he would be as big as Ely and then he'd show him… maybe.

Ethan's only morning job was to take the post from the box next to the gate and separate it into post for Mother and post for the vicar and his wife, then take it to the correct houses. It was unusually helpful of him, but Mother gave him extra money for sweeties if he did so every morning. This morning he opened the house-shaped post box and immediately saw the golden shiny envelope. Intrigued, he lifted it out and was amazed to see it was addressed to him:

TOP SECRET!

Master Ethan Jude

"The Old Rectory", St, Aytas Village. Lancashire.

Very strange! Confused, he hid the card under his maroon school jumper and after separating and delivering the remaining post, he went to the only safe place in the house to observe a secret — Daddy's room. Ely *never* went in there and Mother would be downstairs after breakfast watching morning TV. Pushing open the heavy wooden door, Ethan met Daddy's sad eyes staring out from the bed.

"Good morning, Daddy," Ethan whispered, even though he knew it was useless as Daddy didn't understand anything now. "I've got a secret letter, look!"

Daddy's face didn't move. As Ethan pulled out the card inside the envelope golden dust burst out all over Ethan and his Daddy...

Venus

Venus blinked open her sleepy green eyes and the mural on her bedroom ceiling came into focus, the beautiful flame-haired roman goddess in swirling golden robes, painted by her godmother, Irene, in honour of her namesake. Venus — the goddess of beauty and love. It had been painted to celebrate the arrival of the beautiful fair-haired baby who had been born ten years ago — the daughter of a devastatingly handsome famous actor and his stunning supermodel wife. Their child, in turn, had been picture perfect and the name Venus was given to her. As her feet touched soft, pink carpet pile, Venus looked around her elaborately decorated bedroom. It really *was* fit for a princess, from the mural above to the billowing white curtains at the head of her carved wooden bed and sash windows, and every piece of pink and crystal in between. It was her mummy you see, she loved beautiful things, Daddy too. They had moved from London when Venus was born to the pretty little village of St Aytas, but Daddy still went to work there when he was "on a job" — he was a television actor and was often in magazines, or on talk shows, or at glamorous parties surrounded by perfect people. He was dark-haired and charming and very, very handsome, but Mummy looked like she could have once been locked away in a tower like that of the pearl white fairy princess castle in the corner. Her waist-length wavy strawberry blonde hair cascaded over her milky skin and surrounded what Venus thought was the most beautiful face she had ever seen. Huge green eyes and a soft pink pout had once made Mummy a supermodel. Venus had been beautiful too — until the accident.

She didn't remember anything about it, she had only been eighteen months old when the boot of their convertible car had caught fire. Mummy and Daddy had got out of the front but their seats had jammed and Venus had been trapped. The firemen got her free barely alive and terribly burned all over, especially her hands and her face. She had been in hospital having lots of skin treatments for two years after that and still had to go back sometimes now. The skin grafts hurt a lot and Venus could only ever see tiny improvements to little bits of herself, but Mummy insisted they keep doing them — she says she won't *ever* give up trying to get her "beautiful baby back". Mummy didn't go to parties anymore. Venus had seen lots of pictures at Irene's house of both her parents laughing and dancing — Mummy always in a beautiful dress with her green eyes shining at the camera. Her eyes were always sad now. She was embarrassed of Venus and Venus knew it. She had never said the words directly to Venus but she had often overheard when Mummy has her "traumas" and the doctor comes round, things like "Who is that monster in my princess's bedroom?" Irene always said that somewhere deep down Venus was probably still beautiful, but Irene was an artist with chimes and Buddha's all over her house and Venus knew that was just silly.

There were no mirrors in Venus' bedroom. She didn't need one. She knew every disfigured millimetre of her poor melted face. She had kept a resemblance of her Mummy's big emerald green eyes, but her skin hung around them strangely making them look wonky. Her original lips and nose had vanished completely in the fire apparently, and their man-made replacements looked smooth and shiny and didn't move much. She had no visible ears. Luckily the same length of strawberry blonde locks made a useful shelter from the world's eyes and, apart from school, Venus wasn't taken out much anyway. But she had seen enough horrified faces and heard enough mortified gasps to know she was hideous to other people. Even her parents never kissed her face — only the top of her hair. Her hands were the most difficult thing to hide. Since the fire her fingers didn't want to be separate anymore, so, —despite four operations, —Venus had clumped together hands, almost always in fists. Learning to write neatly had taken a long time and lots of hot, angry tears, but now she won calligraphy competitions at St Aytas Primary School. And she could paint and draw — beautifully. She drew what she loved — the startling beauty of the night sky.

Most children, Venus had heard, were afraid of the dark. Venus loved the night time! The shadowy light of dusk and the first sightings of the moon, followed by the total illumination of the velvet night sky, as humans are left in darkness below. Making us look up every night to the gigantic universe and gaze at its' wonders. She knew every constellation and planet and looked for hours through the silver telescope at her attic window. Bending down next to the window in the horrid bright light of day, Venus spun her star globe. It, and her telescope, were her two favourite things on this cruel planet and it *was* spectacular. Her attic-based hobby was hugely encouraged by her parents and last Christmas they had had a star globe made especially for her. It was just like a normal round atlas but metallic royal blue and had the maps of the stars and planets instead of countries. All the stars on this one, were crystals — white for the stars and different colours for the planets. It was out of this world and Venus loved to touch it and connect in her mind to the stars and other planets where she was sure for some reason there were kinder places.

"Venus darling, you have another card from Aunt Irene." She heard her mother's voice from the doorway. "Top Secret! this one says, perhaps it's another treasure hunt or calligraphy challenge. How exciting! She's stark raving mad that woman I tell you — where *does* she find the time for these silly games?"

Venus heard the shadows of laughter in her mummy's voice as she passed down the golden shiny envelope from Irene, as always with her full name adorned on it: Miss Venus O'Connor. Mummy's hand stroked her hair but as Venus looked up to her beautiful face, now lit by the winter sun streaming in through the window, the laughter vanished from her eyes and she looked sad again. She kissed the top of Venus' hair and scurried out of the room

"Open your letter, darling, and get dressed, I'll make us some nice breakfast before school, OK?"

"OK, Mum." Venus sighed. School just meant another day of Ethan and Anna and all the other village children's stares and giggles. To be fair many by now just stared straight through her ugliness but some still let it bother them. She was opening the envelope absent-mindedly, when...

POOF!

Both Venus and her beautiful globe were covered in golden dust! How had Irene done that? She, gingerly now, pulled out the gold card inside and read — in the most beautiful writing she had ever seen — the words:

An Invitation from The Truth Fairy.

Louis

"Good morning, Louis!" A cheerful voice chirped as Louis' door was unlocked and opened and the UV strip light buzzed into life. "Grubs up! Up you get now and come along to the dining room whilst the eggs are still hot, that's a good boy now."

Louis stared blankly at the chubby, smiley blonde lady he knew was called Tabitha as she turned back to the door as quickly as she had come in moments before. The door was secured wide open now, no more closed doors now until the night time "lock down", for the children's safety only, as there were only two night staff, per night. It would be a huge safety risk to have such "problem children" as those who lived in St Aytas House simply sleeping behind unlocked doors and potentially wandering around. He wasn't in prison or anything. The adults said that. Louis heard *everything* the adults said. Since Mum had died when he was four, he had been around an awful lot of different adults, foster carers, doctors, nurses, counsellors, psychiatrists and people with lots of different fancy titles, who in the beginning had talked a lot *to* him, then a lot *about* him to each other and now talked a lot *at* him with information *they* thought he needed. For the last two years he had been here at St Aytas House in this little village in Lancashire and as he looked around the white clinical room containing a warm bed, a couple of Manchester City posters, a picture of his lovely mum in a frame and his few possessions — he wasn't *unhappy* here. This little village wasn't his *real* home though, he was from a big city called Manchester.

Mum had died in a bad way, he knew *that*. He had been collected from nursery one day by Auntie Sandy instead of Mum and she had been crying a lot. After that, Louis' Nanna, Aunties, cousins and whole family had cried a lot. Louis had cried too because he didn't understand why he couldn't see Mum ever again. *Where* was heaven? *How* could he *get* there? They only had each other Mum used to say, so he'd better find her and *quick*! But nobody would help him and he got angrier and angrier. He had lived with Auntie Sandy for about a year and had gone to his normal school, but he was *so* angry all the time he got in *a lot* of trouble. Nobody liked him anymore. Auntie Sandy got very angry and then one day when he was being *really* cheeky, she had come very close to his face and said:

"Louis Mc Hugh nobody loves you. You're own Mum didn't love you. She went to *Heaven* rather than stay with *you*, even the police said so in *court*."

The police said so! That *must* be the truth! Louis had been *astonished*. He had been six years old. He had not spoken *a single word* since that moment.

Louis' now four-year long silent protest had led him, very quickly from Auntie Sandy's and into some different foster homes around Manchester. He could read, write, was a wizard at maths and could run like the wind, but all was done in total silence. There was nothing wrong with his throat or voice box, as many doctors had said. But he was something they called an "elective mute" — which just means he just chooses not to talk. I could have told them that haha! Louis had thought ironically. He *still* found lots of things funny, but only laughed inside. But being an "elective mute" meant he was *sort of* poorly and so had to be in some type of hospital, not just a normal home.

"Louis doesn't respond to the traditional family setting well," one head doctor had said. Louis hadn't really understood *that* one, but normally he understood everything they said after all the years of hospital talk and tests and fascination with him. He was actually, they said, "super-intelligent". That is how he had gotten to come here to St Aytas House, a private charity hospital for gifted children with "problems". Here he could attend the local schools — thought to be the best in the North West — and was given special classes at the home. His strength seemed to be in maths and physics and his teacher at the home, Miss Joy, praised and congratulated him with all her might in any way she could. He had once overheard her saying to one of the dinner ladies:

"You know some of them you really wish you could reach out and love. But it's hospital policy not to give *any* affection or misplaced sentiment."

After looking up some words, Louis had realised that Miss Joy had just confirmed Auntie Sandy's words, some children you just *could not* love — it *even* said so in the hospital rules. Louis quite liked rules and routine.

As he took his breakfast tray with its neat compartments of food and drink, he caught a glimpse of his shaven head in the canteen's stainless steel. He rubbed it a little — forgetting he was in a public area. He liked it like this — clean and simple. He was always allowed to choose things like his clothes and haircut and did so using written clues and hand gestures. His clothes were mainly black, except of course that *awful* maroon school uniform. His mum had worn mainly black and had *always* worn black eye liner. The hospital *didn't* allow him to do *that* though. He hated school. Not *classes*, just school with all the noise and all the children. Adults he could cope with —

children were an entirely different matter. He had to go to the school to stay at St Aytas House with its comforting clinical rooms and routines. St Aytas Primary on the other hand was a big confusing mass of noise and colour and emotions. Nobody seemed to be in charge at school, Louis thought a lot. Like when that supply teacher had called him *Louise* the girls name, not *Louis* the boy's name (apparently his dad had been French— but Louis didn't remember him) and everybody had laughed and laughed — *especially* Anna and Ethan, who had called him *Louise* every day since. Nobody *ever* stopped them. Anyway, they are probably not loveable too, Louis thought in that moment. That thought was immediately dashed when he caught sight of the golden envelope shining out from his post tray (everybody in St Aytas House had one outside their room). He sometimes received cards and photos from his various foster homes and occasionally staff from hospitals and that, but what was *this*?

Top Secret!

Master Louis McHugh; Room 13 St Aytas House; St Aytas Village; Lancashire

He went back into his room and sat on the bed to inspect the curious card. As he opened the envelope,

POOF!

He and "Moonie" — his Man City mascot teddy from Mum — were covered in golden dust!

His eyes widened in shock and he froze to the bed as his hands continued working without him and slipped out a golden card, on which was written:

An Invitation from The Truth Fairy.

Dearest Louis,

You are cordially invited by me, The Truth Fairy, to attend a special class this Friday,

The fifteenth of November...

At 3pm, when the school bell rings.

Please come directly to the old music room at the very end of the corridor.

It is **most** important that you attend my special friend...

It is equally important that only those invited EVER know about this class

Therefore, please kindly keep it to yourself.

I look forward to meeting you again.

Alma,

xx

The Truth Fairy

P.S. Remember it's TOP SECRET!

What on earth is going on? thought Louis. Extra classes? "The Truth Fairy"? Everybody knows fairies don't exist, don't they? Meeting me again? I don't know anyone called Alma! And she can't know me very well at all — I've kept *everything* to myself for *ages*! And what is all this dust? Was this a strange test by the hospital? Had Louis gone *mad*?

"Louis?" Tabitha was back — oh no! The mess! "Are you nearly ready for school? It's Tuesday, remember? PE today, pack your gym kit."

As Tabitha entered the room Louis stood still, waiting for her reaction to the state of Louis and his bedroom.

"Come on, sweetie, that uniform won't put itself on *will* it?" She smiled at Louis and turned back to the door to continue rounding up problem children for school. Louis looked around him — the dust had totally disappeared, as had the golden envelope and card. All that remained was a white piece of card in his hand that said:

Friday 3p.m.

Shhhh...

Friday 15th November

For four pupils of St Aytas Primary School, the last three days had been the longest days EVER! Since Tuesday morning they had wondered, worried and waited for Friday to arrive. They would have thought it was all just a strange dream if it wasn't for the small piece of white card, they each had in their school satchels, which proved they had indeed been invited to attend a class this afternoon, in the old music room — by a fairy. All four children had kept the secret from absolutely everyone — parents, teachers, hospital staff, everyone. They had hardly dared even look *anybody* in the eye in case they sensed their secret, because each child knew one thing only for certain — they MUST attend this class. They didn't know why, but they knew this class would change their lives forever and, since the golden dust, each had felt much more than just curious about the *purpose* of the class.

Whoever Alma was, she was clear that only those invited must EVER know about the class, so who *had* been invited? For each of the four children this question had burned in their brain and they had looked suspiciously at every pupil in school —

searching for clues in the eyes of others that they may also be in possession of an Invitation from the Truth Fairy. They had seen nothing.

Ethan and Anna, who played together every day normally, had both been unusually quiet this week. For some unspoken reason they didn't want to laugh at the others as much or set booby traps at the moment. Anna had wondered once on Wednesday whether Ethan too had received the invitation, because he was behaving *so* oddly. However, if she asked him and he *hadn't*, then she would have broken the secret and would *not* be allowed to go to the class — which she *must* do. So she had said nothing. On Thursday when Ethan had explained he was a bit quiet because his horrid big brother Ely was home from the army, Anna had been very relieved to have kept quiet. That was a close one, she had thought. The badness had nearly got the better of her once again — but didn't. Maybe, she was getting better?

Louis had continued in silence as usual, but *he* had feared the most that all this had all been his imagination and had checked the white piece of card existed many times a day. In his clinical, scientific world such things simply did *not* happen. Venus, although a tiny bit nervous, was the most excited. She had been waiting for contact from another world for as long as she could remember and she was sure this was just that. Her star-gazing had left her in no doubt that among all of those beautiful stars and planets lay "others".

All of the four children were slightly unnerved to be entering the old music room. It's door — at the very end of the corridor — remained closed at all times and the general belief in St Aytas village was that the room was *haunted*. Even the adults of the village, most of whom had attended the school long ago, agreed that the old music room was indeed haunted by an old village witch who had once tried to take children from the village to fight in a wicked army for evil forces, under the guise of being a music teacher. It was always thought thereafter that anyone who entered the room would be transported to infinite darkness. Teachers and children alike avoided the room and its legendary powers. It was said that St Aytas Church had tried several times to exorcise the room, but had never succeeded. The church, school and community centre were situated in a triangular formation to each other and were hundreds of years old. Many tales of good and evil were alive and told between the three. St Aytas village itself was a mystical place where many strange and inexplicable things had often happened and its people told many different tales and versions of these events. They were all, however, agreed that the old music room of St Aytas Primary was not to be entered under *any* circumstance.

The four chosen classmates, unbeknown to one another had all bravely decided — alone — to break with common belief and enter the old music room at three o'clock today. Butterflies inhabited each of their stomachs as the classroom clock showed the time to be ten to three. Ten minutes ticked slowly by, as satchels were packed and the teacher of class 4B — the class of all our brave heroes — Miss Rubio wished them all a safe and happy weekend. The rest of the class buzzed with tales of weekend plans and excitement for final release from the classroom bubbled and built to a near frenzy. Four members of the class remained silent and desperately tried to swallow the butterflies which were now floating up to their throats.

"BRRRRIIINNGGGGG!"

Four little figures jumped at the sound of the school bell and the classroom door was opened. A river of frantic children flowed quickly along the corridor towards the main entrance and past the headmaster, Mr Johnson, who bade his children goodbye every evening, seeing all with hawk-like accuracy. Four little figures moved in a contraflow to the rest, each so determined and frightened of being caught at their magical business that they didn't notice each other. As they walked, they realised that no one could see what they were doing, other children looked through them, teachers didn't question them. They were *invisible*! This is *brilliant*, thought Venus. The old music room door loomed, its dark mahogany wood and brass doorknob seemed even more intimidating than usual. Four faces stared hard at the door, then all at the same time, they looked around themselves — finally seeing each other.

"You too!" cried Ethan and Anna at the same time and then laughed with relief.

Louis and Venus said nothing, but disappointment stung inside. Why would the Truth Fairy *ever* want to invite these two awful bullies to her class? Venus began to doubt that this was in fact her lovely "others" coming to save her from this mean planet. Louis tried to turn and walk away but his feet were frozen to the spot. He had known this was all nonsense all along, why was he here with these two? His and Venus' eyes met as they both realised that the legend of the old music room was true and, far from meeting with a fairy, they were about to be taken by the ghost of the evil witch.

Just then the brass doorknob started to shine with the brightest golden light. The old door creaked open and four sets of feet marched robotically into the before unseen classroom.

Lesson No 1

The old music room was dusty and dark, the only light coming from a beautiful old stained-glass window depicting Noah's ark and all its pairs of animals. The coloured glass gave a multicoloured hue to the classroom — on whose walls hung old musical instruments of many different kinds. Ancient music stands and torn sheet-music littered the wooden floor. There was a blackboard at the front of the class and four old-fashioned sets of desks and chairs sat in a neat row a meter before it. The outline of a winged figure shone in front of the ancient blackboard, writing on it with a golden chalk. The children starred wild-eyed whilst their feet took them to the desks and their bottoms sat them down at the seats.

"Welcome, my friends. I am so *pleased* that you could all come," said the figure in a musical, velvet voice as it turned to face them.

She was beautiful! Shining eyes of flame greeted them with deep affection from a lilac hued skin. Her long deep purple hair fell in ringlets around her shoulders and the most loving of smiles shone from her silver mouth. Her iridescent wings towered over her like mother of pearl and out from her floor-length silver and lilac robes. A golden aura surrounded her. Just looking into her face, the four pupils felt so deeply safe and happy they almost cried. They had never known a feeling like this and all sat in an amazed and contented silence as She continued…

"My name is Alma. You have all met me before but you don't remember. I have a very important job in the Universe, which is how we know each other, but when I'm here on Earth I am known as "The Truth Fairy". Now I have some *extremely important* and *big* information for you, so all you need to do for now is please *listen carefully*."

Four sets of enchanted eyes gazed upon her unwaveringly.

"Look at the blackboard," Alma instructed

Reluctantly they moved to the blackboard. It was split by the gold chalk into two halves, vertically, each half titled 'I have' and 'I am' respectively.

"So…" Alma continued.

Four sets of enchanted eyes returned to their teacher.

"I want you to think of things you have. I mean really *think* of words and pictures of things you *have."*

Anna thought about her ballet shoes.

Ethan thought about his train set Daddy had built.

Venus thought about her star-globe.

Louis thought about Moonie.

"I'm *so* glad the fairy dust all came off him," he heard deep inside. "It's a bit hit and miss at times, for stains, on Earth."

"Hang on," Louis thought. "I didn't speak! How did *you* hear *that,* you, cheeky fairy?"

"Ahahaha." Alma's laugh tinkled. "I can communicate by *any* means, as can you. Surely I don't need to teach *you* that!"

Louis could not maintain any level of anger and his inside laughter joined with Alma's.

"Excellent job everybody! I saw everything crystal clear! You're all so good at this, I know I have my people." Alma readdressed the group.

"Now, I want you to picture the things you *are...*"

After a few moments Alma started to cry.

She turned to the blackboard and coughed, sniffed and turned back around with the same devotion in her face as before and said softly, "You really *are* good at this my friends."

"So here begins the 'Top Secret' information. Anything you hear from this moment *must not* be told to a living soul. *Until* we meet again. Do you all *understand* clearly?"

A resounding "Yes!" was heard.

"*Fabulous*, then I shall begin. What you *have* my friends are *things*. Your ultimate *things* are your body and your language. You *have* a body and you *have* a language. From these you communicate and gain information throughout your whole life — just like here at St Aytas. They are both *very important.*"

They all understood.

"When I asked you what you *were*, some very powerful words and their images appeared, like bad, sad, mean, ugly, alone, unloved, unhappy."

The children felt *all* of these emotions as Alma spoke them.

"OK now, can you think of one *positive* thing you *are*, try *really* hard."

Anna thought how well she could dance, even Mum seemed proud at her dancing shows *sometimes*. I *am* a good dancer.

Ethan struggled. But then, he was never cheeky at home, to Mummy and of course not to Daddy. I *am* polite (at home) yes!

Venus thought about how well she could draw and paint — and write in the circumstances. I *am* a good artist. She felt something new and strange.

"It's called 'pride', Venus," she felt inside.

Louis was feeling strange that someone could hear him and so thought reluctantly about how clever he was. I *am* intelligent.

"Spectacular images there, my friends. Now can you tell me what part of your body makes you *be* you?"

The children tried and tried. Louis particularly knew *a lot* about the body and this question was driving him *mad*. He *so* wanted to impress her.

"All right now stop, don't waste your energy Darlings, there is *no* answer to that question. You *have* a body and a language, you *are* what is best described in your language as a *soul*... you are a universal energy and part of the whole Universe. Souls on Earth take a body and a family and do their best."

For *some* reason this all made sense to the four transfixed souls.

"So, you *are* a soul.

All souls have four things in common;

All souls are *Good*;

All souls are *Kind*;

All souls are *Beautiful*;

And All souls are *Loved*."

The stress of her velvet tones on each of these special words engraved them on four open hearts.

Four little faces looked confused. Now *this* was totally different from what they had grown to accept. Doubts crept in.

"These are the Truths of the Universe. They are *facts* and cannot be changed. I will tell you more about each to help you understand."

She turned to the blackboard and in the golden chalk drew a symbol.

"Good and Bad, Light and Dark, Holy and Evil — these are all words given to express contrast between the two, but *this* symbol *is* the Universal Truth." She pointed triumphantly to the symbol on the board, pausing dramatically before continuing with feeling,

"In every bit of bad there is a little bit of good

and in every bit of good there is a little bit of bad — to use *words*. So you see one *cannot* exist without the other at *any time*. It is impossible for anything to be *only* good or *only* bad."

Anna squirmed slightly in her seat. She felt hot and was afraid tears were on their way.

"*All* souls are good," continued Alma in the same velvet tones, "souls *are* 'Light'. But every bit of good has a little bad and every bit of light *some* dark. All souls are capable of bad actions but the Universal Truth is that *All* souls *are good*."

Alma paused and imparted one of her glorious smiles upon them.

"All souls are *Kind*. All souls are equal and related as part of a Universal family. Souls have a natural empathy for all other souls no matter what form their Earthly journey takes — animal, insect or other human being."

Hang on — insects and animals have souls! Ethan panicked at this thought. He felt shaky and hot at this part of the lesson.

"On Earth souls can forget to recognise themselves and others as being so. It is NOT your fault. You *learn* the habits and behaviour of those around you as you grow and *forget* the Universal Truths. It is a problem we on the Universal Council see only on Earth, it is a problem with the atmosphere or something — I don't deal in the science of it all, I'm all about Souls." Her lovely laugh tinkled again.

"We have sent many messengers in the past to remind the human race of their souls' *absolute need* to be kind to others in order to remain happy but there is, on Earth, a dark force against us that doesn't want this message to get through. The light *will win* and you four *will* help us."

Four hearts filled with courage. They didn't know *how* but they *would* all *definitely* help Alma however she wanted them to.

"My friends you are doing *so* well!" Alma's smile flashed even brighter than before and she continued.

"All souls are *Beautiful*. I cannot show you a soul in this atmosphere on Earth I'm afraid, but I feel you already *know* you can trust me."

Four heads nodded surely.

"You *have* a body and like all 'things' it can be any shape, size, colour etcetera. It can be damaged, healed, adjusted, ill, etcetera. It can be beautiful to other beings or not. But it is not *you.* You *have* a body, you *are* a soul. *All* souls are beautiful beyond compare to anything you will ever see here on Earth or any other planet. I can see your souls right now and they are simply exquisite! You are *all* Beautiful."

Venus began to cry. She had never heard anyone call *her* beautiful before.

Alma turned back to the blackboard briefly.

Her radiance calmed them all when she turned back to face them.

"All souls are *loved*" they all heard deep, deep within themselves.

Louis started to shake a little. His life for six of his ten years had been lived in direct opposition to this 'fact'. This was what troubled *him*. He absolutely believed this inexplicable creature in her dusty out-of-bounds classroom. She was *clearly* right about *everything* else, but *this*? What about *Mum* then? She *can't* have been wrong! The doctors? All the experts? Nobody *actually* loved him.

"If all of the above are true — which you now know they are, how can any soul possibly *not* be *Loved?*"

Three heads understood, one didn't want to...

"Remember we are all part of one, Universal, loving family, regardless of where, when or to whom we are born. Every soul you meet has a deep Universal love for you, you just need to see and accept it. They may show you badness, unkindness and ugliness but beneath *all* of that they are another good, kind, beautiful soul — one who has forgotten the Universal Truth, just as *you* had; and to whom *you* must reach out and touch. All souls *are* loved."

Five beings were exhausted!

Alma began again after a long pause.

"My friends we *must* all rest. Intergalactic communication *is* exhausting! It is time for you to enjoy your weekends. When you return to the corridor, Earth time will not have altered at all and you will not have been missed. Take time to *feel* what I have taught you."

Four children did not want to leave this magical room, this *feeling*, this *angel*.

"Fear not, my friends, we *will* meet again. At the same time and place on Monday. Until this time, I ask you only *to accept* what comes and what *is to come* and to know all of this knowledge is given to you in *purest love*. Until we meet again, dear friends, remember *one thing* only; DO NOT repeat any of these lessons to those outside the classroom. Until you receive *all* of the knowledge you **cannot** act. This is *forbidden*!" She spoke with a fierceness they hadn't before seen and did not like at all.

"Until Monday…" Their angel had returned. "Please go in peace and love and rest while you can. I have much more in store for then."

She then kissed them all on either cheek, gave each a fierce cuddle and motioned to the door.

Four stunned little figures marched their residing souls back into the corridor.

Even though they had been with Alma for what had felt like forever and at the same time no time at all, they returned to their school corridor. *Looking* exactly as they had before they left it, to all those on the corridor who could now see them again. However, all four children were *actually* changed completely, deep inside.

A Weekend of Miracles in St Aytas
Anna's Miracle

On the morning of Saturday 16th of November, Anna had a ballet exam at her dancing school — "Miss Duerres' School of Dance". At precisely 11am Anna took to the familiar boards of the rehearsal studio in front of three panel judges. If there was one thing Anna could do *extremely* well it was dance — *any* type of dancing. Rhythm came naturally to her, —but the *grace* of ballet for some reason had become her favourite. It was her escape from the "badness". She was as calm as always when it came to dancing and had been in a sort of trance since she had left the Truth Fairy yesterday. Sleep had come very easily — for once in *that* house — and her parents and Lucy had stayed suspiciously distant from her. Mum had even said good luck as she had dropped her off at Miss Duerres' — *unheard of*! Taking in her dark-haired, pretty and tiny reflection in the practice mirrors Anna eyed her treasured scarlet ballet pumps. They were her pride and joy. Instead of the usual standard-issue blush pink satin soft shoes that ALL ballerinas wore, once you passed the Advanced

Foundation grade at Miss Duerres' you were awarded a pair of shiny scarlet satin pumps with matching red leg-ribbons (a dedication to Miss Duerres' favourite film The Wizard of Oz — depictions of Dorothy, The Tin Man and others adorned each studio wall). Other than the exceptionally gifted dancers, you only got to Advanced Foundation aged thirteen. Anna had been nine when she received *her* beloved scarlet dancing shoes.

As the music began Anna started to move, but instead of her usual graceful fluid movements, she was awkward and clumsy, could not remember the routine perfected long before today. What on Earth? This was like a bad dream! Anna panicked, this was impossible, she *was* a good dancer — it was the *only* good part of her, she thought. She tried desperately to take control of her flailing limbs, but to her horror she only found herself in a heap on the studio floor. The music had been stopped and three judges stifled giggles. Anna's face was the colour of her pumps as she fled from the room and into the cold November air outside. She stood panting clouds of breath against the outside wall when,

"Anna Porter! What in Heaven's name was *that*?!" Miss Duerres' voice sounded more cross than Anna had ever before heard. "I had *just* finished telling the judges that you were my *finest* young dancer and what hopes I had for your future when you pulled this little stunt." Her always brightly made-up face fumed from behind her fancy red half-moon glasses and her theatrical arm movements made her billowing layers of coloured winter clothes into an imposing figure as Anna tried to stutter that it hadn't been her fault at all. *Furious*, Miss Duerres had shouted over Anna's half protests.

"You *may* get away with this sort of behaviour at school — I have always been grateful to have never seen this side of you before. But this is a small village, Anna, and I have heard *plenty* from your teacher Miss Rubio who is a good friend of mine. *I* however will not tolerate this outlandishness for *one second*. Anna, you have brought shame on *me*, *my school* and *most* importantly *yourself*. You are a very *bad* girl. As punishment you are to leave your red pumps in my office right now and I will call your mother to collect you. I am *far too* angry to decide whether you can dance at my school anymore at the moment — now hurry along to my office and out of my sight."

To her own absolute horror, it was at this moment that she had kicked Miss Duerres in the right shin.

Tears were pointless Anna had discovered long ago in front of Mum. Mum's Saturday bingo session had been interrupted by a hysterical phone call from Anna's ballet teacher and Anna was now in the back of the family car awaiting *certain* death when they got home. She was *so* angry with herself! She had been totally taken in by all this Truth nonsense and look where it had led her — no longer allowed to dance, stripped of her scarlet shoes and sadder than *ever*.

"Bad to the bone you are, girl." Mum repeated for possibly the twentieth time since she had dragged her from Miss Duerres' office by the hair. She locked the kitchen door behind her and Anna was alone in the cold with her ballet leotard, bare feet and stingy new bruises. "You can stay in there on your own and think about *exactly* what's just happened while we go out for some family time."

Anna would do *just* that. The front door closed and Anna heard the car drive away. She was really alone now, so her tears could finally come — and *how* they came. A flood of hot and angry tears poured at her own badness and more than anything at the disappointment of the Truth Fairy having told her a lie about something *so* important. What *was* the truth then? Tired and totally confused, Anna lay down on the cold chessboard floor to rest her tiny sore body.

From below the kitchen tablecloth something started to shine out. A golden light got ever brighter through Anna's tears. She stared suddenly now frightened at being all alone when she heard a familiar "Woof".

"Hugo?" she cried — peeping under the checked linen. There she saw Hugo glowing brightest gold.

"Yes, Anna my friend, you are not alone *at all*, I am here for you as always." Anna heard an unfamiliar but soothing voice say.

"Who said that?" Anna cried, her scared eyes darting around the now darkening kitchen.

"Me *of course.*" The same voice was coming from under the table cloth.

"Hugo?" Anna whispered staring at her glowing companion.

"Yes, my dear friend." Hugo smiled. "Alma has kindly made it possible for me to talk to you and tell you some things I have wanted to tell you for a *very* long time. Come under the table with me Anna and touch my fur."

Amazed Anna obediently slid under the table and in beside her trusty dog laying her hand gently on his back. *Her own* hand started to glow gold too! Then it crept up her arm with a fuzzy, tickly sensation and across her whole body until she too was glowing gold. She giggled with nerves and excitement as Hugo said, "Follow me!" crawling out from under the table the two golden figures lit up the dull kitchen beautifully. "Right, now climb onto my back and hold on to my collar."

Anna did so without question. The kitchen window's frame began to glow gold and the glass vanished!

"Right! One, two, three, hold on tiiiighhht..."

And with that one golden dog and his little golden human friend flew gloriously out of the cold kitchen and into the bright afternoon winter sky above St Aytas Village.

"Weeeee!" shouted Anna laughing as her stomach flipped and dipped with Hugo's crazy flying. "Hugo this is *amazing*! When did you learn to *fly*? Ahahahaha!"

"Just this morning actually, so I'm a bit wobbly, excuse me. Am I going too fast for you? I'm just *so excited* you see — isn't it *thrilling*!"

"Oh, Hugo it's the *best* feeling in the world and no, *faster*! Ahahaha! I think you're doing a *wonderful* job, ahaha!"

Hugo laughed along with Anna and did a celebratory loop-the-loop!

They swooped and looped and darted and dived all over the village, they could see *everything* from up here! They flew over the park, slid down the library's dome-shaped roof, circled the hospital, waving furiously to all those on the children's ward (who could *see* them unlike everyone else). They zig-zagged over the lake and slalomed the trees of the forest — much to the surprise of one particular sleeping owl! They flew across the triangular formation of the school and into the bell tower of the church — pulling the ropes to sound the biggest bell before flying back out leaving it tolling far behind them. They laughed and they laughed as the cold winter air rushed around them, but far from feeling cold they felt only exhilaration and an untold happiness and, of course, their love for each other. Their countless morning hours together had brought them both so much comfort in their cold kitchen hell but never for one second could they have imagined *this*! As they had done so many mornings, they cherished every moment — *together*.

The sky turned grey and it started to rain.

"Oh *no*," Anna started to complain a little. "We're getting *wet* Hugo!"

"Wait and see!" Hugo called back to his golden passenger.

Moments later a huge blinding beam of winter sun split the grey clouds directly in front of them and *then*...

"Oh, *Hugo*!" Anna gasped. And there had appeared the most radiantly clear and precise full and glorious rainbow either of them had ever seen.

"I *know,*" said Hugo filled with emotion. "We are going to rest for a while at the top of it."

They rose sharply up and caught the upward arch of their hexi-coloured path. Anna fought the brightness of it all to take in every feeling of colour and magic she was experiencing. She was breathless with a rush of something she could not name.

At the very top of the rainbow Hugo ceased flight and Anna climbed down. Now this *was* strange, the rainbow had enveloped them, it was their floor, their ceiling and their walls and yet they could see through it still without it losing any sharpness or definition of colour. They were at the top of it *and* inside it and could see the whole Village below them, and those who had noticed this natural wonder were looking up towards them. Somehow *knowing* they could, they sat. The rainbow supported them — the dog, the girl and their golden auras.

"Anna, now you *must* listen to me," Hugo began. "You *are* a good soul — *all* souls are good."

Anna's smile vanished and she said crossly,

"Hugo, good souls don't go around kicking ballet teachers, *do* they? Or, or, interrupting their Mums' nice times away from their bad little girls, *do* they? I'm *bad,* Hugo. Alma might be able to make you *fly* but she *cannot* make me good — no matter *how many* classes I go to. I thought I'd changed on Friday but just look at what I did today! Good Souls DON'T *do* that."

She started to cry golden tears, which rolled down the rainbow and fell onto the streets of St Aytas Village.

"Yes, they *do*," Hugo soothed, gently nuzzling Anna's bent head back up to meet his kind brown eyes. "Good souls do bad things all the time. But remember in every bit of good, Anna, there is bad and vice versa. Look at this rainbow. From the dark raincloud and the bright sunlight, we get this amazing spectrum of light that illuminates the sky and melts the hardest of hearts. Without the light *and* the rain, it cannot exist. We souls are the same, we have to take the darkness and the light and make rainbows whenever we can."

Anna thought she understood. "So you have a soul too, Hugo, even though you're a dog?"

"No, Anna, I *am* a soul, I *have* a dog's body, remember!"

Of course! She *knew* that and felt silly, but this day had had a lot of ups and downs to say the least!

"Listen, Anna, today you got angry because something you were proud of and had achieved was being taken away from you — your dance classes and your red shoes, and you of all children who *has* so little to be taken away.

"And something I *am*. I *am* a good dancer and I now I can't dance!" Anna interrupted remembering her distress this morning. "That was my positive thing…" she said wistfully.

Hugo smiled at this.

"I know, my dearest friend, but you have so much more too — you just don't recognise it anymore." Hugo told the puzzled Anna. "Every morning we spend an hour together in our silent companionship. It is the *only* time in my day, Anna, where I am not being punished by your parents. You show me, an old soul, my only love and affection in life. You tell me your stories and fears and dreams and all the little wonders of your *amazing* mind. You hold me close and I feel your soul with mine. My journey in this life as Hugo won't be very long but you alone have made it a love-filled existence. I thank you and whatever journey I take from here to eternity I will *never* forget you, dear Anna. I know you better than anyone and I *know* you are a good soul."

Anna's heart felt as if it would burst. She *was* a good soul. They embraced as they did every morning — two golden souls connecting and recharging each other with love and energy, but this time it was from within a rainbow.

"Anna, we must go back soon, I'm sorry," Hugo said after a while. Anna felt her stomach churn and her heart sink at the thought of going from this magnificent rainbow back to the cold kitchen and all that came with it. "There is no magic way through this life, I'm afraid, Anna, but believe me *so much* fabulousness lies ahead of you, my lovely friend. You will get through this testing time with your Earth family and I will be there for as long as you need me, Alma has reassured me of that. In the future you will experience the feeling you felt before, when we were flying, *all of the time*. It's called '*Freedom*', Anna, and you will have more freedom than anyone before this time, you and many other children."

Anna felt that whooshing feeling from before and she *knew* that in the end everything was indeed going to be *fabulous!*

"Come on, sweetheart, let's go back... together we can face *anything*." Hugo stood up and nodded to Anna to get back on. "And whenever it gets tough, we can always picture today."

"Absolutely, Hugo!" Anna exclaimed, climbing onto Hugo's back, feeling braver than ever. "We were lucky souls to see all this and we're lucky to have each other! I love you and you love me. We're going to be just fine."

The little girl and her trusty steed slid down the arch of a beautiful rainbow, flew back around their now streetlamp lit village once more and into the still-glowing window frame.

The kitchen was even darker now and colder still, but neither soul minded one bit as their earthly bodies curled up together under the checked tablecloth once more and they drifted off into a contented rainbow-coloured sleep.

Ethan's miracle

Every Saturday night followed the same routine in the "Old Rectory" — as did most days among this rather odd household of extreme age and youth, but Ethan actually loved Saturday nights in this house. Saturday night was film night at the "Old Rectory" for Ethan and Mother. Sweet treats would be bought in the afternoon from Syd's sweet shop on School Lane and, after dinner had been eaten in the dining room (and a mashed up version fed to Daddy upstairs), he and Mother would retreat to the parlour (it was a *very old* house and some of the rooms had some very funny names Ethan often thought) to watch a film. Not a film on DVD or something downloaded, but a video from Mother's treasured collection of "old classics", from her "hay day". Ethan just *loved* the dramatic stories with their sharp-suited gangsters and super-glamorous ladies in beautiful costumes — or the Technicolor musicals of wagons and singing cowgirls. Ethan loved the music, the dancing, the ways of talking and the fascination of times gone by — for what reason he did not know. But most of all he loved the way Mother's eyes shone when the old films were playing, the way she sang along to all the songs and the wonderful stories of the past she told him after each film. If she got really carried away, she would bring down Daddy's old cine-camera (an old type of video camera) and play silent cine films of when her and Daddy were "courting" and first married.

Daddy and Mother had — before both he and Ely had been born — lived in Africa, as missionaries, in a small village in Nairobi. Daddy had been a Church minister and his young wife had helped the women of the village to be clean and healthy and had taught them and their children some basic English. Looking at the cine films from this time Ethan had — as a smaller child — thought they could not *possibly* be the two old people he was so familiar with. But all of these old films always made Ethan feel close to his mother, when at all other times she was so distant from him. When she smiled with her *eyes* and spoke enthusiastically — which she *only* did on these Saturday nights — Ethan thought she looked *just beautiful*. Mother would drink a cognac on these nights — the only night she would drink alcohol — from a cut-crystal brandy glass, whose partner sat unused since Daddy's stroke. Ethan would drink hot chocolate with marshmallows and both would wear their dressing gowns. Ethan would often fall into a cosy sleep on the big brown leather

Chesterfield sofa beside Mother and later she would gently wake him with a kiss and send him to bed with a:

"God-bless you and love you as *I do,* son."

Ethan really loved Saturday nights.

This Saturday, however, Ely was home. During the regular Saturday afternoon shopping trip, the usual sweeties and chocolates had been bought and Ethan had assumed Ely would be at the local pub (his usual night time home on leave, from which he always returned with a nasty smell and even nastier words to interrupt Ethan's sleep). It was during dinner (at which Ethan remained silent and looking down in the hope that he would avoid Ely's hateful stares) that Ely revealed his plans to *stay in* this evening.

"So, I thought it would be just *precious* if the three of us could watch a film *together* tonight, a war film." Ely addressed his mother in sickly-sweet tones, all the while staring coldly at Ethan.

"Erm, a war film?" said Mother meekly as usual, "well, all right I suppose… I'll get the hot chocolate and the Saturday night 'tuck'" — this was their name for treats — "ready while you put on a film then, Ely. Go and fetch your dressing gown, Ethan."

Ethan had obviously never *told* Ely how much he loved his and Mother's Saturday nights, he just *always knew* exactly how to get to Ethan, instinctively. A war film! How *dreadful* under any circumstances, Ethan thought angrily. But today, when he had nothing but the Truth Fairy's words on his mind, this idea seemed even more horrible. Death and destruction and violence, oh no! His fear kept him silent, as always. He stood up from the table to fetch his dressing gown and Mother moved to clear the table, then;

"No, Mother, no tuck for Ethan — look how *fat* he is getting!" Ely started and Mother turned to look at Ethan — who burned with shame and anger. "It's simply not good for a boy of his age to carry so much weight around, he should be a lean, fit, fighting machine like his big brother."

"I suppose you're right," Mother meekly agreed, taking her faraway eyes off Ethan. "I will get him a glass of milk."

This was *it*! Ethan had had *enough*. Still tired and confused by Friday's class, strained by the presence of Ely in the house and now infuriated by his mother's weakness, the anger bubbled and burned inside of him. From the pit of his stomach he felt a powerful surge that exploded from his mouth:

"Who on Earth would ever want to be like *you*, Ely?" Ethan shouted in a strong voice yet trembling "Or you, Mother, you, stupid old lady. I want to watch a nice film with music and dancing not bombs and terror! I want to eat tuck! I am *not* too fat — I'm *beautiful* and you two are *horrible* and I *hate* you both *so* much! You are stupid, stupid, STUPID!!" He became hysterical.

Ely stood up and flew across the table towards Ethan. Ethan darted and pushed Mother into his path. Ely saw too late and the punch aimed at Ethan's head pounded Mother in the stomach and she made a sickening yelp as she fell to the ground.

"Mother!" the two brothers cried simultaneously as they leapt forwards to help her.

"No!" A forceful voice came from inside the frail-looking old lady on the carpet. "Do *not* touch me either of you. I will watch a film *alone* and you two will get out of my sight for the rest of the evening. Do you understand?"

"Yes, Mother," came two, quiet replies.

"Now go," she said quietly as she heaved her small old frame up onto her dining room chair.

For once Ely was too shocked to do or say anything to Ethan and he didn't look back as he headed straight out of the front door. Ethan shamefully climbed the stairs to his room as the tears began to flow. He didn't want to be alone with these awful feelings of shame and hurt. He had *never* spoken to Mother like that before and it stung him deep inside. The Truth Fairy was totally wrong he was not *at all* kind. He shuffled into the one place he might find some comfort at a time like this, Daddy's room. As he opened the big old wooden door, he saw Daddy lying motionless on the four-poster bed, eyes open and as blank as ever.

"Hello, Daddy," Ethan managed through the tears. "You don't usually see me on a Saturday night, do you? But I've been just *so mean* to Mother you see…"

He could say no more as the tears came faster. He didn't want Daddy to see, but he needed him to be close, so he turned off the green-shaded reading lamp on the bedside table, lay down on the carpet next to the bed, closed his wet eyes and listened to Daddy's shallow breaths. Ethan was beginning to calm down a bit when he became aware of the room getting lighter. He opened his eyes and to his amazement and terror he saw that something on the four-poster bed was glowing gold! He lay perfectly still and breathless for a moment before pulling himself up slowly and peering over the edge of the mattress to see exactly what was glowing… It was Daddy! His whole body shone with a golden light making Ethan gasp.

"Daddy?" Ethan's voice sounded tiny and high pitched, as he gazed in amazement at his father. Too his absolute astonishment, Daddy *smiled!*

"Hello, my son." Daddy spoke! Having not heard it in six years, Ethan still instantly recognised his Daddy's deep, calm voice. Daddy sat up in the bed and opened his arms wide for Ethan to enter his embrace. Ethan collapsed into them and those strong arms encased his ten-year-old chubby frame as he wept tears of relief at the feeling of safety they gave him. He began to tingle and when he looked down, he saw that he too had started to glow gold.

"Daddy…?" Ethan began but could not find the words to continue.

"Everything is *fine,* my son, you are safe. Alma has very kindly made my body 'better' for the evening so that I can tell you some things I have wanted to tell you for a *very* long time," Daddy soothed. Ethan knew that this was all fine then. Oh, how lovely to be cuddled by his daddy, he thought. Daddy kissed him on the top of the head and said:

"Come along, my son, let's take a walk together in the garden, as I have so often wished we could."

"You can walk!" Ethan exclaimed, as Daddy put him down onto the floor and swung his legs over the side of the bed in order to stand. As he stood Ethan saw just how tall Daddy really was — 6ft 6'! This giant of a man gently patted a giant hand on Ethan's head, smiling lovingly down on the stunned young boy.

"I know, it's a *miracle* isn't it! It's only for this one night, so let's enjoy our walk," Daddy replied taking Ethan by the hand, guiding him out to the landing and down the grand staircase.

"Wait! Mother!" panicked Ethan, noticing their golden auras once again. How on Earth would he explain *this*!?!

"No one can see us, my son," Daddy's calm tone maintained as he opened the heavy front door to the November night air. "Let us take in some winter sunshine together, as *you* wished."

"Sunshine?" questioned Ethan and with that the night time faded and was replaced by beautifully warm winter sunshine. Night had become day in front of his very eyes! "Wow!"

The gentle giant and the little boy walked hand in hand through the beautiful English country garden of the "Old Rectory". They marvelled at the pretty winter pansies of all colours, the old poplar trees — tall and proud — the cheeky grey squirrels searching a little late for their winter fare and *all* of nature's wonders around them. At the back left of the garden was a small arch, covered in clematis which in summer would be in bloom. Below this was a small carved wooden bench just big enough for two. Mother called it "The Loveseat" and it was Ethan's favourite part of the garden. He would often sit and trace its intricate carvings of flora and fauna with his fingers. At the top in the centre were carved two lovebirds.

"Let us sit a while, my son," Daddy said motioning to the Loveseat. "I have much to tell you while I can."

They sat. Either side of the arch were two buddleia trees — the butterfly's favourite. Today there were countless different types and colours of butterflies dancing and performing for their enchanted audience of two.

"Gosh it's *good* to be outside in the sun!" Daddy sighed before turning to face his son.

"You are a *kind soul,* Ethan, you *always* have been."

Ethan stared hard at the floor.

"Daddy, you don't know what I did at dinner tonight. How can any boy who is horrible to his mother — an old lady — *possibly* be *kind*!" Ethan lamented.

"Ethan, I know *exactly* what happened tonight and it was *not* your fault. It was a terrible thing that happened to your mother but she is far stronger than you boys have ever seen or than *she* remembers these days. Tomorrow she will feel fine, Alma *assures* me. Ely has *bullied* you for as long as you have existed here on Earth and Mother too, in a different way. It is *all* you have known until now."

"No, *I* am a bully, Daddy! Everybody says so, even the other vicar! I do *so want* to believe Alma, Daddy, I do. I felt kinder from the moment I saw her and I agreed with *everything* else…"

"Ethan, please just *listen* to me," Daddy interrupted still calmly but in a voice that stopped

Ethan talking and do just that. "I want to tell you *my* truth, *my* story — something I never had the chance to tell you *or* Ely." Daddy looked sad for a moment, then continued clearly and with love.

"From being a very young man, I had a 'calling' to work for a higher cause. Something I couldn't see. What your mother and I call 'God' — a greater Universal force for the good. I knew we were *all* connected, like one huge family. I *felt* it Ethan, *so strongly* and so I devoted my life to religion and the teachings of kindness and helping your fellow man until I had passed enough exams to become a vicar and preach *my message.* I always knew my true vocation lay many miles from my English home — in a place I had only seen in pictures and read about in stories — a place called *Africa.*"

Something about the way Daddy said "Africa" made Ethan shiver with excitement and he moved closer to him. Daddy put his arm around his boy and together they glowed as he continued;

"By the time I had earned the right to take part in missionary work abroad I had met and fell in love with your wonderfully bright and fantastic mother with her quick wit. So, we married and we set off on our adventure to a distant continent convinced of our message and *very much* in love. What we found when we arrived, we could *never* have been prepared for, no matter what we had read. Ethan these people had *nothing*. No schools, no medicine, no *water*… children died every day from disease and hunger. Their food was their crop, so the weather could starve whole villages. The worst thing by far, Ethan, was that it was the British People who had done much of the damage to Africa hundreds of years before, when they ruled them."

Daddy paused and Ethan tried to let the story so far sink in.

"As for teaching such people as these to have *a faith,* ha! Ethan *faith* is all many of them *do have!*

And yet what they *are*… oh, Ethan, what they *are*… is a Nation of dancers and singers and *believers*. They *smile* often and complain *little*. Children are grateful for their food and any small item they can fashion into a toy. I had nothing to teach these people, but they had an awful lot to teach *me*. But what I did have was resources and the backing of the Church for fundraising. It wasn't a lot, but it was more than these people could imagine, but *most* importantly I had my *time* and my *energy* and I could *help*. So, for seven years that's exactly what your mother and I did. We built huts and a hospital and a chapel — oh, and, Ethan, the *services*! Colour and song and heartfelt thanks, *every* Sunday… I was happier than I could have imagined anyone could be. Deeply, *soulfully* content, among my African brothers.

Then we found out we were going to be parents. Ely was born in Africa but Mother became very ill soon after his birth. She began to long for England and was extremely unhappy and so with a heavy heart I brought her and Ely back to England and the Church stationed me here in St Aytas, a very special village. But my heart remained in Africa, Ethan. I continued my mission to help others as much as I could here, with kindness and love and words, but I missed the *action*…"

Ethan *thought* he understood and he looked upon his daddy with new eyes. The story wasn't over.

"Mummy was never the same again, Ethan, and neither was *I*. I would look at Ely with all of his toys and food and taking it all for granted and I *hated* him. Yes, my *own* son I am ashamed to say. I wanted to be with all of those lovely village children in Africa with their lovely smiles and their singing and dancing. I never spoke my awful thoughts to Mother or Ely of course, but they must have *felt* it and I am deeply sorry — it was *not* their fault at all and I was selfish. I have had much time to reflect in my illness. So, you see you were not born into a very happy home, my son — I hope this explains some of the behaviour you have seen."

Ethan felt both angry *and* sad at this tale now — although he wanted to hear more.

"You *were* born special though and I saw it straight away, your beautiful kind eyes reminded me so much of the eyes of Africa and you renewed my soul. You were *my* little miracle and I was going to teach you *so* much kindness and love so you could continue my work and be my arms and legs — as I was already an old man by then.

Poor Ely saw this and was — and *still is* — consumed by an awful emotion called *jealousy*, when it comes to you, my son. This does not *excuse* his treatment of you for one second, but I hope you *understand* a little better now."

Ethan felt overwhelmingly relieved. At last someone was explaining to Ethan all the mysteries of his short life so far. How he had missed his Daddy.

"My son, it is not for you to become like Ely or *anyone else*. You are a kind beautiful soul and it is for *you* to show him and everyone you meet how to *be*. That is *your* calling, my lovely son. You will do more than I *ever* did — *your* future is dazzlingly bright. *Be* kind, *be* gentle, *be* you and *help* anyone you can, *however* you can. Remember the ants, Ethan?"

Ethan felt sick at the memory of killing the ants, but he couldn't help but picture them coming back for their fallen brothers.

"*Be* like the ants, my son. Always carry your brothers when they fall. Every soul is your brother, show love to *everyone*. Lead by example and love with all your heart. I spend my hours in stillness and prayer for my universal brothers, this is all *I* can now do. You, my son, can do *anything*."

Ethan felt this with his whole heart.

"Thank you, Daddy."

"Thank you, my son for being *you*. You have always continued to speak to my soul, past my now useless earthly body and you are the *only* person who has done so. Please *always* do so. After tonight I will not be able to speak to you again but please know I am listening with love and pride *always*."

The souls of a golden giant and his golden boy sat deeply contented on a loveseat in St Aytas Village watching the dancing butterflies saying not much at all and smiling all the while — for as long as they could.

Venus' Miracle

On the afternoon of Sunday 17th November, Venus was putting on her new dress bought by Daddy. He had been working in London all week and had returned home on Friday night with a beautiful new dress of deep night-sky blue and covered in silver stars. Venus was always bought beautiful clothes and Daddy had said this dress was for a special party this Sunday (today) at their house but also that the party was to be a secret from Mummy. On Friday night an already exhausted Venus had wondered whether or not she had the strength for *another* secret. He had come into her bedroom very late and Venus had been fast asleep, but after she had woken up, Daddy had been extremely chatty indeed — Venus thought he may have been drinking champagne on the train home...

"You see, Venus, Mummy was *such* a *party girl*!" he had said dramatically. "She would always wear the *most* fabulous dresses and was *always* the most beautiful girl in the room by a mile."

Venus knew only too well how lovely her mummy was — she felt the drastic contrast between them every day. She wanted to tell Daddy how beautiful *her* soul was and for him to be *so* proud, but the Truth Fairy's words rang in her ears and she remained silent. He continued.

"It's no good, Venus, all this hiding away, I mean we cannot change what's happened to you, can we, darling, but we cannot just stay *in* and away from the world either, can we? I mean you're fine aren't you, sweetie?"

Daddy spoke to Venus as if *she* was the adult and *he* needed reassurance. She could only nod, as she didn't really know what to say. So Daddy went on.

"Sunday is our wedding anniversary you see — twelve years, and so as a surprise I have invited some of our old friends from the 'London scene' up to the house for a party. Auntie Irene is taking Mummy to her house while a friend of hers does their hair and make-up then she thinks that we are going for lunch alone. Actually, I've hired an events' organiser for everything else and you and me are going to stay here and make sure everything is just perfect for Mummy, our beautiful princess. What do you say, darling, are you in? Shall we make Mummy happy again?"

This was a silly question, Venus thought, she had wished *so* many times that Mummy would be happy like in the old photos from before the accident, she wanted nothing more. But she was just *so* tired after all of the day's revelations that all she could do was nod as her eyes began to close again.

"That's right, you sleep, darling" Daddy whispered a little bit too loudly, "I have put a special new party dress in your wardrobe for Sunday, full of stars just as you like. Sweet dreams, darling. Remember now it's a secret."

With that he kissed the top of her head and slipped out of her bedroom. Venus had smiled to herself — If only he knew how *many* secrets she knew at the moment.

So now it was Sunday.

Auntie Irene had spirited Mummy away at ten o'clock that morning and at half ten a lady in a sharp black suit and smart black glasses had come in and transformed their house into a party palace of ice swans and champagne and dazzling decoration — all very Mummy. Daddy had put on his wedding suit, which *still* fit him — which was of great importance, Venus didn't know why — and so now Venus was putting on her new dress. It felt lovely, the satin felt cool, yet warming to her skin and the silver-star detail shone, reflecting the multi colours in the butterfly fairy lights in her bedroom. She felt a little bit nervous, but that was because she didn't know anyone from the "London Scene" — and it was always a little nerve-wracking meeting someone new for Venus. People had been gathering downstairs now for an hour or so. She knew she would have to go and greet them eventually but she had heard a lot of door-bell rings and a lot of children's and adult's voices. Children could be so cruel, *adults* could be even crueler.

The fairy mantle clock on her side board said it was two o'clock when Daddy knocked on her door and said it was time. Venus had done her best but Mummy always did a better job on her hair — but never mind she would have to do. Many people were downstairs waiting for Mummy to arrive and when she did there was much applause and shouting — not used to either of these Venus began to cry.

So did Mummy.

Auntie Irene took Venus from the big country kitchen off the entrance hall to the living room and Daddy took Mummy to somewhere else.

"Now, Venus, this is *not* your fault," Auntie Irene chimed. "When that awful accident happened and made you poorly it made Mummy poorly too. She's *not* responsible for her actions, Venus."

Everybody calmed down and returned to the kitchen. For a while the party went on, Mummy smiled and to be fair, Venus thought, everyone was quite nice to her. And then a photographer tried to take a picture of the happy family…

"A magazine! How *could* you!" her mother said.

"I, I, I, I didn't…" her Father spluttered. "Who is responsible for this?" He sounded angry now, his eyes searching the room for the now missing events' organiser.

"Get *out* of my house!" Venus' mother cried "This is *not* a freak show!"

Venus retired to her bedroom and somewhere below her, apologies were made and a party was ended. Goodnights were exchanged from behind her bedroom door and her beloved night drew in.

And then her globe began to glow with the most amazing golden light.

This is it! Venus thought. It's *happening*!

She didn't know what or why but she *believed* and she grew closer to the glowing globe and suddenly, poof! In a cloud of gold dust that no longer startled her, there it was…

Right on the top of the globe was a tiny silver robotic man with purple lights for eyes. He was smiling kindly,

"Hello," she heard deep inside. "Shall we fly to *your* planet?"

"Yes, We *Shall*!" Venus felt with all her heart.

"Touch the globe," came the stranger's reply. "Let's go!"

Venus touched the glowing globe without hesitation and she in turn began to glow gold and feel tingly.

Wow, she thought and then…

Whoosh!

Venus' stomach lurched as she was sucked into the glowing globe and sped through a vortex at break-neck speed.

Geometric patterns of all colours and stars and galaxies and skies filled her vision… like looking through a kaleidoscope. She felt that she was moving faster than a rocket…

And then with a jolt she was still.

And everything was pink. Different shades and hues of pink, but pink none the less.

Pink sand dunes, pink mountains, pink clouds, purple sky — OK *purple sky* but *apart* from that yes, all pink. And *sparkly*, just everywhere, sparkly that's all she could describe it as in her head. And a silvery beautiful light shone all around. She was sat on the top of a hill just within a wisp of candy floss cloud and by her side was her little robotic companion whom by the end of their journey, she *somehow* knew, was named Sebastian.

"*This* is Venus, Venus." Sebastian chuckled "Isn't She *fabulous?*"

And She *was*.

For a long time, Venus could only stare in wonderment at the mystical landscape that lay before her.

Over time her eyes adjusted and yes there was indeed a silvery light from above, but also below them were many iridescent light-forms of every colour and pattern — moving all around.

Amazing! Now they *were* beautiful, Venus thought.

"What are *they*?" Venus asked. "They're *amazing*!"

"Oh, *they* are souls," Sebastian replied matter-of-factly. "That's just how we show ourselves here. I'm still wearing my earth-case, aren't I?"

"What?" a very confused Venus exclaimed.

Sebastian had another little chuckle to himself and smiled knowingly at Venus — he really was a happy fellow.

"Remember Alma's words — you *have* a body, you *are* a soul. Here on Venus souls move freely in their pure forms, without need for an outer case. It is only when we travel to other atmospheres — such as Earth — that we must wear our protective suits, like you humans. I can see yours got damaged, I'm sorry. Does it hurt?"

Venus was taken aback by this direct question — nobody usually spoke so normally about her burns to her. It felt good inside to explain *for herself*.

"Not *really* any more, it's just uncomfortable. I don't remember the actual accident but my skin hurts a lot when I have operations to try and mend it. It was a fire you see…"

"Of course," Sebastian said knowingly once more, "human cases aren't fire resistant at all are they — don't worry you cannot be damaged here on hot old Venus — Alma is protecting you. Oh, how *inconvenient* for you to have an uncomfortable damaged case."

Inconvenient!? Venus *knew* this word — it was used for *small* problems. She had never met *anyone* who thought *hers* to be a small problem before. How interesting! But yes, inconvenient *was* a good word for the situation. She was still alive, she could still do many things equally well — if not better than — other children whose hands were normal. Her face may be ugly but it could see and taste and smell and speak what she was thinking… then,

"It's actually a problem for other people a lot more than it is for me, Sebastian. It's very ugly you see and people don't like to look at me."

"What a strange race, you humans are," Sebastian said in his usual nonchalant tone. "Come with me, I wish for you to explore while you can."

Venus needed no further invitation.

They started down the hill and wound along a pale pink sandy path. As they reached the bottom of the hill and to the level of the wandering souls Venus was quiet from amazement and a touch of nerves.

"Fear not, lovely Venus," Sebastian soothed, "souls *here* are far too concerned with their *own* journey to *judge* or *relate* to other souls in any way other than with *love*. Venus is not a planet like Earth where souls have 'a life' or 'form', this is why Humans believe there *is* no life on Venus. There is, in fact, life in *abundance* of the purest energy forms but on a different light frequency which humans cannot see. The souls of Venus come here to replenish and recharge in times of need, as happens with the souls from Mars — on Mars. None of us souls of Venus belongs here, more than you, lovely Venus. When *you* chose *your* mother and began your life on Earth, she *felt* this and you *reflected* it but fate tore her Earth dreams of perfection apart. She is sadder than you could possibly feel for she *too* is a child of Venus. But she is lost and you are not, and now *you* are being shown again, while in an Earth life, the magical healing power of Venus — and this is *unheard of*!"

Venus was compelled by this tale of enchanting logic, as they moved along the glittering sand path among dunes and boulders of cerise. Indeed, the light-forms meandered around them, only with far less direction, paying them no mind at all.

"Venus, you *must* follow Alma's instructions *most* carefully." Sebastian's tone always remained the same as it was unspoken, but she *knew* the inflections of seriousness all the same, as with Alma.

"You are being shown all of these things for a reason. *You* are important in what is to come for Earth as a planet and the souls hosted there. There, the children of Venus have forgotten their power and *true* beauty. They have been persuaded by a false image of beauty, and have become fixated by their casing. On changing and reshaping them and judging one another. Trying to conform where it is impossible to — look around you, Venus — is any light-form the same?"

She began at this instant to see intricate differences in each coloured geometric light form.

"Souls are like snowflakes, Venus," continued Sebastian. "Each and every one is different and the wonder and beauty is *in* that *difference*. You in your future will remind the children of Venus *and* Mars of their true beauty."

Venus felt the weight of these words on her chest as they started uphill once again to a sharp pink rising of rock, the top of which she could not see.

"You will help the lost children of Venus rediscover their gentleness, their kindness and their care-giving natures. Remind them to look after and help one another. In this way their *true* beauty will radiate from within. Sisters will shine together in all their forms, as will brothers. But this picture of contentment *relies* on you *and* the other children."

Venus somehow *knew* this to be true as they came to what appeared to be the edge of the magnificent rock formation which had now begun to sparkle with pure white crystals, which seemed to be *moving* under their feet! Moving they *were* — towards the *edge*, pulling Venus and Sebastian very gently with them. As Venus' toes touched the very edge of the cliff, she looked to Sebastian with frightened eyes.

"Look down," he said simply and she did.

Over the mile-wide shimmering cliff edge cascaded a fall of pure white crystal, falling a thousand meters to a shimmering crystal pool below. Venus gasped in wonder and held her breath for a moment to capture forever in her mind the wonderment of this scene. She had *known* such a place existed all her short life and here she *was*.

"Oh, Alma, *thank you*!" she felt from deep within her soul.

"We're going inside," Sebastian communicated.

"What!" Venus reacted.

"Yes, into the middle," Sebastian made the situation no clearer with this, from where Venus was standing.

"B, b, but *how*?"

"We will take the stairs." Sebastian motioned with a nod to their left and there appeared a winding vortex of golden stairs deep into the crystal fall and behind it.

They began to climb down them.

Inside the crystal fall (behind the never-ending sheet of liquid crystals), lay coves and caves and tunnels of rock of deep blush tones to all sides of the glowing spiral staircase. Within them Venus could see stalactites and stalagmites and geodes of pink crystal. Beside and inside some of them shone what appeared to be small iridescent light balls.

"The offerings of other souls to planet Venus." Sebastian answered her silent question.

What *is* this place?

They stopped at an opening in the staircase where a glittering platform appeared in the rock. Here the crystal fall was at its *brightest*.

"This is the soul of Venus *herself*. It is a special and sacred place to *all* of us souls of Venus." Sebastian was now shown as a light form of blues and purples with a shimmering white core.

"Oh!" gasped Venus

"Turn and look into the fall Venus. *Really* look," Sebastian commanded gently

She looked into the shimmering crystal mirror and saw, after a few seconds, *the* most *radiant* light-form she had seen yet!

It was pinks and purples with flashes of gold and tinged occasionally with burning scarlet red and crystal specks of black. The patterns were amazingly intricate. Most breathtaking of all, was the brightest white centre of pure light. Venus was transfixed. After a long while she spoke, softly.

"What *is* this, Sebastian?"

"*Who,* you mean," came the gentle reply. "Why, Venus, it's *you*. It's *your* soul."

Venus' whole life changed in that instant. *Never* again would a stare or a horrible word harm her in *any* way. She *was beautiful*.

"See the *intricacy* of your soul, Venus?" Sebastian added to her thoughts. "These are the lessons you have learned in this and possibly other lives — I cannot say too much of this. But even in your short existence *this* time, you have learned *so* much, lovely Venus. You have persevered in the face of adversity and not only honed skills but *mastered* them. You *see* the beauty of the world and you *care* of the happiness of others *before* your own — like with your mother."

Venus absorbed every word — ever marvelling at her new-found reflection.

"You alone in your *very* solitary existence have learned to look up and see your place in the Universe above and around you. Without guidance or example in any real form before you, you *believed,* Venus. This makes you *beautiful of soul*."

Venus felt a peace that *never* left her.

"*Thank you,* Venus," she felt deep within.

"You are most welcome, my child," she received from deep within the soul of Venus.

"Take my message with you back to my Sister Earth and her inhabitants. They *need* our love, Venus."

Venus *knew* she would do just that, for the rest of her days on Earth. She would represent Venus with love, always. She would no longer let the *fear* of the reaction of people keep her *away* from them. Venus had a message to give and to show. She would let her inner beauty shine through and dazzle every other soul she met and much more than that, she would show them *their* inner beauty — reflected in *her* light.

On her return up the staircase with Sebastian, Venus just knew to take a ball of her brightest inner light and now *it* remains *forever* in the soul of planet Venus — in the shiniest of geodes Venus could find.

Louis' Miracle

Sunday evening on the 17th November, as with all other evenings in St Aytas House, was thankfully routine filled and normal. Louis was, as always, grateful. The social area was full of children in the pursuit of various pastimes and games and television programs. They had all been served their usual chicken Sunday roast, which was as always very nice — if lukewarm — and on the usual compartmented tray with some soup and a traditional pudding — today's being syrup sponge and custard. Louis had no trouble eating here at St Aytas House. It *had* been a problem in the past in some foster homes, but then Louis had always been well able to find rebellion and vendetta in creative ways in his silent world. At St Aytas he had nothing to protest about. He was allowed to continue in his secluded existence at his leisure with very little interference or protest from others. They kept him sheltered and fed and warm and *learning* and he in response was even-tempered and even-mannered. *All* sides knew that there was an actual trade-off involved.

As every other night, while the other problem children played board or card games or held great tournaments on the various games' consoles, Louis sat unmoving in the same purple seat under the left-hand high corner television in the lounge area. In the early evenings *this* physics and mathematics super-brain liked nothing better than to watch *the soaps*. The northern ones with the accents he knew so well, that depicted families and people and pubs and problems and fights and all the things that were *very much* on the outside of Louis' world now. Most of all he liked the memories of sitting on the couch with Mum before bed with milk and biscuits and watching these dramas unfold. Before he had *become* one, he laughed to himself sometimes. These memories always made him feel cosy before bed and at half past eight every night he would take himself off to bed. They were allowed to stay up until half past nine at St Aytas House — but *of course* they could go to bed at any time they chose, after dinner.

Tonight, was no different in its routine, like the rest of the weekend had, it continued without *any* mystical incidents. Louis had been more than relieved. He, like the other children, had left the old music room *sure* that this weekend held *something* in store for them all at the hands or *wings* of Alma. He had managed against his usual mind-set to *accept* what *had indeed* happened in the old music room; We *were* all souls and all the rest of it... but what *of* it all? Why was *he*, a boy who couldn't, no *wouldn't* talk being given all this information? What on Earth could he *do* with it. Why was this *loving* Universe trying to take away his only real possessions — his science and hard-learned facts. All this magic couldn't help someone like Louis he thought and nor did he *want* it to. No thank you! He had *really* loved Alma, OK, so he accepted there *was* love in every soul. He knew he now felt *something* even for the other children in the chosen class — *even* Anna and Ethan. Yes, for *all* of them. He had even felt *slightly* more interested in those around him in St Aytas House but Louis had put that down to fatigue.

He would go to his bedroom at the usual time of course this Sunday just the same as ever. When that time came, he gratefully took his tired little body and mind to bed — content to be going to sleep and eager to get the rest of the knowledge in tomorrow's class and finally realise what all this was about.

He didn't ever go to sleep at half past eight. He would just get into bed and read whatever he was reading at the time. You see Louis *always* had a book on the go. Mum had said you should *always* have a book on the go. For Louis these books were about science or the world or strangely enough science fiction which until now he had believed was just that. Fiction. He *had* loved all that. Looking at his current tale of universal star wars, he felt a bit uneasy. Not tonight. He picked up a copy of a science magazine and climbed under his warm duvet. He would take his house coat off after. They called them "dressing gowns" round here, but he liked house coat. It was what they said in Manchester. It was what Mum had called them. He would read until half past nine which is when he would snuggle down under the duvet. He didn't know why but at this time he had always felt a feeling of warmth and safety, just enough to go to sleep no matter where he had been. He *never* had trouble sleeping. This was lucky he had been around enough misplaced children to know. Tonight, would be no exception. So when half past nine came and his bedroom door was locked, he snuggled beneath the duvet with Moonie, as usual. As he heard the staff member's footsteps disappear, he lay ready for the safe feeling to come…

It didn't.

Instead Moonie began to glow gold…

Oh no, it's *happening*!

As he was clutching Moonie, he too began to tingle and then to glow gold in turn…

Everything around him disappeared in a flash of gold light and then he was in darkness…

Glowing gold on a cold hard blue plastic seat, clutching the glowing Moonie. *Otherwise* he was alone in darkness.

His eyes adjusted and he saw he was in among many rows of empty blue plastic seats, still in the dark. This was not right *at all*! He was in some sort of *stadium*. Hang on… he'd been here before…

Then flashes came from a giant screen in the corner of the stadium, followed by darkness and then a picture of a huge blue moon appeared on it.

The stadium's sound system began to play a song Louis *knew*.

"Blue Moon,

You saw me standing alone

Without a dream in my heart,

Without a love of my own…"

He was in "The City of Manchester Stadium" in the middle of *Manchester* — "Maine Road" to the *fans*. He had been here a few times with Mum before when he was *very* little. And "Blue Moon" was Manchester City's anthem.

How on Earth was *this* possible!

Then beside him he became aware of a figure, also glowing gold. He didn't need to *look* — he knew *exactly* who it was, without looking.

The song continued…

"You knew just what I was there for,

You heard me saying a prayer for,

Someone I really could care for…"

He didn't want to turn his head, he didn't want to see *her*.

"But when I looked the moon had turned to dust...

Blue moon..."

But just like his feet had betrayed him into the old music room, so his head turned with *no* permission whatsoever.

It *was* her. It was his mum.

"Hello, son."

No! Louis' mind screamed. That voice was *too* familiar. He didn't want to speak to *her*! *She* had left him! *She* didn't love him enough to stay...

"Son, I'm *so* sorry." She looked exactly the same. OK, glowing gold but the same — even the eyeliner... But no, she looked different. She looked *very* happy. She was *so* calm.

He didn't feel calm. He felt *bloody angry*!

"You *left* me."

Actual words left his mouth. His own voice sounded strange to him after so many years. "*You* left *me* Mum and we only *had* each other."

And then came the tears. Hot, angry tears. His tense little body resisted his Mum's embrace, but not for long. He relaxed and the tears flowed even stronger as he breathed in her familiar scent.

"That's it, son, let it *all* out. It's all fine." Louis' Mum kissed his tear-drenched hair in the cold air and still blue light,

He began to breathe in short gasped breaths and his Mum pulled him in tighter.

"I *am* sorry, son," she continued. "As you are learning right now there are *so* many things we don't know here on Earth while we're alive."

"Am I dead?" Louis interrupted raising his head.

"No, son," his Mum laughed pulling him back into a cuddle.

Louis didn't get what was funny about that.

"I mean *I* didn't know — *you* are getting to learn them now at just ten years old my darling — *please listen.*"

Mum had never had forceful tone at all when she was *alive*. All this was clearly very important — she sounded like Alma, Louis thought. He was much calmer now with Mum, in City's ground, having a cuddle. Even if they *were* gold and his Mum *was* technically dead. She carried on regardless.

"Auntie Sandy was *totally wrong*, she knows it and she's *so sorry* all the time, but she's not allowed to speak to you — it's against the rules. While I'm at it, the rules in the home *are wrong* — all children *need* affection — all souls *deserve* affection. Scheduled or otherwise." She laughed now.

He felt like laughing, sort of, but he didn't.

"*I* was wrong, son…"

"What!" Again, he tried to pull away from her, she held on tight.

"Let me finish." He relaxed into her once again as she spoke. "I was *very* sad at times on Earth and I felt my *only* light was you. When you die like *I* did, your soul is taken to learn some lessons. Alma has been helping me *too,* Louis, and She's changed *everything*. Look at what is *possible,* son. Me and you here now, at *Maine Road*." She laughed again. Alma *had* changed everything Louis thought.

"But I *was* wrong, son, we didn't *ever* just have each other. Listen to what Alma is telling you, you *are* loved by every soul that surrounds you. *I* was loved in ways I never saw until it was too late to be thankful to the faces of those who *did* — until now."

Louis looked up and hugged her tight around the neck, sensing her sadness.

"You're *such* a kind boy, you always were. *Such* a chatterbox…" His mum's voice trailed off and she looked sadder still.

"Don't be sad, Mum, I'm fine. I'm *dead* clever you know." Louis smiled properly for the first time in a very long time.

His mum smiled back with the same face.

"Oh I *know*! I keep a *close* eye on you, my darlin', and I'm *so* proud — *all* the time."

"Do you *watch* me, Mum?!" Louis smiled even more. "'ave been naughty 'aven't I — at times…"

He was still smiling.

Mum was smiling back at him, with the same eyes.

"You bloody *have*!" She was almost *laughing* now. "But I don't know who *wouldn't have been* naughty under the circumstances. Darlin', you've had a *dreadful* time of it since I've been gone — dragged from pillar to post. Poked and prodded like some kind of experiment. You have been *so* dignified, I've learned *so* much from just watching you. You have a strength I never had — or *never knew* I had."

"I've missed you so much, Mum." Louis spoke matter-of-factly and leant forward in his seat.

"I know, son." Mum leant forward next to him, so their matching profiles outlined in gold shone against the blue moon in wide-screen. "I don't miss you because I'm with you all the time, but I miss *this*, I can't chat to you or help you. But I come to you every night…"

"At half past nine," Louis finished for her, finally everything making sense.

"At half past nine…" His mum smiled next to him. He matched it. "Getting you to sleep is the least I can do. But, darling, you are *not* alone, whether *I* am there or not. You *are* part of a *Universal* family, as Alma says. Remember when we used to come here, you were so small but I know you remember, *super brain,*" she laughed.

96

"Remember all the big blokes here, together, singing. Big, tough lads son. Builders, plumbers, Dads, Grandads — all singing, crying and hugging each other over a game. Why?"

Louis remembered these scenes, but he didn't know why.

"Because no man is an island, son" His mum took his head in her hands and their matching faces met fully face on. "No man stands alone. *You* have *so* many answers and a mind which *must* be shared. You have a chance here, with Alma to change the *World,* son. But you *need* to communicate. Don't stand apart from the world. It *needs* your love and you need *Its'*. I was *so* wrong, son, we *never* only had each other. Me and *many* others love you *so* very much, my beautiful boy."

He understood.

"It's going to be dead difficult that, Mum." Louis' tone didn't change.

"Oh, I *know* that, son." And she sounded like she *did* know. "It's going to take an awful lot more effort from *your* position, but you *will* do it. You'll be freer than I could ever have *dreamed* for *either* of us. And you *will* know *real* love all the rest of your days."

And with these words they were no longer alone, the floodlights blinded, the stadium filled around them. On the pitch the team in sky blue scored against the Reds and the crowd went wild. Men, women and children sang;

"Blue Moon,

You saw me standing alone

Without a dream in my heart,

Without a love of my own."

Mum joined in, so did Louis. He was singing!

"Blue Moon

Now I'm no longer alone

Without a dream in my heart,

Without a love of my own."

Louis took in the atmosphere around him. The people were together. For a game, yes, but together all the same. He wanted back *in* and he *would* get there — in the end.

The crown disappeared into the night.

It was just him and Mum. Glowing gold. Louis looked around them.

"I'll see you home, darlin'," she said.

"I know," he replied

"It's been lovely this hasn't it, son."

"Yes, Mum. Lovely. And, I understand." And Louis did.

"And I'll see you tonight…" she began

"At half nine," he finished.

"At half nine." His Mum smiled his smile at him. "I love you, Louis."

"I love you, Mum." He felt it with all his heart, they both did.

And he *did* return back to St Aytas House, but not before mother and son had sat and cuddled and laughed and loved for some time for that once in a blue moon.

Monday 19th November

At St Aytas Primary School, Monday mornings always meant Assembly, at eleven o'clock precisely. All classes would be filed in boy, girl order in their separate classrooms and marched along and filed into class rows in the school hall at the front of the school, next to Mr Johnson's office. There they would stand in nose-picky, head-scratchy, giggly, cock-eyed line-ups before all of the teachers and Mr Johnson himself and sing a collection of hymns, say the Lord's Prayer and listen to stories or watch short plays starring various reluctant pupils — relating to the theme of the week. For these parts the children not performing would sit cross-legged on the parquet wooden floor and generally bother each other in stealth — eyes unmoving from the front in case they should face the wrath of any teacher who may notice. Well, Mr Johnson was the only *real* threat of that actually and he was more *kind-strict* than anything. The other teachers never seemed that concerned with *anything* so much.

Miss Rubio's class filed in as usual. It was their turn to enact the theme, a fact which Miss Rubio had forgotten until she had been calling the register and in a great panic some glitter had been thrown on some pieces of purple cardboard and various words written on them with the help of the class calligrapher — Venus. Afterwards they had been told that the theme was, *of course*, *"The Truth"*.

Four brains had nearly exploded. Already unsure how they were supposed to contain themselves until 3 o'clock that afternoon *anyway* — unable to do anything other than look into each other's knowing eyes. None of them had *dared* discuss *what* had happened to them, but they each *felt* the magic had gotten to the others too. They separately knew they had *all* received a miracle. They had also *all* silently agreed to support each other through this day until they could see Alma once again. Now the fabulous four stifled giggles when their eyes met. Actually, only *they* knew *"The Truth"*.

"Do stop laughing children, it's a *very* serious matter doing Assembly," Miss Rubio pleaded, handing each of them a piece of glittery purple card to hold up at the appointed time. "And *that's* the truth."

This sent them into convulsions of laughter and Miss Rubio walked away tutting and smiling all at once. They all liked Miss Rubio.

Now inside the school hall on the front row, as was customary for the class taking part, the four knowing souls had managed to calm themselves enough to listen to Mr Johnson's opening of the Assembly and offer a decent try of the hymn "All things Bright and Beautiful", which they all heard the words of more clearly after their weekends than they had ever before. Eventually Miss Rubio beckoned them up to the front of the hall with several others and they all held up their purple placards, blinking out glitter from their eyes and standing in an awkward display facing the rest of the school — who in turn, stared blankly and twitched randomly in an entranced sea of boredom. Miss Rubio's words did nothing to enthuse them at all.

"Children, I want to remind you of the importance of 'The Truth'. Of telling the truth to your *parents* and to your *teachers,*" Miss Rubio began in her best teacher tones. She had a very nice lilting, Scottish voice but it didn't help. Eyes glazed and bottoms shuffled. Further *instructions* were to follow, a collective knew — but routine boredom threatened to make them go unheard, as did most others.

"We adults know what is best for you children at *all* times and so it is important to *never* lie to us. You must always *tell us* the truth for your *own* good…"

The four chosen souls' earthly arms began to ache with the unwanted placards and they began to *really* look at the faces of the children before them. Unseeing eyes told of unhearing ears. All four felt uneasy now. The blankness in the eyes of the other children suddenly frightened them. Miss Rubio carried on and for some reason her words started to burn in the ears of all four children at once. Tell the truth to the *adults*! Tell the truth to *parents*; to *teachers*; to *policemen;* and to *doctors*… *Us* tell the truth! *They* have *forgotten* the truth! That's *our* job, they thought together. They looked at each other as butterflies, this time with wings of *fire*, danced in their tummies. As they caught each other's eyes they saw they *too* shone *as flame*. Four sets of arms threw down their placards and still with glitter on their faces, four bodies stepped forward towards the sea of souls before them, still unsure what they were going to do next.

Something about the four figures standing out from the rest was *magnetic* and every eye in the hall turned to face them with full attention. Miss Rubio just stood open mouthed.

"No!" began Venus with a shout that startled them all, and everybody — including the other three — jumped. "It's not true *any* of that actually. The adults don't know what they are doing *at all*…"

All the children in the room sat up a notch.

"Not at all!" chimed in Anna angrily, then a bit more calmly, "The whole world is all just a big mess at the moment because of all these *adults* and their ideas, so we *children* are just going to have to sort it out ourselves."

Eyes in cross-legged bodies grew wider.

"Don't worry *we* know how," Ethan interrupted. "It's all going to be fine because there's this Truth fairy and —"

"Ethan! Anna! Venus!" Miss Rubio sounded desperate. "What are you *saying*?! I think they must have been watching something on TV Mr Johnson…"

"It's not *television!*" shouted a horrified Venus. "Its planets and stars and Universal *Truths*."

"Enough!" roared Mr Johnson, as several teachers moved towards them all.

Children who had never known this level of live entertainment cheered as their three heroes were carried out one by one.

"You are *all* Good," cried Anna as she was carried through the big hall doors.

"You are *all* Kind," said Ethan's feet in the doorway.

"You are *all* Beautiful," Venus laughed very loudly on her exit.

"You are *all* Loved," came a shout from the front of the hall which made *everybody* stop *everything*.

"And *that's* the truth."

It had come from *Louis*.

Silence. Nobody knew *what* to do *then*.

Mr Johnson did. He steered Louis out from the hall with a single hand to the shoulder and to the side of the other three children who were waiting outside his office in the foyer, beneath a huge statue of St Aytas.

The four children remained in the foyer in silence for some time as the rest of the school were marched past them and back to various classrooms on the corridor, pointing and laughing as they went, their elation disappearing by the second.

"I have never seen such a display of *disobedience*," Mr Johnson started after he had smoked a pipe in his office to calm his nerves. This was a *most unusual* situation! He could *only* punish in the circumstances but their words *haunted* him all the same.

"Your parents and guardians have been called by the school secretary and they are coming to collect you now."

No!

This *couldn't* happen!

They would never even make it to the music room.

They would all be *at home* at three o'clock now! They would *miss* Alma completely. They all began to feel sick with panic. Oh, they had broken their word to her so *spectacularly*!

Everything was ruined!

Mr Johnson continued

"I really don't know *what* has come over you all! To say such things, I mean I've never heard such nonsense! Condemning the *police*, your teachers and even your *parents*! Lord knows what *they* will all say! Where on *Earth* you have got it all from is beyond me…"

Venus wanted to tell him it wasn't *from* Earth at all actually, but none of them had the will to so much as look up from the floor. They had clearly totally failed on behalf of the Truth Fairy and now they were alone and grief-stricken to have done so.

As they stood in wait of their separate fates at home, each child realised they would never see Alma again.

But nor would they *ever* forget her truths.

Maybe it was just too soon.

One day, they all resolved silently to each other's souls, they would *make* them all listen.

With that the school bell tolled twelve noon and the world around the children stood completely still.

Lesson No 2

From the very opposite end of the corridor from the entrance foyer where the children stood, they *felt* the musical velvet tones once more, this time with an urgency they were not sure they liked.

"Come to the old music room *at once*. I have arrived just in time it would seem."

The children dared not even look at each other but their legs once again knew where to take them — right past the frozen headmaster and the school secretary, whose mouth was open mid-sentence. Along the corridor past the rooms full of statues of various school scenes. As they travelled along they all felt fear as to what was to come next but they each also felt immense relief. Whatever they had done wrong and however angry Alma might be with them, they would now have a chance to explain and more importantly, to be in her presence once more. Four souls entered the old music room with heads held high and took their places at the desks.

Noah's Ark streamed in its colourful dusty light, but nothing could take away from the power of Alma's golden aura. This time as she turned the four souls felt her fierceness and her still radiant face told them of her unhappiness.

This time she spoke.

"My dearest friends," her velvet tones did not *sound* these words as they had *felt* them before. The children felt deeply upset. "I invited you for your bravery and outstanding natures to impart the most precious of Universal information…"

Four sets of eyes felt the threat of tears. The disappointment in her voice was *too* awful.

"The Universe and I *trusted* you all with the most *sensitive* of truths and then the most *wondrous* of miracles as a thank you for your assistance."

Oh it was a *privilege* four minds wanted to scream, but remained silent.

"We asked only *one* rule be stood by. You were *forbidden* from telling anyone outside of the classroom any of the information given to you — until we met again at three o'clock *this* afternoon. What *actually* happened was at 11.16 a.m.?"

Four bottoms squirmed in their seats.

"You announced to the *entire* school — *including* adults — the *vast* majority of the first lesson."

She paused and met every set of eyes in turn with her enchanting flames.

"The Universe and I can only say…

Four souls awaited Alma's wrath.

"Congratulations! You have passed your first test with flying rainbow colours! Never be afraid to break the rules. You all did *fabulously* ahahaha…"

And with that her laughter tinkled magically around them all and her face melted into the most breath-taking loving smile *yet*.

What on Earth is going on?!? The four simultaneously thought, and then quickly, *How silly* we are! This is not about *Earth*.

They *had* done the right thing after all — and it had *felt* right.

Five sets of lovely laughter rang in the old music room and the four children's auras began to glow gold, as Alma's.

After some time revelling in their freedom and contentment once again, the children sensed there was yet more to be known. Alma's gaze drew back their utmost attention. Once again words were not *spoken* but *felt*.

"Yes indeed, The Universe and I congratulate you all *deeply*. But this is the first of *many* tests of your strength and your character my friends. I will not be able to attend the aftermath of them *all*. How would you have been if your parents had indeed come to collect you? What of the many questions that would surely have been asked of you after the Assembly by *all*? Do you have these answers ready?"

Four souls knew for certain they did not.

"Therefore, my *dearest friends,*" the feeling in her words was back, "lesson two *must* be: *Action, Reaction* and *Consequence.*"

The words magically wrote themselves in the golden chalk on the board as she spoke.

Now what was all of *this*?

"*Action.* As you know so well now, dear Ethan, good thoughts are alone not enough to *feed* your soul. We need *action.*

Do to other souls as you wish to *have done* to yourself.

You *will* fail at times and *do* bad things.

You are still a good *soul.* As today your *intention* was good.

If you do a bad thing, try to take away the lesson from it…"

Anna's soul chimed in proudly;

"Take the sunshine and the rain and make *rainbows* whenever you can."

"*Exactly.*" Alma gave her a colourful smile.

"*Reaction.*" Alma's tone felt very serious with these new words. "You cannot know the reaction of other souls to these Universal Truths until you *try,* as you saw today. Think how new and strange all of this felt to you only a week ago! You have received absolute confirmation this weekend that many souls you meet will never allow themselves to see. You must take some harsh reactions and allow all souls time and space to understand…"

Venus felt she simply *must* tell them all.

"Every time you learn a difficult lesson or you see loveliness in a horrible thing it just makes you *more* beautiful inside. It's *amazing*! We are *all* beautiful souls, no matter what *anybody* thinks."

"*Precisely*!" Alma shone an extra gorgeous smile to the lovely Venus and continued.

"Other people's reactions are *just* that, they belong to *them* and *not* to *you*. You can only stand by *your own* actions and reactions. So make them *count*. *Always* take action when your soul feels the need, but be ever prepared for the *reaction* of others. It may not be what you expect or what you want. So you must always be strong in *your* belief of *your* truths."

Alma paused just in time. This lesson was *definitely* more difficult than the last, but four souls understood everything nonetheless.

They all needed a rest.

At this moment, the musical instruments which had lain dormant in the old music room for many years lifted themselves from the walls and began to play the most beautiful and soulful music any of the children had ever heard and they drifted into a contented rest, together.

A while later five beings came too completely refreshed yet remembering all they had learned.

"My darlings, it is time for us to address *consequence*. Consequence is simply yet another Universal Truth we *cannot* ignore. It is the same for a scientist as for a Buddhist monk. It is the only thing on which *all* of the manmade theories and religions agree. All of the actions of all the souls in existence have consequences for other souls."

These words made the most sense of all to the children. They all had more than *words* to believe in *here*, they had actual and real experience of what other souls had *done* to them.

They all silently vowed there and then to never try and make another soul feel as they had felt in the past.

Alma continued after an Earth-shattering smile.

"As today has shown you clearly, the answers are all *inside* you, my lovely friends, but perhaps now you will all be a little wiser in your approach to the '*how*' we shall deliver our message."

This was the lesson they realised. First had come the truths and now, they must discover *how* to spread their message.

None of them knew *instantly* how they were going to do this for the best — probably *not* like the Assembly this morning though they all silently agreed.

They would need to be more careful, clearly.

Obviously Alma had a plan.

"You are my *first* class of this kind, but you shall not be my *last*," she began to explain. "I have chosen children in villages of all the countries of this world to share and show the Universal Truths to too. They, like you, are special and brave souls who chose difficult lives as *you* did when we *first* met."

With this statement she had lost *all* of the children.

"Let me explain." Alma recognised their confusion. "As I have already told you I have a *very* important job in the Universe. I help souls to choose their Earth mothers and *with* them, their lives. I make sure they are ready for life at that special time and guide them to the start of their Earth journey. *This* is where we first met. Some brave souls, such as you four, choose the most difficult of journeys in order to learn and to teach other souls. As I said in the first lesson, souls here on Earth are *given* a family and they *do* their best."

From somewhere deep inside the four souls *remembered* this to be true. They had all *indeed* met Alma in another time and place.

"However, there is a dark force which wants Earthly souls to remain feeling sad and angry and unloved — this is *killing* our dear Mother Earth. She wants *so* much to be a loving home for all souls. *She* sees the Universal Truths in every one. She needs *help* — and *this* is where *you* come in my dearest friends. She needs your action, your minds, your *force*."

"Like an *Army*?" Ethan shivered at the *very* word and the images of violence and horror it made him see.

"Not an *army*," Alma corrected. "A *Legion*, a brotherhood, a sisterhood, a collective. Your armour is your words, your intentions, your love, your *true* beauty, your kindness, your gentleness and your strength of soul. A Legion yes — but a legion of *butterflies*. As you saw today, butterflies can have wings and eyes of flame and cause *revolution*."

Her words came fiercely again, then gentler than ever.

"Butterflies *are*, in general though, gentle and majestic characters revered for their grace and ability to change."

Four souls had found their new way of *being*.

"You shall not be alone, you will have brothers and sisters across the globe helping to spread your message and alongside you, you will have each other."

Four souls knew a bond had formed between them that would *never* be broken and a look to one another confirmed this in an instant. All felt *loved*.

"You four are the first members of this new legion. We have *tried* the adults in the past, but the truth lies in the eyes of a child, they *accept* and they *believe*. The golden age of childhood is too quickly over but *you* will begin the generation that *doesn't* forget. The Universe trusts you implicitly. You *will* be a brave and powerful group.

You *are* the;

Butterflies Of New Justice.

A legion the world has never known the like of before. You *will* change the world order and you *will* enable the beings of light to conquer the darkness."

Four souls felt an overwhelming sense of pride.

"My dearest friends, take this sign of your experiences."

With this Alma touched each head in turn and with that, upon the head of each child there appeared a golden feather in place of one strand of hair — even shaven-headed Louis received a stub of a feather which he would grow in his own time.

"Every morning touch the feather and repeat three times;

I am a good soul;

I am a kind soul;

I am a beautiful soul;

And, I am loved.

This is *most* important, my darlings — please always do so."

Four souls definitely always would.

Adoration shone from Alma's eyes as she impartcd

"Never forget what the Universe has shown you — *everything* is possible, all souls exist *infinitely* and you are indeed loved *immensely*."

Four souls would *never* forget.

"My dearest friends, our time together draws to an end." Alma herself appeared to be sad at this statement.

Four souls were nigh on distraught. They had longed *never* to hear these words. Yes they knew that all of Alma's Truths were *just* that, but they also knew the road immediately ahead of them was going to be *extremely* difficult for them *all*. Being in this dusty old music room with its feeling of better times gone by and in the radiance of the glorious Alma gave them a sense of safety they knew they would not feel again for some time.

"It *won't* be easy, it *can't* be easy. It is a task only for the brave and the strong, of which you *all* most definitely *are*. I don't believe We could have chosen better souls."

Alma's smile *now* took their souls into an embrace of the warmest affection you could imagine. They were completely enveloped in her and they felt an amazing yet gentle surge of energy recharge them totally. They all — including Alma — had no wish to break from this embrace for some time.

"Right. Any questions?" Alma sniffed.

"Absolutely." Anna surprised herself with her quickness to say, "Why can I not *dance* anymore, Alma?"

"Oh, my dear, you *can*!" she half laughed. "You had so much built a wall around your soul for your own safety — I had to knock it down *quite* fiercely. You will dance once again, with perfection for all of your days, darling Anna."

"Oh, thank you!" Anna almost cried, then said, "but what about Miss Duerres? I *kicked* her, Alma!"

"Anna, Miss Duerres *saw* how your mother took you from the dance school, my darling. She will be keeping a *very* close eye on you from now on, believe me. You have a guardian angel for life in this lady. Your red pumps will dance many more times. And you will show the world how even from the darkest of beginnings can come the very brightest of stars."

Anna smiled to her very soul.

"Ethan my dear boy," Alma added, "you will show Ely the way to the light. Show him love where he shows you hate, however *do not* tolerate violence. Your Mother has become startlingly aware of this side of him, so I *suspect* she will be more vigilant from now on."

Ethan nodded feeling entirely stronger *and* kinder than he ever had.

"Venus my *most* beautiful of souls," Alma shone proudly at her ever faithful and believing Venus. "What *you* will achieve is beyond even my powers of explanation. *You* will bring Venus' souls back to her to replenish. *You* will *save* her species and remind them of their true beauty which lies in their gentleness and tranquillity and inner strength. They will be the *first* to join your legion. As a sister of Venus may *I* thank you from the bottom of my soul."

Still too small in years to understand this fully Venus had seen and had *always* believed enough to simply smile and nod.

"What about me?" came a voice Alma had waited a long time to hear in person

"My darling Louis. What about *you*." Her eyes misted. "Well you can do just about *anything* as you know — that is up to you… but look around you at *who* you now *have*."

Louis took in the other misplaced, imperfect lovely children in the room and he felt that he would *always* have *them* from now on. They radiated love back to him.

"You, Ethan and others will do for planet Mars what Venus, Anna and others shall do for planet Venus." Alma felt serious towards him now. "Don't be afraid. Having considered so much in silence others will listen to what you say, so choose your words carefully. Make them kind. Show the souls of Mars that love, kindness and affection does not make you any *less* strong, but *ever* stronger. You have witnessed life without love and affection (or so you thought) however, now you *know* you are not alone — even that your mother is with you every night for as long as you will need."

Louis didn't get that last bit, of course he would *always* need her silly, but apart from that *yes*! She was *so* right. You need other people. Not just some *one* — others, a community. *That* was what he had loved in the soap operas. People being with and *knowing* other everyday people like *them*. Even Mum had laughed at the misplaced affection thing. He would slowly, hopefully know the love his mum had promised him. He would show others how it was done in the end *he* reckoned. But he really wasn't keen on this talking lark. He would be doing very little of that he reckoned also. But he knew an awful lot about others from his silent perspective.

"I really think we are just about finished here, my lovelies!" Alma sighed.

Four souls were tired and absolutely *fine* with that strangely enough.

"You *are* ready, aren't you?" Alma smiled. "Oh it has been my *pleasure* to meet you all again, you have brought me so much joy!"

She felt exactly the same returned times four.

"We *will* meet again someday," she stated truthfully. "Until then, know my love is *ever* with you all."

"Hang on, what about Assembly?" Ethan and Venus said at once.

"Time is only an *Earthly* measure," Alma smiled. "Try to ignore it as *much* as you can. You will be returned to class in time for lunch having *surpassed* yourselves in placard holding and all in possession of one of Miss Rubio's gold stars. No one will have a memory of your fabulous protest I'm afraid, well other than me and the Universal Council — whom I can safely say will all cherish it *forever*. A *marvellous* display!"

They were all embraced for a long time and once again kissed on both cheeks.

"Oh, my dears, I almost forgot! A little *Earthly* advice while I am here."

The children listened intently once more.

"Food should not contain *numbers* and things you don't understand — your body needs to serve you and your soul so be careful what you put into it. Be careful of alcohol also — I'm sure you have *all* seen its effects on the adults at times. Look to the plants Mother Earth provides for your salvation — she only wants to nurture you. Eat and use only what you need and be mindful always of the waste of yourself and others. Planets, like souls, need love, kindness, gentleness and care. While you are here treat Earth with respect, as she were another soul. I think that's everything, yes… I imagine you are all going to be just fine."

Alma's bright voice contrasted her sad eyes.

Four souls silently assured her they would be absolutely fabulous.

It was the end of this magical adventure, but the start of something so unknown and fantastic for them all that they couldn't feel sad. They had now seen how everything was all connected, they would never feel alone again. And because each of our brave souls *were* just that, they wanted to show as many others as possible. There and then they would set about doing that and so they were prepared to leave the old music room and Alma. They would never be afraid of this room again and it would make a *fabulous* den — no one would ever *dare,* ha ha! Maybe start the Butterfly marching band…

As four *ready* souls turned to leave Alma behind, she called after them…

"My darlings, I love you all *so much.*" And they felt just that. "And never forget the power of a *smile.*"

They never would.

The End

My Dearest Friend,

Unfortunately I am cannot invite every Earth child to attend one of my classes, although I would simply adore to see you again in your lovely Earth form. The Truth is you are all brave and wonderful souls and each of your journeys are just as important as Anna's, Ethan's, Venus' and Louis'. You also have your own talents and skills and problems and struggles. Your Earth self is as gloriously imperfect as these children and the same Universal Truths apply to you;

You are a good soul;

You are a kind soul'

You are a beautiful soul;

And you are loved.

Tell yourself often and see it in the souls around you. **Believe** and you will experience miracles as wondrous as anything seen in St Aytas Village. Miracles of kindness and love and justice.

Just as the other children I need your help.

This is your invitation to be a Butterfly Of New Justice.

As you are a strong, gentle, fierce, beautiful, courageous, kind soul you are perfect to join our Legion. Please accept. Whether you are a soul of Venus or Mars take our messages of hope, love and peace to the souls of Earth. We **are** the light and we **will** conquer the darkness.

Join us.

Until We meet again, darling friend, know that my love is ever with you.

Alma

xx

B.O.N.J. Legion

PENTAGRAM
CHILD

PART TWO

BY

STEPHANIE HUDSON

The Pentagram Child - Part 2
The Afterlife Saga #6
Copyright © 2020 Stephanie Hudson
Published by Hudson Indie Ink
www.hudsonindieink.com

The Pentagram Child - Part 2/Stephanie Hudson – 2nd ed.
ISBN-13 - 978-1-913769-23-9

WARNING

This book contains explicit sexual content, some graphic language and a highly addictive Alpha Male.

This book has been written by a UK Author with a mad sense of humour. Which means the following story contains a mixture of Northern English slang, dialect, regional colloquialisms and other quirky spellings that have been intentionally included to make the story and dialogue more realistic for modern-day characters.

Please note that for your convenience language translations have been added to optimise the readers enjoyment throughout the story.

Also meaning…

No Googling is required ;)

Also, please remember that this part of a 12 book saga, which means you are in for a long and rocky ride. So, put the kettle on, brew a cup, grab a stash of snacks and enjoy!

Thanks for reading x

CHAPTER ONE

KEIRA

TRANSCENDING IN THE PAST

"What do you believe in, Keira?"

"What do you mean?" I asked in that naive way only a child has perfected over the first ten years of their life.

"You told your teacher that a boy in your class was a monster." The doctor in front of me said and I had to bite my lip to stop it from shaking. I found this helped in fighting back the tears but most importantly the fear. Even at that young age I knew. I didn't fully understand it but still I knew. Because it was something about the fear that they loved and that boy in my class was no different.

I still remember walking into the playground that day and forgetting all about the climbing frame I wanted to play on when I heard a sound that would haunt my dreams for years to come.

"Come here little Benny, come play with me." I had never heard the voice before and even as I was still making my way around the corner, I knew there was something wrong with the way it sounded.

"I have something I want to show you." The voice continued and for a second my body stopped moving from fear of what I would actually see. The rational side of me that was only in its infancy of developing knew I should turn around and run. That I should get someone else to help but the different part of me, the one that had been forced upon me on my 7th birthday was overriding safety for one that was being *demanded* of me.

That was a sense of duty I didn't understand but one I couldn't ignore, no matter how much I tried. So I forced my body to make the steps needed and that's when I saw my first 'child' demon.

It was one of those points in your life that even then I knew you could never get back from the consuming horror. I would never be able to claw that sight from my memory no matter how long I dug for it. I could pick away until my fingers were nothing but bloody gnawed bones and I would barely scratch the surface of mental damage done.

So instead my fingers clung to the brick wall for support and I scraped my fingertips along the rough surface just for the proof I needed that this was real and not just another one of my nightmares. But the irritation against my young skin proved that it was indeed real life…*my new real frightening life.*

I heard my classmate, poor Benny Rodgers cry out his terror at the same time a silent gasp escaped my lips.

"What's the matter, don't you want to touch my friend?" The demon mocked and for the first time I lost sight of my fear for a far stronger emotion…*anger!*

"Get away from him!" I shouted without thinking about the consequences for once. I didn't focus on the gruesome sight that was a sadistic chalk white face, one made uneven by patches of scabbed skin. Or the black vertical lines that passed downwards through his eyes and reached his cheeks like some creepy clown sent with the sole purpose to scare the essence out of us children.

Even his hair had changed colour, shape and texture. It now resembled blood red candy floss and was parted in the middle with a thick black line, one that started at the tip of his nose from a fine painted needle point.

No, all I saw was the small demon holding up his t-shirt in front of the terrified Benny and taunting him with the gruesome part of him. It was a face caught beneath his skin that was protruding out of his belly like he had swallowed an even smaller demon, one trying in vain to break free with his teeth.

"Do you want to touch it gir…?" He turned his head as he asked the question but when he saw it was me his question finished with an angry hiss. He dropped his t-shirt and looked back to grin down at the boy on finding he had wet himself.

Just then a teacher I had never seen before came from around the corner and stopped to look and take in the scene in front of her. Only what she saw wasn't what the rest of us knew was really happening.

"Ssshh." The demon said as he turned his head in slow motion without moving the rest of his body and then gently put one pale long finger to his lips. The evil grin he displayed showcased row after row of tiny pointed teeth, all with gaps in between blackened gums.

"Oh Benny, look at what you did." Said the teacher when taking note of Benny's wet school trousers and wrinkling her nose in blatant disgust.

"But it wasn't his fault!" I shouted clenching my small fists and getting my first real taste of injustice. The teacher frowned down at me and the disbelief was clear as day or as clear as

3

what should have been the sight of the demon in front of her very eyes. I remember my anger mounting the longer it went that she couldn't see him for what he really was. Did she need telling? Did she need it pointing out for his true side to be revealed?

"No it was my fault Miss...I...I guess I just didn't realise I needed to go so badly." Benny said giving his lame excuse and I couldn't believe my ears. Why was he sticking up for this demon, the one that had hurt him, I just couldn't understand it!

"That's not true! He made him do it!" I protested in vain, pointing my finger at the demon she couldn't see. She started to cross her arms but I barely noticed as my eyes went past her to see the demon boy had his hand on Benny's shoulder. It was as if his touch was sucking the truth from Benny and making him lie.

Well if he couldn't speak up for himself then I was going to do it for him, no matter what this demon would do to me. However this was the one day that would be filled with lessons that would stick with me for the rest of my days. And as a result, instead of giving me a voice to do good it was going to silence me for *my own good...*

Until the day Draven found me.

"BUT HE'S A MONSTER!"

"You're a Monster!" I screamed at him from the place I remained on the floor with a broken body but far from a broken spirit. The very words took me back to my childhood and like before I found I was crying out for the injustice that lay before me.

"Get away from him!" I screamed, only this time at the evil prick that in my opinion was far too inhumane to have been granted a real name...

Alex.

I loathed the very name. I wanted it wiped out of existence

so that no poor soul could be associated with its evil origins. I tried to bring a part of myself back from the raw hatred but one look down at myself and all the damage he had caused cast such thoughts back to the pits of despair of the likes that Draven had now been thrust into.

I lifted a heavy head, feeling the blood trickling down past my eye and not even having the strength in me to wipe it away. No, I was reserving all that was left in me for one single act of revenge. Just one chance to take him off guard or maybe I would finally learn once and for all how to control what gifts the other world had bestowed upon me.

And what of its King? I turned my head, letting the rest of the blood soak deeper into my hairline and looked towards the altar with a heavy heart at what I found there. It was as if the essence of Draven had replaced his physical form and a shimmering light still clung to the contours of his flesh. It looked almost as though I could have ran my hand straight through him and come away with nothing but a cold lost feeling and a handful of gold, glittering dust.

"Aww, is the bitch missing her faithful hound?" Alex mocked and I reluctantly tore my eyes from what was left of the man I loved and scowled at all the reasons for my suffering. I thought about all he had taken from me and worse yet, what was still left for him to take. My heart was still breaking for my unlikely friend, whose heart I quickly held as dear as family.

Lucius

I still couldn't believe he was really gone. I kept trying to convince myself that it was impossible and that he would once again show up, ready to save the day. But then the haunting memory of seeing the last of the light fade from his eyes was enough of a cold slap of reality needed to bring me back to the devastating truth…

Alex *had* killed Lucius.

"Murderer." I muttered feeling my rage building but still trying in vain to keep a level head.

"Ahh, she speaks again…what was that?" He asked holding up a hand to his ear and smirking at me like there was some cosmic joke that only he knew.

"MURDERER!" I screamed with all hopes of maintaining that calm escaping my willpower. I could even feel the tendons on my neck strain and my lacerated skin on my arms scream in agony as I pounded my fists against the floor. If anything the pain grounded me and fuelled my rage the way I needed it to.

"Kill a few mortals and you're a murderer but bring down an immortal empire and you're a God…go figure."

"I wouldn't mind seeing Zeus imprison your worthless ass this time!" I snapped knowing I was just feeding into all his bullshit craziness but not being able to help myself. I watched as his face first contorted into one of loathing and then just as though I snapped my fingers his face changed and his sadistic grin was back in place.

"Well, well, just look at you…been learning our history have you?" I just sneered at him in disgust and had to hold back the urges of throwing my useless body at him in a hopeless attempt at killing him.

"Go on, try it and just see where it will get you! After all, your friend in there didn't fare so well against me… did he now?"

"Impossible…" I heartbreakingly whispered to myself. I just couldn't imagine it. It was like some deeper part of me wouldn't give up on him and let myself believe what my eyes had seen. There had to be some mistake, maybe part of the plan? Yes, that had to be it!

This thought must have been portrayed on my face because the next thing I heard was his vile laughter echoing around the room.

"Ha! You don't believe it do you…you don't believe I have enough power in me to kill him!?" He finished his taunt with even more laughter. Then as if to prove just how much of a good time he found all this he bent at the waist and rested his hands on his knees to laugh harder.

"None of your kind could kill him!" I said attacking back the only way I could.

"None of my kind? And what is that exactly…? A Nephilim? A fucking half breed bottom feeder?! You know it's that same stupidity that got you all here in the first place. That same narrow minded pathetic waste of space that fills tiny minds, tiny minds that refuse to open themselves up to the possibilities." He said ranting on and spraying the floor with his spit in his haste to get out his words.

"Oh and there is just so many possibilities to releasing destruction on the earth is there?!" I threw back at him.

"Well now you mentioned it, yes there is and let me explain to simple minds why…" I tried to hold back the urge to roll my eyes, I really did…oh who am I kidding, even if I'd had my eyes stapled to my hairline I would have still tried!

"You know what, I think I will pass on your bat shit crazy for today, I think my tank's full!" This turned out the wrong thing to say no matter how good it felt seconds afterwards, in the long run it didn't feel so great for me or my scalp. He was down next to me in a heartbeat and wrenched my head back by my hair so I no choice but to play audience to his sick play.

"Not full enough, so listen up Bitch at what you have to look forward to…" I tried to pull my head back but his grip merely tightened causing tears to escape the corners of my eyes as the pain intensified. He pulled me closer and I became the next victim to his spit sprayed words…words that cast my soul into the shadows of dread and kept me imprisoned there.

"Human eradication. Mortal extermination. The annihilation

7

of Men…Finally the time of personal extinction for the vermin that have been allowed to walk this earth is now and the Titans will not only ensure this, but will strike down anyone that stands in our way!"

"You're INSANE!" I screamed but knew it would do no good from the faraway look of glee he had in his mad eyes. I had to wonder just how long this psychosis had inflicted him or whether he had been born with the sickness and it was being fed from his core.

I found myself trying to focus on finding answers to where this need to destroy so many came from but too much blood loss and that was proving difficult. I could feel myself dying and I found the only benefit to this was that the heinous creature before me started to fade.

"Oh dear, am I boring you?" Alex asked on a snigger and gave me a painful shake like this would help. If I'd had the strength I would have smacked him upside the head and told him he was the idiot! Instead I just seemed to let my body go limp and I slumped from his grasp, which I found was one more blessing to add to my impending death.

All I could wish for was that Draven would make it back to me in time for me to tell him I loved him for the last time. The thought was a crushing one but it was hard to see any other way out of this. I was lying here like a fallen soldier framed by my own blood and having only the strength left to wallow in self-pity for the lost love I had once again found. There was little justice left in the world to find the outcome would be much different from the dire one painted by a mad man.

My body had become numb against the pain and I wasn't sure if this was an inevitable sign of death or just that the pain was being overridden by despair. One not only for those that I had lost but for those I loved which would soon be lost to the world.

I was a creature of habit and that wasn't the habit of giving up but with my cheek to the floor and my skin's pores soaking up lost blood, I knew I didn't have anything left in me.

I knew that I didn't have long.

I wondered if Draven would know the moment it happened? Would he feel my last breath leave me? Would he then be able to give up the fight and walk away? I let myself rejoice in the knowledge that maybe then there would be no war to fight. That with my death he would shatter the vial of blood Alex had given him and with it destroying the key that could release the Titans. My death would save millions and if I had the means to end it right now I would have taken the plunge.

I would have taken it not just for those who I know, not just for my sister, mother and father. Not just for the loved ones I had been born into loving but for the loved ones that had magically come into my life. Frank, my precious little niece Ella, whom I had helped bring into this world, RJ who had become my best friend, and someone for all I knew I had already lost. Someone who had been thrust into a fight that was not her own just for knowing me? How many would continue to hurt and die just for knowing me?

I might have been Draven's Chosen One, but no one chose to have my life infect their own like a disease with only one cure.

My eradication. My extermination. The annihilation of my own soul. And finally the time for my personal extinction so others could live. No, it was not right for me to have one last wish in seeing Draven again and speaking words of love.

No, now I had a new wish…

My date with Death.

CHAPTER TWO

DRAVEN

BROKEN GODS

I had watched many horrors in my countless lifetimes but none even came close to watching the woman you loved in dying agony. Seeing each wound lacerate her body over and over was living a torture of the likes I had never known. The battle that raged inside me was a torrent of emotion flooding my senses with both the need to kill and destroy but also to protect. I knew what needed to be done in order to keep the balance to my people and the mortals we shared this earth with but seeing my girl in danger overrode all of my rational mentality.

So I took her place and could only pray that in my absence she would remain safe. I had to believe that or my demon would take over completely and seeing where I had now come, I needed that belief more than ever. It would be so easy to let myself go completely and free the beast that lived at the centre of my rage.

It also wanted his girl safe and unharmed and anything that threatened that only needed to be eradicated in the eyes of the demon. But what the cretin Alex didn't know and what my Keira had to trust in was that I *too* had a plan.

Belphegor had been more than a little helpful after our persuasive chat and I was surprised when so little force was needed for him to crack. It had been a disappointment really as I had hoped to have relieved some of the mounting pressure I felt from having my Electus taken from me. But one look at me entering that Dublin pub and his vessel had nearly *relieved* itself. After that he had told me all I needed to know about one Alex Cain and his sordid family history.

I had to hand it off to Sammael at the sheer depth of his plans. They had taken root near the very beginning of time. But unbeknown to all of us it was only through the right alignment of the planets and all levels of Heaven and Hell could such a feat be accomplished. And that feat was the key to unleashing the Titans. A key that I now held in my hand at the mouth of Tartarus.

I looked down at the vial of blood in my palm and then back up at the black volcanic wasteland that surrounded the Mountain. I knew where I needed to go and what lay in the belly of the prison, a fact I didn't relish.

Inside the mountain was where the prisoners were kept. Where the worst of Hell's demons that could not be tamed remained forever bound.

The sides of Mount Tartarus weren't made from demonic rock formations at all but something far more sinister. It was a steep maze made from a mass of Devil's soulweed. A demonic plant life that entwined itself with the fossilised bones which represented the mortal victims of each incarcerated inmate.

As each new prisoner was added, so did the walls of the mountain. It grew from the lost souls of the lives taken and in fact became a piece of the guilty's punishment. And all this is spawn from the core in which it surrounds. Its centre was the heart from which true evil was born...

The Titans.

Thinking these gruesome facts made me clench my fist to a point where I needed to remember what I held in my hand. Knowing now that Alex had in fact orchestrated the whole reason I had bound myself to Tartarus was one that made my blood ignite with rage. All this time forces had been at work of the likes I had never known. For an enemy unseen, is an enemy that will come bearing a blade at your back and find a way to pierce your heart from the shadows.

I had always wondered why the leaders of this realm had put certain measures in place to prevent most Demons coming here but I had absentmindedly never put two and two together.

It was around the same time that the last of the Eves was found and finally a stop to her resurrection had been made. It was so blindingly obvious now but at the time I just considered Sammael's reasons were for personal gain and nothing more.

So now it was time for me to face the Demons I had once put there and in doing so putting the whole world at risk.

"Oh yeah, this is a great plan Dom." I said to myself before unfolding my wings and crossing the expansive space. The black surface looked like cracked concrete slabs that had been laid down with flowing lava as their foundations. It almost looked like miniature amber rivers were glowing through the crust.

It was said that when the Titans were defeated they were imprisoned in their once Temple of worship on top of Mount Olympus. Then the mountain they had once called home split open and the Temple fell into the earth and continued until finally stopping at the lowest level of Hell.

The impact rocked the core of the earth enough for magma to flood the imprisoned Titans, encasing their bodies in Hell's natural chains of an unbreakable force. All it would take is one break in the cooled lava that encased the bodies with igneous rock to allow them to break free.

And there was a time when only two men knew what the key was to breaking such a mighty force... Titan blood. Cronus knew this as it is said he was the only being to ever escape the fiery chains of Tartarus. But the once mighty leader and King of the Titans used the last of his powers to escape and had to do so leaving behind his kin, never again to have the strength to return to free them. Hence making it his mission ever since.

There was once a time when many of my kind believed this was the Prophecy the fates spoke of as the release of the Titans would most certainly mean war. And where the last War of the Gods brought new life, another would most certainly mean the end of it.

This was the reason getting into Tartarus was not an easy feat. It might have made for an indestructible prison but what it held at its heart also made it a dangerous one to even exist. But the Titans needed to be kept somewhere and unfortunately with the power of Heaven and now Hell combined, they had little choice seeing as they could not be destroyed.

These thoughts plagued me whenever I came here. But when I decided to use this place as my prison, I only locked my demon to the outskirts. The last time I had touched this place was when making the decision to send Sammael here for his crimes. I had pounded my swords into the earth and called forth the Reapers of Tartarus to drag his soul back with them...when clearly the punishment should have been death.

But thanks to Aurora and her vile family connections I now

had my own VIP access card carved into my very skin, which meant I could walk directly up to the inner circle gates and gain entrance. Which was exactly what I was about to do.

The maze that covered the sheer mountain face was one that, even if a prisoner completed the unlikely task of escape, trying to find his way out of the maze would have sent him deeper into the realms of his own madness. And this would have been long before reaching what is known as the Tartarus crust.

This was the wasteland I had spent far too long staring out at in depths very close to my own madness as a result of being without my Chosen One. But I was a prisoner no more and soon my Keira would be back in my arms with the blood of my enemies at our feet, where they lay slain for their treason.

I swooped down noticing the guards positioned at the battlements as if at the ready for the war we all hoped would never come. Oh my kind had tried before. They thought that by coming in the masses with their armies behind them that they could release the Titans. Foolish enough to believe in doing so they would be granted favour by them or even more delusional, to believe they might even be controllable.

However that time was long ago but no less forgotten. And nor should it be, for the importance of keeping such an event from ever happening was one both Heaven and Hell were even willing to work together in preventing.

As I made my way up the maze surface I knew the only way to spot the cleverly disguised entrance was to look for the largest knot of Devil's soulweed. This was the only thing that grew in this place and it would have been better if nothing had grown at all.

It was like Hell's own version of Japanese knotweed, only this had vines the size of earth's tree trunks and was grey and lifeless looking. I actually took a moment to wonder why it was named what it was. Was it for the way it looked or for the way it attached itself onto the stone corpses and embedded its foot long thorns into the fossilised bones?

Either way Hell's natural parasite grew with as much fury as though the bodies of the damned fed its very roots. I didn't know what was stronger, the deathly vines or the mountain itself. I did however know how far those roots travelled, as I saw the evidence for myself every time I entered my people's crypt. The Tree of Lost Souls was foolishly also known as the Tree of Life but this was not because it represented what it gave but more like what it took away. And like its mother, I knew what the soulweed wanted the most in this world and right now that was my immortal blood.

That vermin Alex had certainly known what he was doing by feeding the Tree of Lost Souls Keira's blood. As soon as it had tasted that brand of ambrosia it had been like an electrical charge to a dead man's chest. The tree was known as the heart to not only my kingdom of the living but also to my kingdom of the dead.

And even the dead still had secrets to keep.

So it was time to go visit one soul that should have died by my hand a long time ago...

Sammael.

I let my wings fold in on themselves just at the right moment to land. I knew that if I hadn't been in this vile realm I would have spent the falling seconds basking in the clean air pushing back at me. As it was however, the second I landed I needed to stretch out my wings in annoyance just to dispel the volcanic black dust this part of Hell was plagued with.

I stepped up to the tightest part of tangled thorns and tried not to think of what the other half of my soul could be going through right now. I should have healed her! I should have insisted, NO! I should have demanded that I heal her before allowing that bastard to send me here!

This mounting rage was more than enough encouragement needed to do what I had no choice but *to* do. I thrust both my bare arms into the hellish plant and let it yank me forward. The second it felt a warm body enter its domain I went forward nearly losing my footing the deeper it dragged me into its deadly breast. I clenched my teeth against what I knew was to come but no matter the anticipation, as it meant nothing the second the needle points pierced my flesh.

Pain was quickly followed by even greater pain as the thorns sank deeper into the pinnacle points of the entwined Pentagrams, the Tartarus symbols carved into the flesh on my forearms. I felt sick. Not from pain… No, I felt sick knowing the very reasons I was forced to take my knife and hand it over to Aurora. To unknowingly hand the fate of my kind and that of Keira's to a lost Titan bloodline.

But it wasn't using Aurora to do it that caused me to force my vessel to keep its stomach acid in place. No it was knowing that we had all been fooled for so long. How could I or any of us have missed the existence of Sammael's son living amongst us for so long? If that wasn't bad enough then finding myself tied to the lowest level of Hell because he had cursed the very necklace I gave to Keira, one that should have protected her...!

Oh yes, I felt sick indeed.

"Fuck!" I shouted, both from frustration at myself and from suddenly being hauled forward and being impaled by even more thorns to various parts of my body. I gritted my teeth and let my body be dragged into the belly of the soulweed until finally it released me by flinging my pierced body to the ground on the other side.

I had been expecting this kind of welcome but it still didn't mean it hadn't hurt like a son of a bitch! I got up on unsteady feet and let the anger inside me fuel my healing abilities, so that by the time I took my first step my vessel showed no signs of weakness.

Directly in front of me stood an arched door of black charred wood in the shape of escaping bodies. My educated guess was this was all that remained when the damned souls of this place had tried to escape these mountain walls. Escaping Tartarus was a useless endeavour and one never yet accomplished by my kind...

Until now.

Knowing what I was about to do went against the grain in every way possible as it was the complete opposite as to why I existed. My job was to protect the realms and for more centuries than I cared to count I had done this successfully. Never once letting my personal life infiltrate this goal. But just one slip into my memory bank at seeing Keira in agony and I was ready to take on all the wrath Hell had to offer just to save one human life. It was perfect insanity and the most beautiful of mistakes to make.

I never understood the meaning of true love and why those who have tasted its bitter sweet nectar would kill for just one more sip...until there was her. And bitter sweet this next action would be indeed...well, if all factors involved got their arses in place to aid me. Because as much as I hated to say it, if there was ever a time to admit that I couldn't do this alone, then that time was now...

Ego be dammed!

I walked up to the faceless shapes immortalised in the massive wood panels and waited to be granted entrance. It wasn't the type of place where you could just barge your way in any more than you could just knock and wait for the butler to answer. After about ten minutes I was just about ready to tear the bloody thing down and have done with it but as if my mounting rage was all that was needed, the door started to open.

A bluish glow emanated from behind the opening making me squint against it for a moment until my eyes adjusted. As the door opened further it was almost as if the space behind it had its own blue moon. I stepped inside and was not surprised that I wasn't that far off.

I had heard about this place but never before seen its haunting beauty. The sound of the echoing doors closing behind me only emphasized the size of the room I now stood in.

"The Temple of Lost Olympia." I felt compelled to speak its name as an emotion I don't usually feel overtook me. If I was to compare such a thing, I imagined it to be as simple as a young boy seeing something from his childhood stories now in the flesh.

The Temple of Lost Olympia was said to be on top of Mount Olympus and also known as the Temple of Worship, but when the mountain split so did the Temple, half of which became the Titan's prison. Knowing that I would be seeing one half was enough but this part was something else. It was as though a piece of Heaven itself had fallen down into the lowest depths of Hell and remained here untouched yet still broken.

The colossal pillars that once framed the great space were now crumbling marble and looked like slabs of broken, stone cogs lay amongst the rest of the rubble. Parts of the many giant statues of fallen Gods lined the long room and remained in various states of decay.

I walked down the centre that had strangely remained cleared of debris and couldn't help but look up at the hundred foot statues in awe. Gods that had once walked these very steps as I and could have gazed upon their own commemorated grand image of themselves.

To be honest I thought it was all slightly egotistical myself but that's what you usually found from the Gods and considering they got most of their power from being worshipped I guess it made sense...well that was until you saw for yourself where that worship got them. Broken and immortal remains in Hell, is where!

I had to shake my head at it all as I frustratingly had to move painfully slow through these parts, knowing what lurked in the shadows of Tartarus...

Harpies.

CHAPTER THREE

DRAVEN

BEAUTY TWISTED UGLY

As if I didn't have enough to contend with, one wrong move in this place and Zeus' throwaways would come by in swarms. Harpies were known as the hounds of Zeus, created for the sole purpose to steal for the arrogant God. He created a new race consisting of four sisters. They were beautiful bird like creatures with the faces to rival any Goddess. Long elegant bodies adorned with half milky skin and plush white feathers. As such they each were gifted with a set of magnificent wings that outshone any Angel known.

But as Zeus started to lose his powers as a God, so did he lose his patience with such things. His beautiful gift to the Heavens turned bitter and with that ungodly behaviour followed. The sisters became vicious, cruel and violent forcing Zeus to banish them to where he saw they would best suit.

It was said that as they fell from their God's grace they were stripped of any power gifted to them. They lost the power of flight and fell first to Earth to then keep falling until they landed in the pits of Hell. Their own feathers circled their twisting bodies as they plummeted to their demise. For our kind to be stripped of our wings there is no greater punishment on either side.

Zeus' wrath sent them straight to the same place he had banished the Titans, giving them what they had grown to enjoy best, a place they could torture freely. In time the once beautiful creatures turned into a form more fitting for their new home. But down here it isn't only the harsh environment that can seep into your very skin… It is the pure hate that can seep into your very soul.

So now they roamed freely amongst this mountainous prison as its shadowed wardens with no understanding of keeping peace within its walls. No, only pain and suffering is their goal…that and the continuation of their abominable race.

It was a sickening thought to know my kind, even the guilty and the worst of the worst would often be forced to lay with a Harpie. But the higher ranking Demons, the presidents of Hell like my father were more than happy to turn a blind eye to the likes of these creatures and their, shall we say, insatiable habits.

I had hoped in what was still considered a holy place that the Temple of Lost Olympia held nothing but bad memories for the sisters. Therefore I assumed it was not only free of them but also their mutated offspring. However I couldn't take my assumption for granted which added greatly to my frustration. Taking steady steps still echoed in the vast space and my unease meant my blades forced their way from my vessel without the mental command given.

"Easy" I soothed my demon, one that I knew was far too near knife's edge. The blue glow that came from behind the biggest statue situated at the end of the room glinted off my weaponry the same way it did from all the pale and broken marble in the room. I frowned down at the giant severed arm that lay fallen from the God it was once attached to and all but heard my Demon growl at the thought.

"Not going to happen my friend." I told him in hopes of eradicating such thoughts. Still I suppressed a shudder, forcing my blades back as I finally came to the end.

I looked back at all the severed heads, crumbling torsos and lost limbs littering the cracked marble floor. I tried not to let my mind give in to torturous thoughts but it couldn't be ignored as I thought back to my own Temple and God's gift to me that lay bleeding out on the floor.

"She'd better live or you bastards are going to find another damn war at your gates!" I snarled up at the massive statue of Zeus himself sat upon a golden throne.

"Seventh wonder my ass!" I said as I walked past knowing that an exact replica once sat upon the Earth for mortals to worship. It was once considered one of the Seven Wonders of the Ancient World until its eventual loss and destruction during the 5th century AD. A destruction I might add that was still believed to be the work of his banished father Cronus. The very one that not only tried to have him murdered as a child but the very same one that ruled over the Titans and was defeated by his scorned son.

Ha and the human mortals thought they had drama to shout about! Forgiving the pun, but Hell, they had nothing on the other realms, myself included.

I rolled my eyes at the whole room, feeling now how once a mind of awe had quickly changed to one of disgust in so little time and so few steps taken. None of them mattered to me as they once had as they all represented the same thing and that was the shit storm they had brought to my home. One Keira had opened the door to…and worst of all, I had fucking let her!

23

I left the temple shaking my head in anger and in doing so barely had enough wits about me to dodge the attack from above.

"Damn Harpies!" I muttered in annoyance looking up from the floor I had just been forced to drop to. I pushed back up from my hands and slapped the volcanic dust from them as I scanned the area. This next space was a courtyard of sorts and was surrounded by jagged mountain rock. It almost looked like black quartz had erupted from the ground and formed natural knife-edged battlements all around us. I say 'us' as it became quickly apparent I was no longer alone.

"Ladies" I said nodding my head hoping they could detect my sarcasm over my anger at being detained any longer than I had to be. Unfortunately this turned out to be a failing on my part as even their rancorous teeth could be seen from down where I stood.

The four sisters stood out from the rest of their smaller offspring but it was not only from size alone but also from their higher positioning. They each had perched themselves at the highest point of rock and surrounded themselves with their family of minions at lower points around where I stood.

Given that only one stood tall amongst the sisters I knew there was a divide in the ranks and if there was one that needed taking out first, it was certainly that one. If there was such a thing as a Harpie with greater intelligence than a common dog then this would be the one

"Mine!" One snarled that was crouched down low and clutched the stone with its clawed hands. All three heads snapped round to the claim and each showed their distaste with a growl. The brazen one stretched out her face like a snake getting ready for the feast and spat at the others like an angry cat. The other sisters followed suit and portrayed the famous Harpie trait of displaying their fangs in anger. They then

stretched out their hideous wings of sagging aged skin, ones void of any feathers.

Even from down here I could see clearly the pot marks left from where their plumage used to be and it marred along the torn withered skin stretched between the long finger bones, ones that powered their limited flight.

They were more like a limp bat, gliding along and only being fed from the negative energy this place emits like one of Earth's power stations. I had to smirk at the idea of fighting these pathetic creatures. Oh yes, they might be greater in number than I but what did they take me for?

It took me back to the day I first warned Keira, that assumption is the mother from which all mistakes are born, of course my little Vixen had gone and threw it back in my face not long after.

For the first time since this mess I couldn't help but smile at the memory. Of course the Harpies took this for something else.

"Look sisters, we have one willing I think." They all snapped their elongated jaws in postulated excitement....well they were soon to taste disappointed in the form of swallowing their own blood and that was a promise.

"Think again Celaeno." I said pleased to see the twisted mix of both fury and shock that I had guessed right. Celaeno meant 'Dark one' and in all the mythology I had heard about these four then it was the dark one that had led the other three to ruin. She held the most of what brains could be had in a Harpie and the other three followed her blindly.

It was said that her obsessive love for Zeus was what drove the maddening need to torture others in a tainted way to gain attention from her maker. Needless to say it backfired but this rage only inflamed their insatiable desire to take men against their will, demon or not.

The other three were recognisable through the power of

elimination as they too had their own descriptive names as their sister. Celaeno had the darker body of the four and was slightly bigger with her longer frame. Podarge was named for being 'fleet footed' so hence was quicker on her feet than in flight.

Aello and Ocypete were the twins, born it was said with their wings tightly entwined. Aello meaning 'Storm swift' and Ocypete 'The swift wing' obviously were named for their talents in the air and I could spot two that remained closer together. Their wings were slightly longer and sleeker in shape, no doubt to aid them with quick manoeuvers whilst flying.

"Willing or not, human you are ours to take!" Celaeno's threat was laughable if she really thought I were a mere mortal.

"Is that so?" I mocked and then looked down at my right hand as I welcomed one of my swords this time. I slowed its release to emphasise the power behind the action and the purple flames licked the blade until it reached the ash floor. I then cocked my head to the side and looked back up at the small winged army that were getting restless.

Celaeno was the only one smart enough to look shocked and as if feeling her anxiety her offspring all whined around her. I readied myself for when her shock turned to blind rage.

"Bring him to me!" She nodded to only two of her lower seated offspring thinking this was all that was needed. Well I couldn't say I wasn't looking forward to disappointing her.

One was quicker in its dismount than the other and swooped low trying in vain to sink its footed talons into my shoulder. Well if it wanted a flying companion then I wouldn't keep it waiting. I twisted at the last moment for it to only brush past me so that I had enough time to quickly grab a hold of its ankle. It snarled down at me as it unwillingly lifted me into the air. I looked down and waited for just the right moment.

"Come on, just a bit higher....there you go!" I said just as I saw the other one coming up underneath us.

"Perfect!" I quickly used my strength in my left arm to pull my upper body up, using its leg as a means to get higher. Then I pulled back my right arm before forcing it forward and plunging my sword into the Harpie's chest. It threw its head up and screeched in a death call up to its mothers.

I pulled back my sword and went into free fall letting go of the dying Harpie and summoned my other sword to come into the play. I had timed it perfectly as the other Harpie was now directly beneath me mid-flight. With one slashing motion both my swords sliced through their mark and both of its wings were severed.

That too called out to its mothers as I landed facing them impacting the ground enough to cause dust to cloud around me. I looked up in time to hear the two dead harpies fall to the grown behind me and I didn't bother reining in my cocky smirk.

The sisters all let out a mournful high pitched wail and I rolled my shoulders in preparation for the retaliation to come.

"I will enjoy making you scream half breed!" Celaeno roared and the half breed comment was enough to make me snap. My wings erupted from my back, proving just how wrong that statement was before I gave them my own promise,

"And I will enjoy mounting your fucking wings to my wall!"

She screamed and that was all her army needed to hear. They all at once left their perches in a wave of blackened wings and came at me where I stood. I waited for the first few to get closer before I spun round on one foot slicing through three harpies at once. Before their bodies had even hit the ground I launched myself up in the air to take the rest from above.

"Let's see if you can keep up with this." My wings expanded and held me mobile above so I could plan my attack. When I saw my opening I went for it letting my wings fold so I would fall, only opening them again at the right moment.

They were still trying to find me when I dropped in the centre and started taking their lives one by one. I had just finished bringing up my sword cutting one in half when I embedded my other blade in the chest of another. I had to use my foot to lever my blade free from its dying form and then kicked it so it went tumbling backwards.

It hit another of his siblings and they fell to the ground in a mass of tangled wings and spewing blood. I landed in time to end its life too before it could free itself from the web of death.

Soon the courtyard was puddled with Harpie blood and butchered remains. I had just used my boot once more to aid me against the head of the last dying offspring and pulled my sword free from its skull when I recognised the cries of grief.

"Unless the bitches of Zeus want to taste the same blade, this is done. Take me to the prisoner Sammael and I will spare your lives!" I slashed my blade down to make my point causing three of the weaker sisters to flinch back.

Celaeno however raked her talons against the quartz leaving deep claw marks in the stone. I tensed my body waiting for the next fight and just as I knew she was about to attack, I unfolded my wings to their full span and let the purple flames ignite in a show of power and dominance. It was all that was needed, that and one last look at all her dead offspring littering the ground around me.

"Who are you?" Podarge asked me and the others frowned at her curiosity.

"King of the mortal realm and son of Asmodeus in this one." Now *this* got a reaction. They all sucked in a sharp breath before they clicked their tongues against the roof of their mouths.

"Master…" They all hissed together and I wanted to roll my eyes. Maybe next time a flying hoard of demons wanted to rip me limb from limb I should mention my father's name….as infuriating as this realisation was, it was a damn sight quicker than engaging in battle that was for sure.

"We shall take you." Celaeno was the one to comply this time and she did so lowering her head in respect. Ok, so maybe not *all* of the presidents have turned a blind eye after all. The fact that it was my father was a sobering one indeed.

I let one of the sisters lead me and wasn't surprised that it was Podarge that wanted the task. She seemed like the quietest of the four or at the very least the more reasonable… if there were such a thing. Maybe I was wrong about their intelligence, as so far the only one to ask the right question was the creature now in front of me.

She walked at a steady pace which was maddening to me. I had to resist the urge to demand her go faster but knew that wasn't the right move. Granted I had defeated their army, one that would take them at least a few decades to recreate. But this place wasn't just a prison to keep inmates where they were sent on lockdown but also a place to lose them altogether.

A honeycomb of every horror imaginable just waiting to be discovered and if there was one thing I lacked, then it was time. The idea of roaming these endless corridors and passageways wasn't something I could afford to do. So for those valid reasons I followed behind the Harpie with clenched fists and grinding my teeth in frustration.

"What must you seek with this inmate?" Podarge asked after turning a corner. I was actually surprised by her question but more at the calm manner in which she'd asked it. After all I had just destroyed her children and I shuddered to think how many of them there would have been if it wasn't only the sisters that could reproduce.

"Vengeance." Was all I said causing her to look thoughtful a moment before nodding her head in acceptance.

"We are nearly there."

"And the Titans, where are they?" I inquired but this time I wasn't surprised by the reaction I received. She snapped her head round and scowled at me through where her wings were joined. She hissed and clicked her jaw in displeasure before answering me.

"No one goes there, not even your father. You will be good in heeding my warning youngling." I had to laugh at the youngling bit. She cocked her head in confusion making me clarify,

"I am older than I look." To which she simply shrugged her shoulders. It was the most human attribute I seen any of them portray as of yet.

"Nothing is older than the Titans or more powerful. Nobody is allowed in the core, not even the Royal blood of the nine." She said looking back when mention of my father.

"And the Venom of God?" I pushed.

"You will have to ask him that yourself." She said coming to a stop at what I presumed was the last door. She held open the heavy slatted wood and nodded for me to proceed her.

"I am not permitted." Was her only explanation and upon looking down at her I saw but a glimpse of the beauty that once radiated from her.

"You're not?" I questioned wondering if there was more to this place than I first thought.

"We are all prisoners here, even the ones that guard its walls." Her response made me want to ask about its wardens then but I was here for a single purpose and that purpose was through this door.

"I thank you." She looked up shocked at such a statement and opened her mouth as if to say something but what she did say I knew wasn't what would have been her first choice.

"I believe his is the last cell." After that she nodded her head once more before leaving me to my mission...

And the inmates of Hell.

CHAPTER FOUR

DRAVEN

INMATES OF HELL

W alking into this level of Tartarus was similar to Earth's prisons in only one way and that was I was now staring down a long pale stone corridor. However that was where the similarities promptly ended. Instead of barred cells being on either side of the walkway there were crude looking pits dug into the ground as if keeping wild beasts hidden from constant view.

The first set of cells were fairly tame compared to the others, being only covered by rows of thick black bars. I will admit that my curiosity got the better of me as I walked closer to the first inmate and looked down.

"Seraphim." I said its name in disgust and it looked up at me to snarl. When most of my kind heard the name of Seraphims, they first thought of angels, but their souls had a

nasty habit of turning sour and now I was looking at the result of that.

Well known to the Egyptians, Babylonians and Assyrians these once angelic figures turned into serpent demons thanks to the first corruption from the serpent Dahaka. In Persian mythology, the serpent Dahaka was the reincarnation of the evil spirit Angra Mainyu. Someone whose evil counted upon the drying of mortal lands and causing famine... hence the foul family offspring reacting to me in this manner now.

I had been the one to put a stop to this plan, banishing Angra Mainyu to Hell but leaving Dahaka to inherit the empty vessel, one gladly accepted. However I didn't discover that part of the infected soul had stayed within the Vessel, polluting Dahaka, until it was too late. Dahaka created the Seraphim as an army to aid in the quest to overthrow my throne in retaliation.

Needless to say this 'war' was quickly fought and won, and resulted in all Seraphims serving out their sentences in Hell as part of the nine Princes' lower ranking army. Well clearly from the looks of it, not all had taken kindly to their new positions, forced upon them thousands of years ago.

The word Seraphim came from the plural of the Hebrew word 'saraph' meaning 'to burn.' This also referred to the burning sensation and inflammation caused by the venom of a snake bite, which was one of their many charms. However it soon became clear that what I only moments ago thought was a tame looking cell was in fact the very nature of their name. This was proven when the Seraphim in question reached up as if to attack me and started burning as soon as its three clawed fingers came in contact with the bars.

Its scaled stretched skin started to blister and split like a roasting pig rotating on a spit and it filled the corridor with not only the smell of cooked flesh but the echoing sounds of agonising pain. Its grey wrinkled face contorted and cracked the larger scales on its domed forehead, causing blood to seep from beneath the cracks. I watched with little pity as its deep set green eyes started to roll back into its low forehead and then its burning body crashed back onto the dirt floor below.

I remembered the creatures all too well and knew how resilient they were to such things. It might not like it at the time but it would be healed and regenerated all damaged skin within the hour, as was the way with Seraphims. And as was the way when the decision to make them the pawns of most legions came to pass. After all, an army that could regenerate itself was one worth keeping close by, if only to keep the enemy busy.

I stepped back and moved onto the next cell, not taking any chances that Sammael was at the end of the row. In fact it was hard at this angle to gauge just how many cells there were in this block, so I let my wings give me the advantage I needed to count them. I was surprised to see only five remained but they were each spaced out by what looked like massive drainage pits simply covered by metal grids.

I couldn't fathom for the life of me why they were here or for what purpose they served. A fact I wondered until it brought me to the next inmate…The Drekavac race.

In Slavic history the Drekavacs were an army of small demons attracted to unbaptized humans and gathered the souls of the unfaithful for their master to feed upon… Deumus Drekavac.

They fed from their terror as it appeared to them as a ghostly figure of an undead child. What mortals didn't realise was that in my world they too appeared as a dying children, using the vessels of sick younglings once death was upon them and never healing their new bodies.

It was still unclear as to why they preferred such a form

over that of an adult or why they would never allow their vessel to age. No, instead they simply allowed their child flesh to rot instead of taking care of their host.

I looked down in distaste at the wasteful vermin that if I had my way, would never be allowed to find solace in the mortal realm. Thankfully Deumus Drekavac had found his demise at the hands of Ragnar's kin and as much as I loathed that damn Snake Eye Viking, he at least rid me of yet another 'Marked' that had been on the extraction list.

But right now, without its master's guidance, was the result of a broken Drekavac dying and its desperate need to feed. If someone else stood in my place now and didn't know the exact nature of what they were looking at as I did, then seeing this small form they would feel only one sentiment and that was pity. In the withering form of a starving child it was unsettling to witness which was a new emotion for me to deal with.

Before I had been introduced to Keira's niece Ella, then my interactions with the young mortals had been limited at best. In fact it was a fairer statement to say they had been near none existent, so before now seeing this kind wouldn't have mattered to me. However now the thought of such a child ever encountering sickness, pain, mistreatment or worse, death, was a difficult emotion to deal with without bringing forth a demon's rage.

Actually it caused so much of a reaction in me that I positioned myself over the cell before I could think too closely into my actions.

"Find your souls release in this act of mercy." I said before discharging the full length of one of my blades, only to be extended into the Drekavac's maggot infested skull, putting an instant end to its pitiful existence.

I frowned in disgust as the blade sank in with little effort and had to wonder how long the creature even had left. Black blood oozed from its eyes and nose, leaving an inky trail along my blade as I pulled it free. I retracted my weapon which left the inside of my wrist dripping with demon blood, one thankfully that was never taken into my vessel. However it did present the problem when battling many a foe that my hands would often be soaked with the blood of my enemies. Well with only my jeans to speak of I had little choice than to smear them with the evidence of what I had done here.

The next set of cells held a mixture of Mephistopheles, a winged demon with giant tusks from its cheeks. Its mortal vessel was patched together using the torn flesh of its victims, stitched in place using its own hair and wearing each patch with pride like a trophy.

Also added to the mix was a Rakshasas, said to be an evil spirit in Hindu mythology with shape-shifting abilities. The truth was it was a demon that would keep shedding its vessel once pregnant with a reincarnation of itself. But instead of being given birth to the way a mortal would, it would come into this world by tearing open its vessels mouth, forcing back its jaw until it broke the skull in two, rendering the host useless. This rebirth could only be achieved down here as the Rakshasas could only survive from the raw demonic energy Hell provided in their young form.

The fifth cell down and with only one more to go finally explained the need for the drainage pits each situated in between the cells. They looked like giant vents and the sight of five dwarfed sized Ukobach demons all held what looked like giant ladles with long arched handles. These lesser inferior demons were not meant for the human realm but sometimes they managed to make it to the surface undetected, which explained why these five were being put to good use.

Ukobachs made up a large part of Hell's workforce and were usually sent to work in the castle boiler rooms for the hierarchy of the Underworld. Given their love of extreme levels of heat this suited them nicely, however these scarred five looked as though they had felt the end of their master's whip a few times before being cast down to the deepest level of Hell.

To look at them you wouldn't have thought much strength could be found in their thin skeletal forms but to see them work such fears were quickly eradicated. Wafer pale skin with the texture of asbestos covered most of their bodies and the sparks that spat out at them from behind the grated furnaces were surprisingly protective. They worked in tandem as they spooned black oil into the slots to feed the constant flames but alas I was at a loss to understand what they could be fuelling.

One looked up at me and I knew from past experience with these demons that all they would see is a vague shadow considering they were almost completely blind. White milky eyes stared at me for a few seconds longer and then turned back to the flames that had caused such blindness. An eternity of staring at the flame would no doubt do that to beings.

It grunted to the others that also gave me a brief look but I didn't expect much else. After all, with lips that were pulled up tight and were pierced to their foreheads I wasn't going to stand around and wait for them to speak.

However their reaction to me seemed strange. They didn't usually interact with those outside of their station and that usually meant anyone higher than them. But now it was almost like they were trying to tell me something. This quickly became apparent when a crank turning could be heard and they all looked up at once. I suddenly spotted the deep rooted chains they all now had a tight hold of and swiftly reacted.

Thankfully I was quick enough in getting out of the way for directly above their cell two halves of a metal door swung open, releasing a downpour of water and flooding their cell in seconds. Even though I had been stood over their cell's bars and directly under where water now poured from, their purpose hadn't been to save me from getting wet…as I was to find out.

The reason for their warnings came as soon as the water touched the core of the furnace, releasing with it bellows of scalding steam. I turned my body at the same time calling forth my wings to shelter behind, igniting my power as protection. I couldn't afford to waste the strength it took in healing my vessel and with it the irritation of receiving second degree burns wasn't exactly on my most wanted list right now.

I stayed hidden until I could no longer hear the water flooding the demons' chamber with my impatience mounting every second. I had heard that time in Tartarus worked differently to the rest of the levels of Hell. That instead of going more slowly it did in fact go more quickly than that of the mortal realm. If I were to guess I would say it had something to do with being closer to the outer core of the earth. That and the 1,430 miles of churning iron and nickel liquid that helped generate the Earth's magnetic field.

Well whatever it was I was just thankful for it as I had already wasted too much time as it was. I shook the water from my wings and I felt the tingling sensation ripple down my spine as my feathers ruffled up in annoyance. Once I heard the metal trap swing and bolt back into place I turned to the Ukobachs' cell, walked back to where I had stood and nodded my thanks down at the five. I received a grunt or two from the wet little demons before they started the whole process over again. They started feeding the reignited flames from the oil that had once again started pouring from different holes in the wall of their cell.

"Last one" I said on a growl as I turned to what was undoubtedly the biggest cell on the prison block. The pit was at least twice the size of the rest and looked by far the deepest. It became clear as to why this was the case as I stepped closer and could hear the unfamiliar sound. It was certainly a fitting prison for such a destructive inmate that was damn sure.

"Aeolus' eye…this is going to hurt' I said shaking my head knowing what needed to be done. Sammael's form couldn't be seen and nor would it with that deadly vortex encasing his cell. Summoning an Aeolus eye was similar to dropping a smaller version of a tornado on top of somebody and expecting them to live a life in its centre for the rest of eternity.

Aeolus, the God of wind and Perses, the god of destruction both were charged by Zeus to create such a force, that the two powers combined were unstoppable to escape and hence this was meant for only the worst prisoners. This he had sent to his brother Hades as a gift to use as punishment to those he had under his charge.

The outcome to this was what I was now looking at and unfortunately what I had to try and destroy in order to free Sammael.

It was a force that not only kept one captive but also literally ripped one to pieces if it was touched. This incredible force had the ability to momentarily eradicate flesh and bone one second but then the power to completely reconstruct the whole body the next. The pain of not only being torn apart was inconceivable but then to be put back together was enough to avoid it like one does death.

It wasn't only witnessing the Aeolus' eye in action for the first time that made me reluctant to get to step closer but it was the monster I had to set free that rightfully remained imprisoned inside. I took out the vial of blood and every fibre in my being had to hold back the Demon in me from crushing it and ending this inflicting madness…but then Keira would be lost as there was no healing her from the curse that bastard had set upon her.

All he had needed to do was whisper a few incantations and gain access to my temple and there was no going back. Oh I could heal her, but it would only be a short fix until the curse would once again take effect. All her old injuries one by one would continue to attack her body over and over until they eventually killed her. And it all started with a cursed necklace ensuring my tie to Tartarus and that massacre in the woods ensuring Keira's tie to death. That was why I couldn't just kill the bastard and have done with it.

I looked up and down the raging twister of destruction to see it rising from the pit now it could feel my presence. It reached up, thinning the taller it got, and resembling that of an upturned tornado as it reached the ceiling.

I had little idea as to why it felt the need to do this, as there were only two ways of defeating such a force. The first and definitely the less painful was to find the one who summoned the Aeolus' eye and get them to renounce its need for continued capture. The second, and definitely the most painful was unfortunately the only option I was left with.

"This better fucking work!" I said gripping the vial tight to my chest and taking a few steps back before doing the unthinkable…

I jumped.

I knew I was screaming in an agony I had never felt before but that was the very point of the Aeolus' eye. To have something created that even the most powerful of demon would experience and that was simple…

Pain.

For a higher being that spent lifetime after lifetime living with pain as a foreign concept then this was something else. Pain when felt for the first time was more than just an experience for the body but it was first and foremost imprinted on the human mind as a lesson learnt. My kind didn't have this as such.

Yes we could inflict pain on each other indeed but this was done using certain powers the Gods had granted us. No, everyday pain that a mortal would encounter was more of a state of mind for my kind. A way in such that one could protect any damage to its vessel with the draining energy taken to heal it.

When we fought each other it was more about the damage done to the inner soul we were fighting against. The very nature of what lies beneath the mortal skin and right now, mine was being torn apart. It was as if it started with the unseen seams unravelling quicker than I could heal.

I looked down at myself and felt my lungs caving in on themselves as my screams overpowered my lungs capacity. I saw my skin shredding away like the wind creates waves of sand over the dunes of the Sahara. My flesh followed creating a red mist to follow my vessel's hide. I felt my fingers being taken away to nothing but the bone and the vial in my fist rattled against its skeletal cage. Every part of me felt lost and for one fleeting millisecond of weakness I almost prayed for a death in which the torture would end.

It finally took hearing my own roar of anguish to realise that my ears had been regenerated. I couldn't decide what pain was worse, that of being torn apart for endless seconds or being put back together again one cell at a time. At some point I fell to my knees and landed on bare bone as the flesh there hadn't yet reformed. I threw my head back and bellowed my fury up at the centre of the Aeolus' eye as the rest of my body came back to me.

When it was all over I knelt there with my bare chest rising like a wild beast that could barely be controlled. I panted, trying in vain to get my body to respond, telling my vessel it once again belonged to me and it was safe.

"I told you I would live on." I heard his voice as a sensitive buzz rattling in my ears and this told me not only did I need a minute for my vessel to compose itself but more importantly that…

Sammael had been right.

CHAPTER FIVE

DRAVEN

VENOM OF GOD

I turned around to find just how Sammael had been spending what was supposed to be his eternal imprisonment and it was a wasted effort when trying not to find pleasure in this. It wasn't possible for me to stay impartial when it concerned my Electus and I certainly wasn't going to try now. No, I was happy to see my enemy living what one would call a life not just in Hell, but Hell's own version of Hell.

Because for someone like Sammael, simply being sent back to Hell wasn't enough. However for a small few being banished back down here was punishment enough as they craved the mortal realm and the hidden power it provided some of my kind. But for others being sent here was just like being sent home, one that fulfilled your every need and fed an addiction you were created into yearning.

I felt nothing but the deepest hatred and loathing for this creature and like I said, I was pleased to see him in the sorry state he was.

"It was nice of them to provide me with a new body wasn't it...although, it is a great deal more difficult torturing one of us without one and this charming little place wouldn't have quite the desired affect if it only had soul matter to tear apart.' I looked down to where a hunched form sat on the floor, one that was covered by black broken skin. It looked like a combination of melted plastic, bubbled around the edges of the multiple holes that it was riddled with and that of worn damaged leather.

What I knew to be his wings barely held any weight to the word. The skin was held together by fractured twisted bones and the knuckles were bent at all the wrong angles, so flight would have been impossible. I took this as part of his punishment, being given wings to taunt a prisoner with something they once had but had now been replaced by something so useless.

Sammael was currently using his to provide a large hooded shelter over his head, so his new form remained a mystery to me. On my next command it became clear why he preferred this position.

"Look at me!"

He raised his head a fraction and I could only see one side of his lip curl in resentment.

"Did you bring my key?" He asked on a snarl.

"First you will look at me" I demanded once again, flexing my fists to get the blood flowing.

"As you wish." And with that he quickly stood and as a result every bone he used cracked and popped with the stilted movement he produced. The way he moved reminded me of not that long ago when motion picture was still in its infancy. That unnatural way in which the actors were captured in a silent movie always seemed more like watching a trapped soul, one that could scream but never be heard.

I shook the thought from my mind and watched as he painfully unwrapped his wings. The jerked movements were almost robotic and slowly revealed the new face of an old enemy.

His skin was that of an old man but strangely without the sight of wrinkles. It had that papery fragility to it often found with age and was marred with liver spots framing his face. He had no hair and his features were gaunt, with hollowed cheeks. A sloped forehead attached straight to what was a nose that was only distinguishable by the two slits I took for nostrils.

The skin was pulled tight across his face enough to cause his skull's features to protrude through, looking as though it could tear at any moment. Thin black lips and a pair of blood shot eyes with the pupils slit at the centres stared back at me, as I took in his new appearance.

I watched as he winced in pain when he extended his wings and at first I thought it was just from the broken twisted way this was accomplished. Then I noticed the change in colour in the Aeolus' eye getting darker and looking to the sides it soon became clear as to why Sammael had been reluctant to move.

The tips of his wings were being stripped away as the space given as his cell wasn't big enough to house his wing span. It made me wonder if this was in fact the reason for his wings disfigurement or was just a cruel part of his punishment after all.

He stood his ground and even lifted his head when I knew all he wanted to do was fall to his knees in agony. If the very reason for my being here hadn't been because of his crimes or ones he would soon be committing, I might have respected him for the show of strength. Instead however the sight of his discomfort was a satisfying one indeed.

I gave him a reluctant nod and he at once folded in his damaged wings, ones that were now considerably more mangled than before. One sat lower at his back than the other and as the tips reformed I could see it start to drag along the floor as he circled me.

"It is a proud day in Hell when royalty comes to visit" Sammael said as I turned my head to let my demon scowl at the enemy at my back.

"Proud is not a word I would use for this day." I retorted as he came back to face me, all the while keeping a suitable distance from the Aeolus' eye.

"Oh but I disagree, for I am proud indeed. You see you being here can only mean one thing…" I raised an eyebrow but kept what I knew to myself.

"My successor has succeeded."

"Yeah...? Succeed this!" I said before I grabbed him by the black rags he wore and threw him into the vortex. I heard his screams of torture but before he could start to regenerate back into the heart of the Aeolus' eye, I did what I had come here to do. I slammed my hand down into the centre of the eye and as soon as the blood I had poured into my palm touched the stone, the vortex vanished.

I looked up as the last of the destructive force evaporated into nothing and then looked down at my palm to see the blood gone from my skin. As Sammael had been too busy with his speeches of grandeur I had already tipped half of the blood onto my hand. What can I say other than I found it a justified act in getting him to shut up.

"Was that really necessarily?" He asked just as soon as his lips had reformed. I jumped out of the pit, cracked my neck to the side to relieve some of the tension and said,

"Let's go asshole." I walked on and cared little for the body struggling to move behind me. With each step I knew a little more of his form had regenerated as pretty soon he caught up to me.

"Give me the key." He demanded and for that alone I wanted to break him.

"You will get nothing until I know my Electus is safe." I threatened making him smirk.

"Ah your Electus, how is the little dear…oh wait I gather if you are here then she's not doing so well…I wonder if she has bled to death yet as I'm sure…" He didn't finish his sentence as he soon found it difficult to speak with his air supply being cut off by my hand. I slammed him up against the wall of the cell block causing the stone to crumble around him.

"Mention her again and I won't be able to stop my demon from killing you." I heard a bone snap before I finally released him. Uncurling my fingers from around his throat was one of the single most difficult things I have done when faced with an enemy. I knew now, right at this very second that my failing, my weakness was not having Keira in my life as I had once thought. It was not being there for her as I should have been.

I thought having me in her life was the cause of her danger but it wasn't, she was always in danger for being who *she* was, not who *I* was. As with I, the Gods had sent me here to defend life in its many forms and they had sent Keira to me to help maintain that goal. To aid us all when the prophecy came to pass but wait…was it to aid…or more importantly was it to…

Rule.

Was she the one in fact needed to lead this army into battle? She had up until now been unknowingly recruiting all the major players in my world. All the most powerful beings that were allowed to find solace on earth were slowly coming together one by one and everything up until this point had in fact been for that very reason.

I couldn't believe it but it took looking into the slitted eyes of evil to come to the crucial decision that Lucius had been right. She was the flame to not only the biggest moths but also every creature out there with wings. It wasn't loving me that put her in danger, it had been the Gods loving her that had.

"Fuck!" I shouted and tore myself away from the soul I wanted to destroy. Before he could say anything I barked out my order,

"Let's get this done!"

We had been walking for what must have been a fair distance, that or my impatience had me close to breaking point. The self-discovery of the true nature of why Keira had been born to the Earth was of little matter to me. Yes, the realisation certainly had its impact on me but it merely cast a heavenly shadow behind her perfection. I wanted Keira back for my own selfish reasons, none of which had anything to do with any damn prophecy! She belonged to me, body, mind, heart and soul and the rest of the world and realms above and beneath it could be damned!

My obvious foul tempered demeanour was all Sammael needed to keep his distance and not speak again as there was no telling what my demon side would do. I could feel it growling beneath my skin, pacing like a captured beast with the bars of my will buckling with every thought. I needed to find my calm in the storm raging inside me and with the lack of my heavenly side to aid me, this was proving even more difficult with each step I took. It was as though the deeper into Tartarus I got the louder my demon became. In fact by the time we finally got to the centre of the mountain I was shaking with unleashed fury.

"It is a gallant show of control, however I am afraid it will not help you here." Sammael spoke just as we walked through the last archway needed before coming face to face with the prison of Gods.

"Not what you expected?" Sammael said as I took in all that was before me.

The prison was nothing like I would have imagined and it was now confirmed that all stories about this place were exactly that...just stories. Chinese whispers that had lost words of truth along the journey on the winds of time.

At the belly of the mountain, in this cavernous vast space stood a magnificent Aztec shaped pyramid. It was built with stepped blackened lava blocks with veins of magma glowing through each giant sized brick. Up the centre of each of the four sides ran a river of the molten liquid, defying gravity and flowing upwards towards the flattened top. At the four corners stood huge Roman pillars of pure white that looked as if they had burst through the lava stone at their bases.

From up here it was clear to see that the small rivers of lava flowed over the top and around each corner where the pillars were each situated. The cooled black rock that stood at each base had burst upwards like an exploding star, so lava couldn't touch it.

It was as though this was all that was left of the other half of the lost Temple of Olympus and its gleaming white marble was therefore untouched by any damaging force below it. It was the only reminder left that this had once been a holy place of worship and it was a staggering sight to behold.

With nowhere else for the destructive force to go, it poured down into the centre of the Pyramid. I could see well enough from up here that the Pyramid was hollow, stepping down in on itself and inverted inwards, creating a smaller version and in the shape of a V.

All around the inside of the mountain was built up of not just rock but years of growth from soulweed roots that had burst its way through the mountain to get to the surface. Looking down at the sea of lava that surrounded the pyramid I realised it was also a feeding ground for the roots of the soulweed. And in turn they acted like a network of electrical cables keeping this place fed with energy.

I looked down at the steep staircase that was so crudely cut into the rock that it barely merited the name. It snaked its way down around the rock face and used each and every natural crevice as a footing. It would take us at least another hour to get down the trail before we even reached the thin arched bridge. One that was the only part connecting you to the rest of the mountain.

"I think not" I said grabbing Sammael by the wings as he started to take on the staircase before me. Then before he could get out a word of protest I jumped off the arched ledge, taking Sammael with me.

We both fell and plummeted down as I refused to open my wings until the last possible moment. When I finally did they acted as a parachute, rapidly slowing our decent enough for me to drop Sammael, forty feet from the bridge. As his body fell I watched as my suspicions about his useless wings were confirmed. He slammed into the narrow stone as my own wings guided me down to where I wanted to be and just in time to grab Sammael before he rolled off the edge.

"Oh how you must want to drop me right now." Sammael mocked looking up at me and knowing full well the inner battle I faced. Just one tiny movement, one slight loosening of my grip on his arm and the threat to human kind would be eradicated. The realms above and below would continue as before and a new day would at least see the light of the sun once more. But if the Titans were released then the only thing that new day would bring is fire and death...Ironic really that the blood spilt from the war of the Gods bred new life in that of mortals and now those that were defeated wanted that life back.

"Oh don't worry, your death will come soon enough, but for now we have business to conclude." I said forcing myself to move in a way that would set him back on his feet. I watched as he straightened the black worn rags he was wearing. It was in the similar style to that of what Buddhist monks would wear only with the added addition of the iron chains that dragged along the floor under the torn skirt.

I turned my back on him and proceeded to walk the narrow bridge that led not only to the Titans but also the end of life as we all knew it. I had a plan set in place but the chances of this working out in my favour were not looking good. Was I really willing to murder the world for one life and with no guarantees to go by?

Well we were about to find out because there in front of me was the key stone that awaited one simple key...

Blood of the Titans.

As we approached I could feel Sammael almost buzzing behind me. This was something Sammael had spent most of his life waiting for. Being once that of an Archangel his deception came at a price indeed but the power he gained more than made up for it. He started life long after the war of Gods and his duty was, granted, an unpleasant one. Life in the form of mortals had grown at an incredible rate and with it, death quickly followed. This was the price mortals paid for their free will and a realm of their own. After all they were created by the death of Gods, it was only fair that they were granted a life of choice as they had little in the first place.

The mistake often made in any religion is not which God made mortals, as many did but it is often how. The blood of the Gods did indeed rain down that day to the beauty below and that untainted blood was the catalyst needed to kick start the evolution of man. The power in that blood is what gave Homo sapiens the power of thought. And therefore both science and religion are one and the same.

So as the world below began the circle of life, the Ouroboros came into effect. Angels of death were needed and Sammael was the first to step up for the job.

"I am curious Sammael, what was it that day? What changed for you to cause such betrayal to your maker?" I couldn't refrain from asking as we neared the end of our journey.

"Maybe you should have asked me this before you banded my lips with metal, condemned me to a life in Hell and murdered the one I loved." His response made me growl angrily before quickly facing him and hitting back with the truth,

"You being silenced was your punishment, Hell was your prison and killing your love was an act of mercy!"

"There is no mercy in MURDER!"

"No, there is mercy when one has begged for death, one you refused to grant her in every life she was forced to live!" I snapped and when he winced I knew I had finally hit my mark but more still, I had just found the answer to my question.

"That was it wasn't it? You were sent that day to take her life?" He scowled at me for a few seconds and the hatred was clear to see until he tore his venomous gaze from mine.

"That day it was decreed that the two last surviving pure bloods, one male and one female were to find death at my hands, yes. I hadn't even known of their existence until the order came, none of us had." He said sombrely and obviously reliving that time so long ago.

"But what had the Gods hoped in keeping them alive so long?" I had to ask.

"It soon became obvious that they were different to the rest of the mortals. For one they wouldn't age, however like the

Titans had learnt, they could die through great injury. The Gods had hoped they would reproduce, like some fucking experiment or rats in a fucking cage! When it became clear of Cronus' plans to release the Titans they knew it was far too dangerous to keep them alive."

"Enter the Angel of death." I said folding my arms and figuring out the rest of the story for myself.

"Yes, enter me! Oh you stand there casting judgement on me when you yourself entered the same forbidden realm in loving a human." At this I laughed but it was without the mentality of humour attached to it.

"You really think you loved her! You took away the one thing that word represents."

"And what is that!?" He asked and for once I felt the tiniest amount of sadness for not just him but for anyone who didn't understand it.

"You took away her choice…her God given right to choose, whether it be to live, love or die. You were no better than the Gods that had kept her alive for their own amusement or their blatant, arrogant ignorance and disregard for one of their own. And when they finally decided to do the right thing by the good of not just mortal kind but of every kind, you chose differently and why…because you lay claim to love her…" I let the anger I felt fuel my words of disrespect for such decisions, decisions to not only ruin the innocent life of a woman but to put every single life in jeopardy.

I stepped towards him and continued…

"Tell me Sammael, did she honour your feelings by loving you back…did she make such bold claims in the face of your own? Did she not put up a fight when you took her against her will, not once, no but with every reincarnated life you forced upon her…is that what you call loving someone?! Because that love you speak about is not only received but delivered back to you in equal amounts. The only thing that girl did against your will was to finally find peace at my hands...one she begged me for!"

"YOU LIE!" He came to rush at me as the truth seeped into his core and rooted there for all to see. I grabbed him and his feeble form, easily over powering him and turned to get him in a lock with my arm banded around his throat.

I wanted to force the difference between real love and obsessive betrayal of free will. Oh I had no doubt he loved her in the only way he knew how but my next words I hoped haunted him for his actions for what little time I knew he had left...

"For real love is about letting them go. It is about doing what is best for not your own gain but for theirs...That is love. And she died in my arms knowing the difference...because I was the one that gave her peace, a peace you had refused her for far too many lifetimes." I pulled tighter on his neck and whispered something that I hoped would finally break him...

"And guess what, she died with a smile on her face and honestly...it looked like the first damn smile she ever gave freely." I finished when I felt him go limp in my arms and finally give up the fight. He slumped forward and I took a few steps back hoping this had been enough to end this madness, one that should have finished the second the light of Eveleen's soul faded from her eyes.

"You can stop this Sammael. You can give Eveleen the memory she deserves and not invite destruction to the realms in her name. You can choose the right path..." As I said this he raised his head where he had remained on his knees. But something I had said made him snap the other way and instead of giving up his resistance he fought harder for it. He raised himself up and stood with his back to me.

"Your Gods and their precious mortals had their time...now

it is time for mine!" He hissed at me turning his head with the last threat before walking past me and stepping up to the keystone.

"The blood of my kin, hand it to me." He demanded.

"No."

"No...? You realise what will happen if you refuse?" Oh I knew alright and I could only wish I had the strength needed to follow through with that refusal, however it was a startling revelation to realise I wasn't. Would I murder the world...I wanted to lower my head in shame but I knew with shame came knowing that my decision wasn't the right one and every fibre in my inner soul knew I was doing the right thing.

"I will give you the key only when I am assured she is safe."

"And I can only do that when I return." This was a hopeless battle of a trust neither of us held for each other or ever would but what choice did I have?

"I demand a blood oath." I stated hoping it was enough to hold up against such a being. The terms of a blood oath were up to the being it was offered from and if accepted then it was binding.

"Very well, set your terms." I felt my tension ease slightly in spite of what I was willing to give in to.

"Upon your return you will free Keira of the curse and swear she will not be harmed by your hand or that of your kin and in return I will let you release the Titans. If these terms are not met or honoured then you will be forced to your knees and await death by my blade once having your will stripped bare and your choices swiftly taken from you...do you except my terms?" Sammael stared boldly at my eyes, raised a hand to his mouth and bit forcefully into his flesh. He never took his eyes from mine as he accepted the only option he had if he wanted to follow through with his plans.

"I accept your terms and leave my blood onto you as it lays witness to our treaty made." He then slapped his hand to mine and I felt the power of the pact forge into one of absolute. Our binding was complete and it was time now for me to fulfil my end of the bargain.

"It is done." Sammael said as he too felt the same force of power bind us. He nodded to the keystone that stood at the top of the arch, situated in the very middle. The doorway was yet to be revealed by the protruding arched blocks but by them being here told anyone alike that this was the door to the Titans' prison.

The keystone was the face of Cronus himself with his mouth open and ready for a taste of his own kin. The blood of the Titans.

I pulled the vial from my jeans' pocket and lifted it up to eye level to see only half of the blood remained. Sammael's slitted eyes widened before they narrowed for a second. I handed it out to him all the while forcing such actions and demanding submission of my demon from emerging.

"Change of plans."

"What?!" I said frowning in obvious distrust.

"You're going to release the Titans." I shook my head unable to think why he would want such a thing.

"Are you going back on our terms?"

"Not at all, the terms I believe stated you would let me release the Titans, and in doing so I need your aid…after all, my wings don't work like they used to." He said nodding up at the top of the arch, one that indeed needed flight to get to. The door when it opened would be big enough for giant Gods to walk through, that was for sure.

"Very well." I took his reasoning for what it was…another deception. One however I had little choice of avoiding.

"Let get this shit over with!" I said cracking the vial in my fist and letting the infected blood of the ancients seep into my palm.

I summoned forth my wings and let them take me until faced with Cronus immortalised in rock and very much a part of his people's prison.

Then I did something that was the very opposite of the reasons for which I had been born…

I brought on Armageddon.

CHAPTER SIX

DRAVEN

TRIPLE CROSSED BY PAST LIVES

The second my hand crossed the opening, was the second my betrayal to my people was fully recognised. It gifted me with the power of foresight and held me immobile and defenceless against the attack. It was as if my blood supply had been replaced by rock and my back bowed, arching with the pain. My wings seized any movement as they too were affected. I was half expecting my body to slump with only my arm anchoring me to the mouth of Cronus. However this did not happen. Some kind of force kept me imprisoned and for the first time in my existence I felt like a living statue.

The other half of the Temple of Lost Olympus flashed in my mind. And that was where the foresight started. This vision granted to me was utter torture and one I was helpless to stop. It showed the Temple of Fallen Gods flood with Lava until stone fingertips reaching up were the last thing on the floor to disappear.

It showed angry Titans with flesh made from black rock and magma running through their veins. These giant Gods stormed through the Temple, as lava splashed up their legs. They smashed any trace that lingered of the Gods they loathed until only one remained. The biggest Titan roared up at the Temple's crumbling ceiling, spitting lava like a volcano before lashing out an arm and decapitating Zeus in one blow.

I felt my eyes rolling back in my head as the vision started to end with a blur of action and I didn't need to see the details to know what came next. The Titans had all run at the mountain walls and burst free from Tartarus. But there was something else in my vision and I squinted trying to focus on what it was hiding in the background of Hell.

"No…it, it can't be…?" I said not sure if even my lips were moving in the real world. But it was the sight of a small mortal figure that stood at the edge of Tartarus as if awaiting the Titans to break free. Titans that I myself had just released…

And with it, releasing Hell on Earth.

The vision's thread snapped and unconfined me at the same time letting go of my hand. I fell backwards through the air onto the bridge and watched from on my back as the keystone and the mouth of Cronus closed. The stone eyes shut and the face of the king of Titans started to crumble away.

I got up off the floor and without taking my eyes from the doorway watched as the protruding stones started to glow. The same symbols that were carved into the flesh on my forearms all appeared one by one on every black stone. But my thoughts were not just on the terror I had invited back to the world but on the small figure in my apparition. One that looked as if it was there for a single purpose. I didn't know how I knew this but that was of little importance. No, what was important was that they were searching for something…

Or someone.

"It's started!" Sammael shouted as the whole mountain started to vibrate around us. Small rocks rained down around where we stood and the floor beneath our feet started to pulsate. It wasn't the same as the way the land trembles before an earthquake hits but more like watching a fast and heavy base line through a sub speaker. The volcanic dust created a fog in the air without being allowed the time to settle.

I turned to growl at Sammael and the cause of what was to come…did he really understand the depth of chaos he was inviting to share his madness with?

"You can't control them!" I shouted over the sound of the mountain trying in vain to hold itself together.

"We shall see!" He said nodding back towards the doorway that had now started to move and create an opening. The rectangular blocks twisted into squares and fell away one by one until the size of a castle door was now an opening. One big enough for any Titan to pass through.

Once the doorway had emerged it didn't stop there. The turning blocks continued to fold in on themselves until pretty soon I and Sammael had to step back to watch as the whole Pyramid caved in on itself. The rivers of lava that had once flowed up the sides became a gushing torrent that fell back on itself, acting like a glowing orange waterfall on either side.

Pretty soon there was nothing left of the structure and all that was left was the heart of evil it had held captive all this time. It became obvious that what had held them imprisoned so effectively was the constant cascade of volcanic matter that was being poured on them from above. Now however, that containment was quickly diminishing down to nothing and leaving behind the frozen ash bodies of angry and defeated Gods.

All of them were looking up at the Heavens they had once been banished from and all were cast with the same haunted empty eyes. Each of the eleven remaining had their arms in shackles behind their backs and the size of chain that secured them to the floor was one you would have found attached to the anchor of a super tanker.

As the last of the encasing lava emptied down past their feet it became the moment of truth for I don't think either of us knew what to expect next. The glowing chains first erupted into blue flames before bursting into ash and landing in the stream of molten rock like grey snow, melting on hot tarmac.

What surprised me was to see each of them not only as carved black statues, but more so to realise they were the size of mortal men. In my gifted sight into the future they were seen as giants breaking free.

They were all male as none of the Titan females were imprisoned. Also some of the Titan men were spared from imprisonment for various reasons that were only to benefit the new Gods' ruling, so that left eleven Titans of both the first and second generation.

We both waited on baited breath for what would happen next and both for very different reasons. Sammael's eyes shone with unshed tears from waiting so long for this day to come. The anticipation showed not just in his demeanour but also the black blood that seeped from his nose and mouth. It trickled down past his chin and when dripping onto the floor the dirt sizzled like acid eating away at the rock.

"Their time is now." He said more to himself and I turned in time to see the Titans take their first breaths in this lifetime. I was just about to speak of his insanity when his next words were said from directly behind me…

"And so is mine!" Then before I could react his arm reached from behind me and with the blade he now held he cut a slice across my chest. I bellowed in rage and spun to face him. His body started to fade and I reached out to grab his robes but the feeling of material in my grasp faded along with him. His last words to me haunted me more than what I was left to deal with…

"Don't worry about your Electus, I have plans for her and they…" He paused and nodded to the freed Titans before continuing…

"…they have plans for you!"

KEIRA

I opened my eyes and never thought such a small action would hurt as much. One of them I closed as soon as I felt liquid trying to soak in. Was I lying in a puddle of water? It only all came rushing back to me when my vision was more a red fog that when cleared I saw the puddle of my own blood I was lay in.

Yep, now I remember…I was dying.

I squinted my eyes and tried to see past what was obviously proof of my last moments on this earth. Well at least the pain was gone and the numb side of death had obviously set in, thank goodness for small gifts of mercy. Now if only that mercy could be extended to small acts of murder…let's say to insane, megalomaniac ex-boyfriends that wanted to destroy the world…yeah, that would be nice and dandy.

"Ah…" I moaned as I tried to raise my head up and it felt like even having these thoughts was bringing back the pain. I closed my eyes again hoping the feeling would pass and instead what followed was a first class ticket to Hell on Earth.

But that wasn't strictly true as I found myself transported back to what I knew as Hell yes, but more importantly what I now knew was a deeper level of Hell… Tartarus.

I remembered that day so clearly it could have been an oil painting hanging on the walls of my brain. I had just told Draven that he should learn his lesson for the next time he fell in love. It seemed so laughable now thinking back to the reasons why he kept so many secrets to begin with and not that his actions were suddenly condoned but more simply understood.

That night I had woken in a different place I had laid my head to sleep and now I knew the reasons as it all seemed so blindly obvious now. Draven's tie to this place was like living with a disease without the need for a cure….until now that was.

And like that night I found myself looking at the same canyon only this time there was no Draven to draw me closer to the edge of the cliff. No, this time I walked those steps with a purpose I didn't really understand. I walked those steps to quell the curiosity something the higher powers were relying on. I walked to the edge to see what they wanted me to see.

The Everest sized mountain lay before me and unlike before the vast space wasn't filled with row after row of soldiers. There was nothing but a vista of volcanic ash and dry crusted patches of dirt that went on until your eyes lifted to the enormous mountain, one I knew held the name Tartarus. I looked one way and then the other and saw nothing but the same dead landscape on either side as far as the eye could see.

"So what do you want me to see?" I asked the forever nothingness around me and definitely not expecting an answer.

So I was a little more than surprised when I got my answer in the form I did. As if on cue with my question the mountain side suddenly exploded outwards as if something gigantic had just crashed into it from the centre. At first I thought it was lava that had burst from within but then that lava started to take form or in this case, many forms.

"Oh God...the Titans!" I gasped before covering my mouth in horror. The giant Gods stormed out one after the other and started to cut across the black desert in no time leaving destruction in their path. Molten rock poured from the opening and for one split second I thought I saw a winged figure looking back at me from what seemed to be the broken remains of what was once a Temple.

I didn't know how I could even see this greater distance than what was humanly possible but I put it down to the vision of things to come. And what was to come was charging at me right now. So I did the only thing I could do, the only thing my body would allow me to do in the face of such destruction. I closed my eyes and let my tears of fear fall down my face. I felt them linger on my chin a second before they fell and as soon as they did I opened my eyes one last time.

It was in the hope of seeing that winged figure once more and I didn't really know why. However what happened did so in painfully slow motion. It was as if everything around me was moving at such a sluggish rate and once my tears left my skin they too became a part of this world.

I looked down at the droplets still on their slow decent to the ground and frowned in disbelief at what was happening. I looked back up to see the Titans too had slowed enough that they barcly looked like they were even moving at all. I knew this was all part of the vision but even then it didn't make any sense. I had been fully prepared to watch the Titans charging at me and only waking up the second they reached me...but what was happening now I couldn't understand what the fates were trying to tell me?

That was until I watched my tears land in the dirt.

An action so innocent as tears from the heart were shed in a place like this and in sight of the damnation to come. What should have been a simple act created an eruption so immense I fell backwards landing on my buttocks. The second my tears had touched the ground it sent a shock wave across the canyon floor and straight towards the Titans. I watched on in awe as the rumbling floor rippled until it centred the Volcanic Gods and then...

BOOM! There was an explosion of black ash that went up in a mushroom cloud as though a nuclear bomb had just exploded. The world around them started to split and branches of cracks spread out like growing fingers reaching out for safety. They finally stopped just short of where I remained frozen in the dirt.

I tasted the dust on my tongue from being unable to close my mouth in shock. And this didn't change when the ground erupted outwards and the Titans started to fall through Hell's outer crust and into the mantel below. Just as the dust cloud started to settle I could clearly make out the bodies of Titans as their lava forms were being consumed by liquid metal.

It burst out around their reaching limbs like chrome death dealers trying to drag them back to the core of the earth. One arm at the very last second reached up and out, erupting free from the ground closing around it. Then I looked on as first the molten metal consumed it, diminishing its fiery veins before the ground sealed around its elbow.

The Canyon floor calmed and when the last of the dust settled all that remained in the vast space was one giant metal arm. It rose up like a monument to what could have happened on this day. I got up from the floor and just as I was straightening myself a great cracking sound echoed in the desert valley. I flinched as the cooled metal shattered from around the arm but left in its place one of black statue limb instead. One whose fingertips were reaching up to the Earth above, one I thankfully now knew it would never see again…

And all from an honest tear shed in Hell.

I woke from the vision coughing out more blood I couldn't afford to lose. But for some reason what the fates had shown me had restored some of my strength…enough anyway to raise my head from the pool it lay in.

Was that all it took to stop the Titans, one of my tears to fall at the mouth of Tartarus? Or was this all a trick and something that could never happen? If anything it left me more confused than before and questioning not only if the Titans had already been released or if I was even human?

I decided to go one step further and raise my body as much as I could with how battered and cut up it was. Having every old injury afflict me all at once was what I could only imagine was like being hit by a car, one that felt the need to back up and roll over me a few times just to make sure.

It made me not only curse being a clumsy human being but also being one that was obviously a magnet for danger. My hands shook as I used weakened muscles to push myself up to sitting and the only benefit to this painfully slow movement was that I hadn't alerted Alex to my conscious state.

He was stood near the altar as if waiting for a sign or something to happen. I could still see Draven's essence floating there and obviously waiting for the rest of him to come back. Well I could sympathise as I was waiting for the same. I just needed him to come back to me now and bring back the proof I needed to know he couldn't go through with releasing the Titans. No life on this Earth was worth more than the billions of people combined. I didn't want to die by any means but knowing what sparing my life would mean wasn't something I was willing to accept.

"Come on, what are you waiting for?" Alex snapped down to where Draven had been lay and I frowned as my suspicions were confirmed. He was waiting for something. He looked like a man possessed or one jacked up on drugs. He couldn't keep still and it was more than just anticipation that had him biting at his fingertips and transferring his body weight from one foot to the other.

He was worried.

I closed my eyes as even I could feel time was getting closer to Draven's crucial decision and I couldn't imagine how it felt having the weight of the world on your shoulders. The realisation of what type of man Draven was caused me to suck in a deep and jagged breath. I knew he was a man of integrity and honour. I knew he could be kind and loving. I knew he could even be funny and damn but every girly cell in my body knew the man was the very meaning of sexy.

But what I didn't fully understand up until right this second was what he had to deal with. It was how he maintained the balance that was so crucial to not only human life but his own kind. The concrete sense of duty that was ingrained within him. Almost like he was engineered for it and I was the spanner in the works that made him question his decisions and act irrationally for the first time in all of his forever's lived.

I was his Achilles heel and I could only pray to the Gods that I wasn't the one that brought him to his knees.

"You can do this…make the right choice…" I barely whispered the words but hoped their strength screamed out

across the levels of Hell and were carried to Draven just when he needed it the most.

However I was soon to find it had all been in vain. Movement in the corner of my eye got my attention and I turned in time to see Draven's essence jerk violently on the altar.

"What are you doing? Get away from him!" I shouted no longer caring if he knew I wasn't unconscious anymore.

"About time!" He snapped and for a second I thought he had been waiting for me to wake. But when it became apparent that I was being ignored I knew this had been the sign he had been waiting for. He turned away and dragged something the size of a body from behind one of the pillars out of view. I could barely make any details out but I saw whatever it was he had covered in a dirty sack.

He dropped his burden and snatched something up from the floor. Revoltingly it looked like a hip flash made from crudely stitched human skin and I had to repress the urge to gag.

He popped the top and started to empty the black liquid all over Draven's spirit. It poured straight through the shimmering hue of Draven's form and dripped down the symbols carved into the sides of the altar.

Each one started to spin and blur telling me something bad was about to happen. The whole sight made me feel sick and my head started to go woozy. The world tipped on its axis and it took me a moment to realise that for now, the world was fine. No, it was just me that was falling. I felt my head slap to the floor for the second time and I closed my eyes to wince against the pain. I knew that due to my injuries I didn't have long but still wondered what was happening now to evoke such a response. It was as if something had passed through from the other side and I had the sickening feeling it wasn't who I was desperate to see.

71

I peeled back my lids in trepidation as one would do when knowing what they would see was going to haunt them. Like watching a scary movie and opening your eyes right before the crucial point the fleeing character is going to get an axe in their back. It was the horrific face of a killer that seemed to imprint onto your brain and flash up in your sleep when you were at your most vulnerable.

Either way I knew what I needed to do and when I opened my eyes I found I didn't need to be asleep to be at *my* most vulnerable. Because I was now the one staring at the horrific face of a killer and this one was straight from my past.

His bare feet were the first thing to come into view. Black dyed skin that looked like they had been dipped in ink stepped closer towards me. The flesh looked as torn up as the trousers he wore and large chunks of skin were falling away almost like the body had begun to rot.

"No…no… What have you done Draven?" I said letting my shoulders slump and feeling the tears force their way out of the corner of my eyes the tighter I held them shut. I tried to forbid what I knew would be the sight of Sammael coming closer by closing my eyes and refusing to look. But the tears wouldn't be held at bay as now I had proof that prayers to the Gods and hopes of the heart meant nothing. Not in the presence of madmen that would stop at nothing until the Earth was nothing but ash and bone.

"Look at me." The demand came and went without my compliance and I half expected pain to follow in sight of my refusal.

"It's about time we met again." The voice changed from the last one and suddenly it wasn't his order forcing me to look I had to contend with, no, now it was my own order *not* to look I battled against.

"Nn…no…noo…its…it's not possible!" I said as I looked

up at the face of evil, one that wasn't holding an axe ready for my back, but he held a smile that looked far more deadly for my mind.

Because my nightmare past was back and this time…

He would get to kill me.

"Morgan."

CHAPTER SEVEN

DRAVEN

SUMMONING

After feigning my shock at Sammael's actions I turned back to the main problem at hand…

"Damn scorned Gods." I said aloud, shaking my head and calling forth my weapons. I stormed towards the enemy with more purpose than ever before and only came to a stop as the first wave was breaking free.

"Well at least I am not fighting giants." I said rolling my neck and readying myself for what was no doubt going to be the hardest fight of my many lives so far. Pretty soon the lava was completely gone from around their feet and the first three stumbled a moment before finding their footing in the open space. It reminded me a bit like an arena and now all I was waiting for was the spectators to get their asses down here and get involved.

As if my thoughts were all it took I felt the ground to the left of me shake as a body landed on his feet.

"I didn't think that stench of a low-life latrine would ever fucking leave." My father said patting the dust from one shoulder.

"You really need to get with the times Asmodeus. When was the last time that was said...Mid second century AD?" I asked just as I saw more bodies drop from their hiding places above.

"Shakespeare had nothing on Apuleius." My father responded with a wink.

"Well I can't argue with his novel The Golden Ass, not considering the protagonist of the novel was named Lucius." I replied on a smile.

"Do you really think this is the fucking time to be talking Greek literature with Daddy dearest?" Sigurd snapped rising from landing on one knee.

"Show some respect!" Ragnar growled at his son after landing next to him.

"Whatever old man, let's get this shit over with!" I frowned at the disrespect he not only showed me but more so his own kin. But then I looked sideways towards my own and realised I was not one to judge.

"I apologise for my kin, my Lord."

"It is fine."

"Not a problem." I and my father both said at the same time then turned to frown at each other.

"He was talking to me!"

"He was talking to me!" Once again we continued the theme and annoyingly said our defensives in sync.

"Tell me you two aren't at it again are you?" My sister said once her and her husband Zagan both landed at my side. Neither of us had chance to answer her question as the first three finally reached us. They all hit out at the same time and our natural instincts kicked into gear as we branched off into three groups of two.

The commander of my guard readied himself for war whilst his Son, the Snake Eye showed off the full extent of his own gifts. The Ouroboros that inked his skin started to spin and merge as one until half his body was a black tattoo. It freely branched out from his hands and attacked the Titan opposing him. The black tentacles caught the Titan in a web of power and it screamed its frustrations out to its brothers, ones ready for the fight and those that were still coming round from an eternity of sleep.

"Sometime before the world ends old man!" Sigurd said fighting to hold on and because of it, launching more liquid rope from his hands. Meanwhile Ragnar was in the process of covering his fleshless skull marred with the holes of every snake bite he had received as a mortal king.

The two twisted horns broke through his back and grew up over his head creating a solid helmet over his face. The horns combined and met with each other, interlocking at his chin like a bone beard. His size had at least tripled, giving him the greater advantage over the mortal sized God.

Only his determined eyes could be seen and they pinpointed the enemy with two tiny white dots in the midst of his pulsating fury.

"BE READY BOY!" Ragnar warned, bellowing at his son before he charged at the confined Titan, one still caught by Sigurd's tangled net of shadowed power. My lead commander lowered his head and ran at the God like a charging bull. Sigurd timed it to the last second and just before his father made contact all his tentacles evaporated. Ragnar hit him with such a force the Titan had little choice than to fly backwards and bouldering into his awakening brothers like pins from a bowling ball.

My sister and her husband were having just as much success working together as Viking father and son. I can't say I was surprised to see my sister's cracked caked skin of the desert sands flake as she smiled in her obvious fun. If there was one thing we all shared as a family it was the joy to be found in fighting what we classed as an equal foe. And husband and wife were no different.

I had seen them work as a team before but never noticed how much it resembled a violent and deadly dance. Each move was executed so precisely that it led into blow after blow with a natural flow. He spun Sophia around by the hands and her feet smacked into the chest of the Titan sending him back a foot. Zagan then used the butt of his double sided scythe to first force him further back, then with spinning motion, repeatedly started to strike the God down with the double blade.

The Titan had no choice but to be forced backwards unable to see the danger he walked into...one being a fearless and deadly but dainty, demon sibling that undoubtedly had a bloodthirsty taste for violence.

So with her being positioned behind the unsuspecting Titan she jumped into a handstand before launching herself up to latch her legs around the God's neck. Then with little more than a readied nod, Zagan threw his scythe towards his wife. She in turn threw her body weight backwards and with her powerful hold on his neck he had little option than to fall to his back.

She rolled at precisely the right moment, reached up and plucking the provided weapon from the air, slammed the blade into the Titan's chest. Its black stone body cracked from the impact around the blade and left a sizeable, crumbling hole when my sister wrenched it free.

It wouldn't kill him but it didn't make the skill of her

combat any less impressive. Oh it would at least slow him down for a moment, which really was all we had to work with. And it certainly gave me a moment to feel proud of my little sister for the bravery and power displayed.

"I think we're up my Maru." Asmodeus said with a grin, calling me his 'son' in Sumerian.

"I would say you are right my Abum" I replied following suit and calling him father in the same ancient language. Then I turned my head to see he was certainly right…It was our turn to play with the Gods.

I waited for my father to turn into his natural form and was surprised when this didn't happen. The Titan had stopped before reaching us to watch his brothers be pushed back and now needing the time to repair the damage made to their stone bodies. So he decided to take us on using a different approach.

"Oh this is going to be interesting." I said dryly as the Titan found what he was looking for… a weapon of his own.

"Remember the horde in Budapest?" I grinned at the memory my father invited.

"Oh they were the good old days." I said getting into the position my father needed me in.

"Shit yeah!" He shouted as the massive, flaming boulder was hurtling towards us. My father lowered his stance, bent one knee to the ground and with his back straight, he thrust his hands forward and clasped them together in the sign of prayer, one of a very different kind. Then just as the boulder would have smashed into him, he tilted his hands and thrust them forwards out straight. He then called forth one of his gifts and turned his body to Hell's red granite starting at his straightened fingertips.

There was nothing in all the levels of Hell stronger than Hell's red granite, so the boulder had no choice but to split on contact, sending two pieces of flaming rock in opposite paths.

As they flew left and right I ran full speed up my father's now granite back and used it to propel myself off towards the Titan. The momentum of the fall helped drive both my blades into the heart of the God, causing him to fall and me to land with my feet on his chest.

One spin backwards and both my blades were free and I landed back next to my father. He moved at a much slower rate in this form but one blow was all it took to crack the next Titan's body. Of course none of our efforts in fighting would ever be enough to kill the Titans but all I needed was time. A time that the Gods needed to repair themselves could just be enough if my plan worked.

What I had hoped to be the case was confirmed every time we sent one back a step broken but I knew once they were summoned back to the mortal realm their powers would be unstoppable. Down here they were still weakened by what heavenly power remained in the Lost Temple of Olympus.

It was why the keystone had shown me them destroying their last weakness but until that power was returned then they were merely a shell of what they could be and what they once were.

Of course that didn't make this any easier, not when the rest of the brothers started to come around and join the fight. Pretty soon it wasn't just one on one but in some troubled moments it was two on one.

"We can't hold them much longer!" Sigurd shouted after using his shadows to fool two Titans into lashing out in the wrong direction and hammering into one another.

"We need more time!" I shouted back in the midst of swinging my swords and crushing the ankle of one Titan and then swinging up in time to take the arm of another, before it took my head off.

"Aww but are we not having fun though!?" Sophia said in

jest before she picked up the severed arm and used it as a bat to knock back another Titan coming at her. Then she discarded the stone limb altogether for what she deemed as a more advantageous weapon. Using a lava cooled stalagmite she ripped from the ground, she swung it round and tripped up one of the Titans. Zagan then at the ready drove his weapon into the body and waited for his wife to repeat the process.

"Here's one for you Viking!" My father shouted to Ragnar as his body slammed sideways into one of the Titans charging at him. This sent him crashing to my commander and the force caused the Titan to fold at the waist around Ragnar's head, cracking him nearly in half.

It was frustrating to see the efforts of my side to then watch as the Titans merely fused back together. No injury inflicted upon them was enough to stick and I didn't know how long we could keep them back for.

"Sophia!" I shouted my warning too late as the first of us received retaliation in the form a blow to the face. The Titan had hit her hard enough to dislocate her jaw and both father, brother and husband bellowed in rage at the sight.

Zagan rushed to his wife's side and my father cleared a path for me so I could take out the one that had touched her. I skidded underneath one Titan as my father dealt with him and came up underneath the one I'd set my sights on. My blade went up and impaled his body in a way that even made me wince with the thought.

I twisted my body up and retracted my sword at the same time, freeing it from the depths of the Titan. I then kicked its healing form away before going to my sister. I lifted her face up to see it had almost healed fully and I knew she was fine when she stuck her tongue out at me before she snapped,

"Stop being a damn girl Dom and go and kick some ass!" I

winked at her and not being one to disappoint a lady's request I did just that.

"Does anyone else think this is going to get fucking old and quick...? I mean these bastards just won't die!" Sigurd said after hitting back at yet the same one he had put down not long ago. The Shadowed King was right, we couldn't keep this up much longer...but my plan was missing one vital piece.

"We just need...!" I was cut off as I put my fist through one of the Titans expecting him to crack only to have my worst fears confirmed when my hand went straight through him. I watched in horror as the Titan I was fighting started to disappear from this world, which could only mean one thing...

"Sammael has started the summoning!"

KEIRA

"You want to lift the curse...? But why? We should just kill her now and..."

"NO!" I listened to this argument play out still suspended in a state of shock. I was currently sat up against a pillar after being placed there by the rotting hands of a stalker I thought long dead. I was trying to convince myself this was all a trick. That this must be down to some kind of hallucination due to blood loss.

"Now do as I say and lift the curse!" The voice of both Morgan and Sammael seemed to merge into one and I wanted to tear my ears off just to save me the pain from hearing either.

"Fine!" I finally decided to open my eyes and witness this little drama. I actually gagged at the sight of Morgan. Not just because it was obviously his corpse that had been somewhat supernaturally preserved by Alex, ready no doubt for this very day. But mainly down to the mental issues I had not only scarred into my flesh but also my mind. All those days of torture by those hands was something not easily forgotten.

Oh we could try and force those thoughts into the forgetful wasteland buried in the depths of our minds but they still managed to cling to the surface, latching on with merely a single word spoken. The smell of damp concrete or the bitter sweet sounds of that damn music box were more than enough for those nightmares to latch onto.

Morgan...no... no it was Sammael...I had to remember that. Sammael grabbed his son by the arm and said sternly,

"And do not harm her in anyway."

"Why?! I don't understand what you would want with the Bitch...AHHH..." At this point Sammael used his painful grip on Alex as a way of not only getting his attention but I can imagine more of way to shut him up.

"I do not need to explain myself to you! Now do as I ask for I am wasting time in bringing forth the Titans." Alex wrenched his arm from his father's grasp and for a fleeting moment I thought he was going to refuse. I didn't quite understand the order not to hurt me myself but I can't say that I was going to complain.

He came over to me after grabbing a bottle of some kind from a vintage looking leather satchel, one that was stained with blood. I can't say that I was looking forward to anything that came from a bag like that but I was far from a position to do much about it let alone start complaining. If it meant lifting the curse then did that mean I had a fighting chance to stop this? Maybe I would discover the key to unleashing my powers, 'cause I had to say that would have been swell right about now!

He came over to me and I refused to flinch in spite of what he had done to me so far. His father on the other hand might have me screaming in fear and I wasn't ashamed to say it all things considered. I could be strong in the face of most things and not to blow my own trumpet but thought I had done pretty good so far in the face of danger.

There had been, crazy, stab happy waitresses, demonic mud creatures, reincarnated horned gods forcing back my virginity before also getting stab happy… creepy demons in warehouses, a team of hired thugs, being poisoned, locked in cells and starved, auctioned off in a giant bird cage…dressed as a damn bird I might add, and I will not even get started on the shit load of kidnappings…oh and the trip to Hell and blood poisoning bit…that was no picnic either!

OK so it was official, how I wasn't dead yet was more than a bloody miracle, it felt more like I should have been a damn cat in my past life….or past nine lives as the way things were looking for the future.

Alex sneered down at me and you could see him revelling in the state I was in. I wanted to say something cocky and smart assed at that moment, I really did but the sight of what Sammael was doing in the background drew my attention. Alex looked back over his shoulder, obviously to see what I was so engrossed in.

"Ah, the summoning begins. I am so looking forward to you meeting the Titans, as I may not be allowed to kill you yet but they certainly will!" I wanted to both cry in frustration and scream the worst of profanities at his taunting words. It had now been confirmed, not only had Draven released Sammael but he had also released the Titans with him. It suddenly all became clear as to why Sammael had prevented Alex from harming me in anyway and was now ordering him to lift the curse…

Draven had made a deal.

Alex stepped in front of me so I could no longer see what Sammael was doing and proceeded to dump the contents of the bottle around where I sat. I was slumped against the pillar and was completely drained of energy, to a point where I had to force to keep my eyes open and myself conscious.

"Oh God what is that!" I said as the putrid stench started to make my nostrils burn and suddenly I wasn't having any trouble staying awake.

"The old sour blood of slaughtered mortals, that's what. Now shut up while I do this, I need to concentrate." Once more my gagging reflex kicked in as the smell of both old copper and rancid meat combined wafted under my nose.

I didn't quite understand what he was trying to achieve especially when he took out his wooden blade and sliced his fingertip with it but I can't say I didn't get pleasure from the sight of himself harming. Now if he could just move a little further up, say to a main artery and that would be magic!

He made a fist to get his blood flowing quicker and then let it drip down onto the disgusting puddle around me. It started to sizzle and boil, popping tiny crimson bubbles the hotter it got. Alex then took out a silver hip flask from his pocket and poured water all over the blistering mixture causing it to bellow with steam all around me.

"Holy water can have its uses." He said just as I started to cough, having no choice but to breathe in the vapour that clouded my body and it felt like it was even seeping into my pores.

"Just let it happen you stupid Bitch!" Alex snapped and I could tell he was holding himself back from kicking me.

"You know, I am really going to enjoy watching you die!" I spat back hoping I wouldn't have to wait long for my wish to come true. Thankfully I didn't hear his reply and I knew he was behaving himself when I didn't feel one either.

No, I had more important things to concentrate on, like relishing in the blissful feeling that had taken over me. The only way to describe it was like jumping into a cool, crystal clear lagoon on a scorching summer's day. It was also sinking into the steaming bath on a freezing winter's day after a hard and hectic day at work. The both feelings totally contradicted themselves I know, but the refreshing sensation you got from one mixed with the comforting sensation you got from the other, were the only way I could describe what was happening to me now.

I found though it was gone far too soon as in what felt like a blink of an eye and I was back to feeling the pain and discomfort I was becoming accustomed to. Alex grunted something in a different language, no doubt an insult or two but seeing that he was now walking away I couldn't give a shit what the dickhead had said.

Besides, now with him out of the way I was free to watch whatever Sammael was up to…was is possible, could he really be bringing the Titans here?

Well I think one brief glance was all that was needed to answer that daft question. I didn't need to have a degree in witchcraft or a doctorate in demonology to know that the giant Pentagram that now filled the space on the Temple floor wasn't there for decoration. And this was proven right when Sammael started chanting a lost language of the Gods, one that sounded like it hadn't been heard in this world since the beginning of time. I don't know how I knew this but I was sure enough that I would have bet my life on it.

I mean obviously that bet would have meant shit right now all things considered, as let's face it, who bets with a bag of torn up money and a Rolex bought from some dodgy New York street seller. Because right now, I certainly wasn't worth the billion dollars some crazy ass Vampire king had once cashed up for me.

This thought instantly brought tears to my eyes knowing all

he had sacrificed for me and in the end it had even cost him his immortal life. It just wasn't fair! He died trying to save me and now Draven had just signed everyone's death sentence right along with him trying to do the very same thing.

As now I had my deadly proof...

The first Titan was here.

CHAPTER EIGHT

DRAVEN

AND ONE BY ONE THEY FALL

"What the Fuck are we waiting for?!" Sigurd shouted in his frustration and I can't say that I blamed him. Unfortunately there had been little time to do much more in this grand plan of mine, let alone enough to explain to everyone what they were fighting for. They just knew that for a short time my father had managed to lift the ban on anyone entering Tartarus and that they were needed to aid in preventing the Titans from escaping this mountain.

I had hoped to have many more to aid us but I hadn't counted on that asshole bringing back an army of the dead to deal with. Half of my council and Lucius' were still there fighting that losing battle of trying to kill what was already long ago laid to rest. They were mindless creatures that had awoken confused and given only one order…to kill the living.

So this was where we found ourselves. Split defences battling it out for the greater good and a divine mortal life the Gods chose to fulfil a prophecy… one that they deemed was *not* this day. The fates were convinced Judgement Day was coming and by all rights to the word that day should have been now. But according to the Oracle, one that was no longer in my good graces, the fates knew far more than we did and we only had to trust that worse events were to follow.

This was hard to believe in the face of Titans both trying to kill you and also disappearing to the mortal realm. I couldn't think of anything more catastrophic for the planet we shared, other than nature's own decision to destroy itself. Because I knew that as soon as that last Titan made it through the summoning that would be enough to alert Cronus from wherever he was hiding and then the power of the twelve would be entirely complete.

Nothing short of Gods from above and below would be able to stop them and this would surely mean the end of the world as we knew it. For Earth would become the next battleground, lain to waste by the carnage that would follow…for there would be little choice than for mortal kind to stand by helpless and watch their world crumble around them.

"I must concur with the Shadowed Soul my Maru, we have little to gain by continuing on this path but much to lose." My father said after breaking one God near in half after lifting his body and slamming it's back down on his solid bent knee. He pushed it aside knowing it would be back up in no time as if no injury had ever occurred.

"NO! We wait, for it will come, we just need more time! It will come…it has to come…" I said looking up at the mountain and for the first time in all my years praying for an enemy.

"Look! Dom another one is being summoned!" Sophia

shouted pointing to the disappearing Titan Zagan had been fighting.

"Oh great, at this rate there will be nothing left to fight." Sigurd said sarcastically after fighting back two at once and the move enabled his father, Ragnar to butt one of them hard enough he went flying to the other side.

"Don't speak so soon…LOOK!" Zagan yelled out his warning as the first signs of power were coming back to them. The more of the Titans that were summoned to the mortal realm the more powerful the ones left here became. Even now I could see their attacks becoming more precise and their movements getting quicker. This became increasingly apparent when one managed to get in a blow to not only my sister but also Ragnar had been brought down once, to which his son had aided him.

One of the larger Titans stood back from the rest as if waiting for something…or in this case…lots of somethings.

"It is Pallas, known as the Titan god of Warcraft…see there… he brings forth his legions…GET READY!" My father shouted to us all and as the fourth Titan was to disappear it generated enough power needed to call on his army.

The floor beneath us started to shake and we all struggled for a moment to remain on our feet. The sides of the platform crumbled into the river of lava beneath us and a large section of the bridge fell into the molten rock below.

I began to worry as pretty soon there wouldn't be anything left to fight on, that or our six broken bodies would be all that remained on one tiny patch of rock surrounded by mountain fire.

My father's warning turned out to be for good reason as the Titan known as Pallas was doing some summoning of his own. I looked over the edge to the blazing depths below us to see the lava forming shapes beneath its scorching surface.

"Oh you have got to be kidding me!" Sigurd said as soon what looked like hundreds of lava figures emerged and started climbing up the sides to get to us.

"Oh that impurae matris prolapsus ab alvo!" Sophia shouted making my father nod in way of appreciation.

"Ah very good my daughter. I believe it was Latin poet Ovid's Ibis… His cursed poem written during his years in exile across the Black Sea for an offense against Augustus…See Dominic, I am not the only one 'stuck in the times'…" He said pulling his hand free from the stone chest of a Titan before continuing…

"…as you may think….It was a good insult indeed, my daughter." I rolled my eyes, hit back at the Titan I was dealing with and then turned to her and said,

"Slimy son of a bitch...! Really?" I said translating what she had said from Ovid's poem, one to which she just shrugged her shoulders and said,

"Well it made the old man happy."

"I heard that!" Our father said before kicking out and then swiping a Titan to the ground before slamming his fist into its head.

"Suck up." I whispered making her wink.

"I hate to interrupt the family BBQ but I don't think anyone of us invited these guys to the party!" Sigurd barked up when the first row of Pallas' army were in sight.

"What do you say old man, should we show them the door?" Ragnar roared his agreement with his son and they both charged at the glowing, skeletal bodies as they clawed their way over the rim. Sigurd was a black shadow, moving too fast to keep track of and hence forth created a confusing fog for the creatures to get lost in.

Ragnar used this advantage to knock all the bodies off the edge and right back into the river of lava beneath us. This was an effective system, one that would have been more so if there wasn't just another twenty bodies to replace them. Pretty soon we not only had Titans outnumbering us to contend with but also a horde of magma fuelled bodies closing in on us.

The only thing in our favour was that finally we were fighting something that could die. One swipe of a blade and they burst into clouds of ash. The major factor not in our favour of course, was there were hundreds of them!

"Sophia, Zagan and Ragnar, you deal with the horde! Keep them back as long as you can. Snake Eye, you're with us." I instructed knowing we had little choice but to work together. He nodded and for once he didn't look like he was going to argue. Um…it looked like he really did pick his battles after all.

"What's the plan?" He asked once he fought his way towards where my father and I were taking out Titans back to back.

"We do have a plan…right?" He continued when I didn't reply and we all watched as yet another Titan was summoned to the mortal realm. In total, only eight remained now and what plan did I have to explain, how I was hoping for a miracle? Yeah that was a great plan but it was all hanging by a thread if what I was waiting for didn't show up soon.

Thankfully I was saved from having to explain my plans as the Titans started to fight as one. It was as if the longer they were free the more aware of their powers they became. And now, obviously more aware of each other as now they started to surround us, to the point where Sigurd had no choice but back up, making us a three sided stronghold.

"Well, King, all I can say is I hope you know what you're doing." He said looking over his shoulder at me and if I wasn't the fool in charge I would have responded with 'me too'. However I just grunted,

"Asshole" under my breath making him chuckle.

"I hope this works my Maru." My father added as he nodded to a fading Titan stood in the ring of angry Gods that were closing in on us.

"As do I or we are…"

"Royally fucked?" Sigurd finished for me and before I got a chance to respond all the Titans ran at us at once. We fought with all we had but by the time they fell we just had others waiting. It was a constant wave after wave of Titans that were growing more powerful with each of their brothers gone. So after fighting seven that dwindled down to three, it actually took more of our combined skills to hold them back.

We barely managed the feat but it wasn't without its consequences as each of us received our fair share of blows and blood spilt from our opponents. I just raised both my blades and twisted my body as I slashed my swords sideways across my opponent's chest, landing on one knee. Then I spun back on myself slicing into the same Titan, taking out his stance with a blade to the legs. As he fell to the ground he left a clear view of the swarm that was closing in on the other three of my comrades.

Ragnar was being overrun with scorching bodies crawling all over him and he spun round in his rage, trying in vain to get them off him. Just as Sigurd hit out at the Titan he was fighting, he ended up stumbling through him as he too received his summoning. I whistled to him to get his attention and motioned to his father. He nodded his acknowledgement and as he made it past me he muttered,

"Not a word, King." This was in regards to him tripping through the disappearing Titan and nearly falling on his ass, which I can't say I would have been disappointed to see right now.

"Time to help our kin." I said to my father after he knocked back one of the two Titans left. The one I had been fighting was still healing so this gave us enough time to help with the horde.

"Tell me father, are you acquainted with Ten Pin Bowling?"

"Uh, no, I don't believe I…" I smiled what I knew was a malicious grin before I grabbed his stone form, swung him around a few turns before letting him go in the direction of what was the bulk of their lava army. He flew at them like a battering ram and a cloud of ash bellowed behind him as he took out one soulless form after another.

He went hurtling off the side of the platform and I waited as his own wings erupted from his back. He possessed some of the largest pair of wings and just at the right moment they burst free. I knew their size played a factor in not just status down here but also the monumental amount of power he held.

They reminded me of the old realms, when Dragons were reality. These demonic princes that were once allowed to walk the mortal realm and prove their worth in the terror induced from others. And therefore not only feeding their egos but drawing in the powerful essence that was fear.

My father was no different as he finally flaunted his true form. His wings spread out in a magnificent display of supremacy and minus the feathers I knew where my brother Vincent inherited the size of his own wings from. They were gigantic and still held a deadly beauty with every large dragon scale that interlocked over the stretched skin. As a whole they looked mainly black but each scale was tipped dark purple with a tinge of forest green the closer to the skin they got.

Then there was the other side of him that I was happy to report no longer resembled an older version of myself. No now he portrayed the three sides to his personality that he was famous for in Hell. On one side of his shoulders were the twisted and curled horns of a ram and on the other were the sleeker, straighter horns of a bull. Lastly his demonic face burned with a lethal determination and he swooped down over the horde and freed his famous temper, breathing fire as he knocked the ranks back into the lava below. He took out a large chunk of the army from above, whilst the rest of us broke away and dealt with the aftermath in the form of the two angry Titans that remained.

It may not have seemed like much to an outsider, having six against two but the power they now held was a force of the likes we had never known. Not only was blow after blow now being defended against but we were now the ones needing the time to heal.

"SOMETHING'S COMING!" My father's demonic voice boomed as he picked up on what the Titan Pallas was cooking up next. His eyes rolled back in their sockets and turned from soulless black to bleached white, glaring out against his charred ash skin.

"Can you stop him?!" I shouted back but it was too late. The mountain rumbled and this time I couldn't be sure that this damn Titan hadn't just triggered the volcano of Tartarus to erupt. We all shook where we stood and even some of the horde had slipped from the edge and fallen because of it.

"BE READY!" Ragnar roared so loud you could hear it through his twisted bone helmet. It was as if he could feel what was coming before the rest of us could. So because of this he bent over as if drawing in the rest of his powers to grow bigger. Whatever it was because of his actions I knew one thing for certain…

It was going to be big.

As the world shook around us, all Pallas needed was the last of his brothers to leave Tartarus, giving him the power boost he had been waiting for…waiting…

For all Hell to break loose!

"CYCLOPES!" My sister screamed as the beasts from every supernatural beings' nightmares erupted through the mountain wall. I looked up as everyone else did the same and saw our war quickly turning into an extermination! There was no creature in Hell, not even at this level that could beat back a Cyclopes, let alone the three brothers that came charging through the rock at us all.

The most ruthless of creatures that were once used in the Titan war against their own kind. Brontes, Steropes and Arges were the sons of Uranus and Gaia but more importantly were also brothers of the Titans. The stories got it wrong in thinking that Zeus released them from the dark pit of Tartarus when it was in fact he who imprisoned them here.

This was easier to do as once the Titans themselves were imprisoned, the Cyclopes turned into immortal stone as there was no fear of their release without also releasing the Titans; reasons because they themselves were the only ones that could wake their brothers from an eternal slumber. One they had just been woken from.

They were giants that the myth of monsters were based on. Creatures with little thought process out of the realms of loyalty and destruction. The chaos they were capable of could level cities to dust in mere hours. And now all that stood in their way were the six of us and a bravery that matched our fallen ancestors, ones that now lived on as heroes throughout the ages.

And we would do the same... for *we* would die the same.

Fallen immortal Kings and Heroes.

"ATTACK!" I roared holding up my sword and running for the monsters that came for us. The remaining Titan, for a time being, was held immobile and I put this down to the exertion of energy used. Still I didn't hold faith that this would last.

However it at least gave us the time we would surely need if we were to defeat this creature as one.

I leapt up into the air just at the right time as all three Cyclopes jumped as one from the side of the mountain. The space we used as a battleground looked half ready to crumble from the impact, as great chunks of it fell away into the glowing abyss below.

The triple beast was three giant bodies of armoured muscle void of the need for skin. It was a mass of solid tissue chiselled for one need and one need only...*strength for crushing your enemy*.

Their heads were covered in crudely hammered iron helmets that sat square to their shoulder as they had no necks. They each had a barred window in the centre for their one eye to see out of and the whole thing had been screwed into their flesh.

This wasn't to protect them by any means but it had once been done to protect us. I knew this down to the three large, thick chains that hung down from the top of the brim around the edge of each helmet. This was also the same for each slatted breast piece they wore; strips of metal that had been forged together with the sole purpose of holding back the beasts in an attempt to contain them if they ever awoke.

Well contain them it had not as all the ends of the chains were bent and broken links from where they had been given the strength to break through. Massive chains of likes you would see on ships and the very same to what had not long ago helped contained their brothers. Well this time they were used to bind the brothers together so they had to move as one, being connected by lengths of chains attached to the gauntlets they were forced to wear. They hung down in swags, giving them limited movement between them and the broken lengths coming from their helmets and chest pieces swung around like wrecking balls.

They roared in anger and growled at each other when one wanted to move one way and the others didn't agree. This was our *only* advantage….so I took it! I let my wings fold so I dropped down on the middle one's back and drove my blades home into their hardened flesh. They went in but only so far and unfortunately for me, not enough to do much damage. It was enough however to set them off in a greater rage. The middle one twisted trying to dislodge me and therefore forcing the ones either side of it to twist with him.

I jumped free, drew in my blades and landed with a roll so as not to get crushed by their colossal feet.

"DOM, LOOK OUT!" I heard my sister scream and I rolled again just before the last Titan could strike me a killing blow. I put enough distance between us to do a back flip until I was facing the approaching Titan storming my way. He was the last one left and because of this, it also made him the most powerful being I had ever had to fight.

"You deal with that! And I will deal with him!" I gave my order knowing that either foe would be a challenge for us all. I decided to let him know what he was in for and I extended my weapons until the tips scraped the floor. He cocked his head, causing his charred flesh to flake at the neck and looked at my weapons a moment before fire ignited in his eyes.

"Don't do it…don't you…." I was cut off in my mutterings when he started to grow his own double blades from his wrists, mirroring my own. I rolled my eyes and groaned,

"This should be interesting."

"Thanatos" The Titan rasped, trying out his first word spoken since the beginning of mankind. It grated along my skin and that wasn't down to knowing what it meant…*Death.*

"THANATOS!" The Titan Pallas thundered after throwing

his arms behind him in his fury. Obviously I wasn't taking him seriously enough, I thought dryly.

"Yeah, yeah…Not today Titan!" I said but then added more after all I got was an angry, confused look back…

"Koprophage!" I said further in response, which meant 'Eat Shit' in Ancient Greek, at which he threw his head back and roared at the top of the mountain.

"Oh yeah, you understood that." I said as he lowered his head and snarled at me.

"You want me dead, then come and fucking try!" I snarled back and at that we both charged at each other with both of our blades igniting at the same time. I jumped and lashed out at him using the momentum of my fall to add power to my attack. He blocked my blades with his own held over his head and they sparked on impact.

I spun my body round and tried getting him off guard but by the Gods he was quick. He blocked every attack and matched me move for move. The last person I had fought with a skill that matched my own had been Lucius when he had still been a member of my council. That thought made my blood burn hotter with the knowledge of what was to become of my old adversary. Death wasn't a pleasant experience for any being but for an immortal it was an even greater loss.

"Lucius." I whispered his name in prayer just before I swiped out at Pallas and barely missed his head. As the move twisted my body I wasn't quick enough to counteract the kick to my ribs, feeling them crack as I flew backwards in the dirt. I flipped up and round on my hands and looked up facing the other battle being fought. In the one second I had spare I saw the Cyclopes trying to kill not only my allies but also *my family.*

The feeling of helplessness overwhelmed my senses and I hammered my fist on the ground in anger before raising myself up for what I knew was the last round. For one of us would die fighting or… die trying.

"Alright, let see what you've got. COME ON!" I thundered at him before I charged once more. He held his stance and the second I got near the real fight began. We slashed out at each other over and over so fast to the human eye it would have been a blur of bodies and blades. I got in my first hit and didn't stop to take in what the damage was, only the need to cause more driving me.

I kicked out, tripping him up and the tip of my swords hit dirt instead of a Titan's chest. I growled in my frustration but then looked up too late to see his blade coming for my head. I twisted saving my face from being cut in two but the blow landed across my naked back.

"Ahh!" I shouted out in pain before attacking right back. It was as if he was getting quicker the more we fought and I was getting weaker. It was only after his blade found its mark on my body again that I knew why. He was drawing in his energy, his greater power from me! I was being drained like my kind does to a human, only it wasn't just leaving me weaker, it was leaving me defenceless!

I went to block with one arm and found my other being held by the wrist to prevent me from striking out with my free blade. He leant forward and said again…

"Thanatos" before he kicked out my legs causing me to land on my knees before him. So this was my time? This was where I would find my death, at the bottom of this hell hole defeated by a God that I myself released?

Then so be it.

I knew of the utter chaos going on around me and the great loss we would all soon endure, in not just our immortal souls but in the rest of the world. But in all this pandemonium around me there was also a moment of peace like I had never known. If this was the end then my mind was welcoming it with only two things...

An image of Keira and complete silence.

I could see the fatal blow coming down at me like a flaming meteorite falling from the night sky. I had no defence left and saw the green cloud of death fall over me as the blow obviously took my life. My last thought was simply the most beautiful thing on the planet...

Keira.

It was access to memory after memory of every time she smiled at me. It was her snorting on the bed after tickling her. It was her drunken ramblings on the couch about tea bags. It was seeing her in a dress and the way the skirt twisted around her and clung to her body as we danced for the first time. It was holding her through the night. It was telling her I loved her. It was making love to her. And it was the way she looked when she ran to me in the lobby and took my hand.

The way she trusted me after all I had put her through...

It was the way she loved me back.

It was perfection.

And that's how I died. Watching perfection...

"Keira." It was the last name I ever wanted uttered from my dying lips.

Then BOOM!

I was unsure what was happening but it sounded like a bomb had gone off and the shockwave rippled underneath me. I expected there to be shrapnel ricocheting off my broken body but I felt nothing. I looked at the green mist in front of me and focused on a pair of wings I had never seen before just as I heard his voice...

"Nope, definitely not Keira."

"Can it... be...?" I said in an awe that was produced by the tiniest amount of hope that seeped into a desperate mind.

"Did you miss me?" I sucked in a shuddered breath to try and hold back my raw emotion of a relief, one so great it was like feeling it for the very first time.

Because if this was real then it meant only one thing…

Life for us all.

"Lucius."

CHAPTER NINE

DRAVEN

VENOM SWALLOWED, SLICED AND DELIVERED

"So I take that as you did miss me." He said smirking as he held out his hand for me to clasp and before helping me to my feet. I looked back behind me in disbelief at the sight of the Titan so broken it was taking longer for him to heal.

"How?" I said in wonder, as not even I knew this could happen.

"What can I say, it must be the God in me." Lucius said looking as smug as ever.

"Don't ya mean the 'blood' in you...? Whats'up Toot's royal beef cake?" The Imp named Pip popped out of nowhere and patted her master on the arm before nodding to me. I had never known a creature like her and was sure I was never to meet another in my lifetimes to come...It was a humbling revelation knowing I could now say that, thanks to Lucius.

"You saved my life." I blurted out finding I obviously had no filter when it came to near death experiences...um, who knew I could be so impulsive.

Pip smirked and just nudged an uncomfortable looking Lucius on the arm, causing him to clear his throat as though trying to find the right words to say.

"Yeah well...old habits die hard I guess." He said making Pip roll her eyes, causing her garish fake pink eyelashes to flutter. I, on the other hand, burst out laughing before saying,

"Don't you mean, there is a first time for everything...*my Brother.*" His eyes widened at the grand gesture I just made and instead of a cocky remark he simply nodded his head in respect.

"Ok enough of this mushy shit, what are you a bunch of silly girls...? What's next a tea party*? 'No, no you can have my Barbie'...'no, no I insist, you can play with her first'*...Bla lala...MAN UP! Come on Bitches, we got shit to fight!" Pip said in her cryptic way that left us both frowning and shaking our heads as she walked away with an exaggerated swagger.

"Translate?" I asked my former second in command.

"Bollocks if I know, but I am pretty sure she called us prissy little girls." Lucius said crossing his arms and staring after his pintsized lieutenant.

"Yeah I got that bit but what's a Barbie?" I asked before I caught sight of one person that was more than needed down here right now.

"I thought you could do with reinforcements." He said following my gaze to Adam.

"We could use some help over here!" Sigurd shouted over to us as they still dealt with the Cyclops. They had managed to get the chains wrapped around their legs and they were currently in a tangled mass trying to break free.

"That won't hold them for long." I said looking sideways to

Lucius and the grin he gave me was one that made his eyes glow with fire.

"That's why I brought my own monster."

I couldn't argue with him on that as I had seen for myself the destruction *his* monster could cause and to say it was impressive was an understatement. We both looked back at the Titan to see him not only on his feet but also it looked like it was finally his turn to be summoned...and our time had just ran out.

"Looks like I'm up...you go and save our Keira girl. I will deal with him." Lucius nodded to the Titan that was looking up at the mouth of Tartarus as if waiting for his calling to the mortal realm.

"Quickly Lucius."

"You know Dom, I think your vessel is getting wrinkles with all this worrying you do." I laughed as I walked away and said,

"Yeah and it's called Keira!" But I couldn't pretend I didn't hear him mutter back to himself,

"That it is my friend...that it is."

I ran over to where everyone stood a fair distance from the Cyclopes brothers all trying desperately to escape their bonds and from the looks of it, they were nearly there.

"Dom you have to go now, you have to get to her before Sammael realises what you have done!" Sophia shouted to me over the chaos and I noticed her limping towards me. The thought that she had been injured made my demon howl in anger. I knew she would heal but that knowledge didn't calm me or the beast.

"DOM!" she shouted my name and I shook the murderous thoughts from my mind.

"Focus! I am fine, I will heal, however Keira will not if you don't get your Hero ass back there!" She was right of course, they could handle it from here but by the Gods only knew what he might do to her when he found out I was capable of stopping the Titans...Blood bound or not.

"Go cowboy, we've got this yo! Oh but could you do one tiny fav before you go?" Pip asked again popping out of nowhere. Before I even had chance to acknowledge her she slapped me on the back and said,

"Good man. Now all I need you to do is hit my Kong." I frowned down at her and shook my head once as if not hearing her correctly.

"I'm sorry?"

"You know, you're the King, now I need you to hit my Kong...King Kong...see?" She said pointing to her chest and the picture of a giant ape hanging from the empire state building.

"I'm still not following."

"I believe my Lord she wants you to punch me." Adam said bowing his head and being respectful as always. Pip jumped up on him and wrapped her legs around his waist, gave him what sounded like a sloppy kiss and then removed his glasses. Then she jumped down and said,

"Yeah, what he said, 'cause then that way when he goes bat shit crazy 'Kong style'..." She said moving an army vest full of badges out of the way and poking once more at her chest before continuing...

"...then that way I don't have to try and stop him from eating you...oh better hurry 'cause those three look like..." I didn't let her finish as I turned to Adam and said,

"My apologies" before punching him across the jaw, causing his head to snap to the side.

"Whoa! There you go...did you hear that crack...I think they heard that all the way back in Lust! How are things back in Lust these days?" Pip turned and asked my father who had returned back to his former self. He grinned down at her and said,

"Very well my child, you should stop by some time and let me show you around." This in the end would have been all it would have taken to set Adam off because at that he broke free from his mortal bonds and became the beast of all beasts.

Abaddon.

"Oh poor baby, he didn't mean it, now did you...this is when you back track Lordy Lust man!" Pip warned as she cooed to her husband, the biggest beast of all. At that moment I would have laughed in the face of seeing my father looking worried for a second, if of course getting back to Keira wasn't my first priority.

My father backed up and Pip patted the massive leg the skin of which was made from the bones of his victims, ones the man part of him didn't even remember taking.

"Hey, it's not him that wants to sex me up, it's those three over there! Go get 'em tiger!" Abaddon turned his head to the way she pointed just as the Cyclopes broke free and roared at the sight of the new beast. I couldn't help but think the three brothers would be in for a shock if they thought they could win this fight. They might all have been the same size but nothing known to man could beat Abaddon...The Dark Lord had made him that way.

I took one last look around as I cast the order for my Angel side to call me back and I smiled when I saw Lucius cracking his neck to the side as if ready for the fight.

The last thing I heard before the battle began was a little Imp's roaring voice shout,

"LET'S GET READY TO RUMBLE!"

LUCIUS

"That it is my friend...that it is." I muttered to myself knowing I had the same affliction that affected Dom and that it was little, blonde and had trouble written all over her...and by the Gods and powers that be, if she didn't survive this then they would find Hell at their gates and me leading the army. Shit, but I would be the next one releasing the Titans if that happened! Well, that was after I sent the bastards back first. Speaking of which.

"Yo, dickhead! Yeah you dipshit, you think you're fighting days are over?" I asked as he looked at me in a quizzical way a dog would look when hearing a new noise. He snarled at me and I saw his body fading in and out, knowing it was taking more out of Sammael bringing this one through.

And good job too or I would have been too late for not only putting a stop to Armageddon but also from preventing Dom's head rolling from his shoulders.

I leant down to one side when the Titan ignored me and picked up a rock. I purposely dug the flesh of my palm into the jagged edge, bathing the stone in my contaminated blood, for there was no other word for it. I had bitten into Alex, like I and Dom had planned in case our worst fears were confirmed from the scumbag. The fact that he was the Venom of God, the offspring of not only Sammael but also the last Titan bloodline combined. This was enough to free the Titans yes, but it had not been enough to kill me!

Of course that isn't saying it hadn't been enough to *nearly* kill me, the bastard! And it had put me in a bloody good coma that was for damn sure. It was a risky plan but what had the alternative been, to watch Keira bleed to death on some fucking altar! Or watch as every last council member of mine died fighting a war we could never win. No, the chance had been worth the pain or near loss of my eternal life.

But the hardest pill to swallow had been the haunting look in Keira's eyes. The point as she saw me slipping away to darkness and her heart-breaking cry of pain was something I would never forget. For I would never imagine a soul so pure and full of love would have ever cried for me. Not in all my years first as a mortal, then as a king and now as I have returned as a God. For that was the only way to describe the infected power that now ran through my veins…

It was the blood of Gods.

And right now my hand was covered in it and therefore made this simple rock a powerful weapon. I threw it up and down, stepping closer to my target. Then said on the third catch,

"It's a hard job, but someone has to do it!" Then I threw it at him, hitting him dead centre on the chest. The impact acted like a cannon ball and the minuscule amount of blood that hit him was enough to prevent his summoning once and for all.

He had flown backwards hard enough to produce a crater in the ground upon his landing and I cracked my neck in preparation for what was to come. He pulled his broken body from the ditch he had caused and healed himself by the time he took his first steps towards me.

"You're a powerful son of a bitch aren't you?" I said on a laugh circling him. He snarled snapping his jaw at me and honestly the sight bored me. All I wanted to do was slit a vein and pour this shit down his throat but I needed to give Dom time to get back to our little troublemaker.

Once that slimy bastard Sammael knew what we had planned all along then I didn't need to venture a guess as to who he would take out his wrath on. And along with every other supernatural being on this planet, we all knew that Dominic Draven, King of Kings only had one weakness. One single ingredient for the recipe of revenge and oh boy, wasn't she just a handful. And I would know considering I too at one time had tried to tame the lioness after stealing her away from the King of the hellish jungle she lived in. She might as well have had a fucking bull's eye tattooed on her back and have done with it!

These thoughts made me angry and I refused to look too closely as to why. It was this damn connection we shared and then there was that moment we shared on top of the tower. My sacred place I went to think, like nobody ever expected me to...

To think about my own soul mate.

I had thought it was Keira and that damn kiss we shared only seemed to solidify that notion. That was before one single vision we both shared caused it to shatter like the fragile glass the fire in my heart had shaped it into. One fleeting moment in time had destroyed what I had felt in the depths of my soul to be true and it had screamed liar to the world.

We didn't speak of it... *ever*.

However, we both knew that we still needed each other, only now that 'need' branched off into different directions, rooted though to only one heart. I closed my eyes and shook off these cryptic bullshit thoughts to get the job done.

"Time to save the world, Luc." I muttered down at myself looking at the blood in my hand dripping to the ground and noticing the way it ate away at the stone like acid...

"Um...interesting. I wonder how this tastes to a Titan?" I said louder looking back up at the advancing God that now knew he was no longer being summoned.

"Let's find out should we?" I said before running straight at him. He saw me coming full speed and decided to match the advance until both of us collided. I side stepped just before I hit his chest and instead he found himself at a disadvantage with an enemy to his back. I kicked out his leg, forcing him to bend one knee and at the same time placing him in a chokehold with my arm banded around the column of his neck.

"You were granted release by your own bloodline, now let's see what happens when you take it back... drink Sama-El!" I shouted wrenching his head back, biting deeper into my own hand and forcing the blood that seeped from my wound down his throat. I saw his dead eyes widen in panic as he understood the ancient word where Sammael received his new name... Sama-El was the language spoken for the true 'Venom of God' but as the fates knew of it from its truer origins, the Blood of the Devil.

He started to choke and as his hands went up to claw desperately at my arm his fingers started to smoke when they came into contact with my skin. I let him go and he fell forward landing on all four limbs. The ground around us started to tremor and I looked up in time to see Adam as Abaddon running into the belly of the centre Cyclopes. He ran with them all being dragged along with their brother to the edge of the quaking platform of rock we all still stood on.

I could tell the fight had been brutal but only on one side, given the amount of blood and injury the three brothers showed on their battered bodies. A sense of pride washed over me as my second in command disposed of the brothers and the last thing heard from them was the death call of three Cyclopes as they went falling into the lava below.

Meanwhile the last Titan had painfully risen to his feet and was making a run for it.

"I doubt he will get far." Asmodeus said coming up to stand next to me.

"I hear Iraq is nice this time of year!" Pip shouted after him putting her dainty little hands together.

"Eh…Squeak?"

"Yeah boss man?" She said looking up at me and flashing me those forest green eyes.

"Don't you think you should go and deal with that?" She looked to where I looked and then realisation hit.

"Oh yeah…you know I knew there was something I was forgetting." She said watching as her husband continued to charge the others that were trying in vain to attempt to calm him down.

"Good girl." I said patting her on her ww2 military helmet, one she had painted an angry cartoon face on the front with buck teeth and glitter pink stars around the sides. I was tempted to ask her about the neon swimming goggles around her neck but knew her answer would have made zero sense, so I let her get back to it.

She ran off and soon made it to Abaddon, taking off her clothes as she went. So by the time she got to him she was waving up at him in nothing but striped over the knee socks, combat boots and that damn helmet!

"She's a keeper that one." Sophia said being carried in the arms of her own husband and her broken leg that hadn't healed yet was the obvious reason.

"As are you my warrior woman." Zagan said looking adoringly at the beauty in his arms.

"Christ is there something in the fucking water!?" Sigurd said coming up next with his father Ragnar behind him.

"And that right there is why you're still single!" Sophia teased before throwing her arms around Zagan's neck and kissing him in abandon.

"Yeah right…So where does asswipe think he's going to get to?" Sigurd asked after his dry response to Dom's sister.

"My guess is he thinks if he can make it out of Tartarus then he is imprisoned no more." Asmodeus said and just on cue the Titan reached the edge of the platform but before he could jump, a huge wave of molten lava crashed up against the rock, creating a wall he could not pass. He tried another way but then same thing occurred until it closed in on him, engulfing his form until there was nothing left but a Titan fighting against an element he could not beat...Tartarus itself.

"It begins." Ragnar spoke after his horns retracted from his face and his lips were free. And he was right, it was beginning. The ground we stood on began to quake harder and the lava that had burst over the sides started to move closer to us. We all walked backwards until it came to a stop and then watched as it formed into shapes.

One black stone after another formed like giant bricks on top of each other from the flowing magma running up the sides. It didn't take long as before we knew it we were all looking up at a black pyramid that looked as if it had been built by demonic Aztecs. Lava rivers defied gravity and gushed up towards the top where I knew it was cascading down on the Titan it held inside.

The very last part to form was an arched doorway with a keystone adorning the top. It had to be the face of Cronus as it was an angry and twisted face of rage. I had to smile when its mouth dropped open as I knew this was the last act needed in bringing back the rest of the Titans.

"Duty calls." I said before releasing my wings and when I heard the gasp behind me I knew what they were seeing...

I had changed.

I ignored their response and flew up to the Keystone. Once more I bit into my hand, vowing it would be the last time today and thrust it into the stone mouth. I felt my poisoned blood beating through my veins and pounding against the walls of my organs like unleashed power trying to break free. I felt it drip from my vessel and sucked in a sharp breath when I felt the key respond as I bathed the God's lock with the blood of their own.

Their blood was their legacy as was their blood their saviour...*My blood was their damnation.*

But then something happened. Something none of us expected, least of all me. For now the price of locking up the Titans became clear. It wasn't just blood they wanted,

It was flesh.

So Cronus' jaws locked shut around the hand I had willingly given them...

Severing it as payment.

CHAPTER TEN

KEIRA

A HERO RETURNS

Sitting here helpless as I watched each Titan appear and knowing I couldn't do a damn thing to stop it was pure torture. My mind was on overtime wondering what had happened to Draven and what was happening to him now that prevented him from coming back. I had at least my hope keeping me sane, one that was being kept alive by the sight of his essence still shimmering on the altar. I had to hold on to the idea that if something had happened to him then his essence would have gone from this world.

I watched as yet another body emerged and became suspended inside the giant pentagram. There were nine now in total and with five stood at each point and the other four stood locked at the corners of where the star met, there was space left for only two more. I dreaded to think what would happen when those last two made it through and from the looks of the evil grin on Alex's face, well let's just say it didn't give me the warm fuzzies!

Sammael stood around the Pentagram chanting and with his eyes rolled back up into his head it looked like he was deep into his summoning mumbo jumbo. They were both turned away from me and it made me think about guns.

That sounds random but I was seriously considering getting one if I was going to survive this! Maybe I could get one of those cute tiny lady guns that strap to the thigh and only fire one bullet. But then on further thought there would be little point given the amount of enemies I was racking up. Hell, by the time the year was out I would be needing a bloody Gatling gun to protect myself.

Movement to my right drew my attention away from the villains in the room and I looked to see Draven's essence shaking violently. I sucked in a painful breath and whispered,

"No...please God no..." It twisted and turned like it was a body being kicked and at one point it rose up arching its back as if it had been struck by something. I knew it was Draven fighting, this knowledge I could cope with, having seen it many times before. But what I couldn't cope with was seeing Draven being beaten, which was how it looked now. A man as strong as Draven made it near impossible to believe he could be hurt, which was why I found it so difficult to believe him dead all that time ago.

But then I would have never thought he was capable of releasing the Titans either but one look to my left and that belief went flying out the window.

"Only one more father and my immortal brothers and I will be reunited by blood once more." Alex said as the tenth Titan came to form. Now there was just one space left and I didn't know what would become of not just me, but the rest of mankind when a figure of a God filled that central space.

I wanted to shout up at the Gods, 'what are you waiting for?!' but then I would only be cursing them again when I didn't receive my answer. Because nothing stood in their way...not God, nor Angel or Demon and certainly not man was left to stop them.

All that was left was a broken girl, whose tears couldn't stop them. If only my vision of a single tear bringing down the Titans was something that could actually happen, because I had those in abundance! I think right now I could take out a whole army with the power of pain behind each drop. I looked towards Draven's essence and just knew when the end came I had to be near him.

So I made this my last mission.

As long as I had breath left in me I would get to him. I took one last look at the two that were busy and decided I didn't give a shit what they saw me doing. I didn't care if they caught me crawling on my belly trying to get to him. I didn't care what they did to me or even if they killed me for it. All I cared about was that my last action in this world was going to be either dying with him or dying trying to reach him.

Because now, all I wanted in what was left of this life was to go home. I wanted to reach that safe place that comforted my heart and warmed my soul. The place I thought about whenever I was afraid or sadness overwhelmed me. The one place in this world that made me feel like I could do anything. It gave me wings to shelter the blinding light of doubt and to soar the skies in confidence. It was a place of solace and understanding. But most importantly it was a place that surrounded me with an intense love that matched my own.

Yes, I wanted to die at home. Every single day having that same choice given would have resulted in the same answer. Because the reasons were so clear and so simple. And they were the same reasons I crawled and dragged my broken body across a sickening temple floor. Through the filth of death and the blood of innocents slain. I gagged, swallowing down my disgust and worked harder. Everywhere on my body hurt but I didn't care. The closer I got to him the more numb I became to the feeling of hurt but the devastation I would feel if I was too late would strike my heart like an icy blade. I needed to make it home, because...

Draven's arms were my home.

So I pushed with my toes and I pulled myself along the floor until my fingernails broke. I used every muscle to breaking point until my body was screaming out at me to stop. But I couldn't ever stop. I looked up to see how far I had left to go and felt my heart flutter when I saw I was nearly there. A few more pushes and I reached out to touch the altar with my fingertips.

"Draven..." I whispered his name, hoping being this close somehow he could hear me. I looked up and knew I had the hardest part to come. Another push and I gripped onto the grooves that made up the symbols carved all around the marble slab. I felt like crying out and shouting as the pain ripped through me like my skin was splitting, but I pushed on. I dragged my weakened body up the altar and feeling only some slight relief then I used my legs together with my upper body.

"Oh Draven." I whispered looking down at his shimmering form that heartbreakingly reminded me of his ghost.

"Draven if you can hear me...come back to me..." I choked back a sob and leant over his face, one that was still hauntingly beautiful even in this form. I put my hand to where his cheek would have been and held myself back from touching it, too scared that I could lose the sight of him. I looked down at him and let a single tear fall as I whispered...

"Come home to me."

The tear went straight through him and his form shuddered

as if he had felt it travelling through his soul. Every tiny grain of floating dust grew brighter and for a miniscule second of hope I allowed myself to believe it had been enough to bring him back to me. That was the second before my heart shattered.

"NO!" I cried out my utter agony as I felt him die for the second time in my life, only this one I was here to witness. He faded away to nothing before my eyes and I desperately reached out to try to cling on to what I could of him. I cried out over and over becoming hysterical in my loss.

"DRAVEN NO! YOU CAN'T LEAVE ME! You can't leave me...! You...you...can't...please...please don't leave me..." I started sobbing out my words in my devastation and I let my body slump from the altar, landing on the stone, cold floor.

"Go get her!" I heard the order coming from Sammael, Morgan, Alex...it didn't matter who. The order meant all the same...absolutely nothing! None of it mattered anymore now he was gone and the only hope I had left was that soon I would follow him into the next life and find him there waiting for me.

I saw a blurred figure coming towards me and I knew it was Alex. I turned my face away and pressed my cheek to the altar and whispered my heart break one last time before I took my own life...

"You left me again."

"I could never leave you...*I promised."* I heard his voice say and even though I let my heart pound in my chest in reaction I knew I must be hearing things. But then I felt his touch and knew nothing on earth or in my mind, heart and soul could create a feeling so beautiful without the one I loved being behind the action. I opened my eyes and gasped as I saw the truth. I felt my lips tremble and my breathing hitch as I tried to take in the air needed to cry.

"Is it...can it be...Draven please, I can't take this heartache anymore...please, please just say something so I know it's not a

121

dream…so I know…" I never finished as he crushed his lips to mine and I couldn't breathe from happiness. Then he spoke over my lips the only words that mattered in the face of death…

"I love you."

Then he heard Alex coming up behind him and turned quickly, creating a barrier between us both.

"NO! It can't be, you can't be here…the Titans would have killed you!" Alex wined out his misfortunes and I heard Draven growl.

"They failed." Draven stated in a dangerous voice that had Alex backing up a step. Draven looked down at me and it was clear he was doing a quick scan of my injuries. I dreaded to think the mess he saw and I wasn't surprised to see him enraged. He turned his head back to Alex and snarled like angry jungle cat. This was enough to get him moving pretty damn quick. To the point he nearly fell over himself to get back to his father quick enough.

"I need to move you." Draven said trying to rein in his temper at seeing me like this. He lifted me up as gently as he could and I tried not to wince. I knew I hadn't accomplish it too well when I heard him growl again. I ignored his reaction and instead used this moment to drink him in. His naked torso was covered in dirt and ash and it looked like he had been fighting a war. There was dried blood on his body in smears and drips that had obviously come from injuries that had healed. So apart from needing a bloody good soak in the tub he was in pretty good shape. I, of course, would have liked to have said the same but without his blood in me I wasn't healing at even near the same rate as he had.

"Here, drink th…" He was cut off and stopped before biting into his wrist as Sammael's voice echoed around the temple.

"You are too late!" I shuddered and Draven ran a finger down my cheek before winking at me. Was he insane…did he not see what was stood around in that circle? My doubt must have been written all over my face because he whispered down at me…

"Trust me, Love." He held my gaze for a moment until I nodded feeling the hope bloom so bright inside me it was blinding and could have blotted out the sun.

"Good girl. Now stay here whilst I deal with some loose ends." I reached out to grab his shoulder but pulled back at the last second, knowing that he would keep his promise…He wouldn't leave me again. He noticed the action and his hard facial expression softened before he kissed me sweetly, like the face of Earth's destruction in the room didn't come first.

"Nothing in this world comes before you…*nothing!*" He told me fervently as if being able to hear my thoughts. I nodded letting him know I understood and let the tears rolling down my cheeks speak for me. He gave me a small smile before getting up and becoming the man I knew had to face the world alone.

"Wait…what's happening?" Sammael said turning back to where the last Titan should have been coming through to see the faint figure vanish completely. He stomped around the circle with the Pentagram inside and looked around frantically. Was it possible? Had Draven found a way to stop it before it could complete?

Alex pulled out his wooden dagger and Draven just laughed seeing it.

"You're going to need a lot more than that boy!" Draven warned and Alex looked around and decided his chances lay better stood behind his father. Sammael was shaking his head in disbelief and then his head snapped up to look at Draven.

"You!" He snarled. Draven nodded once and folded his arms across his chest. He looked like some sentinel warrior stood protecting me and preventing anyone from getting close.

"How?" He asked spitting the question out. Draven just

lifted his chin to indicate where Alex stood behind him and Sammael twisted his head to look accusingly at his son. Alex's eyes widened in shock and as he started shaking his head Sammael must have seen something because he started snarling at him. Then he grabbed him by the collar and bent his head to one side to show off where Lucius had taken his last and fatal bite.

"No...NO! YOU FOOL!" Sammael bellowed at Alex and then pushed him aside hard enough he slid the length of the room. Alex looked as confused as I did but instead of mine his eyes were filled with tears of hurt. Sammael spun back to look at Draven and said,

"Then let their only act in this world be to KILL YOU AND YOUR BITCH!" He thundered in his demonic voice and my skin crawled at the sight of his true form causing the decaying skin of Morgan to peel away, leaving a monstrous sight beneath. He raised his hands to the night sky that showed through the glass dome, threw back his head and screamed,

"ELEFTHERÍA!" The roof exploded and I shrieked as shards of glass rained down like a hailstorm all around us. At the same time the Pentagram burnt into the floor which released all the remaining Titans. They all roared as one at Draven and with the glass acting as a deadly backdrop to such a destructive force they charged at us.

"DRAVEN!" I screamed his name but it wasn't my name I heard him roaring in return,

"LUCIUS NOW!" At that moment I didn't understand why he chose to shout out his name in desperation but at the same time Draven's blades came out on a rush and his body ignited into blue lightning. Where was his demon side?

I screamed again as they were less than a foot from striking him and my hands shot out in reaction.

"NOOOO!" Sammael was now the one screaming as the

Titans first seemed suspended in time and were frozen mid attack. Did I do that? Just as the thought entered my mind the Titans all burst one by one into a black cloud. The dark and smoky fog filled the room making it difficult to see but I heard Sammael's attack before I saw it.

He jumped through the mist with his glowing staff raised over his head and it was aimed straight for Draven.

Before I could utter a warning Draven saw the attack coming and defended himself with one sword and attacked back with the other. What had remained of the Titans was the image of lost souls as the cloud took on shapes of warriors fighting an enemy that was barely there. They lashed out at nothing and it looked more like a re-enactment of the war they had lost all that time ago.

The lighter vision of Gods started to strike them down, coming through the mist like a lantern leading the way. One by one they fell, causing the room to become clearer until soon there wasn't a single Titan left.

I wasn't sure what had happened, whether the Gods had finally come to beat them back or they had been summoned back into Tartarus. Whatever it was the only thing that remained was the fight between old enemies…

A fight to the death.

CHAPTER ELEVEN

KEIRA

DO OR DIE

Knowing the threat to mankind was eradicated helped ease my mind but my heavy heart remained as not all the threats were gone. Seeing the Titans disappear into nothing was of course most of the battle won but that didn't make what I was seeing now any easier to swallow. Draven and Sammael fought in the same style as they had that day on the cliff. The only difference being there was no horde of Gorgon Leeches to aid Sammael and no pet bird Ava to help keep me safe.

I was still sat where Draven had put me and once again I was playing the helpless victim in this drama. There was nothing I could do but sit and wait for Draven to once again win the fight against those who had tried to rip us apart. Oh and of course there was the whole trying to destroy mankind and take over the world business!

Sammael was clearly fighting with his emotions fuelling him as he lashed out with such fury it wasn't having the desired affect he was hoping for. It was giving him a greater strength yes but he certainly lacked Draven's finesse and fighting skill. He struck out, swinging his staff like a bat but Draven simply ducked under each blow and getting closer to him with every turn. Once he got close enough Draven tripped Sammael up so he landed on his back with a crack. But before he could drive his sword down into Sammael's chest he kicked out and took Draven by surprise so his swords clashed against the floor.

Sammael flipped up and kicked his fallen staff up with his foot to catch it. Then he spun round on the same foot but bent low trying this time to be the one tripping Draven up. He used his staff pointed down till the tip scraped the ground and Draven leapt over it at just the right moment. Draven used this to his advantage as before he landed he kicked out at the back of Sammael's head. He fell forward landing on his hands and was taken off guard by being attacked mid spin.

This move meant he lost his weapon again as it went skidding across the floor and this time, he wasn't quick enough in picking it up. Draven drew in his swords before using his power to bring the staff to him making it levitate in the air before shooting to his outstretched hand. Then he brought up his knee and at the same time he slammed it down against it, breaking the glowing staff in two.

"NO!" Sammael shouted still on the floor and no doubt feeling his powers break by Draven's hand. He discarded the two pieces left in his hands behind him and then before Sammael could get back to his feet Draven kicked him hard enough his body slid across the room. He slammed into one of the elaborate stone pillars and a deep crack branched up its length.

Sammael was losing the battle and we all knew it.

"Get up and face your executioner, Venom of God!" Draven demanded walking towards him putting his back to me...which turned out to be a grave mistake.

"Say a word and I will slit your throat bitch! Now on your feet." Alex threatened quiet enough that Draven couldn't hear him. I managed to get on my feet with Alex's arm under my elbow pulling me the way he wanted me. Once I found my footing he banded an arm around my waist and used his other hand to put his wooden blade to my neck.

That stormy night in the woods flashed back in my mind and hit me with a Déjà vu so strong I could barely breathe. I had to remind myself that it was Alex holding the knife and not Morgan that was walking me backwards towards a cliff's edge. I felt the edge of the knife dig in but it didn't hurt as he hadn't yet broken the skin.

Even hearing the glass crunching underneath our feet was reminding me of that night as it sounded like the branches and wood splinters I had been made to walk across bare footed. I closed my eyes and took a deep breath trying to work through all the scenarios and possible outcomes where I wouldn't end up dead!

Once we stopped I knew I was out of time. I had just seen Draven punching Sammael across the face as they now fought without weapons and I wondered if this was some kind of code for Draven. That he wouldn't fight an unarmed being when armed himself.

"Draven! I have your Bitch, now let my father go!" Alex shouted just as Draven was about to break Sammael's neck. He turned his head and the pure Hell's fury in his eyes was enough that I think I would have relieved myself if it had been aimed at me. Draven didn't even think he just let Sammael go, pushing him aside. Sammael seemed confused for a second and took a moment to get to his feet before looking round at the situation.

"Let her go!" Draven demanded and I felt Alex start laughing through my back before I heard it.

"Fool! This is for my father!" Alex shouted and I barely had enough time to mouth the words 'I love you' before I started to feel the blade cut into my skin across my neck.

"NO, THERE'S A BLOOD OATH!"

"NOOOOO!" I heard both desperate cries scream out into the night and just before I thought I would find death, the feeling stopped and all I could hear was a gurgling sound in my ear. It was as though everything happened in slow motion. Draven had first looked at me and saw the last thing I wanted him to know with my time left in this world. But instead of saying it back, he looked past me, behind both of us.

Sammael had panic in his eyes at seeing what his son was about to do and I couldn't understand why...wasn't this what they had planned? Wasn't killing me all part of revenge for stopping them? Well if that was the case then why did Sammael look like his son had just signed his death warrant? Sammael had instantly fallen to his knees and watched what was going on behind us.

The blade fell from Alex's grasp and I watched the wooden dagger bounce on the ground, droplets of my blood spraying on the marble before it stilled. Alex's hold on me disappeared and I stumbled forward at the same time covering my bloody neck with my hand. I turned after saving myself from falling and saw a figure stood directly behind Alex.

Blood spurted from Alex's mouth and then dribbled down his chin when he looked down. Then his back arched as the figure behind him thrust what must have been a dagger further into his back because when he looked down what he found there was the bloody tip of a blade protruding from his chest.

Alex's face was one of shock and I wasn't sure if the pain

had even registered yet because he turned to face his killer. The figure pulled back his hood and revealed the face of death.

"This is for our brother." Seth said before taking hold of either side of his head in his hands and with one simple twist broke his neck. Alex's body fell to the ground with a sickening thud and landed with his head facing the wrong way, making me feel sick.

I looked back up to see the man who had saved my life for a second time...

My Cathedral phantom.

"Seth." I uttered his name as he walked past me with only one focus...

His father.

I wasn't sure what was going to happen next as it wasn't clear how Seth felt about his father. No, the only thing that had been clear was his obvious hatred for his brother, as Alex's dead body laid to rest in a pool of his own blood was screaming proof of that!

I couldn't say the sight wasn't a welcome one, no matter how sickening it was and if it hadn't been a disgusting thing for a lady to do I think I would have gone over there and spat on him! He had killed Lucius and had tried to take everyone else I care about from me along with him. And now there was just one more that needed to pay.

Sammael.

I turned away from scowling down at Alex and turned around to walk over to where Draven now stood looking down at a still kneeling Sammael. I wondered what he was still doing on his knees and why he was no longer fighting Draven when I remembered what he shouted to Alex the moment before his death. Something about a *Blood Oath.*

When Seth nodded to Draven it was all the sign he needed before he picked Sammael up and threw him down on top of the altar they were all next to. He had no choice but to lay flat as the impact would have shattered his vessels spine.

"You can send me back there Draven, you can send me to Tartarus a thousand times for my sins but you know I will find a way…one day, you will see, I will find a way to free them again!" Sammael threatened but Draven just smiled down at him.

"Not this time."

"But you cannot kill me! For I am the Venom of God, I have Lucifer's blood running through my veins! The Dark Lord forbids his…" Draven cut him off with a smile,

"Blood Oath Sammael. When you made that Blood Oath you forfeited your soul and handed its ownership over to me when you willingly gave me your blood. So seeing as you no longer have his protection and my terms were for you to 'await death' should that Oath be broken…" Draven leant down and said, getting in his face…

"And Sammael, I am a man of my word!"

"No! No, you can't do this! I demand a trial! I demand…" He never finished as Seth drew a Katana from behind his back and stabbed his father in the heart. He then, like Draven had done, leant down and said,

"And this is for my mother!" During this obvious act of revenge in the name of his family, he flashed in and out of his demon side. He changed from that handsome chiselled face that could have graced the screen advertising aftershave any day of the week to one that made my spine shiver. His skeletal face wasn't like a skull void of flesh and skin but more like it had been projected on top of his mortal face. Only those intense eyes stood out against the black around his eyes and nose. When he moved it gave it a translucent effect that almost seemed as if it was a face over a face but the two weren't fused together.

He looked back to Draven and nodded, ignoring the ink blood bubbling up around his blade.

"Son..." Sammael spluttered, reaching out to Seth who was walking away. He didn't look back as he said,

"I was never your son, dickhead." And then just raised his hood, the same one I had seen him wearing before with all the straps and carried on walking until he reached Alex's dead form. Seth pulled an artist's sketch from his pocket that was clear to see was a Pentagram. I then flinched when it burst into green flames and he dropped it on his brother. The body ignited as if it had been doused with lighter fluid, burning quickly as though he had been made of paper.

Seth didn't wait to watch his brother burn or as his father died. No, he just left the Temple with his back to the world and without a single word spoken.

I was still looking towards the door he had walked out of when I heard the scream of someone in the face of death behind me. The clashing sound of metal hitting stone quickly followed. I closed my eyes after finally hitting my limit and needing to block out the evidence that this day even happened.

Seth had the right idea putting his back to this world as I couldn't imagine what a lifetime of wanting revenge could do to a person. I remember now what he had said to me that day in my dreams...

'For the one who carries blood in their veins, is one that can bleed and for one that can bleed, can then... die'

He had been waiting for this day. He must have known about the plans of his father and brother and I wondered if Draven hadn't already beaten him to it would he have used the same blood that ran through his veins to send the Titans back? I was still unsure of how Draven did it but I guess I would find out soon enough.

"Keira?" Draven spoke my name softly and I felt him come to stand behind me. I was about to turn round and face him when I felt his hands on my arms stop me.

"I wouldn't look." He warned and instead he moved to stand in front of me.

"Oh my love, it's over now…Ssshh, it's all over." He cooed and it was only then that I realised I was sobbing. Yes I had hit my limit and when I collapsed to the ground I knew it wasn't just mentally. I felt Draven catch me and then lower me the rest of the way to the floor.

"Keira!" Draven shouted in panic. I don't know how I had gone on for this long as it was but my body could do no more for me. It was shutting down and I could feel myself fading away.

"Draven?" I said his name as the sight of him started to blur.

"Dom! What's wrong? What's happened?" Sophia? Was that really her? My head rolled back and I squinted trying to make things out.

"She needs my blood, here Keira, drink…come on, drink now." Draven said putting something wet to my lips. The metallic taste and smell told me it was his blood and I did what he said to save my life. I felt it burning as it went down which was new. I started to feel strange as my body lit up with the knowledge that help was being provided to my failing organs… but it felt different. It was as if there wasn't enough there. I could feel myself start to heal but then something would pull back, like an engine that wouldn't turn over because it didn't have enough fuel.

"Something's wrong…it's not working…but how…?" Draven said to his sister in alarm but then cut himself off as if something had just clicked into place.

"Dom, what is it? What's wrong with her?" Sophia asked and I could just make out her smaller shape knelt next to Draven.

His next words chilled me to the bone.

"It's not what's wrong with her…it's what's wrong with me."

"What do you mean, it…"

"Can't you feel it, I didn't realise till now but…it's doesn't matter, you know who we need, did he come back with you… did he make it?" Draven asked frantically after interrupting Sophia.

"Draven?" I heard his panic and it made my own double in strength. What was happening to not only me but now to Draven as well?

"Dom, there's something you should know."

"Did he make it!?" Draven snapped and I saw her blurred form enough to know she had lowered her head.

"Yes… but not all of him did." She replied cryptically.

"Get him."

"But Dom…"

"NOW OR SHE DIES!" Draven roared at his sister, causing her to disappear from sight.

"Draven listen to me…" I had to stop speaking as I started coughing violently and I felt the liquid erupt from my mouth, knowing it was blood. It was like the blood I had swallowed needed to get out of my body…as if it was rejecting Draven.

"Ssshh now, be still and don't speak." He said wiping the blood from my face.

"But…"

"NO! Don't say it, by the Gods, don't say it because if you think for one moment I just went through all that only to lose you now then you and the fates are wrong!" Draven said fervently.

"But Draven I need to tell you…the last thing… I…" I felt him put his forehead to mine and he whispered,

"I know. I know Keira, but it won't be the last thing you say to me, because I'm never letting there be a last time with us. *There will only be a forever…I promise you.*"

"Then I will pray for it." I said softly letting a tear escape and doing nothing to prevent my head from rolling back for my time had come and I had got my wish. I was going to die with Draven in the knowledge the world was safe, one that would be made safer without me in it.

"LUCIUS!" I heard Draven roar for the second time and I wondered what he was gaining from calling out for his dead friend. Was he waiting on the other side someplace? Was Draven letting him know that I was leaving this world to hopefully enter the next? Yes, that must have been it because the next thing I knew I must have taken my last breath and it was in awe for the next words spoken belonged to my lost friend.

"I am here."

"Lucius, you're…" Draven was cut off when Lucius snapped,

"Do not speak of it! Now, why isn't she healing?" Was I hearing this right?

"Look at me and you will know why." Draven responded in a way that haunted me as it sounded so absent, so lost…*so broken.*

"But how?!"

"We don't have time! We need to heal her as one, like we did once before." Draven stated and I finally knew that I wasn't dead. But more importantly…

Lucius lived.

I was so confused. My mind was conflicted with what I would pray for and what I feared had already happened. I tried to speak but found I could only listen and I could only feel. Another tear fell to the floor, leaving my body on a silent cry. Was Lucius really alive!? Had he really somehow made it back and now I could pray for something new…like my own life to be saved.

"Dom listen to me, that blood I tasted…the Venom of God now runs through these veins and it nearly killed me… We…*I…*" He struggled for words a moment before he said,

"There is no telling what could happen to her if I give her my blood…*Dom, it could kill her.*" He added whispering the grave news to a fragile heart…both mine and Draven's. I heard the man I loved struggle to take this in but a few heavy breaths later he said firmly,

"We have no choice, it is this and we pray to the Gods for hope or it is her death and we damn the Gods with War!"

"Very well. *Then let us pray old friend…let us fucking pray!*" Then in seconds I felt the first wrist being offered to me and I drank it down without needing any prompting.

"Now."

"So much for my vow not to do this again today." Lucius said dryly before placing his own wrist against my lips. I swallowed it down with greater urgency this time and the second it started to go down something magically happened. Instead of it burning like Draven's blood alone had done, it started to cool, like drinking icy water when you're dying of thirst. My whole body started to light up as if every cell had been touched individually.

Four hands started to touch me and caress me in a way I had never known. My body arched and pushed itself harder, firmer against the touch. I heard myself moan in bliss as a warmth travelled up from my toes and fed parts of my body I had never been aware of. I could feel it coming, growing more powerful with each mental wave that crashed into me. Like a crescendo it kept building and building to something greater, something more monumental.

"Ahh…hhhaahaaa!" I let myself scream out my release as my orgasm rolled over me as though I was being crushed by pleasure. My body spasmed over and over, jerking in someone's arms. And then out of nowhere it hit me again, only this time the pleasure was so intense it was almost too much to bear.

"AHHHH, oooohh!" I cried out again as every muscle in my body not only healed itself but felt like it had done so with the intension of pushing each one to its limits! It was the most violent orgasm I had ever had and one that I would be scared to ever experience again.

I started to feel my chest rise and fall with the desperate need for air and soon the exhaustion followed. I opened my eyes and for the first time the world came into focus. The second I did this I wish I hadn't made the innocent mistake as I came back to this world to see two things, things that would haunt me till the end of days.

The first and most gruesome was actually how Sammael had died on the Altar and I knew now why Draven had tried to shield that from me. But the next was far more terrifying.

"DOM!" Sophia's desperate cry chilled my heart and as I let my face turn to the other side, with my cheek still against the marble floor what I saw killed me.

"Draven?" I said his name as though what I was seeing wasn't real but one look into his dead eyes and I knew he was gone. This time I had really done it…

This time I had killed Draven.

CHAPTER TWELVE

KEIRA

THE AWAKENING

Seeing death wasn't something you ever forgot. Yes, for a warrior or a soldier or even a mass murderer, I understood that you could become immune to it. Everyone had their own coping mechanisms. But still, there was something that clung on to you whether you wanted it to or not. Almost like freshly disturbed asbestos fibres sticking to your lungs when you breathed deep. The effects could be everlasting and devastating.

Now I had seen death. I had walked the line hand in hand with death himself and still I was breathing. I had felt the pain and I had beaten it back only to win and fight another day. I had known what it felt like to feel yourself slipping away to that unknown place where doubt was the biggest destroyer of hopes, dreams and faith in that better place. Yes, I thought I knew death.

But I didn't.

I wanted to go somewhere, anywhere that reminded me of life. I wanted the lush green earth to embrace me in its sounds, smells and sights of every day proof there was beauty left in the world. Because right now I needed that evidence that the world hadn't ended and what I had just seen hadn't been real. I needed to know that the world still existed...even if it had just ended for me.

I kept replaying the same pictures over and over in my head. First there had been Sammael's severed head that had started to eat away at itself from the thousands of black maggots that swarmed from his nostrils. They poured down the rest of his face, so that all that remained intact was the top of his head, which was starting to cave in on itself. Then there had been his severed limbs which created the same infestation that seemed to have made up his flesh. Flesh hungry maggots everywhere.

His blood however was like black ink and it filled the pale altar with dark symbols as his blood travelled the carvings. So this was the only way to kill a man like Sammael...to lock his essence within the ancient markings after first beheading him. I didn't know what it all meant or how it worked but I knew that once the blood in the symbols started to evaporate then Sammael really was no more.

It was a gruesome sight and one not likely ever forgotten like all of the deaths I had witnessed, whether it was mortal or supernatural I remembered them all. But it was nothing but a single raindrop in a day of storms compared to turning my head and seeing Draven that way. I heard people trying to say something to me but I couldn't hear them over the screaming. I just needed the silence. I just wanted the isolation to grieve. And definitely didn't need anyone trying to drag me away from his body as I could feel many hands doing.

I remember feeling so angry with everyone! I was angry

with everyone around me trying to keep me from him, even in death. I was angry at our fallen enemies for ripping us apart and using our love against each other. And I was angry at myself for letting them. But most of all I was angry at Dominic.

"You promised! You promised me! You said you would never leave me again! You promised damn you! DAMN YOU!" I only now realised I was the one screaming as I lost all control over my emotions. It was like waking from a dream and finding yourself stood outside in the rain with no idea how you got there. In my mind I had been a small figure of a girl curled up, holding herself in an empty cell and crying quietly for her loss. But in reality I woke to find I was on top of Draven hitting out at his chest and cursing him for leaving me. I was hammering my weak fists down like it would bring him back and throwing his broken promises back in his lifeless face.

"Lucius do something!" I heard someone yell over the chaos that was my heartbreak. I felt myself being manhandled off his body with much more force this time. I started to lash out and fight but then felt a swift slap to my face causing me a moment of shock, one that lasted long enough to stop my wasted efforts in getting back to a dead man.

"For fuck sake Keira listen to me! HE'S NOT DEAD!" Lucius shouted for what sounded like the hundredth time. He shook me with one hand and it was only when I looked down that I realised he had the other one tucked into his shirt that was half open, hiding it from view. I started shaking my head as I processed the words and once they did my eyes widened and my lips quivered before I said,

"Re…really?" At this his anger and frustration seeped from his eyes and he let go of my arm to stroke down my face.

"Really, Keira…he just passed out." At this I lost it again only this time for my entire world of better reasons. I fell to my knees barely taking note of my healed body and the lack of pain before crying out my utter relief. I felt Lucius get down next to me and I threw myself into his body taking him off guard. I burst into uncontrollable sobs and felt him put an arm around me, pulling me closer to his body by the waist.

"Is she going to be alright…bbb…bossman?" I heard an emotional Pip ask that sounded like she was still sobbing herself.

"Give me time alone with her, there are things I need to explain. Take the King back to his bed, for he will need the rest if he is to…" I felt Lucius hesitate before deciding not to continue.

I don't know how long it was after Lucius had turned everyone away when I finally got myself under control but by the time I looked up he was still holding me with one arm.

"I can't believe you're here." I said in a croaky voice that had been abused this last twenty four hours. Lucius' eyes got soft, causing handsome little lines to appear at the corners.

"You thought I had died?" He asked and I choked back another sob and decided it was safer to just nod.

"I am sorry my little Keira girl." He said sincerely.

"What happened back there?" I asked nodding back towards the Temple exit and where I knew the crypt wasn't far away. He took a deep breath and looked away. I knew he was trying to find the right way to tell me and it looked like he wasn't looking forward to the task.

"Will Draven be alright?" I asked and then thought of another question,

"How did he stop the Titans? Or was it you, is that why he called out your name?" Soon I had him laughing and shaking his head at me.

"You don't change do you? Even facing death doesn't slow you down." I gave him a frown in return, one to which he just laughed at again before giving me a playful frown back, mimicking me.

"Right Mister, emotional girly outburst is done, time to talk" I demanded pulling away from him and folding my arms. I expected him to do it back at me but then I remembered his hidden arm.

"Are you injured?"

"Bloody hell woman! How do you expect me to answer a single question if you don't ever shut up!?" He said pretending to be dramatic.

"Ok answer that one first." I said nodding to his arm.

"No. If I am going to explain what happened then I will do so on my own terms…now not a word or so help me I will gag you." I couldn't keep the smirk from my face after he winked at me, even when I rolled my eyes at him it lost its desired effect as I was grinning.

"Do you remember when I first found you in the Temple?"

"Yes but what has…" When he lifted up his finger to shake at me I held my tongue and the impulse to ask yet another question.

"I didn't rescue you straight away."

"You didn't?" He raised an eyebrow at me and I threw up both of my hands in defeat,

"Hey give me a break, if there is always one poor sap that gets left out of the loop it is muggins here…besides, that wasn't really a question, more of a prompt to get your ass in gear with the story telling."

"Have you finished?"

"Can I get away with saying maybe?" I asked making him roll his eyes.

"Right, getting back to the point. When I saw what he was doing the last parts of the puzzle fit into place. We knew what he had planned and I crept back from the Temple to inform

Dom. We both decided that if I couldn't get you out in time then there was only one back up plan."

"And that was?"

"We needed his blood. We both agreed that he wouldn't kill you as he needed you alive to bargain with Dom for your life. So seeing as there was only one way to release the Titans, it just happens to be the same way to lock them back up again…hence needing his blood." Lucius finished taking me back to that horrible place in time when I thought he had taken the fatal bite.

"But why didn't you tell me any of this!" To this outraged demand he both gave up trying to stop me asking questions and just cocked his head to the side as if it was obvious.

"Come on Keira, we all know your acting skills are utter shite. Besides, I needed Alex to believe and if you believed then so would he. But hey, if it makes you feel any better it did put me into a coma."

"Oh yeah, that helps, thanks." I said sarcastically before hitting him on his arm, the one he didn't have cradled to his chest. He laughed once and then it was if a memory had him frowning again.

"You know if there had been any other way then we would have…" I stopped him by putting my hand on his leg.

"I get it. Don't get me wrong, I wished there had been another way and would have loved to have been spared the heartache but if it meant saving the world and killing the bad guys, then who am I to complain." When I finished I looked up as during my little speech and admitting my heartbreak at seeing him die I hadn't been able to look at him. But when I finally met his eyes all I saw there was the respect he had for me.

"I think we should continue this conversation on the move, if Dom wakes he will do himself an injury if he finds you are not by his side." We both got up and I tried not to make it obvious that I was staring at his arm. We walked the length of the temple and I noticed him giving me a side glance.

"You know you are about as discreet as an elephant hiding behind a lamppost." I rolled in my lips to stop my smile and said,

"I don't know what you mean."

"Oh now this is different, Keira's playing coy." I shot him a look and did a pathetic attempt to growl at him making him laugh.

We were now walking back through the house part of Afterlife and it was the first time I'd stepped within these walls for over a year. It had been an insightful journey back but I managed to keep my emotions in check as he told me all that had happened. Of course his side only went back so far and if I wanted the rest I would have to get that from Draven. Well, when he awoke of course.

He decided it wasn't the best idea to walk me back through the crypt considering there was quite a lot of shit to clean up… these were his words not mine. I found out that Alex had left the army of the dead to keep the rest of Draven's council and half of Lucius' busy.

Vincent had led the fight seeing as it would have been impossible for him to have helped his brother in Hell, being the Angel he was after all. So he and the others had helped to hold them back before they could become overrun. Pip and Adam had also been helping in this but they couldn't afford Adam turning into his beast for fear it would be too hard to contain him. So as soon as Lucius had regained consciousness, both of them followed him into Tartarus, after being assured by Draven that he could get his father to bring down the barrier for a short time.

He also told me about how he had saved Draven's life and I was surprised, given his cocky nature when this wasn't said in a boastful manner. It was said as a matter of fact and as I threw my arms around him and started to sing his praises (obviously not literally, as my singing voice sucked and that was one victory song no one needed to hear.) This was in fact the most uncomfortable I had ever seen him look.

Hearing about the Cyclopes brothers had my fingernails trying to embed themselves into my palm but I had felt so proud when hearing how Adam had defeated them with ease. I had also laughed hearing what Pip's part in all this had been and I was looking forward to being with my friend again.

In truth the overwhelming need I felt to be with them all right now was getting stronger the closer we got. I could only put it down to what it must have been like knowing your family was off to war and nothing inside you felt right until you saw for yourself that they were safe again.

The hardest part in all this was what was happening now and what Lucius had to tell me, which all started with a simple sounding question,

"So why did Draven pass out?" Lucius closed his eyes a second and then stopped walking. I didn't realise until I was a few steps ahead of him and as soon as I saw that he was no longer with me I too stopped. I turned to look at him and knew instantly this wasn't just something like jetlag for a demon after a battle. No his face said only one thing…

"It's serious…isn't it?"

"I am not going to lie or try to play this down because not only do you have the right to know but I also think you will be the only one able to help him." I frowned and instead of bombarding him with questions as was my usual trait, I simply nodded for him to continue.

"Dom had no choice but to enter into Tartarus with only his demon side, leaving his Angelic side behind in the fear that a place like Tartarus would destroy that part of him." I let this sink in for a minute giving my brain chance to catch up with exactly what this all meant.

"But it didn't destroy that part of you?" I asked knowing that since the ritual of the Triple Goddess that Lucius too now had his own heavenly side. Hard to think looking at the cocky bad ass who stood opposite me now but with the spear of Longinus embedded beneath his wings I saw that day what he had become when trying to save my life.

"That's because I now have the Venom of God running through my veins. There is no being alive, no matter their power that would have control over Tartarus the way one who possesses that blood does. Not Angel, Demon or mortal. That was what we counted on."

"Alright, I get that but that doesn't explain what has happened to Draven now. I mean I saw him, he fought Sammael and he seemed just fine!" I started to protest until he cut me off just before I could start my rant again.

"Keira, he came back through and into his Angel side. He fought well against Sammael because he was weakened from his summoning and made a blood oath for your life. He made him swear on his soul and what would happen to it if he or his kin were to hurt you was up to Dom to decide."

"So that's why he fell to his knees when Alex cut me?" I said to myself feeling the last of the puzzle pieces to slot into place, creating the last scene to the story. Lucius nodded and then continued,

"So you see Sammael had no chance against him, the only

part of our plan we didn't account for was his other son to show up to take his revenge…that and the payment I and Dom both had to pay for our part in the Titans…*unknowingly.*" He added bitterly and I looked to his injured hand that he still kept hidden. Well at least he would heal quickly and all I could hope for was the same for Draven, whatever it maybe. Thoughts of me playing nurse for a few weeks all of a sudden didn't sound half bad at all.

"Oh Keira, I don't need to read your thoughts to know your innocence, however intriguing it may be to my kind, is getting in the way of reality." I frowned looking down and so very close to putting my hands over my ears and repeating over and over, 'Don't tell me'. I didn't think I could cope with much more and especially not after everything we had endured together. Not when what felt like we had only been reunited for a fleeting moment before the beauty was ripped from us with the threat of death on both sides.

"It's his demon side this time Keira."

"What do you mean?" I asked after he blurted this out.

"It remained in Tartarus."

"What!?" I shouted thinking this was unbelievable. I mean bloody hell could we not catch a freakin' break!

"I only realised myself what it all meant when I locked up the Titans. I had to leave payment for the act as did Dom for when he released them." He said grimly.

"So you're telling me he had to leave half his fucking soul!" I shouted getting outraged at the injustice.

"Keira calm yourself."

"Calm myself! Are you for real!? I can't bloody calm myself and I will tell you one thing for a bag of chips, if Sammael or that dickhead Alex was here right now then I would kill the bastards all over again, human or no human, most things died with a racket to the head!" I ended this outburst when Lucius started laughing at me and after trying to get my breath I asked him angrily,

"What?!"

"A bag of chips...really?" I folded my arms across my heaving chest and snapped out my defence,

"I'm a Northerner, deal with it!"

"Oh, yeah, I got that bit love." Lucius said smirking and I rolled my eyes at him. He shook his head at me and then said,

"Let's get going should we."

We were both silent a moment and I knew, despite all the banter, he was giving me time to take it all in. I couldn't stand the silence after a while and knew we were close to Draven's bedchamber. It was almost painful to think about walking through that door again, so I needed a distraction.

"Great, now I'm starving." I said faking being snippy and also realising I couldn't actually remember the last time I had eaten a decent sized meal. He laughed and said,

"And would it be fish with this bag of chips?"

"Who me...? No way, pie every time!" I said wondering how far I would go right now for a proper Northern meat and potato pie! Lucius laughed again and said,

"Come on Pie girl, if I remember correctly we are nearly there."

"Ha! Don't call me that in front of Pip or Toots will fly out the window and I will be rechristened Pie Girl forever more."

"Isn't that the truth...don't worry, it will be our little nickname from here on out."

"Don't you dare" I said in warning.

"Have no fear your secret Pie addiction is safe with me." I groaned and then my stomach followed suit making him chuckle.

"I'm sure there will be food when we get there."

"I thought you were taking me to Draven?" I said noticing

that we had come a different way and were heading for the marble dining room.

"I am but first we need to do something before I leave."

"You're leaving...? But why?" I asked almost in a panic I couldn't contain.

"I am not one to relish in admitting this freely or pretend this is something I find easy to say, given that it is a feeling I have never encountered before but here goes…" He took a deep breath, stepped closer to me and then dropped his bombshell on a whisper.

"*…I am not strong enough to help anyone…not like this*" It wasn't easier to hear but I agreed with him, as I couldn't imagine for a being as powerful and mighty as Lucius what it must have been like. Which is why I should have let it go but my worry and care for him couldn't do that.

So I asked the question I dreaded hearing the answer to, as I already had an idea on the horror hidden behind that shirt.

"What was your payment Lucius?" He gave me a sad smile that didn't reach his eyes before he pulled out the evidence of what Tartarus had chosen to take from him.

My hands flew to cover my mouth as I gasped at the side of his badly wrapped arm that was missing a large portion of it. A bloody stump bound with strips of cloth was half way up his forearm and it all started to get blurry as the tears prevented my vision.

And then they overflowed with just one sentence…

"They took the hand of their jailer"

CHAPTER THIRTEEN

KEIRA

HEAD OF THE COUNCIL

We walked towards the grand dining room in silence and I was thankful we didn't have far to go. I wanted to say the right thing at that moment but found there were no words that came to me. It was as if everything I thought to say would get stuck in my throat before I had chance to get them out. So in the end Lucius placed it back inside his shirt and said,

"It will grow back...*in time,*" muttering this last part as he walked past me. By the Gods how I wanted to say the right thing at that moment, but what do you say to something like that, 'If you get a hook and an eye patch chicks will dig it!' ... Yeah, I didn't think so. I was just happy to hear that it would grow back for him as many others, being us mere mortals, didn't have that luxury.

Thankfully I was saved by the fact it became quite

obvious Lucius didn't want to talk about it and he certainly didn't want my pity and I could relate. But instead of not saying anything we came to the door and I patted him on the back and said,

"You're still hot, so suck it up." I hadn't known until I said this that it was exactly the right thing to say, judging by his smirk and the wink he gave me.

"Thanks kitten, but while we are on the subject, I would love to return the compliment but..." He looked me up and down and it was the first time I saw his nose twitch. I followed his gaze and I could feel I wasn't half as sexy when my nose wrinkled up in disgust.

"Oh God I look horrible!" I said taking in my pitiful appearance. I had on the last thing I wore when Alex took me and what surprised me the most was that I hadn't lost my flip flops. And it was a good job too for when that dome roof had exploded. I mean don't me wrong, it wasn't like I could have gone shopping in them any time soon. Nope, there was only one place these babies were going after today and that was at the bottom of a bin, along with every scrap of clothing I was wearing.

My denim shorts were the only thing I wore that wasn't ripped but they were no longer blue but now burgundy from being soaked with my blood that had long ago dried. My vest was torn at the strap and just hung down on either side. My shirt had long been a lost cause when I tried to use it to stop the bleeding on my arms and it had become another casualty of war. I couldn't see my face but I knew it was covered in dirt, blood and God only knows what else and I wasn't even getting started on my hair.

"Yes you do but tough shit because it's time to lead your council." He said pushing the door open over my shoulder.

"My what?" I said as I felt him gently push me into the

room that was full with everyone and when I say everyone I mean…*everyone!*

"Uh…Lucius?" I said under my breath knowing he was behind me. I could feel my heart racing as everyone stood upon my entrance and waited for me to take a seat.

"You will be fine." He whispered back, leaning in to my ear making me shudder. I turned my head back to look over my shoulder and said more loudly this time,

"Are you kidding me?" To which there was a few sniggers in the room…well to be fair I knew it had just been from Pip as I turned back to see her biting her lip trying not to laugh. She gave me a little wave and Adam gave a sideways glance and the corner of his lip lifted at seeing his wife happy once more.

I let out a nervous noise and shrugged my shoulders giving them all an awkward smile.

"Go take your seat, Keira." Lucius said holding out his arm to the head of the table where Draven's empty seat was waiting for me. It was one of the saddest sights I had ever seen and the very last thing I wanted to be doing now was trying to fill his royal shoes.

The last time I was here had been at their family breakfast and it had been such a light hearted event, however one that seemed a lifetime ago, not days I could count with my hands. He had looked so indestructible sat at the head of his council in that high backed chair. The same strange symbol that sat at the top of the throne glared out at me like a beacon of hope and I felt my own birthmark tingle at the sight.

I closed my eyes for a second longer than a blink and my mantra of 'You can do this' repeated in my head as I made the steps around the full table. Eyes followed me and every face looked near beaten down with the events that were now happening. They needed hope and reassurance that I could do this and all *I* needed was Draven.

Lucius followed me round the table, staying at my back until I reached the top. There he held out the chair for me and everyone waited for me to sit down before they did the same.

"As was instructed to us by our King, Keira is now the head of this council in his absence and all decisions are hers to make and her ruling is final." They all freely acknowledged this, all apart from me and it had me blurting out,

"He did what!?" Everyone's reactions to my outburst were different. For a start there were those that I had no idea were even involved in what had happened today. Like Sigurd who was smirking at me and Ragnar who had coughed to hide his laugh. Zagan was hiding his smile behind his hand and Sophia elbowed him frowning before giving me a warm smile in encouragement.

There was of course Pip who was giving me two thumbs up and one look at what she considered 'Fighting gear' had me smiling. Adam bowed his head, showing me the same respect he freely gave to Draven and I was so touched to have everyone's support.

Even Takeshi, who looked drained of energy, gave me a small grin before nodding his head. Ruto sat looking bored but when he caught my eyes on him he winked at me. The only ones missing were Liessa and Caspian from Lucius' side and of course Vincent. But as for Draven's brother we didn't have to wait long.

Vincent walked through the doors as if my thoughts had drawn him there but one look at his grave face had me shooting from my chair.

"Is he?!" I couldn't finish that question but the panic was crystal clear. Vincent took a swift moment to look at me and he too tried to hide his smile.

"He is still unconscious and I think he will be this way a while longer but right now it is the best thing for him." I wanted to ask him more about it...actually what I really wanted to do was run from the room to go and sit by his bedside and not move until he woke up but one look at everyone and I knew the most important thing I could do right now was suck it up and do Draven proud.

So that's what I did.

I cleared my throat, sat up a little straighter and started this meeting the only way I knew how and I went with my gut and did what I thought was right by Draven's people....by *my people*.

I waited for Vincent to take his seat, one that was next to me as I had both the Draven siblings either side of me, giving me their support.

"First I would like to thank everyone for the parts they played in...in..." I struggled to find the right word for what everyone had done until Sigurd spoke up and said,

"For saving the fucking world honey, call it what it is." And then he winked at me. Ragnar growled his disapproval, one that his son ignored.

"Yes, as Sigurd so articulately put it... for saving the world. But as you all know now we have to save its King, so please, if anyone has any ideas then don't be shy." I said actually crossing both my fingers in my lap under the table. I heard Lucius clearing his throat next to me and I looked up to see him smirking down at my hands. I took a page from Sigurd's book and ignored Lucius as he had done with Ragnar.

"If I may speak, my Queen?" Takeshi asked bowing his head.

"Oh I'm no..." Lucius put his hand on my shoulder to stop me and I took the hint and carried on with a more formal,

"Yes, please continue."

"I am being blocked by something and had been of the mind that Sammael and his kin were the only ones involved but I no longer believe this is the case. I think whatever we plan we need to have care in whom we put our trust." He said looking around the room and each nodded their acknowledgement.

"Agreed then. Nothing leaves this room." I confirmed and thought I hid my shock well because inside I was a wreck with worry and my mind was chaotic with questions.

"And what of the Viking, he is not on this council?" Ruto spoke up and Sigurd turned violent eyes to the youngest one in the room.

"Careful boy or you will see what this Viking can do with only a finger." He said holding one up and letting it turn black before a slight mist escaped his fingertip.

"And you will see what I can do with a blade, old man."

"ENOUGH!" The demand I was shocked to say came from me as I had stood up and hammered my small fists on the table top. Everyone went deadly silent as I stared each of them down before I spoke.

"I vouch for every person in this room. And I ask you to all remember that it wasn't long ago that many of us were enemies yet here we sit, all as allies with a common cause. If anyone doesn't like that then there is the door but I am telling you now, everyone that stays are going to be working together as one, so before I make you kiss and make up I suggest you both shut it and quit the shitty remarks. Because then the next threat to be heard will come from me." I saw Sigurd looking smug at Ruto so I continued with…

"And the next finger I see held up in anything but a question will find me biting it off! Am I understood?" Sigurd folded his arms across his chest and leant back in his chair before nodding.

"Ruto!" Lucius snapped out his name and he flinched at the sound of his King's disapproval in him.

"My apologies, my Queen." Ruto said to my surprise.

"Good. Now that's settled let's move on shall we." I

finished retaking my seat like I wasn't a trembling mess inside. My heart was pounding and I could only hope no one around the table could hear it. This was something I didn't hold much hope in considering there were Vampires in the room, speaking of which Lucius leant down and muttered softly,

"You're doing fine, just keep breathing."

"Kick ass Toots! Boo yeah girl power!" Pip said with a massive grin on her face and doing a fist bump in the air. Sophia smiled and I tried to hold mine in but let my gratitude be shown through my eyes.

"Calm yourself my sweetheart." Adam cooed tipping her army helmet to one side to speak in her ear.

"Now, does anyone else have anything to add?" I asked hoping this time it wasn't just more bad news because I was hitting that limit again and the last thing I needed was to lose it before I got the chance to be alone.

Vincent was just about to speak when the door opened and in walked a woman I loathed.

"Aurora." She swept into the room as if she owned the place and when she saw me sat at the head of the table she did a double take. She wore an elegant, vintage looking chiffon dress which was a black see through material on top of a cream underdress that was cut across the shoulders and had sleeves that finished at the elbow. The full skirt complimented her long legs and to finish off the look she wore a belt that was two feathers back to back, in the shape of leaves and she wore her hair plaited to one side.

She was stunning as always and I don't think I let on how painful it was seeing her. Sophia hissed at her, one she ignored and Vincent rose from his seat.

"You are not welcome at this table." She stood at the only empty seat, one I knew would have been for me if Draven had been sat in his rightful place. She didn't show any emotions on her face to whether she was hurt or upset by Vincent's statement. No, she just stood in front of the seat looking regal and well, like the Goddess it was proved she was.

"I have not been formally removed from my council place and this is a council meeting is it not?"

"You know damn well why you weren't informed!" Sophia snapped and Aurora twisted her head slowly to look at Sophia.

"Do I?" She asked with that irritating singsong voice of hers.

"Don't play coy Aurora, it doesn't become you." This snide remark shocked me when it came from Zagan.

"You locked Dom to Tartarus!" Sophia shouted but even under this pressure she didn't looked at all phased.

"Yes I did, upon his request as I am not a very good royal servant if I don't obey, now am I?" She countered making Sophia rise out of her seat. I knew that we needed to hear her out before a brawl started and as much as I would have loved to have seen Sophia rip into her, now was far from the time.

"I want to hear what she has to say." I said and Sophia shot me one of those 'really?!' looks that I just gave her a little shake of my head in return. She nodded and then sat back down accepting the little kiss on her forehead from Zagan in comfort.

"Thank you my..." I cut her off as there was one thing I couldn't stand right now and that was any bullshit acts of loyalty.

"Let's get one thing straight, you don't like me and I certainly don't like you but none of that matters when the King's Demon is locked to Tartarus. So if you can help then say what you have come here to say, if not, then you can leave." I finished my little speech and I was happy to report that I saw one tiny second of rage cross her face at me before she plastered back on her composed smile and sat down.

"I believe I am the only one who can help the King."

"Yeah right." Sophia commented dryly.

"I would have warned the King this could happen *if* I had been informed of his plans to enter Tartarus." She said and it was clear she wasn't happy to have been left out of the loop.

"And what would you have done after that Aurora, take up arms and fought beside us, 'cause that would have been a first." Sophia snapped.

"This isn't helping Aurora." I informed her at which she bowed her head to me, and the respect was about as sincere as a snake's.

"His Demon is locked to that place permanently now because of two things, one because he asked me to do this seeing as I am a direct descendant of the Gods and secondly because of this it was the only thing the Titan Cronus had the power to take." She finished feeling quite pleased with herself from the looks of things.

"But why would Cronus even need to take something like that when Draven was the one releasing them?" I asked as it didn't make much sense.

"You wouldn't understand, you're just a mortal." This turned out to be a grave mistake to make as Sigurd wasn't the only one on his feet as most were around the table.

"Insult her again and we will see how difficult it is to behead a Titan's descendant!" Sigurd threatened and I saw a moment of panic before she composed herself.

"I merely meant that she has not spent enough time in our world to understand such of the workings of higher beings."

"You mean the workings of mad and broken Gods." Vincent said also coming to my defence. Aurora didn't respond to this but I could see that something behind those cool eyes snapped, she was just keeping a lid on it.

"Please, everyone sit. We know the situation Aurora and how we all came to be here so try not to bore us with what we

159

already know and more of how we can resolve it…can the tie to Tartarus be reversed?" I asked feeling this conversation was going nowhere fast and to be honest, as well as needing to get back to Draven as quickly as possible, I was also shamefully desperate for a bathroom stop.

"The tie to Tartarus can be severed yes but only by the person who created the binding and also…" She stopped and tried not to smile at what she was about to say next.

"Oh by the Gods miss prissy fancy pants, just freakin' say it!" This came from Pip who for the most part had been quietly watching it all play out. Aurora turned to glare at her and started speaking but only looking at me at the end,

"…and also the one reason the binding was made. And it was made because of her." Aurora nodded at me but this wasn't some big shocker she was hoping for as it was blindingly obvious as to why Draven would do something so foolish. Hell, it seemed as if I was the only reason in this world any supernatural being did anything foolish! No, everyone knew this was just a pathetic attempt to try and make me sweat in front of all these people.

"This isn't news to us Aurora so try and stick to what can be done." Sophia said looking bored and at her fingernails.

"Very well, the only thing that can be done is if I enter Tartarus whilst I presume your father still has the barriers down and lift the binding."

"And you can do this?" I asked feeling a new hope bloom but just wishing it didn't come from the Uber Bitch in the room.

"I can." I released a pent up breath but as always did so too soon for she wasn't finished.

"But I can't do it alone."

"I am sure that won't be a problem as we are not short on council members willing to go with you." Vincent said and all at once each member thundered their fists on the table top in a show of their support for the cause. Sigurd said,

"Hell, I would feel better knowing someone is keeping an eye on the bitch anyway...! No offense." He added looking to Aurora which wasn't sincere at all.

"None taken, barbarian." She responded curling her lip in disgust.

"As touching as that all is, there is only one that must accompany me." She continued and I knew something bad was coming.

"Who then?" Takeshi asked frowning at her as if he too knew who she was going to say...

"The King's Chosen One...Keira."

And then there was chaos.

CHAPTER FOURTEEN

DO OR LOVERS DIE

I held my head under the blissful cascade of water so much longer than was needed, seeing as I couldn't get any cleaner. I can't say how wonderful it had been scrubbing my skin free of dirt and blood or any evidence of the horrors I had encountered only hours before. But this was not how I first welcomed the new day.

No, first I had an outraged council to deal with, including the snarling Vampire at my back who looked ready to tear Draven's ex in two!

"If you think I'm letting you anywhere near her!"

"No way Bitch face, you can go and swivel on a broom!"

"Not happening!"

"The King would never allow it."

And so it continued.

I felt myself holding the bridge of my nose with my fingers and suddenly I knew what it felt like to be Draven. I held up my hand and tried to contain the situation before Aurora found herself getting lynched.

"Please, let's just think about this a moment." I said and just when I thought it would have been Lucius and Sigurd to shout out their disapproval with me first it was actually Vincent.

"There is nothing to think about." I shot him a look to see him ignoring me and frowning at Aurora, who was looking slightly smug…what did she have…a death wish?!

"Aurora I will do it. Now please leave us." I said spinning the room into shock.

"The Hell you will!" Lucius said at the same time Sigurd said,

"The fuck you will!"

"Aurora." I ignored the two Alphas beating their chests at the little woman and said her name again in warning. She looked about ready to protest but one look around everyone in the room that was close to killing her and she stood. I waited for her to leave the room before I looked up at Lucius.

"Can you have Ruto follow her?" He knew why I asked this to be done as he too didn't trust her. He nodded to Ruto and without an order given verbally Ruto got up and slipped from the room silently.

"You can't be serious!" Sophia said leaning closer to me.

"Yeah Tootie, my home girl here is right. I mean if you are looking for adventure then me and you do tequila before climbing some sand dunes, 'cause trust me that shit is funny to watch…do you remember how much sand you got in between your a…" Pip was cut off with a hand to the mouth when Adam flashed embarrassed panic before she spoke what we all could gather was a sandy and uncomfortable experience between the two lovers.

"Look guys, we are out of choices here." I said but then jumping when Sigurd shouted,

"Bullshit!" To which I just gave him a pointed look that said please don't argue with me on this.

"Ok so what is the alternative here because if anyone else has any bright and shiny ideas then please speak up…" I said waiting for the room to go silent as I knew it would because in reality we had no other options. The only one who could free his Demon was the person who had locked it there in the first place and the reason he agreed to it.

Everyone looked at each other in the hope that someone would say something but there was nothing. It was sweet and touching how they all wanted to protect me and the loyalty I felt warmed my fragile soul.

"Unfortunately people this is our only option. We may not like it…I mean shit, Hell is the very last place I want to go to right now but I went there once in hopes of freeing Draven and this time I get to actually do it. There is no talking me out of this and like Lucius said, my ruling is final."

"Now wait a minute, when Dom said that I doubt it was thinking you were insane enough to go on a suicide mission with that spiteful bitch!" I pushed my chair back a bit to look at him head on.

"So are you saying your word isn't trustworthy?" I asked knowing I was backing Lucius into a corner. He growled down at me and if I knew there was nothing he was backing it up with I would have crapped myself.

"You know it is." He forced out through gritted teeth.

"Then it's settled, I get to make the final decision as is according to our King."

"Fuck! You are making a mistake, woman!" Sigurd snapped almost going red in the face. He had his hood back as you could see his eyes and the snake that was circling one iris in sight of his rising temper.

"He is right, this will not end well Keira." Vincent said adding his doubt to the mix.

"Ok, so tell me honestly as I can see everyone is avoiding it like the plague…"

"Oi, can't we let that drop, I mean that was how many lifetimes ago! And they eventually got over it." Pip said nodding to the room after throwing up her hands dramatically. She was obviously referring for her innocent part in the spread of the Black Death back in 1603, one she was punished for, which was of course how she met half of her husband...*the terrifying half.*

"Alright Pip, my bad for bringing it up. What I meant was can anyone tell me what I really want to know, which is what will happen to Draven if I don't go through with this?" One look to Sophia's sombre face and then to Vincent's I already knew and that was why nobody wanted to tell me.

"He will die won't he?" I said swallowing hard and forcing the question past my dry lips.

"He will get weaker by the day. He can last a time but the fight first with the Titans without his angel side and then to do the same again without his demon was too much for him, along with…" Zagan didn't finish as I already knew what pushed him over the edge and it was the reason I was sat here and no longer slowly bleeding to death.

"I get it. So we have no choice."

"The hell you don't! You can chose to live that's what you can do…Look it's shit, I get it, I really do but do you really think the right option here is to not only lose Dom but you as well?!" Sigurd said and it came easier to him than anyone else in this room because he didn't have the same connection to Draven that we all did…however no one but me argued his point.

"Losing him when I am able to do something to stop it is not an option for me and I wouldn't want to live in a world where I chose differently," It was at this point people were starting to get that they couldn't change my mind. I could tell from the deep sighs of defeat that travelled the room.

"So the only thing we have to plan for is when this all goes tits and belly busters up over our heads and asses...! Am I right or am I right?" Pip asked the room and I shook my head at her version of being serious.

"Yeah Squeak, that is what we must do." Lucius said and she beamed at him before confirming what we all knew,

"Great! Well that we can do because I will tell ya one thing for a Bucky o'Hare toy and that is, that Bitch has a stick up her ass for a reason and it's not so she can look taller!"

"I think in that Pip we can all agree. So I have a plan." I said and for the next hour we all agreed on what needed to be done. There was something not right about Aurora and her offer to save Draven. Not unless it was for her gain, so the only plan now was to find out what it was and before I found a knife in my back in the depths of Tartarus.

I was kind of hoping we were all just being paranoid and that some small part of her actually cared whether her King lived or died. But counting on that would have been not only foolish but down right dumb!

Once things were settled I rose from my seat only to have Sophia clearing her throat like there was something else to deal with. I froze with my hands on the armrests before straightening.

"Uh...we kind of have another issue to deal with." She said and I sat back down. I had to refrain from Draven's trait of holding the bridge of his nose once more and just closed my eyes instead.

"And I was so hoping that dawn would bring better news." I muttered thinking about taking early retirement from the royalty business.

"We still have your friend..."

"Yeah, you know the pink one with righteous dress sense!" Pip added and suddenly I shot up in my chair.

"RJ?!" I shouted her name feeling so bad that I had forgotten all about her. Ok, so it's not like I hadn't been a bit busy worrying about the world ending and a million other things that all included death but still, I should have checked.

"Is she?"

"She's fine but we had a little...uh, well something happened when I ..." If Sophia was tongue tied than this was definitely bad.

"What she is trying to say is that when she came to it was when we were all fighting an army of the dead. As we were a bit busy at the time all we could do was protect her but..." Vincent stopped mid flow and I gathered this was the part that no one could get past.

"That Seth dude is totally in Love with her!" Pip shouted suddenly making us all jump as she clapped her hands and bounced in her seat.

"WHAT?!" I shouted back thinking it was unbelievable.

"Forgive my wife, she is a hopeless romantic and gets carried away." Adam said only Pip was having none of it.

"I am not hopeless, you loved that candy thong I made you wear for Valentines, and even more so when it came time for me munching the front, beside my nipple tassels didn't exactly last long and you said..." In the end Adam decided the best way to shut his wife up was to grab her face in both his hands and kiss the words from her brain. All I can say is it must have been good because Pip came up for air with the biggest grin...and amazingly, no words followed.

"So let me get this straight...he's not in love with her and she is all good?" I asked and one look to Sophia combined with Pip's giggling meant this was far too much to hope for.

"Ok, someone please explain." I asked thinking any minute now and a Mount Vesuvius sized migraine would hit.

"So RJ seeing what she did obviously didn't go down so well." I asked.

"Oh man, she proper freaked and I mean Jack Torrance style! But it wasn't like we gave her an axe or anything so she could break down doors shouting 'Here's Johnny! At us, no she kinda just started screaming 'this can't be real' and shit, so then we knocked her out…but not like hit her or anything just…"

"I think I get it Squeak." I said wondering if this day really could get any worse or should I expect it to start raining black cats and broken mirrors anytime soon.

"I'll take it from here Mrs Ambrogetti, thank you." Vincent said and she blushed.

"I made her sleep and we were just trying to figure out what to do when she wakes when Seth walked through the crypt. It was obvious he was leaving… that was until he saw your friend."

"And then BOOM! Instant attraction…or will it be more like fatal attraction seeing as he's the broody, loner killer type? Do you know if she has any pets…say like a pet bunny?" I couldn't help it this time, I burst out laughing at my crazy friend and nearly kissed her for at least lightening the mood.

"So what happened?" I didn't want to ask, I really didn't as I very much doubted there was little I could do.

"He walked over to her, picked her up and simply asked us the way. Ragnar showed him to a sitting room where he lay her down and he has not left her side since." Vincent said answering my question.

"Has anyone tried approaching him?" I asked and turned to Sophia when she started speaking.

"Yes, Zagan and I went in there whilst you were with

Lucius and tried to explain what needed to be done before she awoke."

"And what needs to be done?"

"She needs to have her mind believe it was all a dream and wake up in her own bed." Zagan spoke this time and I nodded thinking this was definitely the best option by far, however I was waiting for the massive 'but' to follow, so beat them to it guessing for myself,

"And I gather he wouldn't let you." I watched as Zagan, Sophia, Vincent and even Ragnar all looked at each other.

"Uh…not exactly." Sophia said and thankfully quickly continued,

"No, he told us, you can try but it won't work and I quote 'She is different'. So we tried and he was right, nothing…after that all he said was 'Leave her to me' which left us little option to do much else."

"But what if he hurts her?" I said in a panic getting up to go to her. Lucius looked at everyone and must have gathered for himself enough to know this wouldn't happen because he placed a hand on my shoulder and said,

"I think there is evidence to believe this is the last thing on his mind."

"He is right, from the short time we were in there it was clear he would guard that girl with his life." Ragnar said with his arms folded.

"Well durr Odin, he so wants to Marvin Gaye her!" Pip said holding herself and swaying to something she started humming.

"Translate?" I asked Adam who smirked before saying,

"She means the song he sings 'Let's get it on' and before you say it Pipper Winifred Ambrogetti no one wants to hear about *that* time." He added when she got excited for a second as the obvious 'that time' popped into her head.

"What did she call me?" Ragnar asked his son.

"Our old Gods father. Think yourself lucky you got the God of War because she called me Loki the God of Mischief earlier...fucking God of mischief....*I couldn't have had Thor could I...I even look more like the dude from that movie for...*"

"Have you finished?" I asked Sigurd who was muttering to himself and Pip patted him on the arm and said,

"Ask daddy for a hammer for your birthday and I will upgrade you to the hot one."

"I think I am dreaming...Lucius am I dreaming or are all council meetings like this one?" I asked looking up at him over my shoulder.

"No, just all *my* council meetings are like this one." He responded wryly, shaking his head when looking at the trouble maker in question...*Pip.*

After this meeting was finished everyone left knowing the plan. A decision had been made that Seth should be allowed to deal with RJ. I didn't like it but there wasn't much I could do. The guy could scare the monsters from under your bed and he had just saved my life for the second time, so how bad could he be?

I could only hope that what everyone had told me was enough to keep her safe but I couldn't help but feel sorry for what she was about to go through when she woke. I remembered it well and how hard it was to take but at least I had my gift on my side...if you could call it that.

Having years of seeing the impossible does somewhat help the situation but granted I wasn't thrown into the deep end quite as much as she. For starters I hadn't witnessed my first battle till after Draven told me he loved me, so that counted for something didn't it? Yes, this should be a rule, no battles until after the third date at least.

I decided this was one of those things I had to put to the back of my mind and deal with later because I needed to have my full wits about me or this could go very, very bad...and to be honest, I was terrified. So I walked to the only place I could find my sanctuary...

Draven's bedchamber.

"Hello old friend." I said running my fingers down the door panel and looking down at the handle as though it would bite my hand off. I don't know what I was so afraid of but this room held so many memories for me it was like opening a vault that I had locked away with the firm intension of never opening again.

Only now, here I stood ready to throw myself back into this life, starting once more with a quest for truth. Well at least this time it was a quest for truth when Draven wasn't the one being forced to lie to me, for reasons he himself had created. No, it was in fact trying to find out if there was a traitor amongst us as well as trying to free Draven from Hell.

"Alright mister, I'd better be winning girlfriend of the freakin' year or we are going to have words!" I said out loud before opening the door. I don't know what I was expecting, maybe a part of me had been expecting it to have been changed completely in my absence. I had thought a lot about this in the time we had been separated, more time than I would like to admit. But I always wondered if he, like I, would find it too painful to look at the room the way it was when we together.

I remember telling him in his office how I could never walk back in this room without him loving me. It had been so hard to get the words out but I had been so terrified of opening my eyes and finding myself standing in this room. It seems so silly now, after everything we had been through in the last twenty four hours. It was just a room. The only way it could hurt me was if I myself let those memories hurt me. Because for all that time apart I still tortured myself with the past. I still tortured myself with the memories of what we did in this room. The declarations of love, the laughter, the mind blowing sex and even the arguments…they weren't just in this room, they had forever lived on in my mind.

And the mind is the most dangerous place of all.

So no, the room hadn't changed, not one bit. Huge tapestries still hung on the walls, injecting colour of the past against the stone. Masculine heavy wooden furniture still sat in its place and even the couch I had first been placed onto that night was where it had always been. I would remember that night till I could no longer remember my name. The very first time I set confused eyes on this room and my mark was still stained on the fabric from a wound given to me from the first of many enemies to come.

But I was wrong. The room had changed. One very significant change and that was this time I wasn't the one injured. This time I wasn't the one lay on the bed or couch helplessly waiting for Draven to fix me. No, the room had changed alright and the proof of that lay on the bed in my place.

"Draven." I whispered his name as though he was just sleeping and would soon wake up rested and fighting fit like always. But after a few more steps closer to him I knew this would never be the case. He even looked different. His skin was much paler and the dark shadows under his eyes gave his handsome face a tortured look. He didn't look peaceful in his slumber at all and I wondered if he was trying to fight his way back to us.

"Try…try and fight. I need you…oh Christ how I need you…" I said collapsing next to him. I sat by the bed and my movement must have made his arm fall down for the next thing I knew I was holding it to my chest and crying into his skin. I convinced myself a few times that I felt him move but it was nothing more than hope playing a cruel game with me. As I said, the mind was a dangerous thing and mine was making me suffer.

"I love you Dominic." I said into his palm before kissing it like somewhere in that locked abyss he could escape from and he could hear me. Like my voice could act as a beacon in the darkness. I waited and I waited but it became obvious…

My light wasn't bright enough.

I don't know how long I remained there but I must have nodded off because Sophia had come in and told me I needed to eat something. I decided even if Draven did wake the last thing I wanted was for him to find me looking the way I did right now. So this was when I let Sophia lead me to a different room so that I could shower and eat.

I didn't want to leave him but I needed to face the heart breaking reality that my presence wasn't doing what I had prayed for. It wasn't like in the fairy tales or the movies where it takes just a few words of love spoken and the fair princess or handsome knight wakes. It isn't just the sound of your voice that breaks the spell or a single kiss that makes their heart beat again. No, it was a twisted dream I lived in believing that was all it took. Not in this world…not in my broken world. And speaking of broken worlds…

"Are you decent?" Lucius asked from behind my borrowed door attached to this borrowed room.

"Yes, come in." I said as I had finished my shower, washing with products I hadn't remembered using, eating food I couldn't remember tasting and dressing in clothes I hadn't remembered picking. I was on autopilot, flying in a mission I only hoped I would come back from.

"That's a shame." Lucius said joking at finding me dressed. I rolled my eyes at him as I zipped up my hooded sweater. It might have been summer here but it was a bit cooler than Italy had been…although thinking about it, wouldn't I be better off with some kind of metal warrior woman bikini, considering I was going on a mission to Hell? Lucius had gone to stand by the shaded part of the room and had poured himself a glass of wine from the decanter there.

"Is it hot in Hell?" I asked making him start spluttering out the first sip of wine he had taken. Then he started laughing and shaking his head at me.

"You know this is not a good idea, right?"

"I know but sometimes the only idea you have left doesn't mean it's a good one, it just means you have no other choice… do or die remember." He turned away from me and looked out at the view without getting too close. He looked thoughtful for a moment before he spoke again.

"I wish…" He started to say something then shook his head and decided against it.

"I will look into things my end but I have decided to leave Adam and Pip here in case they are needed and if this goes down the way I suspect it will then…" I didn't let him finish. I walked over to him and put my hand on the arm he had at least re-bandaged and was now hidden by a black sling.

"Then that's why if things go bad then you need to come back… you will be needed here. If I don't make it, and Draven doesn't wake up then you have to take his place. You were his second in command once and not only that you are the only one that can keep the balance of both sides." I said knowing that I had convinced him to come back for only one reason and that was because of what I had decided to do to save Draven.

"I hope your loyalty for those you love doesn't get you killed one day." At this I laughed,

"Well I survived you didn't I, surely that counts for something." At this he smiled looking down at me and then he pushed a piece of my damp hair behind my ear before he whispered softly,

"That it does, love." I swallowed hard before laughing nervously.

"Then stop being a pansy ass, I think that sling has made you soft…should we swap it for a pink one?" I teased making him fake a growl at me.

"Come on, we'd better get going, I have a Hell to get to." I said turning but then I felt his hand on my arm holding me back.

"I have to tell you something." One look at his face and I knew it was going to be one of those 'oh shit' moments…I wasn't wrong.

"You're going to react to some things down there."

"What do you mean?" I asked frowning up at him.

"Aurora doesn't know this, nobody but Dom and I know and you must keep it that way."

"Lucius, what are you…"

"We changed you Keira." He blurted out as if he had been trying to tell me this all along.

"What do you mean…tell me?" I said feeling my heart begin to pound in my chest, readying my body and mind for his confession.

"When we gave you our blood, when we saved you…when I gave you…" He took a deep breath and hit me with the truth of what I now held inside of me.

The blood of our enemies…

"I gave you the Venom of God."

CHAPTER FIFTEEN

KEIRA

NOTHING CAN HURT ME NOW

When I first found out that I was going into Hell to save Draven the last thing I expected was that I would first need to take a flight back to England. But that was exactly what I was doing now. I was sat opposite Aurora on one of Draven's private jets making our way to Birmingham airport.

It had been an emotional goodbye between us all. One made more so when I came to saying goodbye to the man I loved who couldn't say it back. I decided to write him a letter telling him all the things I wouldn't be here to say in person for when he awakened. And all I could pray for when that happened was that he understood why I was doing this. I needed him to know my plans from my own words and he needed to know that I would stop at nothing if I could save him…as he had done for me.

Turning my back on him lying in that bed for the last time was beyond hard, it was excruciating. I had spoken to Vincent and Sophia separately before our official goodbyes explaining to them what I had done and to try and help Draven understand that we had no other option.

But from the looks on their faces, they weren't looking forward to the task. As Vincent predicted from Draven's diminishing health, he doubted his brother would wake from this until his Demon had been reunited with him. One look at Draven I was inclined to believe him, as with each passing hour he was looking worse for it. No, time was of the essence and this long haul flight was the last thing we needed!

I sat for the best part of our flight silent and frustrated. Of course this wasn't helped every time I looked up and saw Aurora's calm face, as if she was simply on her way to the Bahamas or something.

Actually she looked more like she was on her way to a business meeting in her dark grey suit. This was complete with a ridiculously tight pencil skirt, power bitch hair style scraped back into a tight bun and what I knew were Louis Vuitton shoes, only due to their red soles and hearing about them enough from Libby over the years.

She also wore a pair of black leather gloves and I really did wonder if I had to remind her we were going into Hell, not staying the night at the Plaza in New York. I looked away from her after getting aggravated and thought back to this morning.

Hearing what Lucius had to tell me wasn't easy at first knowing I had that asshole's blood in me but then he got to the benefits and I had to say, it certainly eased my fears about where in Hell I was off to.

He told me what it meant having this blood or more importantly what it meant to have this power inside me. In reality I didn't feel any different but he assured me that being down there, in the lowest level of Hell, then that wouldn't be the case.

The only good news in all this was it would mean being a mortal in Tartarus wasn't going to suck as much as it sounded. Because I would be the only being down there with the power of Titan blood. Even Titan descendants like Aurora didn't have even a tenth of the power that the first generation had. I put this down to all the incest hence weakening the Godly gene pool.

But whatever it was it didn't matter as long as I kept this just between the three of us. Only Lucius, Draven and now I knew that there were now three beings in the world that held the key to unleashing the Titans and that thought was a truly frightening one. So not surprisingly I tried not to focus on this part and more on the bit about being kick ass down there.

Before I left I had found Sigurd outside getting on his bike before I too had to leave in the Limo that Sophia had provided us to get to the airport. I ran over to him and asked,

"What are you doing?"

"I'm leaving, got shit to do." I frowned up at him and was about to rant at him about honour and the fate of mankind and…well anything else I could guilt him with when he burst out laughing, bursting my rant bubble.

"You should see your face Lille øjesten, you look ready to self-combust…chill out honey, it's my back up plan." He winked at me, turned the key and then kick started his bike until it roared beneath him.

"Back up plan…why, where are you going?" He grabbed my chin playfully giving it a little shake as he said,

"The Cheshire Cheese." Then he was off and out of sight as he kicked up the gravel and summer dust behind him. I didn't understand why he hadn't just travelled with us as he knew we were leaving for England, so I could only assume he needed to see someone else first.

Once we had all found out the details from Aurora things after that became a little bit more complicated. For starters everyone questioned how Aurora could gain access to something called the Janus Gates. I remembered hearing this name before and it only hit me on the flight over when it had been.

It had been that perfect night of the New Year's Party in the Temple and where not only did Draven and I have our first dance but that was also the night Draven took my second virginity.

I looked out at the clouds resting my chin on my palm with my elbow to the arm rest as I tried not to think back to how perfect my life had been back then. It seemed to be the only time we had together without the world against us and us having a break from revenge, hatred or greed for power.

No, instead I focused on the story Draven had told me in bed one night before the party so that I would understand what they were celebrating. It was to celebrate the Roman God Janus, who the month of January was named after. I remember that he had two faces one looking to the past and the other to the future.

I also recalled that he was the God that controls all doorways into the past, future and the end, which made sense considering the end was rather Heaven or Hell for most of us.

So I understood why these portals were called Janus gates and obviously Aurora knew of one that went straight to Tartarus. I gathered that this particular gate only worked when Draven's father had pulled down the barriers, to which Sophia had assured me would be for some time longer.

The most important thing I remembered was that Janus was actually the oracle Pythia's father, which given her cryptic fate shit completely made sense. You could just imagine Sunday dinner round in that family's house…'Can you pass the carrots daughter'....'I could father, but are the carrots really there if a rabbit doesn't see them grow?'...I laughed to myself thinking this was exactly how it would be having met her myself and after spending the summer playing her cryptic games of fate, that only led to heartache.

I liked to think everything we had been through was for some greater reason and the fact that we had both been played like saps was all just for the greater good. I spent a long time after finding Draven in Italy cursing the Gods and basically telling the fates where they could shove it. I had turned my back on their world pretending it was for the best but I knew the mistake I was making.

Because deep down there has only ever been one path for me to take in life and even sat on this plane off to where I was headed, I knew I was still walking that path. The only time I had veered off was when I ripped off that necklace and said goodbye to Draven for what I had believed was the last time.

Nothing about the last ten months in my life had felt right. Just like I was living through the motions hidden by my own shadow cast through a bitterness that wouldn't die. But none of that mattered now. Not after learning the truth in Draven's heart and that of my own.

Because one thing became so clear in what I was doing now. That when you were truly this much in love with someone honestly, there were no lengths you wouldn't go to just to protect the one you loved. I understood that now but more importantly, I understood Draven's actions had been justified. I too, if it meant saving Draven's life, would fake my own death so that he could live and one look at Aurora and the Gods only knew what she was capable of.

We had said little to each other for most of this trip and it had got to the point where I needed to know about where we were going. The place Witley Court had been mention during the last meeting we had which had been to iron out any issues with the plan. When Aurora mentioned about the Janus gates, everyone knew where we would be traveling to...Worcester, England.

"So, this Witley Court, is there anything I should know?" I asked trying to sound polite at least.

"Why should there be?" She asked raising one perfectly plucked eyebrow, making me worry about my own. I could only hope I wasn't starting to resemble Burt from Sesame Street's Bert and Ernie! Given her snippy tone I knew she had clearly dropped the fake loyalty act.

"Oh I don't know, say because I am trusting you here to be my guide into the lowest levels of Hell and bring me back alive after freeing my boyfriend's demon from a prison *you* sent him to...so yeah, I would say any information you can give me right now would be classed as a big heads up and help immensely." I said sarcastically making her lip curl up at me in disgust. Then something must have clicked with her because her shoulders slumped and she dropped the attitude.

"I know you don't trust me and after your track record for pissing people off, I guess I don't blame you." She shocked me by saying this and I frowned at the comment about me pissing people off...*what by... breathing!?*

"But I truly want to help my King and as I am partially responsible, I feel it is my duty to make things right."

"Uh huh." I said nodding my head and I think I would have been more convinced if she dressed as Santa and told me she started work at the North Pole in an hour! There was nothing sincere about her noble statement and I was half tempted to grab her arm and give it a yank across the table to check all that hadn't been written on her skin.

"So this Witley Court, aren't the owners going to mind when we rock up and ask to use their Janus Gate to Hell?" I said and you could tell one look from her frowning at me and she obviously didn't get my humour.

"Are you right of mind? Of course that isn't going to happen! To start with it's not the type of place you would live in and secondly…"

"Why? Not fancy enough for you?" I asked interrupting her.

"More like dilapidated… really, does Dominic not tell you anything?" She said shaking her head to herself as though I was a lost cause. I silently saw red at hearing the way she said his name and felt the ache in my hands when I realised I was twisting the bottom of my t-shirt in both hands until my fingers hurt.

"Well most of the time we are too busy doing far more enjoyable stuff and conversation kinda gets in the way." I said making it clear not to go down this route with me.

"And how long have you been back together again after your yearlong split?" She said smirking at me and it was at that moment I was thinking of joining a very different kind of mile high club…the murdering kind!

"Look, are you going to tell me about this damn Witley Court or do you just want the bitch fight and lets be done with it!?" I said and at that moment if I would have been the bone popping type I would have cracked my knuckles in some super cool badass way…but to be honest the sound gave me the willies.

"A lady doesn't fight." Aurora said and I laughed out loud.

"Yeah right! I wouldn't let Sophia or Pip hear you say that, you would get your ass kicked!" I thought it a wise decision when she didn't reply but the sour look on her face said it all really. On both sides I thought my chances against her looked good seeing as miss prissy pants was too above her girly ass to fight me but on the flip side, it didn't bode well for me going into Hell with some wimpy Angel that couldn't fight for toffee! Which reminded me to ask,

"So if you're an Angel, then how is it you're ok in Tartarus yet no one else is?"

"Because I am a Titan goddess and it was the power of my ancestors that made Tartarus. All who hold our bloodline can access the prison boundaries." I wanted to roll my eyes at her arrogance.

"Yeah well I wouldn't boast too much love, if I had been related to the Manson Family I wouldn't write a song about it." At this and the mention of her family I had obviously hit a nerve. Her face twisted into an angry scowl but I continued,

"And you must need the barrier down or you wouldn't have checked with Sophia at the meeting."

"I can gain access to the outskirts of Tartarus as the barriers only prevent you from getting inside the mountain but to enter through the Janus Gate, I would need the barrier down, yes this is true" She added reluctantly.

"So you only locked Draven's Demon to the outskirts?" I asked feeling hopeful.

"I did, but when he unleashed the Titans, that locked his Demon back inside the mountain, due to the marking I had to carve into his arms."

"You did that!" I shouted outraged at what I was hearing. She rolled her eyes at my reaction and said,

"Everything I did was because it was asked of me. I cannot just tie anyone to Tartarus with the click of my fingers you know and this is the first time I had ever done anything like this." She said all this looking exasperated at having to explain herself, but yet she carried on.

"Try and remember Dominic is different. It's not like there are many of us walking around with both Angel and Demon inside of us. First I had to ensure the two sides would split, which is what half of the symbols are for."

"Ok, I get it you had no choice, yada, yada, yada! So now we are off to this Witley Court...what's so special about this place anyway?" I asked to a bored looking Aurora who had turned to look out of the window.

"That you will find out when we get there." And that was my cue to shut up if ever I saw one. I gave a humph sound and noticed she picked up a newspaper that was folded on the table between us, but not before I caught her satisfied smile, one she tried to hide.

If it wouldn't have looked blaringly obvious in such a small space I would have got up, walked away somewhere I could go and screamed in frustration at having to deal with her!

I hated her and not just because she was Draven's ex, but mainly because she was a massive bitch face that just loved trying to make a fool out of me! But I wouldn't stoop to her level. okay, so maybe I had already stooped a bit by rising to her haughty and rude comments but the best thing I could do now was just ignore her.

She was a means to an end and that end was my only goal now...

That end meant having Draven back.

CHAPTER SIXTEEN

KEIRA

BACK TO AFTERLIFE

Thankfully Aurora and I both learned quickly that there was little point to us actually speaking seeing as we both couldn't stand each other, which meant that I spent the rest of the flight torturing myself with beautiful memories of my time with Draven. It had taken me a bit of time to realise that this was the exact plane we had travelled back in when we stayed at my parent's house for Christmas.

I remembered my shock when hearing him say he was flying the plane. I mentally shook my head at thinking back to when I had heard his voice coming over the speakers asking me to join him in the cockpit. I still remember what he had said like it was yesterday,

'You don't want me to come back there do you, Keira?' I had laughed knowing that he would have as well if I hadn't chickened out and lost the battle before it even began. There was never any point as Draven always won with me. He would give me that sexy commanding voice and I would be a goner, powerless to say no. For a start he knew all my weak spots and I was ashamed to say there were many.

I remember freaking out when he talked about me being his co-pilot and laughing at my reaction to it. In truth all he had wanted to do was show me one of the most perfect skies I had ever seen. There had been something about being in the front of that plane with all that vast blue space in front of you. There weren't many places in the world where you could look out and not see anything living in front of you as far as the eyes could see.

No plants, no wildlife, and not a single person that could invade our moment, just a blue ocean with not a drop of water in sight. It was the closest to heaven any living creature would ever get until their dying breath. Nothing manmade for your eyes to see but the plane we sat in and down there it could have been any time in history and we wouldn't have ever known.

Because up here nothing ruled.

There was nothing owned to fight over. There was no religion to forbid or curse. And the power of the sky could destroy the mightiest of armies or destroy nations with just one storm. If we were nothing but targets for the Gods above and below, then we were nothing but grains of sand to the sky.

And looking down at the world slowly coming into view, I had never felt this be as true as it did now. The different shades of green patches were getting closer and closer until the roads looked filled with toy cars. Was that what we were to the higher beings…toys to powerful children, keeping them entertained with the choices we made? Sometimes it felt like that and now I had to wonder how entertaining the choice I was about to make was going to play out for them?

We landed with a bump and as I usually did I closed my eyes just when I felt the wheels hit the runway.

"I never liked flying in one of these things." Aurora said and I had to laugh at that.

"An Angel who doesn't like flying?" I asked and I was expecting a scowl not the little smile I received.

"It is a funny notion I guess, considering if this plane had crashed I would have been the only one to survive." Ah, so that's what made her smile, the thought of my death. Well that was reassuring for the hours to come... *not!*

I gave her a fake smile and then rolled my eyes when she looked away. Oh yeah, this was going to be a riot, I thought sarcastically. The plane cruised slowly away from the rest of the planes and I saw a black car waiting for us. I yawned not being to help myself as the lack of sleep was catching up on me. I was surprised I was still going but when I queried it with Pip and Sophia they had both explained that was due to the blood from Draven. Well I knew one thing, I was definitely not looking forward to the jetlag once it caught up with me as I might end up sleeping for a week.

I had tried to sleep on the plane a few times but my mind had been too jittery to relax enough. I couldn't really blame it all things considered. I was starting to lose count of the people who had tried to kill me, so now being sat across from someone who was smiling at the thought of me dying in a plane crash wasn't giving me the BFF vibe.

Before I knew it we were off the plane and I was once again stood on English soil, smelling the English air that seemed to always threaten rain. I smiled at the thought of English summers and how unpredictable they were but I had to smile at the bright sunshine we were getting now. Well I could only be optimistic and take it as a good sign because it was that or people saying, 'well at least it was sunny the day she died'.

189

We both folded ourselves into the car, one of us more graceful than the other but at least I could say I received a smile from our chauffeur. Aurora didn't strike me as the type of person who was nice to what she considered the hired help and her attitude wasn't only reserved for people she wanted to maim, like yours truly.

Not a word was spoken to the driver and I gathered he had already been given his orders, so I let myself sink into the expensive leather seat I knew belonged to a Mercedes, thanks to the badge I recognised and looked out of yet another window.

I watched the busy world getting on with their lives and whether it was stuck in traffic on that long commute or arguing in the car with a loved one, it was still a simple life I envied right now. None of them knew how close they had come to the end and I was thankful for that. I really was but the smallest part of me, the selfish part, wished I didn't feel so alone and out of my depth sometimes.

You would think by now that I would have been used to things like this happening and in a way I was but it always made you face each day wondering if today would be your last.

It made you create a list in your head of things you needed to do. The people you loved in this life and what it would mean to you just to hear their voices for the last time. To tell them what it has meant to you having them in your life and loving them the way you knew they loved you back. It was breathing deep, looking down at yourself one last time and whispering the last words you wanted to die saying.

Yes, it felt like I had prepared for this day and done these things far too many times in my short life… and honestly,

I was tired.

I must have nodded off not long after we hit the M5 as the next thing I knew the sound of wheels crunching over gravel was jarring me awake. The creepy part was waking to have Aurora looking at you like she wanted to peel my face off and use it as a victory flag. This look didn't last long before she graced me with one even creepier and with a fake smile plastered on her face she said,

"We are here."

I would have said, 'No shit Sherlock' but words fled me because one look out of the window and the breath-taking Witley Court stood there in all its broken glory.

Aurora waited for the driver to open the door for her and I watched as he handed her a fancy, old fashioned umbrella. I leant closer to the window and looked up to see the unusual sight of a clear blue English sky with the sun beaming down at us. So I could only surmise that she knew something that I didn't,

"Big shocker there, Keira." I muttered to myself as I opened the door and got out of the fancy car.

"Please Miss allow me to do that for you." The driver came rushing over and I don't know what he was going to help me with bless him as I was already out of the car. I thought he was going to leap at me when I started to close the door myself, so I left it making him smile at me.

"Thank you." I said and he tipped his chauffeur's hat at me and one look to Aurora and I knew he hadn't received the same gratitude from that giant cow bag! I had nicked 'Cow bag' from Pip when I heard her call Aurora it the last time we spoke, so I thought it was quite fitting.

This was proven even more so as she walked up to the small gate and nodded to it expectantly. There was a woman sat next to a little hut off to the left and after saying something I couldn't hear into her radio, she stood up. I just made it to Aurora in time to hear her saying,

"I am very sorry Madame, but the house is closed today due to unforeseen circumstances."

"We are the unforeseen circumstances, now open the gate." Aurora snapped and the poor woman fumbled enough she dropped her radio before scrambling to pick it up and open the gate.

"Uh…I am sorry I was told the owner was coming, a Mr…"

"A Mr Draven yes, we are here in his stead." Aurora snapped out as she walked past without sparing a glance at the poor woman.

"Oh…oh, right ok, can I give you a tour or would you like two of our audio guides?" the lady asked having to shout the last bit up at Aurora as she walked ahead. I stopped by the nice woman who wore a pale grey shirt with a logo I couldn't make out and a pair of dark grey trousers.

She was looking very dejected by Aurora's rude behaviour, so I patted her on the back and said,

"Feel sorry for me, I have had to deal with the Bitch all day." Then I gave her a wink and walked on, leaving her smiling again.

I walked up the sand coloured gravel forecourt in utter awe.

"Draven owns this?" I asked myself and instead of Aurora answering me she just turned her head and snapped,

"Are you coming?" I ignored her and didn't even have it in me to growl under my breath, because nothing the cow bag said would spoil this moment for me.

Witley court was a shell of the stunning show of wealth and riches dating back from hundreds of years ago. What welcomed you was the impressive sight of a stone building now lacking a roof and the glass in what were too many windows to count. The building was in a U shape with the two wings of the house either side of an impressive entrance, which was made even more so by the twin towers situated either side of the grand steps.

These steps led up to the imposing front that was made up of six massive, classic Grecian style columns that curled like rams horns at the top. The whole building looked to be made from the iconic Bath stone that was pale but seemed to age beautifully. The roof was long gone and all that remained was the stone balustrades that stood along only one wing, the tops of the towers and the entrance.

I saw Aurora's behind sway up the steps, taking each one like a lady just helped out of a carriage and for a second I was assaulted with images from the past; tall hats and suit jackets with tails, lavish dresses sweeping along the floor and the butlers and footmen hurrying to assist the wealthy guests.

Horses getting impatient to be freed from the burdens they pulled, and the whole place being lit up from open windows, filling the summer night with the sounds of the party in full swing. But curiously amongst these strange flashbacks were the sight of two huge bronze lion sculptures standing guard on either side of the entrance door.

And then it was gone with the disappearing sight of Aurora. I shook my head and followed her footsteps feeling myself being drawn to the place. It was easy to see this place in history being one of splendour and luxury but more importantly a status symbol of the wealth you had acquired through business or if you were lucky enough, through inheritance. But either way this was the place you threw the grand parties.

This was the place you invited royalty.

Or this would have been the case if I didn't now know who its real owner was. For now all I wondered about was what they could have used this place for and more importantly, why did it look like it had all but the stone burnt down?

These questions bombarded me with every step I took up to the entrance. I passed through the columns and turned to look back, taking in the breath-taking view of the grounds and the stunning countryside of Worcester beyond it. There was a massive lake surround by woodland and trees that looked older than the building itself.

I heard a cough of impatience behind me and it broke the moment of appreciation for this part of the country I now found myself in. So I turned, looked up at the arched main doorway that was decorated with an almost Celtic design carved into the stone. But instead of Celtic knots found in the borders they were in fact Tudor roses, carved with very skilled workmanship as most still looked perfect even to this day.

I looked both left and right before walking through to see the two towers either side and exposed part of the red brick from where you could see the roof to the entrance would have been attached to the towers. So this building must have once been red brick but at some point changed during no doubt one of its many alterations.

"Would you like a tour or would you like to save Dom's life?!" Aurora shouted back to me as I could just see her stood on the other side waiting for me. I wanted to shout some clever and sarcastic comment back but to be honest she had a point. So I swallowed the insult and hurried my ass up trying not to lose focus.

The rest of the inside that I could see was like the outside only less preserved. It was still a shell of its former glory, but one made even more so by the obvious fact that it had at one time been stripped of everything. The walls were bare brick with a few sections still with what was once elaborate plaster work attached to them. There were a few exposed beams and the ones not weathered through years of exposure to the elements, had so much fire damage they were black strips sandwiched between red brick.

It just seemed to be room after room of open space and you were left with only your imagination to connect the dots. I knew these grand houses were filled with salons, drawing rooms, saloons and sitting rooms although in most of them I wasn't actually sure what the difference was, other than in the ballrooms and dining rooms of course.

I walked through what I presumed was once a grand entrance hall and onwards to what could have been any one of these rooms from my list. I looked up to the first floor to see what must have been a bedroom at one time as there was a part of a cast iron fireplace still fitted there.

I would have loved to have gone exploring in all the different rooms and read all the history plaques they had dotted around the place. But Aurora was still waiting and I knew time was of the essence.

I walked down the centre and out of another highly decorated door, one that was done in the same style as the front entrance. The only difference was that there was a half-moon shape carved into the top of the arch that was filled with what could have been a grape vine. Well that would have been fitting considering the amount of entertaining these walls would have seen throughout the years… and no doubt the amount of wine consumed.

But what the view beyond opened up to was nothing short of incredible!

"Wow." I said in awe, one Aurora merely scoffed at before dropping a bombshell.

"Well it is certainly better situated than the next place he chose for our council meetings that I will agree with you." She said in all her snobbery.

"What do you mean…no, this couldn't have been…"

"The first to be named Afterlife? Yes, it was indeed, that was until the battle."

"Battle?!" I shouted now looking around and understanding more about why it stood the way it did today.

"Come on, we have only two minutes until it starts." She said ignoring my one worded question after moving her leather glove to one side to look at her designer watch.

"Until what starts?" I asked not surprised when she started walking down the many steps in front of us and thus continuing to ignore me. Of course why should she stop now when she had the art form so perfected? Oh but to have the power of laser beams from my eye balls, I thought bitterly whilst scowling at her back.

I thought for a moment what she had said and looking round at this grand place I could understand why Draven would have picked it. I remember him once telling me that not all the meetings he held were at the Afterlife I knew and for as many years as Draven has been in charge, there must have been quite a few properties Draven owned. I decided to put it from my mind for the moment before I got too lost in my thoughts. No, once again I had to remind myself that I needed to stay focused, especially when it came to Aurora.

I stood on what I knew was named a portico due to all the Greek mythology books I read as a child. It was a sort of columned porch leading to an entrance, like the one at the front of the house I had come through. But it could also refer to the walkway of many columns that was connected with a roof, like the one I now stood in, the one that lead on to this beautiful sight in front of me.

If I had thought the front of the house was impressive then

this was taking it up another level! I felt dwarfed by the Roman style pillars looming over me. But as I stepped out from their shadows into the warm sun, there I was greeted by a vast landscape of green carpets perfectly maintained. The beautiful flower gardens interlinked by their sandstone gravel pathways, framed the setting seamlessly. And what held centre stage in all this magnificence was the awe inspiring central fountain.

I had to walk closer to make out exactly what it was but from here I could just make out the figure sat upon a winged horse rearing up. The nearer I got to the dark figures the more I could make out that it looked like the tale of Perseus and Andromeda. I knew my history and this one was a favourite of mine, as I used to watch the 80's movie Clash of the Titans. However unlike the movie and more to the original story, the sea monster in the statue looked more like a dragon being slain by Perseus, as he sat upon his winged steed Pegasus.

I saw Aurora was now stood not far from the small stone wall that surrounded the large body of water the fountain sat in. She was facing it like she was waiting for something and after her 'two minute' comment I guess she was. I made it down to her and waited, thankfully not having to wait too long, God forbid considering her preferences on being made to wait.

The sound of the water fountain starting up filled the quiet and peaceful countryside and before long the amount of pressure built up sending powerful jets of water high into the air. I could feel the light mist of water whenever the breeze changed direction and it felt blissful against my skin in this summer heat.

Around the base of the fountain were sea creatures with curling fish tales and their heads thrown back with their mouths open so jets of water could erupt out. Each was covered in a thick blanket of moss depending on where the water drenched them the most.

"Was this what we were waiting for?" I asked over the sound of crashing water, one made louder the higher the main water jet travelled. It was the one coming from the beast's mouth as now I could see Perseus thrusting his mighty spear into the creature. I had to restrain myself from giggling out loud as that thought transformed into something quite rude and I blamed it on the half-naked Andromeda stood there playing helpless damsel.

"Now you will see why Dominic owns this place." She said producing an old coin from her suit jacket. She flashed it up at me held there between her fingers and I could see it was solid gold with a face on each side.

I wondered if it was the face of Cronus seeing as he was the King of the Titans or was it this Janus God? Whoever it was I didn't get to find out as the next thing I knew she had thrown it into the fountain's pool. The murky water wasn't deep and you could see all the other coins tourists had no doubt thrown into the fountain over the years hoping their wishes to be granted. Well I could only hope that coin had double the strength, for my wish needed to be lifesaving.

I looked back at the grand structure expecting something to happen at the house when my head shot back round as a rumbling started. The water started to ripple and wave as if the floor was moving underneath and I wasn't wrong. Suddenly large stepping stones emerged. Coming up one by one they all led to the immortal legends glistening in the water raining down on them.

Aurora barely waited for the last stone to appear before she was balancing her ridiculous shoes on the wet and no doubt slippery stone. I mean I was wearing converse high tops and even I was worried. But just as she stepped out she pulled at the umbrella hooked on her elbow, held it at arm's length and then pressed a button, releasing it at just the right time. She held it up over her so she wouldn't get wet and not giving two hoots about me as I was left to follow, getting soaked as I went.

"You know I am sure if you would have mentioned this bit, I would have brought an umbrella too." I said shaking thanks to the unexpected cold shower.

"Um, it must have slipped my mind."

"Yeah right." I said behind her knowing that she was about as honest as a peeping tom saying he was only there to check out her curtains!

The spray from the fountain battered down on her umbrella but the power of the fountain was almost deafening and I wouldn't have heard her if I hadn't been stood directly behind. Although come to think of it, not being able to hear her wouldn't have been a bad thing given that everything she'd said to me so far hadn't been worth hearing.

I knew we were waiting for something else so I didn't bother asking this time. Rather that or this was her idea of a joke and if that was the case then at least I had enough water around to drown her in. Thankfully I wasn't allowed too much time for my temper to rally up so I didn't have to elbow her in the water just yet, because what appeared next was what I assumed was the appearance of the Janus gate.

All around the base in between the sea creatures were massive upturned clam shells to collect the water in until it overflowed from the gaps. The one directly in front of us started to fold upwards which pulled and stretched the moss, snapping it free from the stone. There was a grinding sound before it created enough space that a hidden doorway materialised.

"After you." I said over her shoulder looking down at the dark and damp passageway, one there was no telling how far it went down. All I could think about was 'Christ but I hope we didn't have to walk our way down to Hell, because no amount of sessions on a Stairmaster or hours at the gym would prepare someone for that climb'…and I was about as unfit as they came!

"Thanks." She answered dryly and this wasn't just in her tone thanks to that damn umbrella, which she now cast aside before stepping through the doorway.

So this was it…

My doorway to Hell.

CHAPTER SEVENTEEN

KEIRA

DOWN THE RABBIT HOLE, WHERE THE BUNNIES BITE!

"Do you have to continue with that infuriating sound?" This 'infuriating sound' Aurora was speaking about was my teeth chattering due to it not only being freezing down here but also that fact that I was soaked through to my bra! I felt as though my nipples could have cut glass and I was half surprised they hadn't poked holes through my t shirt they were that erect.

"Well I'm human and some spiteful brat didn't tell me about the waterworks so I could bring my waterproofs, so excuse me for making a sound, but hey, here's an idea, why don't you take off those ridiculous heels and ram them in your ears...I will help if you like." I snapped after having quite enough of her shit.

"You know, I don't know what he sees in you and that vile

humour of yours." She said smoothing down her perfectly dry hair and looked over her shoulder at me, like some spoilt little rich kid. I just laughed which echoed through the tunnel we were walking down.

"Yes, well I like to think he was temporarily insane when he was with you, so I guess we're even."

"We loved each once but you wouldn't understand." At this I lost even more of my cool.

"Oh I understand alright but it sure as Hell wasn't love, so let's call it for what it was and not bullshit each other shall we? He thought you were beautiful until he got to know that beauty didn't reach your heart and you *loved* the power being with him gave you!" At this she whipped round and hissed at me, making me take a step back. Not because I was scared but more because I was taken aback by her losing her calm and collected demeanour.

"You think you're so clever, don't you?! But you have no idea what it was like living in the shadow of this great 'Chosen One' he was really meant to be with!" She shouted and got closer and closer the deeper in her rage she lost herself to.

"Can you imagine what that would feel like, to love a man and know that no matter what you do, that he will one day leave you without a second thought for another woman?" My back hit the side of the tunnel and if my back wasn't wet already it would have been from the dripping bare rock.

"No, you couldn't possibly. And you wonder why I am the way I am, why I am bitter. You can't know what is in my heart. Truthfully it is the love I have for my King that has stopped me from killing you and saving him the heartache, I myself have had a taste of." As I listened to all this, my mind was split between feeling sorry for her and not trusting anything she said to be real.

Yes her words were powerful and she knew just the right

thing to say to get many on her side but I wasn't dumb. I had been fooled by her kind before and was immune to such behaviour after dealing with my cousin Hilary for so long. So I did the only thing I knew to do and that was not to bullshit her with fake sympathy. But to merely nod, giving her the time to calm down again before saying,

"Well I guess then I should say thanks for not trying to kill me."

"Don't thank me yet…" She said turning away from me making my eyes grow wide before she added,

"I am taking you into Hell after all." And then she continued down the stone steps.

The light from the opening only offered us so much before the deeper we went, the more I had to rely on the sides for guidance. Aurora was using her phone screen to light the floor in front of her but for me being at the back of her, it was about as helpful as a chocolate teapot was to a diabetic.

I was tempted when we finally came to the end to shout three Hail Mary's I was both that exhausted and was happy to report we weren't walking all the way to Hell. No, we came to a door that Aurora pushed with little effort before it swung open, allowing us both entrance.

"But I thought the door at the fountain had been the Janus gate?" I asked looking round in utter amazement.

"This is the Temple of Janus, where all the doors and portals to each realm of Heaven and Hell lead too." She said having a change of heart after her outburst and answering one of my questions. I looked around and if I lived to be a hundred I didn't think I could have counted all the doors this place held.

I wondered could there really have been that many places in the other realms? But if I really thought about it, if Heaven and Hell were each the same size as the surface of the earth then there were a lot of places you could visit. I gathered if they hadn't been in the mind to recycle souls then they would have all been overrun many centuries ago.

I looked around the main room thinking a giant could have lived here quite comfortably and still have room to stretch. The room we were stood in was an Octagon shape and branched off in eight different directions. The long arched passageways continued on far beyond the eye could see and each, like the main room we were stood in, had seven levels of doors all linked by balconies running the full length.

It reminded me of a massive library, only instead of displaying books there was every kind of door imaginable. There were tall doors, thin, wide, and squat. There were old, new, slatted, panelled, carved, ramshackle, paint chipped, stripped, bleached and varnished.

Round, square, I could even spot one that was the shape of a star. There was the weird and wonderful, like one I could see as I spun round in awe that looked to have been made from an entire tree root. Up on one of the higher levels there was one made all from broken mirror pieces that looked to have been laid on bloody foundations.

It was all incredible and something you could have stared at for hours and still spot something new with every turn of your head. Even the great wooden spiral staircases that were situated at each corner of the Octagon shaped room were amazing. All of them were highly decorated and carved in different styles, each a different shade of wood than the next. And each of them was what connected all of the floors together, so you could get to every single door.

The only common theme there seemed to be that all of the doors held some kind of keystone above them and they held a different symbol carved into each one. I gathered this was instead of door numbers and it made sense seeing how many ways numbers have been written down throughout the ages.

But symbols have always been the one form of communication that unites us all. I couldn't think of one single country or race that didn't use symbols in modern society, even to this day and it was something we had all carried from our ancestors since the beginning of time for us mortals.

"This way." Aurora said and I turned to find she was stood at the centre near a giant water feature. The enormous amount of water that was being pumped to create it made me wonder if it had something to do with the fountain above us.

Whatever its cause or use, it was incredible to witness. It flowed the full height of the room looking like a water tube big enough you could have fit a car inside it without getting it wet. I frowned as I got closer and wondered if what I was seeing was real? The water wasn't falling down but it was in fact raining upwards.

"That's amazing." I said reaching out with my hand, one I found slapped away to my great shock.

"Don't touch it!" Aurora shouted at me and the panic in her voice told me I should heed her warning.

"Why, what...what is it?" I asked looking up at it and feeling drawn to whatever power it held.

"It is what powers all the gates here. It channels the power and essence of Janus himself."

"So it's not a gate then?" But even as I asked this question I knew that it was but what I didn't know was where it led to.

"Oh it's a gate, it's just one that's forbidden to be used by anyone who's not worthy." She sighed when she saw my confused face and continued,

"One needs to be judged first and to be judged by Janus, he does so by not only looking into your future but also into your past and more importantly, your reasons." She said flicking her fingers so I would move further back.

"So if you don't pass his test you don't get to use it, I get it…"

"Oh no you don't. If you don't pass his judgement then you don't get to go home. If that were the case we would have every one of my kind down here trying their luck. No, there is a reason no one wants to be judged and that is the punishment if you fail." She actually shivered a few steps back before turning round to put her back to it. With this reaction I gathered it must have been a bad thing to fail then, so I asked, following after her,

"But wait, what does it do, what is the punishment?"

"What does it matter, just leave it be Keira." Hearing Aurora actually saying my name was enough to make me drop that question but there was one I really wanted to know and this was one I wouldn't give up on.

"Ok fine but just tell me, where does it go?" She stopped in her tracks and I saw her defeat when her shoulders slumped.

"It goes everywhere and anywhere. Just think it and it will take you there. The past, the future, some place in the present, anywhere you want to go as long as you think about it hard enough when you walk through, that's where you will find yourself. It's dangerous and foolhardy to try."

"But why, I mean it must have worked for…"

"It has worked for no one! As the Janus gate only allows the worthy through they don't take the chance for selfish reasons. Only the most worthy cause will be allowed to pass through its essence and to this day, it hasn't found one." She looked past me when she said this, as if she had lost someone dear to her through this same foolish act and I finally let it go.

She walked away and I looked back one last time. There was something that kept me held there, like it was luring me in and I wondered if that was part of the power it held over people. Was that why there were those crazy enough to try it? Either way I found I was no different and it took an irate clearing of Aurora's throat to pull me back into the now.

I walked away wondering something else and that was why when I needed to get into Hell, nobody had told me about this place back when I was trying to save Draven? Was it because I was human? I jogged the last bit of distance between us and had to ask,

"Last year when I tried to…"

"I did wonder how long it would be before you asked." Aurora said, back to being irritatingly cocky and I almost cursed myself for the question.

"Only my kind can come to this place and most are not worthy to open over half of its doors. Try and remember, for a human to get into Hell or Heaven, usually they do have to be dead." She shot me a look as if to say, should we test this theory and instead of rising to it I just said,

"Well I guess lucky me considering I was allowed in and I gather I still am now or this has certainly been a massive waste of a girly trip." She rolled her eyes at me once more not getting my humour and I wondered if there was any humour in the world she did crack a smile at.

"Yes, I think it has been established that you are obviously different." This was not said in that warm, loving way. No, more of an 'I hate that you're different and more special than me' kind of way. When she turned her back to me I knew it was obvious this conversation was over, so in my saturated clothes I squelched my way after her.

I had started to get worried when she started walking down one of the endless corridors and the only benefit of that I could see was that by the time we reached the end I would be bone dry again.

But thankfully this wasn't the case as after only a few short steps down there was an open archway. This was ornamented with painted scenes of both Hell and Heaven on carved stone that was designed like a frame within a frame, stepping down in on itself. It was beautifully painted but the primary colours used were blues depicting Heaven's side and reds doing the same for Hell.

"Stunning." I whispered as we passed through. I would have thought given the door that the room would have been just as spectacular but other than pale, bare stone walls there nothing other than the reasons we were here.

Two doors.

"I gather we take the black one." I said and she didn't respond. It was a large round room and opposite each other two doors protruded from the curved walls like statues in their own right. The black one I spoke of had a huge block frame and it looked to be made from cast iron. It was crudely made with what looked like desperate souls trying to escape and reminded me of the wall of souls that attacked me that day when I first found the Temple.

All tiny hands and faces pushed themselves against the forged metal as if being caught in the making process trying to escape. I looked to the other side and saw the white door of carved marble framed by Roman pillars, reminding me of the entrance to Witley Court.

The door was split into four panels and each held heavenly images. Gardens and a celebrated feast were in the bottom two, whilst the two on the top held Gods on thrones. The last scene showed a great battle with half naked men wearing large elaborate helmets on horseback.

When I took a step closer I noticed something important and my head snapped between the two doors.

"It's a story of the great battle." I said out loud making Aurora huff. Well I bet she would considering her ancestors lost and these doors made it blindingly obvious of that. The

Heaven's gate told a story of peace and serenity being shattered by the mutiny and divide between the Gods, then after the battle came the feast for victory. The opposite door told only one story, which was the outcome of what happened to the Titans.

"So if that door leads to Tartarus, then this door leads to…"

"Not all places in Heaven are safe to travel to. It's not all divine power that keeps everyone in check…how do you think the first demons came to be?" She asked and it was obvious she was feeling superior having this knowledge over me.

"So you're saying that the first demons came from those that went against the original Gods" I said which wasn't a big shocker but knowing my weakness for gaining answers and knowledge into more about the supernatural, I couldn't help myself.

"To want something different in your life than those around you doesn't make it wrong, that is why not all Angels are good and all Demons are bad, we just all envy mortals." I frowned at this but from my face alone I didn't need to ask the question.

"Look around you, does this look like we have free will to you? No, if we want to make our own choices we must leave our home and be cast aside into your world, only to find we have even more rules to abide by there. But you mortals, the Gods gave you the world to do with whatever you chose and let you live your lives without limitations and after being created by the blood of my…"

"Eh, hang on a minute, there is a bit of a difference here considering *us mortals*, ones that *you* envy, have not even the same amount of power you guys hold in your little fingers!" This time I was the one stomping up to her as I continued my rant letting my anger bubble hotter.

"So don't talk to me about injustice when my people have to go through the pain of watching loved ones die or feel the pain and suffering of illness! Ever even had a cold Aurora, ever had

STEPHANIE HUDSON

a snotty, cracked nose, a throat so sore every swallow feels laced with razors or a cough that keeps you up all night? And that is just one illness everyone experiences at least once a year, I am not even going to talk to you about Cancer! So I think all things considered, immortal being that you are, we are more than even!" I finished and only then did I realise I had backed her into the door to Hell.

"Fine. Do you want to back off now?" She said and it was then that I recognised what I saw in her eyes…

It was fear.

That night quickly flashed back in my mind and it was the night I had almost killed her. I can't believe I hadn't thought about it till now. But in truth I put this down to how I would block out that part of my life as it was too much to bear thinking about. And that night was no different. That very moment I walked into Draven's bedroom and saw her there it had been like a red cape to a bull. Something inside of me had snapped and what came out was a power of vengeance of the likes I had never known. I had in fact prayed for the very same power to come to me in the Temple with Alex but it was as if I had been running on empty.

"Aurora, what happened that night back in Lake Como, I just wanted to…"

"No!" She shouted, moving out of my way and when she took in my look of shock in the sight of her reaction she said,

"Please, let us not mention it again." I nodded and left it as it was, feeling that no more could be said.

"Shall we go to Hell?" I asked instead, changing the subject for one definitely more dire and dangerous but without a doubt far easier to deal with. Because going to Hell was a piece of cake compared to having a heart to heart between two people who obviously hated each other.

"I think that would be best." She said and it was the first

210

time I got to see a glimpse that she did in fact have at least a slither of humour running through her serious veins.

She put her hand in the small pocket in her tight suit jacket and I had noticed her doing the same thing in the car before I nodded off. It almost looked like a nervous habit as this was the third time I had caught her doing it. Only now I realised what it was and I had to wonder how many of those coins she had in her pocket, because this time she pulled out a slightly larger one.

Then she surprised me when she bent on one knee and my first thought was how she managed it in such a tight skirt. This wondering of mine was eclipsed by her next action and I watched with a raised eyebrow when she slid the coin underneath the door. Well what did I expect, a coin slot like on a fruit machine or if you wanted a can of coke?

Whatever she had done it was clear this wasn't her first Rodeo, as the next thing I knew the door to Tartarus was opening and as I walked inside I received my next big shock of the day…

Tartarus was a Temple.

CHAPTER EIGHTEEN

KEIRA

SAVING MORTALS AND FREEING DEMONS

I looked round in wonder at what would have once been a magnificent place to see. We were in some kind of broken Temple that quite obviously had been a place to come and worship the old Gods. But it was hard to imagine why it would be down here in a place like this. So once again I found myself asking the question,

"What is this place?"

"This is the Temple of Lost Olympus." She said stepping over the fallen remains of what were once great and mighty statues of her ancestors. If I thought the Temple of Janus was large then this was its older, bigger brother! The statues alone were like buildings left to rest on their sides. Huge severed arms still holding onto their weapons reminded me of Jurassic trees fallen after a storm.

"But why is it here?" I asked following after her and

climbing over the smaller bits of debris. I could practically hear her rolling her eyes!

"Mortals…" She muttered before she carried on.

"This temple used to be on top of Mount Olympus but after the last battle between the Gods, Zeus forced the remaining Titans back into this place. Once there he then used the last of his power to bring forth the greatest storm this planet has ever known, striking down his own Temple and using it as a prison, one that took them straight to the lowest levels of Hell." She said this scowling at the statue of the God she obviously held responsible.

"And this is what remains?" I asked looking back around the room.

"No, this is only half of what remains, the other half…well I guess only Dominic knows what that looks like…this way." She said and I knew enough by this comment what she meant. After making our way across the vast room she came to what appeared to be a hidden door. I frowned and said,

"Is it not that way?" I pointed to the large door at the end, next to the only statue that remained mostly intact and you could tell it was the main man himself…Zeus, the one Aurora clearly detested.

He was sat upon a huge throne as if looking over his domain and now I guess he was forever to be punished also, considering all he had to look at now was the result of such a war.

"No, Dom went this way. I can feel his presence as if he walked these very steps." Once again I found myself frowning that she could 'feel him' and I knew it was irrational, but I didn't even want her thoughts to feel him, let alone her jealous hands. Not only that but it annoyed me that she made out she could feel his presence when I had the strongest urge to go the other way.

In the end I didn't say anything but just followed blindly as we went off in the opposite direction to what I felt was right. The entrance to the next room was half crumbled away and I passed it as quickly as I could in fear that it would all come crashing down on me. I let out a sigh of relief when making it through and growled under my breath when I heard Aurora chuckle because of it.

We walked into a dismal looking space that reminded me of what a tunnel to Hell would look like, which wasn't surprising considering where we were. It was made from a kind of mosaic style only instead of using tiles, it was clad in black rock that looked like shattered glass. It was as if someone had smashed a massive slab of it and then tried to piece it back together again.

Once again I was worried about the light situation, or lack of it more like but in the end I didn't need to worry. Aurora's dark shadow walked over to one wall and lit something that was hanging down, almost like a giant match. Once it was lit she picked it up and put the end to what I could just make out was a small hole in the curved wall. I heard the sizzle and then it was like a tiny bomb went off as the flames must have travelled behind the walls.

One by one small windows carved all along the tunnel lit up and provided us with enough light to be able to see how far down it went. Well one thing was for sure, I would certainly be getting my wish of being dry again long before we got there.

I couldn't tell you how long we walked, but two things I was thankful for. One, I was now mostly dry and two we didn't have to see the bottom of the tunnel before reaching our destination.

As we had been walking down I had noticed there had been plenty of arched doorways to choose from and it looked to me as though these could have been different cell blocks. Well it was a prison after all so it would make sense.

It was hard being down to here to get an accurate scale on how big the place was without actually seeing what was through those doors. But one thing I was sure about, if they had all been cell blocks, then that meant we were utterly surrounded by the most dangerous demons ever known.

"I can assure you it's this way." Aurora snapped impatiently over her shoulder and this was getting old pretty damn quickly. I felt like I was being rounded up like cattle and having such a thought in this place sent a shiver through my body.

We entered yet another corridor and I had to wonder how many were in here as the movie Labyrinth sprang to mind. At least this one was slightly less depressing than the last. It actually reminded me of a gallery from a castle only void of the family ancestry on the walls. It was a wide, tall walkway that only had one slatted door at the end. Above sat a scary looking statue that almost looked positioned there to guard the place. It was of a winged creature that was sat in an awkward position, all bent and scrunched up so it could fit on this small plinth above the door.

"Wow that is one ugly looking Gargoyle. I mean I have seen scary at Afterlife but this one takes the biscuit." I said the closer we got and after catching up to Aurora.

"That's no Gargoyle." Aurora whispered in vain as the creature started hissing at us. It was obvious it had heard us and only when it jumped down did I realise it wasn't an '*it*', no, 'it' was a *she* and she was not happy.

No wonder I thought she had been a statue, considering her skin was like rough old stone, weathered by nature. Her wings were a combination of an injured bat and a bird after having all its feathers ripped out. It was almost painful to look at and the long finger bones that ran through the wings crawled through me like nails on a chalk board. Her face was no better and the snarling didn't help as her elongated jaw stretched further to allow for her many rows of teeth to snap at us.

"Eosss!" The creature hissed what sounded like a name and it was one I was sure I remembered hearing before.

"Podarge" Aurora responded angrily and I gathered it was the creature's name. It became obvious they knew each other when it finally clicked where I had heard that name before...

Eos was Aurora in Latin.

I mentally went back to only days ago when Draven had told me who Aurora really was. She was the Goddess of Dawn and the painful thought of such beauty clogged up my throat so I couldn't speak. I tried to focus more on the truth and that was just because someone had a beautiful name and the title to go with it didn't make them a beautiful person inside. I knew this and knowing her, boy did I really know this! And evidently so did Podarge if the way she was snapping her jaws at Aurora was anything to go by.

"Why are you here?" The creature snarled with venom as she looked from her to me.

"That is none of your business Harpie you know who I am so you would be wise to have respect when speaking to me!" Aurora replied standing straighter as if the sight of greater posture was something to be feared.

"Oh I know who you are and of your traitorous ways."

"What is she talking about?" I asked turning to face Aurora wondering what I was about to hear.

"Nothing!" Aurora bit out at me and what I now knew was a Harpie just laughed in response with a high pitched cackle.

"You call betraying your master nothing?" The Harpie informed me and my mouth dropped before I shouted,

"Draven...? Why you…"

"She's talking about Zeus." She said cutting me off before my murderous rage could build.

"Oh...well that's alright then I...uh...I mean, how could you do that?" I said looking accusingly at Aurora and changing my tune when seeing the angry Harpie taking a step towards me. Aurora just rolled her eyes and then quickly diverted her aggravation to someone other than me for a change.

"My business with that ruthless bastard is my own and does not concern the likes of you and your abhorrent kind."

"Eh...yeah good one." I said sarcastically when the Harpie looked even more enraged and started to go into attack mode. She crouched low and opened her frail looking wings as if she was about to pounce. Aurora looked at me sideways a second before sighing as if she was about to do something she really didn't want to do.

"You die traitor and with it I will cook the flesh of your mortal over your burning corpse to share with my sisters!" I grimaced as she said all this just having images of them all singing Kumbaya whilst waiting for me to roast over a Goddess fire with an apple in my mouth. Actually one more look at this winged Diva and it would be more like them all singing 'Hell ain't a bad place to be' by AC/DC whilst waiting for Scouser Al a carte to cook!

"Seriously though, do you have any friends?" I asked which she ignored by focusing on our main problem.

"Zeus should have killed you!" Aurora shouted making Podarge charge at us. Aurora pushed me out of the way just in time before the Harpie could dig her talons into my shoulder to no doubt fly off with me. I fell to one side stunned that Aurora could have possibly just saved my life and watched in shock as business chic turned into office deadly. She spun on her heel and ran at the Harpie that had landed on her hands and one bent knee. As soon as she saw Aurora running at her she pushed off the ground with her toes and started matching her speed towards her.

I had to wonder what they were expecting would happen when they just collided with each other but it became obvious that only one of them had a plan. As Aurora continued to run towards the Harpie I saw her put one hand behind her back just before she reached her target. The flash of metal only caught my eye for a split second before she was coating it with blood. She sidestepped at the last second and spun on her heel once more only this time she held out her blade for a single purpose. The razor edge sliced into the Harpie's neck and as Aurora continued spinning around to the creatures back it slit half of its throat open.

The Harpie stumbled back holding her gaping neck in shock but Aurora didn't give her chance for much else. No, she tripped her up till she was on her back looking up at Aurora with pleading eyes and reaching hands. What the heavenly Aurora did next was shocking because without any care or mercy she brought her knee up before hammering it down and stomping on the Harpie's face. Her thin stiletto heal first impaled her eye before travelling through to her brain, killing her instantly till Podarge was no more.

Aurora wasn't even breathing heavy and for someone who thought it wasn't correct for a lady to fight, she was bloody ruthless at it!

She looked down in disgust, smoothed her hair back and pulled her foot free taking the impaled eyeball with her. Then she walked past me, pulling down her jacket saying,

"Fucking Harpies."

After the Harpie incident we were both quiet as we walked what I hoped was the last stretch to wherever Aurora was taking me. I still couldn't get over the shock of Aurora saving me from getting mauled to death by Podarge. It would have been the perfect opportunity to have gotten rid of me once and for all. So did this mean we had her all wrong…was she really here to help Draven?

I wanted to think so. I wanted to think the best of people and give them a chance without my own personal issues with that person getting in the way of my judgement calls. I had little choice in trusting her when it came down to it as this was literally the only option we had left and honestly, there wasn't a second thought in risking my own life if it meant saving his. So who knows, maybe we would both die trying. These thoughts made me break the silence as we came to another slatted door that looked the same as the previous million it felt like we had already come through.

"That Harpie could have killed me." I stated using this as my only chance to plant the seed.

"Yes, it could have." She said looking back at me in all seriousness.

"Could you have still freed Draven?" Aurora stopped walking at my question. Her hand automatically went into her jacket pocket where her fingers played nervously with something I couldn't see.

"It wouldn't have mattered." I frowned at her response thankfully making her elaborate.

"If you die, then bringing back the King would only mean my own death, one I would have no choice but to forfeit for his own."

"Wait, I'm confused. Why would you die if something happened to me?" I asked coming to stand in front of her and stopping her from storming ahead which was something she was obviously good at considering I had spent most of this trip staring at her tailored back.

"It's simple. If you die and Dominic comes back to find you gone then, like you and everyone else, he would merely believe I had killed you for my own gain. Therefore I would not live out the hour upon his return." I contemplated this for a moment and then thought now was a good a time as any.

"Then I should probably tell you, if you gave him a lock of my hair and told him the last thing I said to him, he would know I must have asked you to tell him goodbye." Aurora's eyes widened and then she asked the question I knew she would, one whose answer she believed could save her life.

"And what is the last thing you said to him?"

"I will see you again on the other side." She gave me a thoughtful look and then nodded her head in understanding before saying a word I never even thought she knew the meaning of, let alone be able to form the word.

"Thanks." I seriously thought I was going to choke on my tongue in shock just hearing it and in true Aurora fashion she rolled her eyes from the look of shock on my face.

"Come on, it's just through this door." She said and the knowledge was like music to my ears. I walked past her as she held the door open for me which was completely out of character. I put it down to our sort of heart to heart, or more like mutual understanding on my untimely death should it horribly occur.

The room she followed me into this time was definitely one that I knew what this place had been filled with.

"Draven's demon is in this prison block?" I asked looking at the floor and seeing the dug cell pits.

"It is in the end cell." She said nodding to the end of the long room. Not that I had seen many cell blocks in my life but I imagined it looked very similar to the ones we had in the 'mortal realm'. Of course both types held monsters of society, only these were more the 'live under your bed and eat your face off' than just your regular murdering kind.

I walked past keeping mainly to the side furthest away from the scary looking inmates that reminded me more of a bunch of captured, angry beasts. The long pale stone corridor was something I wanted to run down just to get closer to Draven's demon but I not only wondered what it would look like but more how it would respond to me. I had seen Draven a few times when his demon had been more dominant and it had scared me at first but just like the rest of him I knew it would never hurt me.

So making the decision I went with my impulse and ignored everything unimportant in the room and ran for it.

"Keira?!" I heard Aurora shouting my name in question and multiple things all started happening at once. First I heard the grinding of metal as though a massive crank was turning and then overhead the sound of rushing water. I stopped to look up after only making it three quarters of the way down the cell. Then I heard my name being screamed by Aurora before I felt a body tackle me to the ground.

"Umpf...! Hey, what are you...?" I never finished as I looked up to find Aurora on top of me, pinning me to the floor and being silenced by the sight of a huge pair of glowing wings erupting from her. The wings encased us both in a golden dome and when the water could be heard gushing from an open trap, I thought it was a bit overkill saving us from both getting wet. However this thought quickly fled when I saw the look of pain on Aurora's beautiful face above me.

I wanted to ask what was wrong but the sound of the water was as loud as if we had been lying next to Niagara Falls. Then came the heat that started to seep in and suddenly it clicked as to what caused her pain. I was horrified and left feeling helpless as Aurora once again saved me and this time it would have no doubt been a torturous death. Thankfully it stopped not long after it started and Aurora closed her eyes in what looked like great relief.

Even after enduring what she had to in order to save my life she still managed to get off me gracefully. She even offered me her hand and I took it still in a state of shock. I got up off the floor and saw all her golden feathers ruffle as if to shake off the water that still clung to its tips. She could see I was about to ask so she answered me before I got chance to ask.

"It was the furnaces." She said as if this would mean something to me. She held out her arm for me to precede her and I turned muttering,

"Alrighty then." I walked past the large trapdoor above one of the cells, one that looked to have little demons working their ugly little asses off. They shook off the obvious downpour and started back to their shovelling. Water still dripped from where the two half-moon doors met and I could only hope it wasn't something that happened every other minute.

"We have plenty of time till the next one." Aurora said as if hearing my anxious thoughts.

"And how much is plenty of time exactly?"

"Well that depends how long you want to drag this out for?" She responded back sarcastically and I smiled.

"Ah, there's the Bitch I know." To which she smiled and winked at me making me laugh. I turned my back to her and continued down till we came to the last cell. I took a deep breath, bracing myself for what I would find but then the realisation hit me like one of Zeus's thunderbolts.

"You have no idea." She said as I approached the edge of the hole only to find the truth,

It was empty.

I turned around slowly and the face looking back at me

wasn't one I could trust, even though it had saved my life. No, the face looking back at me said only one thing,

Betrayal. Betrayal from a person who had been waiting a long time for this day to come. She put her hand behind her back and I thought I knew what was coming, but oh how wrong was I. She brought the small blade that was like a shorter version of a samurai sword and held it in front of me.

"I lied." Was all she said before she grabbed a chunk of my hair and then…

She pushed.

CHAPTER NINETEEN

KEIRA

FOOLED ALL ALONG

I fell backwards, landing hard at the bottom of the pit with a painful thud. I cried out and shook my head trying to make sense of what had just happened. I looked up to see Aurora stood at the edge holding a handful of my hair that she had cut just before I fell. If I hadn't just felt like my spine had been run over by a Mac truck then I would have jumped up and grabbed her ankle. The bitch had pushed me in and the only reason I could fathom was that she wanted Draven for herself. But if that was the case then why did she save me before?

"Why?" I asked gritting out the question between my teeth. She started laughing and it was the ugliest I had ever seen her.

"You ask me why?!" She shouted down at me and that once cool calm façade was now long gone.

"Yes I want to know why! Why would you save my life if only to leave me here to die!?" I screamed back at her.

"Oh I am not leaving you to die you unfortunate and pathetic mortal. Oh don't get me wrong, if I could kill you I would relish the act but alas no, he needs you alive." I scowled up at her trying not to show any weaknesses and with it the haunting realisation someone else out there was trying to hurt me.

"Who?" At this she just started laughing again and the sound lashed out at my nerves.

"Oh you'll find out soon enough, don't you worry about that."

"And what of Draven, are you just going to leave half of him down here too?" I asked hoping the only reason she had taken my hair was so that she could get away with bringing him back without him killing her.

"I must say I am surprised everyone was gullible enough to believe I needed you down here with me to free his demon. No in truth…"

"Oh this will be rich, do you even know what that word means?" I said hitting back and interrupting her.

"When it is beneficial to our cause, then yes, I know what the word means…for example, it is the truth when I now tell you that I could have freed that asshole's demon from anywhere in the world if I wanted."

"What!" I shouted feeling like such a fool for playing into her hands like this. After all every single person at that table had tried to talk me out of trusting her but I agreed to go only for one reason…I had been desperate.

"Then why…?"

"Oh come on! Isn't it obvious? Once those barriers go back up do you know how hard it is going to be for even Draven to get to you? And now thanks to you he will think you dead, so cheers for that." She said waving my hair back at me.

"Draven will reach me, you won't be able to stop him." I said knowing I was right, he would stop at nothing to save me.

"No but as I said, thanks to you he will think there is no one even left to save and besides, he has men that will come for you soon to hide you in another location, one where no-one would ever have a hope in finding you." She finished by tucking my hair away in her pocket giving it a pat like it was her life insurance.

"So this is your grand plan for revenge is it, to leave me here, tell Draven I am dead and then what? You think he will jump straight back into bed with you?" Again, with that infuriating laugh of hers.

"You really are one dumb bitch aren't you?" She said shaking her head as if she couldn't believe I hadn't figured it all out yet. I really wanted to respond by informing her how she was actually the dumb bitch considering she was doing the classic movie baddie cliché when they tell the goodie all their plans. So what she didn't grasp was that I was pumping her for as much information that I could by acting stupid. Because it all came down to one simple truth, baddies all had massive egos that wanted the last word and that last word was always so you would know how clever they were.

She crouched down low and I finally got to see what she had hidden away in her pocket. I gasped at the sight of my purple diamond necklace hanging by the chain she held in her grasp. Her eyes widened in sight of my distress and she smiled down at me.

"Who do you think was the one to switch the necklace in the first place?"

"You and Alex were working together?" I asked and my plan of feeding her ego was working alright. Christ what was next, her singing like some damn canary?

"Ha! You would think that, no I must confess he played his

part well but that puppet Sammael had no clue about our back up plan, one that was sure not to fail and well, here I am, staring down at the proof of that…and I must say it does suit you." She winked at me after looking round at my hole.

"However it is missing something."

"A gun?" I said and she gave me an evil grin, followed by,

"Oh no, I wouldn't give you the easy option out."

"The gun was for you, bitch!" I corrected her wiping the foul grin from her face.

"You think you're so quick don't you, well let's see how quick you are with an Aeolus' eye to keep you company." She said and I frowned having no clue what she was talking about.

"But first I think you should see me follow through with my promise as I set free the Demon King I imprisoned." Ok none of this was making sense and it was time to play dumb again.

"I don't get it, you aren't doing this to get back with Draven but you're not doing this as revenge either, so what's your angle here exactly? Because I gotta say, I am failing to see the point of locking up Draven in the first place if you're trying to get away with the not so unique, crazed bad guy take of the world shindig…which by the way this shit is getting old and has been done to death! Seriously can't you be like Gru and try and steal the moon or something?" I said and for once I was smirking at how confused she looked.

"Who the fuck is Gru?" She snapped as I had obviously knocked her evil genius mojo.

"Evidently someone shit loads smarter than you." I responded like I was bored and hopefully buying myself some time. Time for what I didn't know but hey, they always stalled in the movies and considering we were following the theme, I went with it.

"Don't worry, that whole fucking Draven family will get what's coming to them but for now I will play the game as I did when we were together and get what I need from having them around. But I came here to get you out of the way and I have done my duty in that part so time to bring lover boy back and you know what…"

"What?!" I didn't really want to know but short of a few rounds to the head with a baseball bat there was going to be no shutting her up, so I played her game. She lent down further and said,

"I am really going to enjoy watching his fucking heart break!" Which was at the point when I lost it. I threw myself forward and jumped up clawing at her face and feeling satisfied when I felt her flesh curl under my fingernails. She screamed out and fell back as I too landed on the dirt ground.

"Bitch!" She growled and I laughed giving her a taste of her own medicine. I had never seen her looking so ugly and the angrier she got the more twisted her looks became. It was like her other self was the black and evil soul shining through and the beauty of the dawn was no more, consumed completely by the destructive storm building inside her.

"You think that's funny, then you can laugh in the face of your lover's heartbreak!" She said before smashing the necklace on the side of my prison and the thing shattered like fine glass. Purple rain fell from the two wings that kept it safe and one foreign word spoken and that storm she had been holding back exploded.

"Enjoy your Aeolus' eye and I will enjoy my new lover, Seth is waiting for me…*be good…*" Her malicious voice trailed off into the nothingness that started to surround me. It picked up speed until I was enclosed in a hurricane that forced me into the centre in fear of being sucked up and away.

I screamed in frustration and couldn't believe I had once again not only been captured but also trusted the wrong people. Aurora I had never trusted but Seth? I had thought after he had saved my life and put a stop to his brother that it meant he was on our side. So none of it made sense? Was this their plan all along, to wait until the last possible second to find if Sammael failed then to intervene and come out of it looking like the heroes?

Well whatever it was, I would have to figure it out later as I had a much bigger problem to face now and that was the shit storm that was raging on around me. The noise was deafening and my screams of anger could barely be heard by my own ears so I didn't hold out much luck on being heard by someone who could free me. For starters I didn't even know what this thing was and I was tempted to just see if I could run through it. However knowing this place I thought taking the more cautious route was my best course of action.

Of course this decision didn't come to me in seconds but more like after being sat on the floor for half an hour with my knees to my chest, comforting myself anyway I could. I thought about not only what I could do but also of all the things that could be happening now? I knew that Aurora must have been in league with Alex at some point as she had been the one to change the necklace. I also knew that it must have been the key to unlocking his demon so I could only hope that by her smashing it against the wall it was enough to release him. I wondered if that meant he was awake now and being told of my death.

It was all too heart-breaking to think about and as I sat there on that hard dirt floor, I went through every emotion known to man. I went through the anger, the self-pity, and the sheer desperation in not knowing if Draven was alright. The worry that he might not get my letter explaining everything or the devastation he might have to endure thinking I was dead. And I certainly knew what that particular pain felt like.

It was all these thoughts combined that made me get up off

my feet and try something I wasn't sure wouldn't in fact just get me killed for real. But what were my other choices here…to wait for some demon thugs to come and get me, taking me to Gods only knew where. At least here people knew where I was, ok so they couldn't get to me but I had to trust in Sigurd's backup plan. Of course it does always help when you know what the actual backup plan is but that was broody, lone ranger types for you. They were a complete pain in the ass when it came to situations like now!

"Ok, here goes." I said for no reason as not even I could hear myself. I decided it was now or never, so I reached out with my fingertips and closed my eyes…

Which turned out to be a big mistake.

I started screaming and this time it could be heard. The pain was unlike anything I had felt before as I had never had my fingers stripped from skin and flesh. I pulled it back to me and felt my stomach turn at the sight of my three fingertips topped with bone. I turned and bent just in time to be sick to the side, bringing up the small amount I had eaten that morning. I kept being sick with both extreme pain and the thought that my fingers were now lost to me.

Tears streamed down my face and I cradled my hand to my chest being careful not to touch the ends. Then the other pain started, again one different from all the rest and by the time I had finished bringing up nothing more than bile I noticed something was happening. The new pain I was enduring was one I didn't mind so much when I found out the cause. So considering it was from putting my fingertips right again I slumped down to my knees and watched in amazement as my fingers reformed back to how they had always been. I was sure even the length of my fingernails was exactly the same.

"Well I won't be doing that again!" I said swiping my lips with the back of my hand. I looked down and stared at the floor until my sight went blurry. But wait, what was that? I was staring so hard I started to focus on a darker patch on the floor that for some reason was drawing me in. I don't know if it was just my mind playing tricks on me or even my hope getting the better of me but either way I couldn't seem to look away.

I bent over and not knowing what I was really doing I started to touch it. Remembering what happened last time I got too curious this time I quickly touched it and yanked my hand back. Thankfully there was no pain, so I did it again and again just to make sure before leaving my hand there. I frowned down at the patch as if waiting for it to do something more and after it didn't I started to get mad.

"Just do something you stupid spot!" I shouted irrationally wondering if losing your mind just added to the torture. I clawed at it hoping there was a hidden edge but there wasn't. I banged it with my palm hoping it would activate some kind of mechanism, like something out of Indiana Jones. But no, there was nothing and the more worked up and frustrated I got the angrier I became. In the end I lost it completely and before I knew it I was forming a fist and punching the ground.

"You stupid, stupid, stupid son of a...oh..." I was shouting at it one minute ignoring the pain of punching it until one of my knuckles started to bleed. The second time I hit it some of my blood smeared onto the floor and after that I was left in utter shock. Because now the deadly vortex started to disappear like a cyclone running out of air and with nothing left to power it, the tunnel of what had felt like razor dust started dispersing quickly.

Once I watched the air settle I got up on my feet and looked down at my hand. I turned it round and poked at the cut on my knuckle with my other finger. I collected some of the blood on the tip and brought it up to inspect it.

"Uh." I said and I don't know what I was expecting exactly

but I was a little disappointed to find it wasn't bright green and glowing. No, it looked no different than it always did and it was sad fact to admit but I had seen quite a lot of it over the time I had known Draven.

"So what now?" I asked myself finally being able to hear my own voice. I looked around the small cramped space and suddenly regretted not ever getting into rock climbing as a hobby.

"Ok, so new rule, if I live through this I am going to a survival army camp to learn kick ass survival skills!" I said as I jumped up at the first jutting rock that looked like it would make a good hand hold. I missed the first few times but got it on the third. I had already eyed up where I planned to put my foot and my converse squeaked against the rock before I could dig my toes in. I looked up as I hung there feeling like a plonker considering I had no clue what I was doing.

"Give me ivy any day of the week!" I huffed out before launching myself up to the next hold. I just managed to grip on but I didn't think I could hold it long as the strain hurt my fingers. My final triumph came when I thankfully reached the top of the ledge and by this time I barely had enough strength to lift myself up. I did this with no grace whatsoever and I grunted as I flopped onto my belly and dragged myself along until only my feet were dangling over the edge.

By this point I could only lay there panting trying to catch my breath.

"Gym Keira, you're getting your ass to a gym…" I said out loud to myself looking down at the floor with my forehead on my folded arms in front of me. I then took a deep breath and dragged my legs over the side when I heard a haunting sound.

"Oh shit!" I shouted scrabbling to my feet and making a run for it. I recognised the sound of the crank turning from before and all I could hope for was that I could make it to the door in time. I pushed myself like never before and ignored all the snarls and growls from the inmates below. They obviously had their own way of dealing with this torture but I wasn't going to wait around and find out if I could!

I saw the door coming closer and started chanting,

"You're going to make it, you're going to make it, you're... going...to...make...IT!" I shouted this last one out just as I flung myself against the door before the doors above swung open and a torrent of water escaped the small space into the cell below it. I grabbed the handle not waiting around to find out what happened next,

Only...

It was locked.

CHAPTER TWENTY

KEIRA

WHEN DID THIS TURN INTO A DAMN WESTERN?

I closed my eyes and could do nothing but wait for whatever Aurora had endured the first time round. I thought about all I had been through in my life trying to save Draven and knew it would come to this at some point. My endurance as a mortal could only stretch so far and evidently something would have to give, snap and break. And out of them all I would have put bets on the human going first.

Which was why, even though I wasn't brave enough to open my eyes and watch what my death was going to be, I refused to panic in the face of it. I refused to give in to my fear but in truth I just wished my body would follow my mind. Because all that was happening in these short and few seconds left was my whole body shaking waiting for the pain of death. My face was pressed to the door like I had the jaws of a predator breathing against my skin. My chest rose and fell with heavy gulping breaths that were out of sync with the way my limbs quivered. And beads of sweat rolled down my face to join the silent tears I shed. It was my end and with it...

I fell.

"Dang, what the Sam Hill?!" Ok, so I must admit, that wasn't the first thing I expected to hear when getting into Heaven. But then again neither was landing sideways into a hard body before being spun around violently and at the same time covered inside a big cape. I heard the door slam and after that the protective arm around my waist went slack.

"Tis alright now little lady." A gruff voice spoke and the strength in it made me a little reluctant to come out from under what was now obviously his long jacket. However when I did I couldn't hide my shock at who I was faced with.

"You're...you're a...uh...what are you?" I said stuttering as I struggled to form that sentence in sight of this mystery man.

"How'd I do you for little Miss, the names Bill." He said taking off his brown top hat and bending at the waist. I half expected all the things he had attached around his hat to come off but nothing moved.

"Uh, well I guess I could be better considering I'm a human stuck in the lowest levels of Hell and was about to be scalded to death because some bitch double crossed me and pushed me into a pit surround by a flesh eating twister..."

"Could be worse." He said making my mouth drop open as he put his hat back over his shoulder length, curly dark hair. I didn't need to ask what was worse because one look of disbelief on my face and he elaborated,

"You could be dead." To which I could only nod and agree with him.

"Time we vamoose little lady." Bill said walking past me, leaving me feeling bewildered. Was this guy real?

"Your name's Bill?" I asked thinking this must be a joke Hell was playing on me.

"Yup."

"Let me guess, first name 'Wild'." I said unable to help myself. He stopped walking and looked me up and down. One eyebrow went lower and then he said,

"Have we met before?" To which I nearly burst out laughing.

"Umm, nope, definitely not because don't take this the wrong way but I think I would have remembered you." And this couldn't be a truer statement. Because the very last thing I thought I would find down here was a bloody steampunk cowboy!

"They call me Wild Bill Hickok." He said tipping the rim of his hat and again my mouth opened like a damn fish.

"Wait! Are you telling me you are the Wild Bill?" I said in disbelief. I mean the Wild West wasn't my forte or anything but there was a handful of famous cowboy names everyone knew and Wild Bill was about as famous as they came.

"The one and only, darlin'." He winked at me and then turned on his metal heeled boots and walked away expecting me to follow.

"Ok, so even if you are who you say you are, why should I trust you, cowboy?" I said knowing he had saved my life yes, but knowing that Aurora needed me alive and that there was someone coming to get me, I couldn't really trust anyone at this juncture. So I started backing away and he looked over his shoulder to see me putting distance between us. He rolled his eyes once before turning back to me and then held up his hands, on which he wore cut off fingerless leather gloves that were cracked with age.

"Tis alright now little lady, don't you be fearin' of old Bill."

"Don't come any closer, cowboy!" I said as he started to

walk closer to me. I didn't want to trust those midnight blue eyes no matter how kind they looked.

"It's Keira right?" Bill said and then my heart started to race when he pulled out a gun from one of his holsters and pointed it at me. I nodded and swallowed hard. I was just about to resign myself to the fact he was going to make me follow him at gun point when he surprised me by saying,

"Then duck and get behind me." I didn't even hesitate to do as I was told when I heard the familiar sound behind me of a Harpie's hissing. I ran behind him as I heard the shots going off and by the time I turned all six Harpies were on the floor and trying to drag their damaged bodies away. I half expected him to blow the smoke from the end of his gun but instead he just scattered the floor with empty shells and refilled it again from the bullet stash on his gun belt. He then rolled the revolver back in place with a flick of his wrist and once it clicked home he walked closer to the wining creatures dying on the floor.

One looked up as he approached and snarled before saying,

"She killed our mother." And Bill looked round to me with an eyebrow raised. I lifted my hands as he had not long ago done to me and before I could speak my defence he said,

"Double crossing Lickspittle?" I frowned and said,

"Uhh…If that means bitch then yeah, that's her." He nodded once and then without looking down he unloaded all six bullets into each of their heads. My mouth gaped open at what seemed to be the theme being round this guy seeing as he didn't even look to aim once. He didn't even need to look to make sure he had killed all of them, he was that confident in his skill. No, he just spun his gun round his finger and holstered it like the coolest cowboy in the world. Then to make it even cooler he started walking, stopped next to me and said,

"I'm no cowboy, I'm a lawman," and then carried on walking.

"Holy shit." I whispered in awe of the guy. One I was definitely sticking with like Winnie stuck in the Poo!

"Hey wait up!" I shouted as I ran to catch up with my new protector.

"So who sent you?" I asked looking up at yet another tall man making me think I should start asking people to buy me high heeled shoes this Christmas...! Did they do converse high tops with heels I wondered? Well if there was one person on this planet that would know it would have been Pip that was for sure!

"The Big Bug." He answered...or at least I think he did!

"Sorry?" I asked shaking my head.

"Why? You ain't no Corncracker." He said confusing me further.

"Ok, so now I am lost..." He smiled at me, scratched his beard and ran his finger and thumb down either side of his thick moustache that reminded me of handle bars on a motorbike.

"You said sorry but you don't strike me down as stupid like some buck tooth farmer that could eat corn through a picket fence."

"Uhh...O...kay...well thanks, *I guess.*" I said left utterly confused now and wondering if he was complimenting me on my teeth.

"Good, now let's vamoose." I wanted to ask what he meant but seeing as he'd said it before I just put two and two together and was surprised I didn't get 66 reasons to be confused. I started to follow him and tried to take in everything about his appearance. He wore massive heavy leather boots with wicked looking spurs attached in deadly spikes. They were very detailed with scenes of a skeleton riding a motorbike drinking whiskey and it reminded me of the comic Ghost rider.

I was happy to report his beige trousers were void of tasselled chaps but instead had the manlier gun holster strapped to his thigh along with a long thin sabre hanging down. The other side held his bigger gun that fit snuggly in the holster that attached to his thick gun belt, one that was decorated with rows and rows of bullets.

"Look in your fill sugar, old Bill doesn't mind." He said looking sideways and catching me eyeing him up. Obviously he was taking my interest in him the wrong way.

"I am just trying to way up why you're helping me?" I said honestly.

"Usually I would say I owe a demon a debt."

"So that's not the case this time?" I asked making him smirk. He had a handsome face that although a little weathered, it just added to his charm. He had little laughter lines in the corners of his eyes which reminded me of Draven sometimes. His eyes were kind and thoughtful, which dangerously drew you into trusting him. His hair looked a little wild with some curls tighter and perfectly formed as opposed to the ones that were more of an unruly wave.

His nose looked to have been broken at some point but didn't by any means detract from his handsome features. One of which was a dimple that became a creased line half way up his cheek and only made its appearance when he smiled. It was the type of mark that I could imagine a lover caressing after affectionately making him laugh. I don't really know where that thought came from but it was so strong I blushed.

"No, although I do owe him my soul." I almost missed his answer when getting lost in my thoughts.

"You owe a man your soul?" I asked horrified.

"You're a bit of a biddy little lady ain't ya?" He said and again there was that dimple.

"I don't know what Biddy means." I said and he laughed before saying,

"Probably a good thing seeing as it would just make you

more biddy." He sniggered and turned a corner. I frowned at his back and huffed hating not knowing what a stupid biddy was.

"So, are more of them going to be after us?" I said letting the biddy comment go after deciding this was a far more important question that needed answering. I could only hope of course that I would understand the answer.

"I would think so, but don't worry little lady, I got plenty more bad plums for 'em for when they do." Uh, I wanted to tell him that I don't think rotten fruit was going to cut it until I realised he meant bullets when I noticed him patting his gun belt.

"Are we going back to the Janus Gate?" I asked trying to keep up with his long legged stride. He was about the same height as Draven but it became obvious that Draven took my shorter legs into account when we were walking together. Now though, I was practically jogging next to Bill just trying to keep up.

"Yeah, that's what I'm fixin' on doing but I reckon we need to get a wiggle on." He said and I hid my smile at hearing the way he spoke. It was almost as bad as trying to understand Pip and I would have said, if she wasn't blissfully married to Adam, then this guy would have been the perfect second for her.

"Okey dokey" I said sounding like an idiot, one he looked at like he couldn't understood a word I said, which was just laughable considering who I was speaking to.

"You have all your saddle bags in the right place?"

"Eh, yeah thanks." He nodded and I rolled my eyes as soon as he turned his back and started walking again.

We continued on pretty much down the same path that Aurora had led me down but for some reason we seemed to get to our destination a lot quicker than before. I put this down more to despising the company in Aurora than the fact that I had to practically run to keep up with Daddy Wild West long legs here!

"Oh thank God." I said out loud and received a disapproving frown from Bill.

"Now I've gone and taken a cotton to ya, so don't you going spoiling that purely purdy self of yours by cussing little lady."

"Uh…come again?" I asked wondering what on earth a purdy was.

"No cussing and taking the Lord's name in vain." He elaborated and I snorted in disbelief. This was a demon I was speaking to …right?

"You're serious?"

"As serious as squatting on your Spurs." He said and just his face alone answered my question.

"Alrighty then." I said making him tip the rim of his hat at me again before praising me,

"Good girl".

I was left standing there looking a bit bewildered by the guy. I mean I know that not all demons are bad guys as I have learnt many times before this day but God fearing demon folk that don't like swearing? The mind just boggles.

"What the Sam Hill!" Bill shouted from across the Temple, causing something I once again had no clue to what it meant echo around the room.

"What is it?" I asked climbing over one of the giant fingers that looked like a tree log. I almost got stuck with me straddling it in between my legs and my mind flooded with so many rude jokes I had to bite my lip. This was to stop from obviously upsetting the gentleman cowboy, lawman steampunk dude but also to stop from breaking the cardinal geeky sin and that was when someone starts snorting at their own jokes.

"The gate, it's gone…it's…why that Cultus dung eating…"

"…Bitch?" I said finishing it off for him so that he didn't

have to be the one cussing as he called it. He didn't agree but I took his growl as one aimed at Aurora and not me.

"So what do we do now?" I asked like one of those annoying sidekicks that ended up being more of a hindrance than any help. However even knowing this I still couldn't help from asking the irritating question, the poor guy.

"Hell fire and horse feathers!" He said ignoring my 'Uh?' and continuing on,

"First thing is to get out of this Shindig little lady." He reached out his gloved hand for me to take as he helped me over the rest of the broken limbs on the floor.

A short time later and I had seriously hit my limit of playing the lamb and following blindly behind people I either didn't like or didn't know. Wild Bill Hickok had been quiet for most of the endless walk through Tartarus and for the most part we came across no one. I did notice though that when we arrived at some doors, Bill stopped me so he could listen to what I gathered was whether or not the coast was clear. There had only been one incident where Bill had to take care of, and when I mean take care of I actually mean spear through the chest with his sword.

The creature he dispatched looked like a guard of some kind as he was clearly wearing a uniform, one that hid his face from view. I had to admit I was glad if some of the creatures in the prison cell I was locked in with were to go by.

I nearly asked at one point if all cowboys had swords as he was the first I knew of. Ok, so my Wild West trivia was lacking at best but really, a sword? Unless he was at some point part of the Cavalry, speaking of which it would have been nice to see Tartarus stormed by the Afterlife crew but I guess I couldn't complain considering I was still alive thanks to Wyatt Earp here.

As we walked I started to notice even more about him and that included the poker hand he had attached to his hat.

"Are you any good?" I asked nodding to his hat that held a pair of black aces and a pair of black eights that looked slightly blood stained. He smiled down at me as he held open a door for me that led into a massive spiral staircase which was half covered by the biggest looking thorns I had ever seen!

"The dead man's hand." He said and my frown was all he needed before he continued.

"That's what it's known as, the dead man's hand, on account of the fact that I died holding that hand." I almost tripped up on my step and tumbled down the neck breaking fall.

"You died playing poker?!" I shouted in my shock. I mean it was true, I didn't know the guy but still hearing how someone died from that living breathing person's mouth was a shocker for anyone.

"I did and when I was winning too that dang boot-licker but look at me I could yarn the hours away, you be careful of the soulweed little Miss." He said pulling me a step further away from the deadly looking thorns that looked like spears desperate to feel blood at their tips. I took his advice and started to concentrate on my footing in this giant tunnel going straight down. Being in this place I didn't think we could actually get any further down but here we were and from the looks of things, we were heading deeper into the pit that was Hell.

"I thought we were trying to get out of here?" I had to say after stewing on the silent questions I had for too long.

"We surely are but there is only...wait." He said breaking off what he started saying when a shadow fell over us and we both looked up at the same time.

"Well Butter my Butt and call me Biscuit. That's a lot of bad plums I'm gonna need."

"I really need to learn how to fire a gun" I said after Bill's comment about needing bullets and his response had me laughing in the face of danger,

"Well darlin you're in luck, because here comes your target practice!"

"You're darn straight!" I said making sure not to swear but taking one of his guns from him and trying to act confident with it. Because there above us was a swarm of Harpies by the hundreds...

And they were pissed!

CHAPTER TWENTY-ONE

KEIRA

SPINNING UNDER CONTROL

You could have dropped a double decker bus down the centre of the staircase and it wouldn't even have touched the sides. Which meant it was unfortunately big enough for Harpies by the hundreds to come flying at us from above. Wild Bill held his guns up ready and I did the same but he looked like he was having second thoughts. He looked to the centre of the staircase with one raised eyebrow like he was calculating his next move.

I couldn't believe how calm he seemed in the face of such danger and it helped settle my own nerves. There was just something that drew you in around Bill that made you trust him and his judgement…well that was until he grabbed me around the waist, pulled me close and said,

"Trust me Little Bean." The endearing nickname made me nod but my eyes widened as he walked us backwards to the edge of the stairs, closer to the immense drop. I found myself now with two dangers to whip my head between and now I was the one calculating which was going to be worse...Falling to my death or being torn apart by ugly bat women!

"I want you to stick to me like a grey back, you got me?"

"Uh not really. But I will hold on if that's what you mean." I said having no clue what a grey back was. He winked at me before he reached my arms up to hook them around his neck...

Then we fell.

He had walked us backwards off the edge together and I screamed as we fell down the centre. His long jacket tails flapped up around us and with Bill's arms extended straight up he fired shot after shot up at the Harpies. I turned my head to try and see what was happening and just saw Harpies dropping like flies and spiralling out of control, crashing into the sides of the staircase. I would have liked to have asked what was going to happen when we hit the bottom but I thought now wasn't a great time seeing as he needed his wits about him.

I still couldn't see the floor and couldn't express how happy this made me that was until I felt a Harpie get close enough to dig her talons in my leg.

"AHHH!" I screamed as I felt the tips of claws dig in my flesh and through my jeans.

"Eat lead Varmint!" Bill said and just as the Harpie raised her head to snarl at him he shot her in the face blowing most of her jaw off. Then a swift kick to the head and she finally let go.

"Hold on!" Bill shouted and I knew without looking we had reached the end. I closed my eyes and heard the whoosh instead of the last sound I thought to hear which would be our landing on solid ground. Instead the noise I heard was one I could never forget and one I used to dream about whenever I was far from Draven...

It was the sound of wings.

I opened my eyes and looked to see two massive copper coloured wings that were incredible. They were made up from what looked like thousands of knitted wire feathers that looked far too delicate to take on the strain of keeping two bodies in the air but that was what they were doing. He had unleashed them at just the right moment to save us from breaking every bone in our bodies from the landing. He brought us upright and I looked up to see Harpies still continuing to travel down at us in a spiral pattern.

I heard the raining of bullet shells and for both our sakes wished he was one of these new age cowboys that was packing a semi-automatic from the movies that never ran out of bullets!

"We gotta move!" He said clicking his revolver back and firing at the closest grey bodies that looked to be dive bombing us. I looked all around the round empty space that was mostly covered by the thickest roots of what he called soulweed but managed to spot a door.

"There's a door!" I shouted over the sounds of bullets flying hoping his amazing skills at shooting things extended to his ability to hear frantic screaming.

"GO!" He shouted back and I frowned at his back as he cocked the hammer back with his palm for a quicker fire.

"I'm not leaving you!" I shouted back and he shot me a look of disbelief over his shoulder.

"Dang Loco She stock!" He said shaking his head before firing off another two rounds before swapping to his other loaded gun.

"Run and I will cover you as I follow!" I nodded for no reason as he couldn't see me anyway but I did as I was told and ran for the door. I winced and covered my head with my arms as one of the Harpies snuck through and came for me. It was just about to reach out but then after a brief look of horror on its snarling face it fell to the ground. As it fell the sight of Bill stood there behind it with a smoking barrel aimed right at us. He nodded to the door and then turned just in time to get one between the eyes. There was no doubt about it the man had skills with a gun that was for sure.

There was no door handle on the arched door so I pushed it with all the measly strength and I jumped when an arm came from behind me and pushed along with me. I like to think it was our combined strength that made the door open but really who was I kidding, it was all from the demon at my back.

We almost fell into the room and as I was stumbling forward trying to catch myself Bill was already slamming the door behind me. I turned just as he was fitting a large plank across the door slotting it into the iron holders to keep it locked. All I could think was to thank any God that was listening for it not being locked before we came through it.

I leant over putting my hands on my knees to catch my breath not from running but from the massive adrenaline rush I had received through being chased through the air. I was by no means an adrenaline junkie which was funny considering the amount of crazy shit I had no choice but to do!

"Bloody Supernaturals with wings." I muttered making Bill laugh, which I had to admit wasn't a bad sound to be hearing right now. It seemed to relax my shattered nerves and after another deep breath I was back to normal. It was one of those deep belly laughs that he actually needed to throw his head back to let it out.

I smiled but hid it by pulling up my jeans to check out the cuts on my leg from the now dead Harpie. Thankfully it wasn't too deep and had already stopped bleeding.

"So, what now, cowboy?" And before he could say it I beat him to it,

"Sorry, I meant Lawman." He nodded behind me and I turned from his smirk to find an opening.

"And do we know what's through there?" I asked just as the banging started from the other side making me jump.

"Not sure but I'm reckonin' there ain't no Harpies in there."

"And how do you know that?" I asked trying not to jump again at the sound of them trying to break the door down.

"Because every one of those she devils are *out* there trying to get *in* here." Ok so he had a good point and this became emphasized even more when the first cracks started to appear in the door.

"Ok let's go!" I shouted.

"Good choice little Miss." He agreed and stormed past me grabbing my hand and pulling me through the opening. We jogged on through the dark passageway and I was glad he kept hold of my hand so it was easier for me to keep up when he half pulled me. We were nearly through to the other side when we heard the echo of a door being smashed through. The light at the end was bright enough to give me hope as it lit up the fact we didn't have much farther to run.

We burst through the opening and only one thing escaped me,

"Oh Hell no!" This of course was in response to the river of fire that cut off any means of escape. The space we walked into was a huge cavern like an underground air pocket in the mountain. I couldn't actually tell what the river was but at least it wasn't lava. The liquid looked like black water and was covered by a fluttering of blueish flames dancing on the surface. It was almost like there was an invisible layer of gas feeding the fire. I looked around and counted at least ten holes in the rock face where the dark water poured from and cascaded down into the river below.

"What do we do now?" I asked only to find him near the edge by a strange looking boat. It looked as if it was made of cast iron and held together by strips of metal and riveted together. It was bent, twisted and charred and there was absolutely no way I was getting in that thing!

It was a long, wide rowing boat and as I walked closer to Bill I was horrified by what I saw. There, mounted on the sides, were six mutilated bodies that had no legs. Each had all four limbs amputated above the joints with their arms removed for a purpose. On the sides of the boat closest to the water these poor souls had prosthetic contraptions that attached to the oars for rowing. And if that wasn't torturous enough then they also had their eyelids and mouths sewn shut. It was disgustingly dreadful.

"Oh no! No, no, no I am not getting on that thing, for starters I remember my last boat trip in Hell and that was quite enough for one lifetime thank you very much."

"I'll grant ya it ain't no Mississippi river boat…" At this my laugh interrupted him and I looked past him to the creature at the stern of the boat that obviously controlled the disfigured lackeys. She too was missing her limbs and also mounted in what looked like an iron chastity belt. The obvious difference was that not only was she a woman, if her large naked breasts were to go by but also attached to the metal stumps on her arms were long whips that were meant for only one purpose.

"You think?" I said in response to the Mississippi comment. He nodded behind me at the shadows of Harpie bodies making their way through the passageway as they were nearly here.

"Okey dokey, creepy ass boat it is!" I said walking past him to said creepy ass boat.

"I thought so." He said in all smugness, one I would let slide in light of the killer horde that wanted to render me like the unfortunate limbless souls that were strapped to this boat. To be honest the balance of insanity only just tipped towards me getting on the boat and if my rock climbing had been any better, then I might have taken my chances playing spider monkey.

Once on the boat Bill stepped up to what I presumed was called the captain creepo and I watched him pull a leather coin bag from his pocket. He then flipped her a coin which amazingly she caught in her mouth and then swallowed it. It kind of reminded me of the action of a sea lion and I wasn't far wrong in thinking about this like a freak show. If that was the case then did that make Bill the ring master?

In the middle of the boat was a black worn chesterfield couch with an overly sized high back that curled over at the top. I sat down in it not knowing what else to do and half expected to be cast off this death ride for doing something wrong. Bill came to sit down next to me and we set off just in time as all the harpies had just burst through the opening at once.

"Won't they just be able to fly and get us?" I asked looking frantic with worry we would be sitting ducks out here, ripe for the limb picking.

"You watch now, it will be like hazing a tenderfoot."

"Uh…a what now?" I asked having no clue what a tenderfoot was. In the end the sight of them all stopping near the edge and snarling as we drifted further away from them caught my attention.

"Why won't they fly…oh…eww" I cut myself off when I saw one try its luck and as soon as it flew over the water it caught alight and was burnt to ash in seconds.

"No don't you go worrying that pretty little head of yours darlin', anything in this boat is safe as long as it stays in the boat, you get me?"

"Oh yes, loud and clear." I said thinking he was going to be hard pushed even getting me out of this damn thing once we got to wherever we were going. I let things settle in my mind or more like the racing of my heart calm down and I only accomplished this if I didn't look at the gruesome creatures that were powering this boat. The sounds of the lash hitting flesh made me flinch every time she threw her whip and I got the feeling Bill wanted to comfort me but didn't know how. However I did receive a pat on the leg and an 'It's alright little lady'.

For what felt a long time nothing was said and after giving my mind time to bombard myself with unanswered questions I had to speak out.

"So let me get this straight, Aurora somehow managed to close the Janus gate, the way we both came in?"

"I reckon so and she wouldn't have done it alone either, I'd bet my whiskey on it." He said patting a hip flask that was tucked into his leather waistcoat pocket. I couldn't see what was written on it but I was sure it had a picture of the devil on it.

"Seth." I said his name on a hiss knowing now they were in league with each other. It made me wonder if his fake concern for RJ had just been a ploy to stay at Afterlife for this reason and if so, what were they planning exactly? And another thing I couldn't understand was why they needed me alive or more importantly *who* needed me alive?

"You think that's the Boot-licker that helped the charlatan trick you down here?"

"She mentioned leaving to be with him so it all makes sense why he didn't help us at the Temple until the very end." I said looking out at the vast wasteland we had been travelling down for a while.

"Temple?" Bill asked and I turned back to him and offered him a small smile before saying,

"It's a long story." To which he nodded back to the wasteland and said,

"I think we got time Little Miss."

I had to laugh and looking at the blue flames flickering in the line we travelled down as far as the eye could see I decided he was right, we certainly had time. So I said the one thing that was necessary if I was going to tell him all that had happened,

"Call me Keira."

The rest of the way we both shared information with each other. For example I told him everything that had happened to do with not only what was happening now but also what had happened last year with Draven pretending to be dead so that a prophecy that claimed he would take my life would never happen. When hearing this he referred the fates as being as useful as a bull with tits to which I burst out laughing in a fit of snorts. I think at one point he was worried I couldn't breathe because he started patting my back and he continued to do so until I held up my hand and said,

"I'm good."

In return he told me that this was the only way he knew of that could get us out of Tartarus because unless you had the right payment then it wasn't possible. I asked more into this and he told me that having the right coin to pay the right ferryman was not something you could easily come by and with the barriers back in place it was literally the only other way in or out now the Janus gate had been disabled.

I remembered my own coin and the way it had taken me straight to the Prince of Lust or better known as Daddy Draven. So I gathered this was the way everything was done around here and in some way it made sense and I looked at it almost like a bus token. When I said as much it was Bill's turn to laugh.

When I asked him what he was in Hell exactly he told me he worked as a bounty hunter collecting the souls of the 'wanted' or 'marked' as they were also known. I was really keen to hear more about this but as soon as I mentioned

Draven's name he shut down. It didn't take a genius to know there was obviously no love lost between the two and even though I really wanted to know I decided to leave this well alone. So instead I asked more about the 'Dead man's hand' he had in his hat thinking that as he had already mentioned this once before it obviously wasn't a touchy subject.

He explained his story and told me he was mainly remembered for his services in Kansas as sheriff of Hays City. But he also was a marshal of Abilene, where his ironhanded rule helped to tame two of the most lawless towns on the frontier. As you can imagine he said this with pride and I could understand how he accomplished this seeing how good a shot he was. I didn't know much about the Wild West but what I did know from listening to my Grandad talk about watching his westerns was that the only thing that mattered for a longer life back then was how good your shot was.

I asked him if this was the case how he ended up playing poker and his answer was simple.

"If ain't no longer broken then it don't need fixin now does it." To which my answer was just a simple sounding,

"Ah."

"Besides, after one particular gunfight I no longer had a taste for using my lead for killing." This surprised me and I wanted to know more but I could tell not to push it as his face said enough…guilt.

So after that he moved on to his other talents and that was usually with a deck of cards. He told me how he was known to be able to shoot all six rounds without sighting his pistol at the ace of spades from fifty yards away. Each was of course a direct hit at the spade, which was ironic he always used this card considering he was holding it when he died.

I asked him about it and was surprised he talked about it with ease. He told me while in Deadwood Dakota Wild Bill

Hickok became a regular poker player at Nuttal & Mann's Saloon. One afternoon a man came in and sat down at his table to try his luck but he didn't know at the time his own luck at who should be sat opposite him and the offer he would receive. During the game the stranger told him he had heard about his recent brush with death by one young drifter by the name of Jack McCall.

Jack McCall had the belief that if he killed himself a famous gunfighter that he too would become famous for the act. Of course he was right but that fame wouldn't last him long whilst still breathing. Less than a year later after avoiding his trial it only took two days once they had in him custody to find McCall guilty and on March 1, 1877 he was executed by hanging. And to the rest of the mortal world that was the end of it. And if the person he had been playing poker with at the time hadn't have sat in that chair opposite him then it would have been.

But instead he gave Wild Bill Hickok, famous gunfighter of the west an offer he couldn't refuse. He told me at first he thought that the man was not sound of mind but after proving to him he had certain gifts that could not be proven as false he decided getting drunk was the best answer.

"Well it was either finding my answers at the bottom of a bottle or at the end of my gun."

"So what happened next?" I asked him, almost forgetting our grim surroundings and folding up my legs on the seat like a small child getting lost in the story.

"Well I got full as a tick and after taking my last shot and talking too fast and thinking too slow, I agreed if he won the game I would accept his offer." I smiled knowing he obviously lost but I still had to ask,

"What hand did he win with?"

"Royal flush, yeah, that Big Bug city slicker had me good! I just put my hand on the table and the next thing I know that Dang, Young Whippersnapper, a boy so slow he couldn't catch a cold had shot me in the back like some yellow belly, lowdown, dirty, sneaking polecat and then ran out the door before my head hit the table!" He said slapping his hands together to add the sound effects of him hitting the table.

"So what did you bargain for?"

"My soul." He said calmly as if he was talking about making a deal for a horse and a packet of tobacco.

"In exchange for what?!" I shouted a bit too loudly.

"Calm your little britches Miss Keira, it all turned out just shiny." He went on to explain that the reason this 'Big Bug', which I found out was cowboy slang for big boss man, had come to that table because he'd heard of his skills at finding people. Of course none of those skills meant much if they belonged to a mortal so all the boss had to do was sit back and wait for something he knew was about to happen.

Bill had given him his soul in exchange for eternal life as a demon on the grounds that as soon as he completed the job he would be granted his soul back and be a free demon to do as he pleased. I had thought this wasn't a bad deal until I found out that he still hadn't completed the job, hence still having a 'Big Bug' to answer to.

"It ain't all bad, not considering we became pretty good comrades over the years spent together, besides his cause is a sound one." Bill said playing with what I now noticed was a strange coin hung from a black leather thong around his neck. It almost looked like two coins back to back held together by what looked like…

"Is that a bullet?" I asked getting distracted and reaching over to touch it.

"Hey what ya…" I didn't hear the end of what he said because as soon as my fingertips came into contact with the coins I was a goner! The last thing I felt was my eyes roll back up in my head and my mind went blank.

———

"Hey now, come on little bean, your horse is getting restless." I heard Bill's voice speaking to me and felt fingers prodding at my face.

"For fuck sake Jim, she doesn't have a bloody horse and probably doesn't understand a fuckin word you say!" I felt myself frown at the voice that was familiar but one I hadn't heard in a long while so I couldn't be sure. And who was Jim?

"Bill? Where's Bill?" I heard myself ask in a croaky voice that was starting to get panicky.

"Calling me Jim might not be firing all rounds Corncracker, seeing as she knows and trusts me as Bill!" I could tell it was Bill's voice saying this without any doubt so had to wonder if Jim wasn't his real name?

"Come on Darlin' open those pretty eyes for us." I had to wonder who the 'us' was and knew the only way I would find out is if I did what he asked. So I opened my eyes and Bill said,

"Good girl, now this here is the Big Bug I was telling you about." As soon as my vision cleared like it does first thing in the morning after a heavy sleep I ended up shouting the one name I least expected to…

"Jared?!"

CHAPTER TWENTY-TWO

KEIRA

RIDE EM OUT COWBOYS

I couldn't believe when I woke up I was bombarded with the craziest sense of déjà vu and there was an easy answer as to why. I not only opened my eyes to the handsome sight of Jared stood over me but also the sight of an entrance to an entirely different type of Hell.

"Is that the Hellfire caves?" I asked getting up slowly and putting a hand to my head as I felt like I would pass out again at the slightest movement. I didn't know what had happened when I touched that damn coin but now I felt like my mind had been violated!

"It is Kitten." He almost purred my name and it took me back to the first time we ever met in his underground fight club. A pair of silver grey eyes was all it took for me to fall apart and burst into tears. I felt myself being picked up and placed in someone's lap and when I heard Jared's soft voice whispering in my ear words of comfort, I knew I finally felt safe.

"I made it…I…mmm…made…it…I…" I sobbed feeling the past hours of life threatening experiences finally float away just in the arms of someone I truly trusted and one I called friend. Poor Bill didn't know where to put himself and in the end told Jared he would give us a moment alone.

"I know pet, I know." He hummed smoothing back my hair. It took me a while to pull myself together and I felt embarrassed after my meltdown but I knew the whole experience had just topped my limit. There is something so mentally challengingly about survival that when it is achieved you become so overwhelmed and thankful for it that you need to get it out and express it anyway you can. Some people shout and dance about it. Some people pray and offer their thanks to the Lord they believe in. And some people, just like me, bawl like a baby to the first person they care about.

"You good?" Jared asked me after I had finally started breathing normally and was no longer washing his t-shirt disgustingly with my snotty nose. I tried to wipe it as I moved away to which he just laughed.

"No worries Kitten, you should see me drool after a pretty girl when I'm…"

"All beasty?" I said interrupting him on a laugh and he smirked at me.

"Yeah, all beasty." He repeated shaking his head at me and running a hand over his dark charcoal colour hair that for once was free from its usual leather tie.

"Eww by the way." I said as he gave me his rough hand to help me up. You could tell he was a biker alright just from the look of his hands, well that and his boots.

They were the same cracked leather ones I had always seen him wearing with the laces only tied halfway up the calf. One flopped over more than the other and heavy buckles gave them that bad ass look he seemed to have down so well.

"I will give you 'eww' in a minute if you don't get your sweet ass on my bike." He said nodding to a group that must have been his biker posse.

"Why, where are we going?" I asked noticing his mammoth sized brother whose black skin looked like silky chocolate you just wanted to lick. He too was a handsome man but it was hard not to be afraid of him as the dude looked like he could snap my bones and then use them to pick his teeth after a Keira BBQ!

"Where do you think Doll, we gotta get you to a party!" He said winking at me.

"Uh, I think we have got more important things to think about other than a party, don't you?"

"Oh I know you won't want to miss this one, not considering who will be on the guest list." I almost snarled out her name,

"Aurora."

"The one and only Titan bitch."

"But wait…" I said reaching out and holding him back by the arm. He stopped, turning back to me and followed my gaze to where Bill stood shaking hands with some of Jared's men.

"It complicated, Keira." I knew he was being serious when he called me by my given name.

"Then uncomplicate it for me, Jared." I said proving two could play that game. He rolled his eyes and ran a hand down his face in exasperation. He smoothed down his black wiry beard and pulled it more into a point which I knew was a habit of his. His almond shaped eyes held my wide ones for a moment before he closed the distance between us.

"Do you not think we have more important business to get to?" At this I made a huff sound before starting my rant.

"Yeah I do, but I have just had it to my neck and back with

being double crossed or betrayed by people that are supposed to be on our side. For God's sake I just spent over six months with a guy whose only real intension was to kill me and take over the world with a posse of old, pissed off gods that got their asses handed to them and kicked into Hell. So excuse me if I find it hard to trust again." By this point he held up both his hands in surrender and said,

"Alright, alright, you have a point Pet, don't go all bat shit woman crazy on me."

"Tell me about you being Mr Big Bug." He winced and said

"I fucking hate it when he calls me that… Jesus."

"Yeah well he isn't fond of anyone swearing either." At this he rolled his eyes again only this time it wasn't directed at me.

"Yeah well let's just say he's stuck in 1876 and being a demon hasn't curbed his religious views or damn Western manners." Jared said grabbing my arm and pulling me over to the flint stone wall that framed the courtyard and entrance to the Hellfire caves.

"Ok so I take it you trust him?" I asked and he gave me one of those 'What do you think' looks.

"Hey, like I said, you can't blame me. Aurora said someone would be coming for me and I know Bill saved my life but I have to be sure on this one. Because whoever Aurora is answering to then she made it clear that they need me alive and if it had been left up to that Bitch then I would be roasting over a spit with an apple in my mouth and playing host in a Harpie buffet." Jared growled at the mention of what had gone on and finally understood that I needed answers.

Jared went on to tell me how Sigurd had turned up at his club and as soon as he mentioned my name Jared knew it meant trouble. I asked how he had reached him so quickly after I left but he just winked at me and told me he had his ways, so I left it at that.

I was thankful when he told me how he had come to know Bill and that he was in fact the man that had sat opposite him that day in the Nuttal & Mann's Saloon in Deadwood, South Dakota. He told me that he had heard about the talents of the famous Wild Bill and knew he needed him for a job, one he refused to tell me about.

I wasn't surprised when he skipped past this bit considering his face said it all. It was obvious that this matter was one that was both personal and painful for him, so I didn't push for it. All I needed to know, he assured me, was that he sought out Bill for this job and once it was over then he would be free to live his immortality anyway he chose.

He became a member on his council and through the years working together they formed a friendship.

"I mean shit, if I could I would have offered his soul back decades ago but once you become blood bound then it can't be taken back. In the end it wouldn't matter…"

"What do you mean?" I had asked him and he shook his head and looked away. For a few minutes I didn't think he was going to answer me.

"There was a reason he was in Tartarus, Pet."

"Yeah I know, he came to save m…he wasn't there to save me?" I asked when he started shaking his head.

"He was there as a prisoner." I gasped and my hands covered my mouth in shock. I had no idea this was why he was down there and that his break out only mirrored my own.

"Alright, I am going to cut a long story short and we will leave it at that so we can get the fuck outta here and stop this Bitch." I nodded my understanding and waited for it.

"Something happened a while back and he took the fall for it in hopes it would take him to those who could help with his mission. It's fucked up complicated shit that I am not going into no matter how much you give me that puppy eyes crap, but just know that when it came down to it he followed my orders to save your ass and gained his freedom by doing so from the one that sent him there." I was still trying to digest this when a terrible thought occurred to me.

"Oh no, please don't tell me…"

"Yeah, it was your lover boy that sent him to that shit hole and only his word or the word of his next in command can give the order for his release…Lucky for you we all had a backup plan that even you didn't know about. King Vamp got Snake Eye to track me down and seeing as I was responsible for Jim's soul, I was the only one who could communicate with him."

"So you were his possession officer?!" I shouted making him groan. I remembered Draven telling me about them not long after I had first discovered the Temple.

"Yeah, some shit like that." He said and if I didn't know any better I would have said he looked embarrassed.

"So you guys knew Aurora would double cross me?"

"We had an idea yes. Lucius tried to warn the King about her deception long before they became enemies but well, to be blunt your boyfriend can be a stubborn dick sometimes."

"Oi! I mean I agree he is a stubborn ass on occasion…" He gave me a pointed look tipping his head at me and I rolled my eyes before I said,

"Ok, ok, so yeah most of the time but still, you could be nicer about it." At this he laughed and it was booming.

"Oh Kitten, we are Kings, do you really think we give a shit about being nice about it! He rules his realm, one we all live in but there are plenty of creatures he can't ever rule. The shadow lands of chaos, the demonic beasts of my kin thanks to my Hell's bite, the Vampires Lucius creates…do you think he controls them all?"

"Well I…uh…well to be honest nobody ever really explains

it to me, so excuse me for just guessing." I said getting snippy making him smirk.

"And there's no need to be a smug bastard about it." I snapped. He laughed and said,

"But I am a smug bastard, Kitten it comes with being one of those arrogant Kings." And then he winked at me.

"So where is this party we are talking about?" I asked and he smirked down at me before pulling something from his leather biker jacket that looked older than most men. The bright green envelope was covered in mermaids that on closer view were actually mermen dressed as women as they all had boobs and moustaches.

"Pip!" I shouted knowing that it couldn't possibly be from anyone else. Jared nodded as I tore into the green paper and was instantly met with googly eyes that sprung out at you when you pulled it free. I laughed when Jared groaned,

"Jesus."

I opened it up and had to shake out the confetti shaped like little pink willies and my little ponies. It read...

'That's right bitches, it's my party and your ass is invited!
So what are you waiting for, you don't have long to go get me a
present and I don't want no cheap ebay crap from China you
hear!
Boozy punch is included along with a punch up from boozy men
lol ;)
Bring your shanizzel and be ready to dance like no one is
watching, (although everyone will be watching, as it is a party
you dune buggy! So bring the funk to my funky town and be
ready to have the time of however many lives you have lived!
Be there or be the square in this bitchin' heart shaped hole!
Boo Yeah!
Love Pip

P.S...Oh yeah, I should mention it's at Witley Court and starts when the last mortal is out for the Devil's count!

"Witley court?" I asked looking up at him.

"Been there before by any chance?" He replied sarcastically and I looked down at his feet and decided to get him back by saying,

"You know sparkly penis confetti and tiny my little ponies suit your bad ass hotness persona, I would so keep it." He looked down seeing it scattered all over his boots and groaned again.

"Ha! Yeah well when you have so much bad ass hotness it can pull off anything." He said being all cocky and I laughed.

"Then I am so buying you a rose petal tutu for Christmas this year." I said walking past him to where Bill was walking back to the group of bikes. Jared caught up with me and then calmly whispered in my ear,

"And if you do you will find yourself over my knee before New Year."

"Smug royal bastards." I muttered under my breath. I was just following him over to where the other bikers stood when I thought of something else I wanted to know.

"Wait!"

"Bloody Hell woman, you're worse than a nagging wife!" Jared said stopping and storming back to me.

"Yeah, like you were ever married." I said but it was one of those awful moments in life when your mouth speaks and your brain doesn't think that it might not actually be a wise thing to say quickly enough. His face said it all.

"Oh Jared, I am so sorry I didn't know and..." I stopped speaking as soon as he held up his hand.

"Its fine, just ask what you were going to ask and lets not speak of it." I lowered my head feeling guilty and only when I felt his fingers raising my chin could I look at him. His beautiful almond shaped eyes and deeply tanned skin, gave him an exotic look but it was when his startling silver eyes that were ringed by a thin black ring looked at me like that, that's when my guilt doubled. He must have seen it plain as day because he laughed once.

"Don't feel guilty Keira, you didn't know, in fact, not many do." I nodded so he let go of my chin.

"Does Bill know?" I asked this and his response answered more than just one of my questions.

"Yes."

"You knew didn't you...that he was going to die that day?" I asked referring to when Bill was shot in the back of the head. Jared's reply shocked me.

"Who do you think tipped Jack McCall off?" I was mortified by this response and started stepping back. How could he do that?!

"How could you..." He took only one step towards me and said

"He didn't know it at the time but he was in the first stages of Cholera. He would have been dead soon anyway and I needed him sound of mind to accept my offer, not vomiting and shitting all over himself in a bed somewhere dying of thirst." Ok so the way he said it did make being shot in the back of the head sound a much more appealing way to die.

"Ok, so you've made your point." And yes, he very much did with that disgusting mental image of how people died back then if suffering from that particular disease.

"I thought so."

"Umm..." I started to say something before he could walk off again and his shoulders slumped and he muttered a curse to himself.

"Just one more question."

"Of course there is." He commented dryly, one I ignored.

"Why do you call him Jim?"

"Because his real name is James Butler Hickok and because it is my way of showing respect for a soul I own."

After this shed load of bombshells about a man I didn't really know but had saved my life, we walked over to Jared's men all stood around their bikes. I recognised a few of them from the battle we were all involved in last year and it was a weird thought to have. So much had happened since then and just like history was repeating itself we had come full circle. Only now I was the one who was supposedly dead and soon Draven would be told as much with the evidence of my hair and message used as proof of the fact. I didn't know what Draven would do when he woke, if that hadn't already happened but I could only hope he would read my letter and understand the reasons I did what I had no other choice but to do.

He of all people should understand the lengths some people would go to for love. I had once thought that pain, suffering and hatred had been the strongest emotion a person would act upon but after all we had been through together I now knew differently...

Love conquered it all.

"Are we gettin' a wiggle on or what?" Bill said pulling me from my thoughts. Bill was looking at us both stood slightly away from everyone else. I gave him a little smile and as soon as he saw it he gave me a nod as if this was all he needed. It was a sweet gesture and I was starting to grow a soft spot for my new friend.

"Head up!" Jared said before catching a small helmet and stuffing it down on my head.

"You did that just to shut me up, didn't you?" I said lifting the visor so I could speak again.

"Well we wouldn't want this pretty little head of yours to get hurt now would we human." Orthrus said just before he started his engine.

"Cut giving her shit, Orth!" Jared said scolding his brother.

"Ignore him." He added turning back to me and squeezing my hand for encouragement.

"You still remember how to ride one of these things right?" Jared asked Bill as he led me round to what I gathered was his own bike.

"Don't make me clip your horns Big Bug, I ain't no Cultus Corncracker!" Bill said getting irate putting his hands on his hips and making his long jacket flare out at the sides.

"Weren't you Hell bent for 50 years?" One of the other men asked and I gathered this meant the length of time he was imprisoned for.

"50 years?" I whispered to myself in disbelief.

"53 but who's countin'." Bill said like it was nothing. I was beginning to notice that Bill was completely different around other guys than when we were alone and I put this down to old fashioned manners, ones that obviously didn't count around his fellow men.

Jared nodded to one of his men and in less than a minute he was wheeling a new motorbike in front of Bill making him whistle.

"Well it ain't no Crowbait that's for dang sure!" I didn't know what a Crowbait was and so was surprised when it was Orthrus who leant closer to me over his bike and shouted over the engine,

"A Crowbait is a shit horse."

"Ah." Was all I could manage from shock that he had spoken normally to me. Bill's ride at first glance looked like

271

what I can only guess was a Harley type bike. But it was clear to see it was custom made and no expense spared. There wasn't the normal lavish chrome work and fancy glossy paint but instead rich shiny brass and copper.

The bike looked like it was made from parts of an old fancy steam engine. In fact it wouldn't be hard to believe that it could run on coal and I wondered if it had a steam whistle in place of the horn! It most definitely went with his 'Steampunk look' that was for 'Dang' sure.

"Are you jesting with me Big Bug?" Bill said nodding to the name and I bent at the waist to see what he was looking at.

"Annie?" I read out the name hand painted on his bike's tank and Bill smoothed his hand over it like it was his baby.

"Well I knew you always wanted to ride her." Jared said making everyone laugh and Bill just tipped up his hat at him and winked, mounting his Annie.

"Then let's go for a ride and see if I can break her in."

"Am I missing something here?" I asked looking back to Bill's Big Bug.

"He had a thing for Annie Oakley. Now get on Kitten, time to crash a party." Jared said and all at once the men mounted their bikes and started up in a chorus of roaring engines.

"Annie Oakley as in the cowgirl?" Jared didn't answer me he just patted his seat as a way to get me to hurry my butt up.

"What bike is this?" I asked as I cocked my leg over the leather seat to his sexy looking black bike.

"Now this beautiful girl here is my Triumph Rocket III Roadster and no, before you ask I don't have any pansy ass name for her, now in the words of my lawman here 'get a wiggle on darlin'." I laughed, did what I was told and Jared shouted,

"Hellbeasts, roll out!"

CHAPTER TWENTY-THREE

KEIRA

THIS IS WHAT I AM PACKIN'

On the road we certainly were a sight to be seen and I had to feel sorry for all the people who tried to take pictures of us as we rode past. We just seemed to leave a stream of people all looking at their broken phones in utter amazement and confusion as to why it had happened.

I must say I did slightly let it all go to my head as most would, because I gotta tell ya, being on the back of Jared's bike and riding with his posse made you feel dangerously invincible! Most of the time everyone gave us a wide berth even on the motorways. I did feel a bit bad at one point when driving through a town and one of the mothers dragged her child inside as if there was going to be some kind of shootout. People slammed doors and shops' signs were suddenly closed for the day.

But I suppose putting myself in their shoes and looking at it as an outsider these were all wise decisions to make. It wasn't as though I could even say that if they knew them better they wouldn't react this way but this was most definitely not the case. Because let's face it, if people had seen half of the shit I had seen then they would be moving to the wilderness and learning how to survive on berries just to hide.

I heard Jared saying something as we slowed down about the dickheads behind us and I braved turning my head to see a black Range Rover behind us with tinted windows trying to cut them up so it would split the group. I saw one of Jared's men trying to motion the driver to pass them all but he was having none of it. Orthrus outright gave him the finger and this was when he chose to make his move. He cut us up on the slip road, enough to make Bill, Orthrus and another of Jared's men have no choice but to swerve so they wouldn't get knocked down.

The car passed Jared, me and two others of Jared's men giving us the wanker signs as they passed. I felt Jared's growl vibrate through him as I had my arms around his waist and was holding on for dear life. They then sped off no doubt thinking this was the end of their fun, what they didn't get was it had only just started for the ones they had pissed off…And one thing was for certain, they had pissed off the worst type of wrong people you could imagine.

They mustn't have known this road as it wasn't long until we were all faced with a set of traffic lights. The two lanes were filled with our bikes on one side and on the other was the blacked out 4x4. Bill came up alongside me and Jared at the front and for a hopeful second I thought the idiots next to us would get ignored. If I'd have had the opportunity I might had done the whole 'it's better to ignore them' speech. Although one look at how angry the guys were and I think I might have skipped it seeing as I had witnessed first-hand what these guys all changed into.

"Hey, nice hat asshole, what you packing under that jacket, a BB gun?" The guy said to the right of us in the passenger's side after rolling down his window. He looked like some punk ass rapper wannabe with pasty white skin and a bad attitude. You could see the car obviously had people in the back as well, as he turned in his seat to seek the praise of laughter from his asshole friends.

"Jim…" Jared said his name as a warning when he heard him growl. Bill didn't look at them, he just continued with eyes in front but I noticed his hands on the handlebars gripped them tighter until the leather on his gloves looked strained.

"Hey and look at the pussy we got over here lads, great pair of tits on her!"

"Oh shit."

"Fuck yeah."

"Here we go." All three comments came at the same time in response to Bill finding his limit. The idiot that had made the comment had his head turned once more to his friends and didn't see as Bill kicked down his stand and tilted his bike to rest. The asshole had just turned his head back around and started wagging his tongue between his two fingers to mimic oral sex when he found himself being dragged out of the car window.

The skinny guy twisted and kicked out his legs screaming about being let go. Bill calmly dropped him to the floor and pulled out one of his guns pointing at the guy's head.

"This is what I am packing." Bill said looking down the length of his gun to see the petrified guy nearly choke on his own tongue through fear. I looked up to see all the other guys scrabbling to get out of the car to help their friend, obviously not spotting the gun till it was too late. They all approached Bill and without even looking at them Bill pulled his other gun and shot off three rounds.

"Holy shit." I said when seeing that without a single glance their way, Bill had shot one guys phone from his hand, another guy's joint from his mouth and the furthest guy's baseball cap clean off. The guy on the floor saw all this and quickly peed himself as he started begging for his life. His friends had all run away shouting for help like they were being chased by the wrath of God.

"Pppp…please man, don't kill me, I didn't mean nothing by the bitch…Oh god!" This turned out to be a mistake because he started to cry again when Bill cocked back the hammer at the reference to me being called a bitch.

"I think you owe the little lady an apology prairie coal." Bill said and the guy looked confused to what he called him.

"He means horse shit, now get on with it asswipe!" Orthrus shouted leaning back in the saddle of his bike with his massive arms crossed.

"Shit yeah, I'm sorry, I'm sorry, totally…please man let me go!" The guy pleaded for his life and Bill gave it another few painful seconds before he flipped his gun on his finger and back in the holster. He didn't say another word, just got back on his bike and started it back up again. Then he reached into his jacket and pulled out a card.

"Jim."

"Can't have them botherin' any other of these good folks, now can we?" Bill said nodding to the queue of cars behind us, in response to Jared's warning. Then he flicked the card through the window of the black Range Rover and suddenly flames ignited from inside the car.

"Shit man!" The guy said scrabbling up and half tripping up thanks to having his trousers falling down his legs due to the questionable fashion guys chose when fastening their belts half way down their backsides. I didn't get it and I was thinking after today and showing everyone his batman underpants that neither was he.

We all rode off with the sight of black smoke bellowing behind us from leather and rubber burning and a queue of cars too afraid to move...oh and not to forget a half-naked tosser that had wet himself!

After that I was happy to report there were no more incidents to speak of and other than a sore bum and strangely enough achy abs we were arriving at Witley court just as the sun had started to go down. We had only been on the ride for just over an hour but I was really looking forward to the second the bike stopped so I could hop off. Although there was a strong possibility I would be walking like John Wayne with a saddle stuck in between my legs minus a horse...it wasn't going to be a sexy swagger by any means!

We all pulled into a car park and it must have been the front entrance to the park as last time we had pulled right up to the house. The wheels all crunched on the gravel making even more of an impact to our arrival. I was glad to see no one was around and the opening times as we passed the front entrance told me everywhere was long ago closed. The time of year threw you off what time it was with the sun going down much later, as it must have been getting on for nine o' clock. I was more than happy about this fact as I think the sight of a gang of bikers, a blonde girl and a guy looking like Paul Newman dressed as Butch Cassidy would have been a worrying sight for anyone.

And even more so considering the sign on the door stated clearly this was an English heritage tourist site which meant lots of families and retired folk with possible bad tickers...not really a place you want to chance scaring people. But if there was ever a Kodak moment it would have been now with us all walking through the gift shop after the locked door was clicked open.

And even more so walking up the pretty garden paths that led to what the signs told us was the main house.

It would have reminded me of a rock band MTV video if we all had guitars, microphones and half naked girls dotted about the place. Let's put it this way, we definitely needed heavy rock music playing in the background as it was one of those moments in movies where you're excited about the good guys turning up to kick bad guy ass! I think the only thing we were missing was one of the dudes at my side cracking his knuckles and one of them pumping a shotgun with one hand. Of course in my case it was more likely them turning into giant dogs and Bill tipping his top hat at the bad guys before he shot them. Either way if it meant that bitch was gonna get it then it would be worth watching on the big screen!

We all turned a corner and saw a beautiful lake that looked so picturesque with the sun going down.

"Aww that's so pretty." I said forgetting my bad ass companions and the fact they would give two hoots about the way the trees reflected back in the shimmering water.

"That's nice princess, ooh and look over there, a perfect place for me to dump a couple of bodies that won't be found till next spring." Orthrus said coming next to me and pointing towards a dark patch in the surrounding plant life. I looked back over my shoulder at him, stretching my neck and he winked at me and smacked my butt as he walked past.

"Damn mutt." I grumbled and I heard his booming laughter that was similar to his brothers.

"I heard that little girl." He shouted back and I carried on turning my gaze from the lake and back to where I could shoot daggers from my eyes at his back.

"I know you could!" It wasn't my finest come back of the decade but it was better than my first option which was a rock to the back of the head.

278

"You coming, sweet cheeks?" One of Jared's men asked as he passed me. He had a rounder face which made him look kind and jolly. He wasn't over weight but he had a slight beer gut on him that actually suited his stocky frame. He had brownish green eyes that smiled even without his lips doing the same.

"Don't you take any notice of Orth, he's a cocky shit." I smiled at him as we walked side by side and he was one of the ones that had said 'oh shit' when Bill had gotten off his bike. This told me two things, one he had been around longer than fifty years and two he knew Bill as well as the rest of them.

"The name's Chase and before you say, it's not because I chase cars or cats or any other crap dogs chase because they're mental!" I laughed and it was nice for once not having to look up too far at one of them. He seemed to be only about four inches taller than me which was unusual for these guys because I had thought you weren't allowed in the club unless you were over six foot!

"Keira." I told him my name and he burst out laughing, which was a cute chuckle that was almost like a hiccupping noise.

"I know sweetheart, everyone and their preacher knows who you are in my world." This made me blush and he nudged me side on.

"Stop flirting with the chick and hurry your ass up, lover." The other guy who said that was taller than Chase but just as wide. Because even though height obviously wasn't a factor anymore the muscle mass definitely was. Wait...did he say lover?

"That's Otto, my husband." I coughed and snorted at the same time and it was one of those moments where you really wished you could be cool. But jeez, I wasn't going to deny it was a shock. Not that I had any problem with it as I believe marriage was for love not gender. But I just hadn't been expecting it.

"Smooth." He said laughing again and taking the micky out of me and he so had a right to. In the end I just nudged him sideways back and we both continued walking grinning.

It didn't take us long to reach the house and it was very clear there was a party going on but wait…

"This is the wrong place, isn't it?" The one called Otto looked back at me and was clearly amused.

"Come on Kitten, I think we'd better get you to the fountain, but let's head round the side so we're not seen." Jared said taking my arm and leading me off once we got through the gate.

"But…but…" I tried to make sense of it all as only this afternoon I was here and it was still a ruin not the palace it looked now. The once stone shell was filled with not only the sound of hundreds of people in full swing of a party but also floors, ceilings, windows and a roof.

"How is this possible?" I asked looking round at a glimpse of the beautiful furnishing inside.

"For some of my kind creating something like this is nothing more than a thought and something they could do in their sleep." I found what he was telling me incredible as I walked past the massive windows that each showed exquisite and lavish chandeliers hanging down and sparking in the candle light.

"My sister Libby would love this." I said mentioning my sister for the first time with anyone but the Dravens.

"The interior designer?" Jared said and I was shocked he knew who she was.

"Now the mother after Ella was born." I corrected him and I didn't know why I did but it was strange feeling to be so at ease talking about my sweetheart niece.

"Ella?" He asked with a frown I couldn't understand. I was about to answer him when something caught my eye as the fountain came into view. The whole back of the house was lit up by paper lanterns lining the pathways and massive flames burning away at the centres of various naked sculptures that were involved in different sexual acts. Like one male statue was chained by his hands behind his back and had a ball gag in his mouth. It was all made of metal and the bodies all had holes in so the fire inside could be seen. They were incredible but weird at the same time. Some were dressed with metal tutus and Santa hats that even had little bells attached.

I laughed out loud when I saw one wear a metal mankini.

"Oh yeah, this is Pip's party alright." I commented when I saw a bunch of waiters walk past struggling on roller skates and wearing those inflatable sumo suits. Talk about trying to make it mission impossible whilst serving canapés.

"I am starting to worry about meeting this Pip." Jared said and I snorted unable to help myself.

"You should be but whatever you do don't insult her and don't mention anything about what she's wearing unless it's a compliment…actually I wouldn't do that either if her husband is anywhere near her." I looked to Jared and saw the disbelief there in one raised eyebrow but I only had to say one name and his face changed very quickly to one of shock.

"Abaddon."

"Oh shit."

"Yep, oh shit is right." I said in agreement as if there was one Demon I ever needed on my side then Adam's would be the one I wanted fighting in my corner every time.

"But wait until you meet her, she is fabu…" I stopped speaking as soon as the central fountain came into view and I saw the figure stood there waiting. I suddenly felt like I couldn't breathe and I took a step back bumping into Jared.

"You...you planned this?" I asked feeling my throat clogging up with emotion.

"I did." He said leaning closer to my ear and without another thought I took off running. I didn't think about the danger. I didn't think about who could see me.

I just didn't think.

I just ran.

Because stood there at the fountain was the only person I needed to see back on his feet. The only arms I needed to feel. The only lips I needed to kiss and the only person right at this moment that I needed to tell I loved them...

Draven.

CHAPTER TWENTY-FOUR

KEIRA

PIP'S WORLD

I was running one second and then my brain kicked into gear and I stopped as soon as I saw who had approached him.

"Aurora." I cursed her name as I spoke it through gritted teeth and knew that I had a very important choice to make. Which was why I backed up slowly into a shadowed corner of the house to watch what happened next.

"What are you doing?" Jared must have seen me backtracking but not yet seen why.

"Look." I pointed to where Draven stood and the world's biggest bitch was walking up behind him.

"Then what are you waiting for, we all know she and Seth are the traitors." I shook my head and without taking my eyes off the two of them I said,

"Something doesn't feel right. I can't put my finger on it but you have to admit, why go to all this trouble…? Why wait till now when there were so many other occasions she could have double crossed me? No, something doesn't feel right and the only way I can find out is if she still thinks I am in Hell…this is my only chance." And it was true. I hated it but it was true. I couldn't let my selfish need to be with Draven ruin what might have been our only chance to catch Aurora in the act so we could understand what she and Seth had planned.

I had to wait. And worse still I had to make Draven wait.

"She's just told him he needs to let you go."

"You heard that?" I asked shocked from such a distance away.

"Must be the animal in me." He said and winked at me making me roll my eyes. I saw her put her hand on Draven's shoulder from behind and he shrugged it off without looking at her. Draven had his back to everything and was just looking out at the fountain as I had done this morning. It was almost as if he was waiting for me to come walking back through the way I had entered.

"What she's saying?" I asked Jared with the K9 hearing.

"I am sorry for your loss my lord…"

"Oh please." I muttered before he carried on translating,

"…if only I could have done more to save her life but she was so stubborn and refused to hide whilst I fought off the Harpies, then of course she…" Aurora was cut off before she could take her next breath as she found half her body suspended over the water being bent backwards with Draven's hand around her throat.

"Do not speak her name EVER!" This was one comment I didn't need Jared to tell me as I heard it being roared from all the way over here. Oh yeah, he was angry alright.

"I'm thinking your boyfriend is pissed." Jared said as we watched Draven fling her back around and release her in a way she only just managed to stay on her feet. Aurora said no more but slunk away after straightening herself up and smoothing down her long evening dress.

"This is my cue." I said knowing I had to follow her.

"Did you leave the rational part of your brain in your helmet?" I just gave him an unimpressed look to which he added,

"Good point, you never had one." I gave him a frown and shook my head.

"Look the point I am making is if she sees you and knows there is a chance of you ruining her plans, whatever they might be, she will kill you this time." He said and I guess he had a good point, so I said the only thing that came to mind,

"Grab me that clown."

"What?" I nodded behind him where one of the guests dressed as a demonic clown was walking this way.

"You're not serious?"

"As a hellhound peeing on your sofa." I responded making him growl.

"Funny."

"Look just grab me the damn clown!" I said never expecting this sentence would have ever crossed my lips…clowns creeped the willies outta me!

"Fine one clown coming right up, my lady." Jared said reaching out at the right moment to drag the clown closer to us.

"Sorry about this but do you think I could borrow your wig?" I asked politely and Jared groaned. Then he just snatched the poor guy's neon green curly clown wig off him to which we both received a shock.

"Really?"

"You're shitting me?!" I and Jared both said at the sight of the poor manhandled guy that was left with the exact same curly afro wig only in a different colour.

"What, I like wigs." The guy said in his defence and Jared let him go and muttered,

"I'm thinking it's safer I don't meet this friend of yours."

"I wonder how many he had on." I asked as I let my hair down to twist it up and put the wig on, secretly offering thanks that it wasn't sweaty. I looked round the corner as I stuffed up the loose bits back into the wig, only to see Aurora was making her way back into the house.

"Oh that's just perfect, nope would never guess it was you...wow in fact who are you and what have you done with the daft blonde I was with?" I smacked him on his arm and said,

"You could be helpful you know."

"I got you the wig didn't I?"

"Yeah and now I need your jacket." I almost laughed at his horrified face.

"Oh hell no! That is not happening Kitten!"

"Don't be a wuss, I will get it back to you, now hurry up as she will be out of sight any minute." If I hadn't been in a rush I might have doubled over with laughter at the sight of Jared looking torn...man, he must have really loved this jacket.

"Alright but I swear if anything happens..." He said as he shrugged out of it and handed it over...*reluctantly.*

"Yeah, yeah I'm puppy chow, got ya! Ooh perfect." I said slipping it on and finding a pair of sunglasses in the inside pocket.

"What'd you want next, my wallet!?"

"Sissy." I called him.

"Thief."

"You will get over it, now how do I look?" I said putting on the sunglasses that reminded me of the terminator.

"Like Keira only in a fucking stupid wig, shades and my most prized possession." I just groaned at him and his helpful ways.

"Well it's all I've got so I will just have to roll with it." I said and was about to walk away when he shouted for me to wait. He then jogged over to one of the female guests and said a few things to her. Next thing I knew he was jogging back to me after she had dug something out of her handbag.

"Time of the month…did you need a tampon?"

"Haha, funny little shit ain't ya?" Jared said with fake laughter.

"It must be the wig." Jared tried not to smile at my comment but I could see him fighting a smile.

"Come here and hold still." He pulled me closer to him and repositioned me so I had light on my face. Then he produced the item he'd borrowed from the woman waiting and I felt him draw a circle on my nose.

"There! Every clown needs a red nose."

"You're enjoying this aren't you?" I said sarcastically up at him and he nodded winking at me.

"There she is, walking through the crowd." Jared said looking over me and I turned to face the window I had my back to, to see he was right.

"You go and I will assemble my men to take the exits in case she runs. Shout my name and I will hear you."

"Ok, got it." I said seeing the side entrance and deciding this was my best bet.

"Oh and Keira…" I stopped to look back at him and saw he was both worried about letting me go but obviously the sight of what I was wearing was making him smile.

"Take care of my baby." I rolled my eyes and said sarcastically,

"I will guard her with my life." Then I patted the jacket and was off out of sight.

I wasn't going to lie, I felt like a grade A idiot but on the plus side I actually felt a bit underdressed next to all these crazy characters. The room was filled with a mass of colour and this was what I could imagine was Pip's dream wonderland looked like. Or at least the people she would allow into it.

From what I could see of the room it was incredible and like stepping back in time. Of course you had to cancel out all the added extras that were obviously chosen by Pip. For example the ball pit in one corner that was filled with different coloured neon paints and lit up with a black light so everything was glowing. At the moment there were three people wrestling and one woman who looked like she was having a jolly good time playing with herself...if you know what I mean.

Then there were the giant ice sculptures dotted about the place for the sole purpose of drinking absinth though ice. One was carved into the shape of a massive rollercoaster and someone had their mouth on one end and a waiter (this time dressed as one of the characters from the goonies) was pouring green liquid from the top. In fact the only reason I could tell some of the staff were there to do a job was by the frilly spotted aprons they were made to wear.

One who walked past me offering people turkey twisters on sticks was dressed as one of the Thundercats and in a pink frilly apron this was quite a sight to be seen. The inside of the building that could be seen was back to its former glory and the plaster work alone was breath taking. I only wished I had enough time to look around but all of the little glimpses of the house I was seeing were only from scanning the room looking for Aurora's blue dress.

I just turned in time to see her as my eye was caught by one of the entertainers blowing fireworks from their mouth instead of the usual fire breathers. The dancing coloured sparks had just finished when I saw the bottom of her dress disappearing from sight as she walked up the staircase on the opposite side of the room.

I think I was in the entrance hall but it was so filled with people I couldn't tell for sure. All I knew was that it was a long room and had an open balcony running all the way around above us showing us the first floor. Right ahead of me was an open doorway showing the staircase beyond it and was framed by two roman pillars either side of it.

I pushed and ducked my way through the best I could and I was thankful nobody was taking any notice of me. I saw the stairs branch off both left and right but missed which side she had taken. I finally managed to get myself to the other side when I had to slip past a man dressed as a bear in a rockabilly style dress...he was even wearing a head scarf tied into a big red bow on the top of his animal head.

I ran through the opening thanking my lucky stars that not many people wanted to linger out here and ran up the staircase picking the left side. By this time Aurora was out of sight but thankfully when I reached the top there weren't many doors to choose from. One door was to my right and facing me there was an open doorway that led onto the balcony which then had one at its centre. I was just about to try the first door when I was met by a familiar face.

"Pip?!"

"Toots?!" Pip threw herself into me after having a moment of shock at seeing me not just in the flesh but no doubt with what I was wearing...although knowing Pip this might have been an everyday wardrobe choice.

"Oh by the power of Grayskull! Thank my lucky star knickers! I knew it! I just knew it! I would have bet my paper plate collection that you were still alive and kicking and I told Adam as much!" She said getting so excited about seeing me I had tears welling up.

"Hey, don't you start crying now or you will ruin all your birthday makeup!" I said referring to her eyes which were painted with a comic book scene over each eyelid. Although I had to admit, it looked like quite a pornographic one. I dreaded to think about the poor girl that had to paint the 69'er through her eyebrow. I had to laugh because one part of her eyebrow's hair was left unpainted and acted as the pubic hair for one guy. They even had little speech bubbles, one saying, 'Are all you guys on the same team?"

Of course now one of the bums was dripping down her cheek because of her tears and I couldn't stop myself from saying,

"You have ass on your face." To which we both burst out laughing as I tried to wipe it away.

"Yeah well you look like Rudolph at some 70's disco!" She said as her come back and we were both off laughing again. So much so for a moment I had completely forgot what I was here for.

"Pip, I saw Aurora come up here, do you know where she went?"

"That bitch! You know she told the king you were dead! I mean none of us wanted to believe it but then she handed him your hair and…"

"Pip, I know, I know! Now focus, I need to find her and discover what she's up to before she finds out I got out." At this Pip's face got very serious and even with the porn painted on her face, it was a very scary sight to witness.

"What did she do to you?"

"Now Pip, just wait a…"

"TOOTS TELL ME!" She screamed in a rage and then a door opened and I was quickly shoved into a doorway recess and Pip shouted dramatically,

"TELL ME YOU'RE STILL ALIVE SOMEWHERE, OH

MY DEAR SWEET CARROTCAKE…YOU WERE TOO
YOUNG TO DIE!" And then she threw up her arms and started
crying.

"Do you need a pill or something?" I heard Aurora ask her
in a shitty way and Pip just jumped up off the floor she had
slumped to and said,

"Nope, I should be fine, I just miss my friend so much…are
you sure she's like dead and shit?" To which Aurora just replied
in a curt manner,

"Yes, quite sure." And then slammed her door shut. I poked
my head out from behind the recess and Pip said,

"She's in there." I had to laugh.

"I know Pip."

"So what's the plan Stan?" She asked following me and I
stopped and held her back by the shoulders.

"My plan is to try and sneak in there and see what's she up
to, your plan is to inform the others."

"Wow, Big boss man King is going to shit rainbows when
he knows you're still alive!" I almost choked on that mental
image.

"Not unless he's taken Unicorn pills, now is there any other
way into that room?"

"Sure, it's the state room and has access through that door
for the maids and other poor lackeys there to doing the bidding
of posh twonker donks and toffee nosed tw..." I held up my
hand cutting off her rant before it got too explicit.

"I've got ya. Ok, so I came with a few …uh…friends."

"You mean biker dudes that turn into rip your face off dogs,
right?" Wow, she was good.

"Yeah, that and a cowboy who's not in fancy dress but don't
ask. I asked them to cover the exits in case she runs. But I need
to know, have you seen Seth?" Pip frowned at me and scratched
her green hair that was all in plaited bunches with the blue ends

all curly hanging down and bouncing with her erratic movements.

She looked utterly adorable.

But this, combined with what she was wearing, was just something else. It was a short dress with a tight top that moulded to her little breasts and had tiny plastic toys attached to the black material, ones that looked as if they had been collected from Kinder surprise eggs.

But it was the skirt part that was really amazing and took me back to my childhood. It was made up of massive material flowers and each one was a different 80's cartoon. From the ones I could see there were He-Man, She-Ra, Jem, Gummi Bears, Rainbow Bright, Snoopy, Carebears, My Little Pony (both original and new) even ones like Galaxy High School, Chip n Dale and Muppet Babies. In fact it looked like she had made each flower from kid's old bedding sets throughout the 80's.

"You mean the dude that's all loco about Pinky?" She answered and I dragged my eyes away from her dress.

"You mean RJ...he's still got RJ with him?!" I said getting panicky and completely forgetting this factor when Aurora first mentioned his name.

"Uhh well Yeah! The dude won't let the righteous babe out of his sight." She said this like it was obvious.

"So he's here, you've seen him?" Pip cocked her hip to the side and thought for a moment and then her eyes got wide like it had just come to her. I followed where her gaze went and suddenly my heart started pounding.

"Don't tell me."

"Sorry sister, but your Pinky promise pal is in there, with both of those vipers." I closed my eyes and prayed for RJ to be alright. I could only hope that my time wasted out here hadn't been the time needed for RJ to get hurt. I felt bad enough that I was the whole reason she was in this mess to begin with.

Now I just needed to figure out a way to get her out safe and survive doing so.

"Ok, new plan, forget my solo mission, it's time to call for the Cavalry." Pip stood to attention, gave me a salute and said,

"You can count on me Tootie Sargent!" And then she ran off down the stairs wearing a pair of baby pink wedge shoes, with unicorn horns sticking up on the front surrounded with white fur. I was still shaking my head wondering how she walked in those things let alone ran in them.

I waited till she was out of sight and then decided it was now or never. I opened the door, walked into the room and immediately heard voices. I crept through the room after a quick scan to make sure I was alone and walked over to the adjoining door where the voices were coming from. I pressed myself to the panelled door and waited to see if I could make out what was being said but was disappointed to find I couldn't. I was also disheartened to find I couldn't make out RJ's voice and I could only hope and pray that she was still alive.

Well there was only one way to find out.

So very slowly I turned the handle, moving it by the tiniest amount so as not to be detected and then finally managed to unlatch the door enough to push it. I was just thankful nothing squeaked or creaked but by the time I opened the door and saw what was happening in the next room, nothing could have prepared me for what I saw...

Violation.

293

CHAPTER TWENTY-FIVE

KEIRA

FIGHTING FOR A HOMECOMING

Inside the room I watched in horror as Seth was chained to a metal bed and a naked Aurora was sat astride him riding his manhood with obvious pleasure. Seth looked strange and half drugged as he kept falling in and out of his demon side and shaking his head erratically. One thing was blindingly obvious and that was Aurora was taking him against his will.

She was raping him.

I wanted to shout blue murder to get her to stop and leave him alone but I knew I had to be careful, especially since she had a gun lay next to her on the bed.

"STOP IT! LEAVE HIM ALONE!" RJ shouted from the corner of the room where she was tied up. She had seen me and the first thing I noticed was the cut bleeding on her lip and a nasty lump on her forehead as if she had been struck. Her makeup was streaming down her face in black lines like she had been crying angry tears.

"Silence or I will shoot you and it might ruin the moment!" Aurora threatened picking up the gun and pointing it at her as she continued to ride the unwilling Seth. He must have had some knowledge of what was going on because he shouted up at her,

"NO! Don't hurt her or you will never get what you want!" I gritted my teeth and dug my nails into my palm to stop myself from racing in there and trying to save the day but I just couldn't risk it. I didn't know what exactly she wanted, although it should have been quite obvious considering the act. But then again, I doubted she went through all this just to get her rocks off with someone she had taken a fancy to. Either way I couldn't risk RJ's life, not again. So I had no other choice than to wait for others to get here.

"Oh but I think I know what you want! Then so be it, have your little punk." Aurora said after looking between the two both trying to save the other. Then she started laughing and threw her head back and by the time she looked down again she had morphed in to RJ. I sucked in a sharp breath which was masked by RJ's gasp of shock.

"No...no...you're not her...you're not..." Seth kept repeating to himself over and over and closing his eyes as tight as they would shut.

"Look at me, it's me...just open your eyes lover." Aurora cooed in RJ's voice and just as he was about to open his eyes RJ shouted,

"IT'S NOT ME! IT'S A TRICK!" But this just ended with her finding the curtain she was tied next to wrapped around her, preventing her from speaking. I almost called out in fear she wouldn't be able to breath but the material stopped just covering her mouth and leaving her free to breathe through her nose.

"Now look at me and I will show you what you truly want." Aurora said and it was messing with my head let alone what it must be doing to poor Seth. She rode him harder making him cry out and open his eyes. This was his first mistake as it was obvious he couldn't hold back his desire for the fantasy. Oh yeah, he had it bad for my friend alright.

The real RJ's eyes were wide and tear filled making me want to run over there and comfort my friend but I was rendered helpless.

"That's it lover, I can feel how much you want me, how much you want this body." She touched her pert little breasts and then ran her hands up into her pink tousled hair and Seth remained as his demon form this time.

RJ looked even more shocked and I was surprised she hadn't passed out by now. Although I suppose this wasn't anything compared to the battle of the dead she had witnessed. Ok so I could now see a long future of paying out some hefty psychiatric fees but let's face it, it was the least I could do after this shit storm I had landed in her lap.

I wanted to look away from the disgraceful act but when she put a vial of something blue to Seth's lips I needed to know what she was doing. She dripped it into his mouth and he looked so lost and deep into the lies she was feeding him he didn't even notice. Then she downed the rest of it, swallowed and eyes that weren't her own rolled back up into a face that didn't belong to her either.

"Yes...make me yours, join with me, fill me...fill me!" Aurora shouted and Seth gripped on to the chains that held him pulling enough that they snapped. I thought he would take this moment to escape or at least do me a favour and snap her bitch neck but he was too far gone from this world. Whatever she had given him had made him truly believe it wasn't anyone but RJ he was making love too. He flipped her over and hammered into her quickly finding his release.

Aurora screamed and quickly transformed back to herself making Seth instantly realise his mistake. He flew off the bed backwards and shook his head over and over as if it was a nightmare he was trying to banish from his mind. He scrabbled over to RJ and pulled her huddled form to him making sure she was alright. The shackles still encased his wrists and the lengths of chain he had snapped still hung down from them.

"I'm so sorry, I'm so sorry…"He started chanting as he held onto RJ as tight as he could fearful if he ever let her go. I looked back to the culprit and as soon as I knew that RJ was safe I made my move. She had just picked up her dress and was bending down when I ran in the room and grabbed the gun she had left on the bed.

"What the…!" Aurora started to say but stopped when she saw it was me…that or a mad biker clown that had just sprung into the room and was now pointing a gun at her. Any other time and I would have laughed just thinking about what a sight I must have made.

"Don't move bitch!" I shouted like something out of a bad cop show. Aurora laughed and said,

"And who do you think you are that you will be able to stop me!?" I was about to say when it was actually RJ that answered her.

"Keira…is that you?" I smiled at her and that was when Aurora dropped the evil villain victory look for one of pure shock.

"NO! It can't be…but…it's…it's impossible!"

"Not for this Scouser!" I shouted back and whipped off my glasses, throwing them to one side so she could see my face and I had to admit, I felt like a bad ass!

"Ahhh!" She screamed and threw herself at me, knocking the gun from my hand and tackling me to the ground. I twisted before she could kick me and stuck out my foot tripping her up so she landed flat on her back. Then I jumped on her, straddling her waist and started punching her in the face.

"You want sex! Buy a vibrator you raping bitch!" I shouted in her face as I lifted up her head by the hair and smashing the back of her head back into the floor. I had lost my temper before but this was something else.

"Help her!" I heard RJ shout to the still naked Seth and his response would be something later I would laugh at.

"I'm not sure she needs help, Rachel." Did he just call her by her first name Rachel? Thinking this I received an elbow to the face which threw me to the side allowing Aurora to get up and run off. I got up and shook my head at the same time running from the room in hot pursuit feeling my adrenaline kick in like a drug called kick ass!

"Come back here you coward!" I shouted as I followed her out of the next room and back into the hallway. She disappeared down the staircase and raced around the corner down the next lot of steps into the crowd. She looked back to see me still coming for her only she ran straight into an angry Imp holding a folded chair like a bat.

"Take a seat, Bitch!" She said as she let it rip, smacking the entire chair into her face, knocking her clean off her feet. Her nose burst and now, added to the black eye I had given her, she wasn't looking quite so beautiful anymore. She got up on wobbly feet and I don't know what came over me but I leapt off the staircase straight for her. I flew through the air to the sound of Pip screaming,

"FOR SPARTAAA!"

And then I landed on her. We both went down and skidded forward as the crowd parted. She tried to crawl away but I reached out and grabbed her ankle and yanked her back. I was like a woman possessed. It was as though all those times I had wanted to scratch her eyes out and strangle her with her own hair had all come rushing back to this moment and I just couldn't stop.

I found myself on top of her again and it was a vague feeling that my knuckles were hurting from punching a face.

"Here, use this!" Pip said pulling my shoulder and handing me something pink. I didn't even think I just grabbed it, raised it high and was about to bring it down on her head full force when I heard the one thing on this earth that could stop me...

Draven.

"Keira?" He said my name and I paused mid murdering action. I looked up and saw him stood at the end of the room with the crowd parted down the middle. I had no clue as to what I must have looked like as I remained sat on his ex-girlfriend amazingly with my wig still in place, if not a little skew-whiff. I also looked up to see what I had been about to smash into Aurora's bloody face and found to my horror I was still holding above my head a giant penis shaped piñata.

I remained frozen in position for a few more seconds, panting and very much like a naughty deer caught in head lights.

"Uh...hey." I said not knowing what else to say considering this wasn't the beautiful, running over the meadows into each other's arms to the sound classical music scenario I had dreamed of. No not especially when quickly after he said my name all the rest of the crew came rushing in and stopped dead when everyone saw me the way I was.

"She found the baddie." Pip said defending me and dropping the next item she had been ready to pass me if the giant paper penis filled with treats hadn't done the job. I looked to the side and then up at her saying,

"Really…? An inflatable boob?" She shrugged her shoulders and then offered me a hand up.

"What were we gonna hit her with next, a sex shop?" I muttered dryly.

"Maybe." She muttered back and Aurora had just started to try to get up when Pip bent down, pulled her up by the dress and said,

"Bang Bitch!" Then cracked her across the face with her fist, putting my punches to shame as she let her go to flop back to the floor now unconscious.

I looked back up to see Draven was still clearly in shock and I pulled the wig off my head, letting my hair fall down my back before I said,

"Sod it!" And then I ran at him and finally got my meadow moment. He opened his arms at the last moment and picked me up as I crashed into him. I burst into tears as I felt his arms band around me and held me to him.

"You're here, you're really here." He whispered into my hair and I cried harder. I heard everyone around us cheering and clapping at the sight of our reunion and I smiled into his neck.

"I'm here, I'm home." I whispered back and it felt like long blissful moments that I wanted to cling onto for forever. Just being back in his arms, knowing it was now all over made it finally worth it.

And then the music started and someone gave an old soul a guitar,

So a cowboy could start singing…

As I travel here in this world, well I'm just a pilgrim passing through,
But Abraham told me of a city, where God's foundation's standing true

When I come to the crossing of that river, don't you weep
because I'm gone
Just tell all my friends and my loved ones, that I finally made it
home.

Then Bill stopped singing to play his solo on the guitar and I felt Draven squeeze me tighter to him and we both looked sideways at Bill when he started back up again.

Now I can almost see my mansion, but this mortal body clouds
my view
Day by day it's getting clearer, the life of glories shining
through
When I come to the crossing of that river, don't you weep
because I'm gone
Just tell all my friends and my loved ones, that I finally made
it home
Just tell all my friends and my loved ones, that I finally made it
home.

It was a beautiful song and one sung with such soul that it nearly had me balling all over again. I knew it was about death but for me and for Bill, it was simply about coming home.

And like I had said before,

Draven was my home.

CHAPTER TWENTY-SIX

KEIRA

MORTALLY HURT

"Keira!" Sophia shouted pushing through the crowd and running into me. We embraced as sisters and again I found myself being bombarded with emotion. I managed to hold in the tears but you would have thought the amount I had cried in the last year and half I would have been immune to emotion by now, that or my tears should have dried up long ago.

But there was something about a happy ending that brought out the humanity in all of us, even Bill who hadn't seen this side of the world for over fifty years. Because even though we were all different deep down, at the root of our core there was something the same in all of us. Race, gender, beliefs and sexual preference, strip it all down to its bare bones and we filled our lungs with the same air and we pumped blood around the same hearts. It was only our minds that made us who we were, nothing more, nothing less.

We were dangerous if we wanted to be and we were loving if we chose to be. It was that simple. And this brought me back to the destructive being on the floor that *wanted* to hurt. No-one made her that way, she chose that path.

"Let me at her!" Sophia said letting me go and storming over to Aurora until Vincent stepped in front of her.

"I think there are only two people here that can make the decision of what to do with her." The Angel in my life said, nodding to me and Draven.

"Well you already asked me once not to kill her." Draven said looking down at me and I blushed remembering my letter.

"What are you talking about, my Lord?" Adam asked coming up next to his wife and prying what looked like a priceless vase out of her hands, one that she had at the ready for when Aurora woke and it didn't take long for it to happen. As soon as Adam had moved Pip away we heard malicious laughter.

"See." Pip said mimicking the action of smashing her over the head. Adam just shook his head at her and we all allowed the battered Aurora to struggle getting to her feet.

"Oh how I enjoyed watching you both suffer!" She spat at us and Adam had to literally hold Pip back with an arm around her waist.

I had to say I was tempted to allow her to spin her delusions for longer but I couldn't wait. Oh this was going to be so good and damn satisfying.

"You really think you made us suffer?" I asked stepping forward feeling Draven keep only a step behind me. The entire crowd was watching this all play out as if it was the night's entertainment.

"Oh I know I did! The look on his face when I told him his

little bitch was dead! And yours when I left you in that hole!" I heard Draven growl behind me and everyone in the room took a step back but me. No, I just started laughing harder and soon her smirk dropped when she finally realised she had missed something.

"You really are a stupid cow aren't you...I mean she really fell for it didn't she?" I asked Draven looking back over my shoulder and he just folded his arms across his chest and said,

"That she did, love."

"What the fuck are you talking about!?" She shouted shaking her head and getting more worked up.

"Get a clue! He never thought I was dead you dumb bitch!" I shouted at her relishing the sight of her jaw dropping.

"Oh this is going to be good." Pip said nudging Adam and getting excited.

"I...he..." She stuttered for words.

"I left him a letter telling him what I had planned and knowing it was more than likely you would double cross me, I told him as much."

"But that still doesn't..." I cut her off again only this time by laughing first then Draven got his part of the plan in.

"You gave me a lock of her hair and told me the last thing she said to me... but she lied." At this Aurora's face twisted into an angry snarl.

"Then why let me live?!" She growled out the words and Sophia looked as if it was taking everything in her not to rip her throat out.

"Good question." Draven said down at me calmly before then snapping in his rage and storming past me to grab Aurora by the throat and pin her to the wall.

"Whoa!" I said thinking this was it, he was really going kill her and I didn't think I could do much to stop him. I mean, yes, I had not long ago been trying to kill her myself but now...

could I really stand by and watch my boyfriend kill someone with his bare hands.

"Eos Titaness, you are charged with the desecration of a sacred Janus Gate, conspiracy and treason against your King, your attempt at disrupting the balance in which we live by and…" before Draven continued he squeezed her neck tighter and lifted her further so she couldn't breathe, then got closer to her face and said,

"…even if your attempts at trying to destroy my kingdom weren't reason enough for your punishment, trying to KILL MY ELECTUS WAS!" He roared in her face and dropped her to the floor where she was left gasping for breath. Then he looked down at her with nothing but disgust on his face when he said,

"You were honoured with a place at my table and on my council. You had more than our kind could ever wish for yet you threw it all away and for what, power? Well let me tell you something Eos…" He leant down, lifted up her head forcefully by her chin and said,

"There is no power in Death!" And then he left her face fall and walked away after giving his sentence. He looked to me and just as his eyes started to soften she started to laugh. He looked back and you could feel the whole room chill from the sound. It was nothing short of madness.

"If you think there is no power in death then you are mistaken *my Lord!*" She hissed the 'my lord' and then spat on the ground.

"You think you hold the balance then you are wrong! You think you rule over this kingdom, you are wrong! You think I did any of this without honour WRONG! MY HONOUR WAS NEVER YOURS!" She screamed getting up and again started laughing. Everything in the room stopped and even I, the only mortal in the room could feel something coming.

Then from above Seth ran to the edge of the balcony as if

something had only just now hit him. She looked up at him and blew him a kiss and then started to fade from the room but not before she told us of her victory,

"Long hail Cronus and his REBIRTH!" She shouted this last word just as Seth jumped down over the balcony hoping to land on her but he landed with a knee to the ground where she once stood.

Aurora was gone.

"NOOOOO!" Seth screamed and then punched the floor, splitting the wood beneath his fist. He remained frozen in place with all the muscles on his naked torso bulging. He had found his trousers but still remained barefoot and shirtless. He didn't have the bulk as most of the other men but his slim frame was defined and full of strength.

We were all left confused or at least I was having no clue as to what any of this meant.

"Tell me she didn't…" Draven trailed off when Seth raised his head and his glazed eyes said it all. And this was when it finally all snapped into place.

"Titans." I whispered and Seth's eyes found mine before he once again lowered his head in what looked like the deepest shame I had ever seen on anyone before. Then he raised himself up without a word and walked to the door. The crowd parted for him and every eye in the room watched his departure in silence.

RJ came running from the room above and flung herself at the railings of the balcony before shouting his name,

"SETH!" He stopped with his back to everyone and you could see his naked back tense.

"Seth?" RJ said again this time as a question and you could hear the devastation as a wobble in her voice. But that heart break only became something you could actually hear when he finally walked away…

Without one word spoken.

RJ burst into uncontrollable sobs and ran back into the room above and I looked to Seth as his figure walked through the pillars and down the steps into the darkness. He didn't turn around once but I knew he had heard her heart breaking. And one thing I was certain of and that was he felt it breaking as well.

For long moments nothing moved and only the sounds of a broken mortal girl could be heard echoing through the house and for once, it wasn't coming from me. I walked up to Draven, placed my hand on his chest, looked up at him and said,

"I have to go to her."

"I know." He said putting his forehead to mine and gave me a look that mirrored my own. It felt as though parting now would tear apart our souls. That was the worst thing about being the people with responsibility, he had to deal with the consequences of Aurora's actions and I had to deal with Seth's. We owed it to the people we cared for when really our first choice would have been each other. All I wanted was to find my solace in his arms and close the door on it all.

But we couldn't.

And so we didn't.

By the time I got to the bedroom I had an angry RJ to deal with not the emotional, mascara mess I was expecting. She had pulled off all the sheets on the bed and had stuffed them into the adjoining bathroom tub and poured what smelt like bleach all over them. I walked over to close the bathroom door before I passed out from the fumes.

She had obviously smashed a mirror against the wall as there were shards scattered on the floor where she had been sat tied up not long ago. To be honest if she had been free sooner I think she would have probably been right next to Pip passing me shit to bash Aurora's head with.

I found her stood by the central window in the room looking out over the gardens and staring at the fountain. She looked to be holding something and as I stepped up to her I realised it must have been his t-shirt. She was twisting it over and over in her hands and I remembered doing this a few times myself. It was as if holding something in your hands helped you focus on channelling your hurt to an object, instead of letting it fester in your heart.

"He left." She said without looking at me.

"I know."

"He left." She repeated again and I had to bite my lip at how upsetting it was to hear.

"I know, honey." I said again not knowing whether to pull her to me for a hug or to go and hunt down one broody bastard named Dickhead!

"Just like that…*Gone.*"

"I'm sorry." And I was. Because if anyone in this world knew how she felt at that moment it was me. This was when she finally turned to me and with tears in her eyes said,

"He didn't even say good…*goodbye.*" She hiccupped and stumbled on the word 'goodbye' and I found I too had tears welling up for my friend.

"He's a fool."

"Yes but…but…" She burst into tears and threw herself into my arms and said the rest of her sentence into my hair,

"But he's not a fool in love."

This was when her knees gave out and I caught her, lowering her to the ground as she wept into my arms. The only thing I knew to say to her was one simple fact,

"You're not alone." Which made her cry harder and hug me tighter. I didn't know if it was the right thing to say and I didn't think I would ever know but it felt like the right thing to say at that moment.

RJ cried until she was spent and when I pulled back I saw a different RJ looking back at me. She had always been so tough and so strong but now void of all makeup and with tear stains down her face she looked so young and vulnerable my heart melted all over again for my friend.

"What the Hell is happening Keira?" She asked and I actually laughed making her smile at last.

"I would normally say you wouldn't believe me if I told you, but after what you have seen then I think you're the only mortal alive that would."

"Ok, hold up…*mortal?*" She asked raising her hand to stop me.

"I think we need to talk."

"Shit yeah, I'll say."

We got off the floor and she followed me into the other room so we didn't have to be reminded of what had happened in here. I found a much smaller room that was sweetly furnished and of the likes you would have found in most period homes around the country that had been preserved for the public to visit.

We both sat on the flower print bed and I set to the mammoth task of telling her everything I knew from the very beginning. And after a lot of swearing and 'I knew it' from RJ my tale was finished and I certainly was in need of a drink!

"Well shit me and call me a TellyTubby!" Yep, my friend was back.

"I know."

"That's…that's…"

"I know." I repeated again and I knew she needed time to digest all this.

"So why do you think she did that to him?" RJ asked now

she had calmed down considerably. Because the first time I mentioned Bitch's name, let's just say she hadn't found her happy place.

"I'm still not sure but when she pushed me in that pit she mentioned Seth as her lover so I thought they were together in this. But that must have been her goal from the beginning…but wait…Oh course, I have got it!" I shouted jumping from the bed.

"What? What is it?"

"This whole thing has been about Seth all along. I couldn't figure out what had taken her so long…why strike now when she could have betrayed me and Draven over and over, why wait?" I said walking across the room and back as I played it all out in my mind.

"I don't understand, then why now?" RJ asked and I stopped facing her,

"Don't you see, it was only ever about Seth. He has been in hiding all this time, even to the point that not even his brother knew where he was. And Seth knowing what blood he carried…"

"The Venom of God?" RJ asked and I added,

"Not just that but the blood of the first, the last pure blood of the Titans! So that's what she wanted all along, she waited for him to come out of the woodworks to save the day and extract his revenge. All she needed was to keep me and Draven out of the way. So she pretended I was dead, which kept Draven busy but still allowed her freedom as his council member. All she needed was enough time to get Seth to herself…"

"And time for the bitch to rape him!" RJ jumped in shouting out her crimes and horrifically laying witness to it as I.

"And then she is…oh God…oh God now, it can't be…could she?" I said as finally the worst thought came to me.

"What!? What is it…Keira!" RJ shouted after me but I had

311

already run from the room and down the stairs to try and find Draven. I ran into Otto and Chase who caught me so I wouldn't fall in my hurry.

"Whoa, careful there you could've…"

"Draven! And the rest of them, where are they?!" I shouted feeling myself shaking from what I knew.

"Calm down, they are having a meeting, I am sure they will be done soon."

"NO!" I shouted loud enough that everyone in the room started staring at me. I looked around and felt the heat in my cheeks so decided to take a deep breath and say,

"It's important…"

"We can see that sweetheart." Chase said interrupting me with a smile.

"Please."

"We will take you to them." Otto said and nodded for me to follow. We walked through the crowd and Chase leaned closer to me and said,

"They're locked away in the Green Salon." Then they both led me through the biggest part of the people still in full swing of the party and into what looked like a ballroom. The room looked to be about 70 foot long and the ceiling looked higher than the other rooms I had been in which allowed for the enormous chandeliers. There were eight of them all hung down like crystal fountains and all of their candlelight was flickering off the gold leaf that decorated the hand crafted plaster work on the ceiling and walls.

It was an incredible room and if I hadn't had the most important discovery to tell everyone then I would have taken the time to admire it more. But instead I raced to the far side of the room towards the double doors that were closed, cutting off the party on the other side. I left Chase and Otto behind and before I knew it I was pushing both the doors open as if I was trying to make a grand entrance.

Everyone was there all sat in any available seat with Draven stood by the window with his back to everyone. He turned when he heard my dramatic entrance and before anyone could utter a word I shouted what I had come here to say,

"She wanted his sperm!"

CHAPTER TWENTY-SEVEN

KEIRA

THOSE HARD TRUTHS

Ok, so with deeper thought I could have worded it a better way and one less obvious considering what she had forced him to do but still it made an impact. The room became split with two different reactions. In one half their jaws dropped and confusion was written all over their faces and the other, which included most of the men, including the Draven brothers all looked ready to burst out laughing. I rolled my eyes and said,

"Ok, so I could have reworded that but what I meant was to explain why she needed his sperm." Draven's eyes went soft and he smirked when looking at my nose...what was he looking at my nose for? He walked over to me, pulled me the rest of the way inside and closed the door. Then he tipped my chin up and said,

"You look adorable but this is making it very hard to take you seriously." Then he pulled off his cravat that I had only just noticed him wearing and used it to wipe the red lipstick from my nose.

One word...*Shame.*

"Uhh...oh yeah, thanks." I said feeling that shame colour my cheeks and only wished he could have wiped the red away from them also.

I finally took this moment to really look at him as he undid the buttons to his shirt allowing his neck to be seen and I had to stop myself from attaching my lips to it and sucking. The way he was dressed reminded me of Mr Darcy and he looked so powerful in this period costume that I almost forgot what I had rushed in here to say.

"You were saying, my love?" Draven asked giving me a look that said he knew what I had been thinking and his eyes flashed purple. I leant in and said,

"Can we bugger off when I've told everyone?" I asked on a whisper, one that everyone had heard if the sniggers were anything to go by.

"Most definitely." He replied with a promise in his tone and I beamed up at him. We seemed locked in this silent stare that was as if we were trying to undress each other and express without words what we wanted to do when we were finally alone.

Someone coughed in the background and I looked to find Lucius stood there leaning casually against the window close to where Draven had been stood. I had noticed most people when I had been busy trying to beat the crap out of Aurora but now scanning the room I saw everyone was here. Vincent, Sophia and Zagan along with the rest of Draven's council including Takeshi and Ragnar. Also there was Ruto, Adam and Pip from

Lucius' side but now added to the mix was Sigurd, Jared and his brother Orthrus....oh and a Cowboy.

I think if one more supernatural dude walked in it would look more like a Gold's gym convention thanks to all the muscle and testosterone in the room. I was actually surprised to see everyone was dressed up apart from the obvious ones, like Sigurd and the two Hellhound bikers in the room. I almost wet myself when I saw Lucius dressed as a steampunk pirate and I didn't have to think too hard on who the culprit might be.

Speaking of the rainbow in the room I looked to see Pip was curled up on Adam's lap and she was playing with his braces.

"So I was saying…"

"Sperm!" Pip shouted and I wasn't sure whether Adam wanted to laugh or to smack his forehead at his wife's behaviour.

"Uh yeah, thanks Squeak."

"No worries, Toots, I've got ya back girlfriend!" She said making a fist and pounding her chest twice like some kind of symbolic gesture for the sisterhood.

"So we have all gathered that Aurora's whole plan was to get to Seth from the very beginning."

"That's what we were just discussing but none of us can understand why she would gain anything from it." Vincent said calmly.

"Because she's a fucking nut! Let's just put it down to calling a bitch a bitch and that's that!" Sigurd said leaning forward from his chair and raising his hands to slap them back onto his knees before getting up.

"Excuse my son, my Lord, he is…" Ragnar started to say but got cut off from Sigurd,

"Don't say shit old…"

"You need never excuse your son, Ragnar, not when he

aided Keira as he did." This shocked everyone when it came from Draven and even more so when he continued,

"As far as I am concerned I not only trust everyone in this room with my life but also owe you all a great debt indeed." This of course blew the wind out of Sigurd's sails and Jared crossed his arms over his chest with a smirk.

"Besides, he is right...she is a fucking nut." Draven added and everyone laughed, all but me who very rarely heard him swear in front of me. Sigurd came over to him, smacked him on the back and said,

"Nothing like watching your crazy ex being beaten up by your girlfriend to pull the stick outta your ass, eh?" I nearly swallowed my own tongue and for a split second worried for Sigurd's life.

"Something like that." Draven said turning to me and winking.

"Ok now I know I am in the twilight zone." I muttered to myself.

"You and me too, Lille øjesten." Ragnar said coming over to stand next to me and place his big paw on my shoulder. I looked up at him and said,

"Hey big guy."

"I hate to be the kill kicker in all this mushy shit but are we ever going to find out what the hell the bitch wanted?" Orthrus said before taking a swig of the bottle of beer he was holding.

"Seth is not only the last blood line of the Titans but also has the Venom of God in him right?" I asked and Vincent answered me.

"This is correct and I know where you are headed with this but it would be impossible."

"So she couldn't have his baby, even after I saw her take that potion crap, force him to take it, made him find his happy mojo by posing as RJ and riding him to get his rocks off and then getting preggers with his baby, someone that she can reincarnate as Cronus?" When I had finished the room not only went quiet but it looked like everyone was about to have a heart attack! Bottles fell from lips, jaws dropped, eyes bulged and those in chairs sat forward.

Oh yeah, I had dropped a bombshell.

"Come again?" Sigurd said looking at me like I was now the Oracle.

"Could it be possible?" Vincent asked his brother who was stood motionless still taking in what I had just said.

"Surely not…Dom?" Sophia said getting from her chair.

"And you're absolutely certain this is what you saw?" Draven asked me, ignoring his siblings.

"Trust me I only wish I could erase the sight from my mind but I think the damn scene has been burned to my retinas! So in answer to your question, yes I am very sure." Draven turned away from me to face the room and said the one thing that was certain to make me swear…

"Then our war is not over."

After that it became a battle to keep everyone calm and under control but I had to say that Draven had this mastered to a fine art. I learned that having a lot of alphas in one room was not the calmest of places to have a discussion about someone who obviously wanted to take over the world.

Draven had asked his father to look into the whereabouts of Cronus after the business with the Titans to be sure it wasn't him who had set this whole thing in motion. But unless you were on Lucifer's own council then you had no right even asking. Thankfully though his father held his seat at the table with pride, so he was looking into it.

I had asked the obvious question which had been why

Aurora had waited for Seth to appear and not just used Alex? Because I had to agree with Pip when she said that Alex would have rode that crazy train all the way home…and I had to try and stop from laughing when she started with all the sex hand signs.

But according to Lucius and the research he had looked into, Seth was born after Alex or more like Cain, which was what his first name really was. Cain and Abel, like the ones born to the first Eve were reincarnated just like Eve was. But unlike Eve this had only happened the last time she was alive before Draven put the poor woman out her misery.

Sammael had succeeded in creating his offspring with Eve the first time but after he was banished from Heaven after they found out what he really was up to, he was serving his sentence and by the time he got back out the sons had all died. One of course by his kin's jealous hand when Cain killed Abel in a murderous rage. Eve would then know lifetime after lifetime of being taken against her will by Sammael in the hope of recreating the key he needed to unlock the Titans.

Only as before, Seth was the only one who was born a half breed, a Nephilim the result born from angelic beings mated with humans. It was hard to imagine Sammael as anything angelic but he did in fact start life as a high ranking Angel and only became the Venom of God when he betrayed the Gods. So when Cain was born he was in fact more demon than angel due to his father's tainted blood and had no human in him at all. So the likes of Aurora, being an Angel, would not have been able to create an offspring with Alex.

Which was what made Draven's father and Mother so special. They were, and remained to this day, the only two souls connected enough that they defied their laws and created life despite them being Demon and Angel.

But this wasn't where it ended or the only reason why Seth

was the only one able to create a child, one needed with the pure blood of Titans to become a new vessel for Cronus. Lucius explained his findings when looking into Seth included ancient script of the Qumran.

The Dead Sea Scroll spoke of the 'Children of Seth' and how they would be condemned for their fates foresaw them rebelling against God and all Gods alike if ever allowed to live on earth. Of course this didn't mean much to Lucius at the time but now it all made sense. Seth was the one they had waited for all along and Sammael and Alex had been played by Cronus and Aurora.

Yes they no doubt wanted to free the Titans but Cronus still obviously needed a pure blood vessel and with Aurora being a Titaness this was already half the puzzle complete. But as always Pip explained it best the only way she knew how... being blunt as ever,

"So some little magic voodoo and hocus pocus, a little party trick turning into Pinky and BAM! You had yourself a recipe for a baby megalomaniac Cronus...! Wow nursery would be Hell on training wheels with that kid around! I mean what's his dummy going to be made of, fire and brimstone?! Geez Maneez!"

Of course the major problem we had now was that none of us had any clue where Aurora could be but we knew one thing, she had planned this all perfectly and for a long time. I remained very quiet during this discovery as I felt responsible for letting this happen. If only I had known the importance of stopping her actions. I had stopped myself at the time in fear for my friend's life but now, well could I really have put everyone else at risk to save one human life?

Draven continued to look at me during this whole discussion with nothing short of concern. It didn't take a genius to guess where my thoughts were leading me to and the guilt was no doubt written all over my face.

"We were all fooled and for more years than I wish to repeat." Draven said and Sophia, Pip and I all scoffed at the same time.

"Not me, I always thought she was a lying bitch!" Sophia said and Pip raised her hand and added,

"Me too! Total skank attack." Draven then looked down at me and I held up my hands and said,

"Don't look at me like that, she was your ex, I was always going to hate her ass, even if she was a bloody saint."

"Fair enough." Was his only comment.

"Women's intuition is basically like having a bullshit detector with tits or fun bags...do we all prefer fun bags?" Pip asked looking around the room for an answer.

"I like fun bags." I said and Draven coughed a laugh.

"Sorry darlin' I'm a tit man, it kinda kills the sex vibe when a dude with a dick says the word 'fun bags' during the act." Sigurd said and for some reason I blushed. Orthrus however was in full agreement and said,

"Fucking 'A', brother!" and slapped his hand to Sigurd's. All the women in the room rolled their eyes at the same time and just like that the tension that had once been there was gone and talks of 'The Bitch' were over...

For now.

"Time to party like it's the 80's! One tequila, two tequila, three tequila, FLOOR!" Pip screamed as she handed out shots from a belt she now wore that had test tubes all the way around.

"Is that blood?" I asked stepping back, thankfully into Draven's arms.

"Yep, fresh out the virgin! Ha look at your face! Look at her face Kingyo, she thought I was serious. No, it's just food dye." I laughed and took one but my smile only lasted until she said,

"Nah, the virgin blood was in the macaroon you just ate, ooh time to put more paint on the bouncy castle!" Pip said running off and I think I started to turn green.

"She's joking again..." I looked up at him and smiled and then he added,

"It was just regular blood." And then winked at me.

"Why you!" I said turning round and poking him in the stomach, which of course was still rock hard and had no give to it. Mine however, had lots of give to it when he did the same back and it also came with a little snort.

Not long after we had finished our meeting Pip had dragged me away to get me in my dress. As soon as she said the word my heart dropped at the idea of looking like a walking sweet shop but thankfully I was nicely surprised. The top part of the dress was corseted and was plain black satin that fit perfectly. When I asked her if she had had it made to fit she just winked at me and told me to get my sweet ass downstairs soon as we were bobbing for poisoned apples.

The skirt part was what normal people (Not Pip) would consider the 'mad part' of the dress. It was ripples of sheer white material edged with thick ribbon at the bottom of the short skirt that were all bright colours of the rainbow. It curled around me and flared out in waves. It was sweet and pretty and I felt like a little girl wearing it.

I nipped back into the room I had left RJ in to check on her to find her fast asleep on the bed. She looked completely worn

323

out but was still in her oversized hoodie and black ripped leggings, so I covered her up and took off her shoes.

"Please be safe in your dreams." I whispered to her and left the room as quietly as I could. I was just twisting up my hair and tying it with the rainbow ribbon to match that Pip had given me as I bumped into someone.

"Lucius."

"So you made it." He said raising his eyebrow at me in that chastising way that told me what he really wanted to say was, 'I told you so'.

"See, it all turned out in the end…well, kind of." I added trying to hold back my guilty face.

"Well I don't know, I am dressed like a damn pirate." He said making me laugh.

"Let me guess, Pip?" He then held up the hook that she had obviously stuffed over his severed hand and said,

"You think?" making me laugh harder this time.

"The annoying little Imp doesn't even have the decency to fake being sensitive to my cause."

"You have met Pip right?" I asked looking him up and down thinking that she might have made him a Pirate but at least she made him a hot one. Captain Jack Sparrow would have had competition on his hands.

"Yes, undoubtedly so." I smiled knowing that he adored that little Imp, no matter the hard ass act he played.

"So you arranged with Sigurd to help spring Bill out to save me."

"That was the plan and one that worked nicely I think, considering what we had to work with." He said looking me up and down with a smirk and I blushed.

"Ha ha, very funny. But seriously you could have told me I could be expecting a cowboy to show up and save the day."

"Like you told me about the letter you left Dom?" Ok so he had a good point.

"Yeah, I thought so."

"Then I guess we are even." I said in my defence.

"I guess we are." It quickly became one of those moments that you didn't know where it should go but before it became awkward you wanted to end it. My time around Lucius was difficult to explain as there was always going to be a love there that was different to what I held for anyone else. It wasn't bad, it wasn't wrong, it was just different. We had been through a lot together and when I had thought he was dead I had felt the same searing pain of loss that I had done when I thought I had lost Draven.

Yet the love I had for both of them was separated by a very strong and prominent line. It was the same line I had with Vincent, Draven's brother and between Sigurd and Jared and anyone else who was dear to me. But I would say if that line was ever smaller on one side then it would have been for Lucius. And that was a confusing can of worms I never wanted to open.

"I have come to say goodbye." I looked up at him and noticed for the first time I had known him, he looked tired.

"Why, the party is still…"

"Let's just say that I would rather miss what I suspect is to come and let's leave it at that." He said cryptically. I frowned and it deepened when I noticed the little black veins around his forehead and down his neck. I wanted to ask him about it but I could tell now wasn't the time, not when I saw the flash of pain he was trying hard to hide. And I knew it was the physical kind.

I nodded and he gave me a small smile that didn't reach his stunning steel grey, icy blue eyes. Then he put his hand on the back of my neck, pulled me close and kissed my forehead…

Then he let me go.

He started walking away but I shouted down the staircase to him,

"Lucius?!"

"Yes my little Keira Girl?" My heart tugged hearing my pet name and I closed my eyes a second too long.

"Are you alright?" I asked and his response nearly broke me,

"No…

But I will be."

CHAPTER TWENTY-EIGHT

KEIRA

WONDERFUL WORLD

I couldn't help but feel a sadness I had to hide after saying goodbye to Lucius but it seemed to be a recurring theme for the both of us. It felt like there was so much more we both had to say to one another but neither of us wanted to go first, or even listen to the facts. But I knew one thing and that was I hated seeing Lucius so broken.

I shook my head slightly to get the morbid thoughts from my mind and tried to focus on the arms that held me from behind. When I had first walked back down from my goodbye with Lucius to find Draven again, I had been swept off my feet by someone I didn't even know could dance.

Vincent.

The music was playing some catchy beat and I laughed as he twirled me around and just smiled when my feet fumbled the steps and messed up. I think I must have stepped on his feet more times than not. It was when I was being spun for the third time that I caught sight of Draven watching us.

He had his arms folded and was leaning against one of the pillars just watching us both. I thought he might have wanted to cut in but then his look said something so much more. It was the type of look that made you feel shy, even with the one you love. I must have started blushing because he laughed. It was a beautiful sound which was why it was hard to keep my pretend scowl. If anything though, this just amused him more.

Vincent and I continued to dance until the song finished and once it had he looked down at me.

"I think he has been made to wait long enough, let's torture him no longer." I smiled and then bit my lip knowing there wasn't much I could say to that. I was about to pull away when Vincent's arms wrapped around me and pulled me in for a hug. Then he kissed my cheek and whispered in my ear,

"You saved my brother. You risked your life to bring me back the biggest part of my own. I cannot thank you enough and even a lifetime of doing so will still not amount to what it means to me. You are my world's strength and I can only hope I find a love like yours one day." He pulled back to see the tears running down my cheeks, so he reached up and wiped them away with his thumbs. His crystal blue eyes glistened with emotion and for that one moment in time it belonged to us and no one else in the world.

After that I found myself back in Draven's arms with the party continuing on around us. Which brought us back to Pip and her fabulous ways. She bounced off into the crowd and I couldn't take my eyes off her.

"You love that little Imp, don't you?" Draven asked me from behind and I bit my lip to stop it from wobbling.

"I really do." I said swiping the tear away before anyone saw it. It was strange for I had been in Hell facing perils, fighting Harpies, facing imprisonment in something that would rip me apart yet coming through all that and finding my family on the other side was what made me cry the most. It was feeling blessed and loved. It was being allowed the time to reflect and feel proud that you had the strength when you most needed it.

It was simply living and being thankful for it, because no matter what you went through in life there was always a way out, you just had to fight for it. You just had to find the strength and push yourself through the shit and come out clean on the other side. But the one thing you had to keep you going was that when you hit rock bottom, at least you had something hard to help push yourself up against when reaching the top. And let's face it you couldn't get much lower than Hell's version of Hell!

So that was why I cried more now than when I was close to death, because even though there can be strength in your tears, there is double the amount of love in them. And that's what my tears now were for. They were for the love of my friends, for my family and more than anything else, they were for the man I loved at my back. And as long as we had each other that was all that mattered…

We could face anything together.

"Well then, you will be glad to know I picked up a birthday present for her." I snapped my head round and looked up at him with wide eyes.

"You did?"

"I did, from the both of us of course." He said and he bent to one side to pick up a gift bag I hadn't even noticed was there. I had to laugh at all the comic book characters that covered it and the massive multi-coloured bow attached to one side.

"What is it?"

"You will find out." He whispered and then nodded to Pip who was twirling in the middle of the colourful crowd like a child lost in her own wonderful world. To look at her you just had to smile and admire her beautiful spirit. Holding her skirt out and spinning round and round on her own listening to the heavy rock music that you would never have put her actions of dance to but it didn't matter. She didn't care for such things and neither did anyone else.

She was perfect just the way she was.

And she was my perfect friend.

Suddenly the music stopped and Pip started clapping and chanting,

"Cake, Cake, Cake!" Everyone in the other rooms tried to cram into the room to see and Draven and I stepped closer. Then from around the corner four people emerged each carrying a pole attached to the corners of a table top.

"Oh...my...God." I said at the sight of Pip's cake where there was only one word to describe it...insane.

"I think this is her biggest one yet." Sophia said coming to stand by us with her own present in her hand wrapped and ready to hand to Pip. I looked back to the enormous cake as they set it down on a free table, taking up the whole space and one that could have sat six for dinner.

It was amazing and stood about 6ft tall. In fact I don't think if the guys carrying it hadn't been Supernatural the four of them wouldn't have got it in because that thing must have weighed a ton! The best way to describe it was a giant waterpark with the main water chute starting at the very top. There was a tunnel at the top that looked to be the start of the ride and where the carriage would come racing from. Then there were twists and turns and even a loop the loop all around the cake that was like a snowy mountain.

There was also an icing figure of Zeus stood at the top of the mountain holding a sign up with both arms above his head, it read,

'Pip's Water Works'

"Brilliant!" Pip shouted laughing at what it was named and then she bent over double and let out great belly laughs that even made her wheeze uncontrollably. I think it was the Pip equivalent of the Keira snort.

The rest of the cake as it went further to the bottom became a sea with the arm of Poseidon rising out of the base. He had his famous trident in his hand and a dragon style sea monster's head rose up from behind the arm and became the end of one of the water slides disappearing into its mouth. The centre of the cake was obviously earth as it was all different greens from the hundreds of tiny trees the ride passed through.

Dotted all around the cake were smaller rides like it was in fact a whole fun world filled by this crazy amusement park and you could tell Pip absolutely loved it!

Adam came up from behind it and Pip ran and jumped in his arms. I think he was dressed as a Jedi Knight and I was surprised he was looking so tame considering Pip must have dressed him. But I guess seeing as she had a thing for 80's pop culture, it fit in with the theme of the party…which of course was madness.

"Thank you, thank you, thank you!" She chanted bouncing in his arms and he beamed from making her so happy.

"That's not all my little Winnie, there's a surprise waiting at the top of the mountain."

"YEY! Is it that rainbow pony tail butt plug I wanted?" She asked clapping and I heard Draven cough and lean down to say,

"Did she just say…"

"Yeah, she did." I whispered back shaking my head and trying not to get that particular mental image.

"I don't think I could have fit that into the carriage, love." Adam said laughing and then pulled a big lever that was on his side of the cake. It was a candy pole, with red and white stripes and a big exaggerated red ball on the top. He pulled it towards him and you could then hear the cake coming to life.

The icing clouds above Zeus started to move from one side to the other. Then a rainbow went behind the mountain and back round again. The tiny rides at the bottom started to move and fairground music started to play. Even tiny little icing figures started to slide down the water chute into the dragon's mouth and every time one disappeared there was a tiny little scream.

But the best part came when the tunnel door opened at the top and the little carriage emerged. It followed the track all the way round the mountain until it came to the end near where Adam had situated Pip. There in the little carriage was a black velvet box, tied with a comic book ribbon and the whole gift matched her dress.

She squealed and grabbed the box before yanking the ribbon off impatiently then she snapped open the box and started screaming with delight. Everyone cheered even though none of them knew what it was, although it was obvious it was a piece of jewellery.

"You got it! Oh my peanut butter cups! You got it me! You remembered!" Adam, looking like the dashing Jedi picked up his wife and swung her round before showering her with kisses. Then he put her down and she shouted,

"I love you, I love you, I love you! Now put it on me!" To which Adam started frowning and growled,

"Not here, love." He said making her laugh.

"Ok cave man, I won't get my dairy pillows out, no need to

go all possessive about my Jubblies…here look what he got me everyone!" Pip shouted holding up the box and showing us the beautiful silver heart with an arrow going through the centre. At the end of the arrow you could just see the tiny green emerald embedded there. It took me a while to figure out what it was as there was no chain attached to it but then the whole 'Dairy pillows' and 'Jubbly' comment clicked and I knew it was a nipple piercing. I looked at it again and saw that the arrow went through the nipple and fixed to keep the heart in place around it.

"It's so pretty." I said and even though I couldn't see myself getting my nipples pierced this was one piece of jewellery that could have changed my mind…it was very cute.

"As pretty as it may be nothing will be piercing this delectable skin of yours other than my teeth." Draven hummed after getting his lips close to my ear. I shuddered in his arms and almost groaned as I put more of my weight back against him. We hadn't even had our first kiss yet and I put this down to we both knew what would happen when 'It' finally happened.

"I need to get you away from here. I'm finding my patience to have you is at its last strength." As he said this he pulled me more forcefully back against him and I could feel his solid erection was backing up his words of need.

"Oh no, now you two can just stop that for a minute, I am opening presents!" Pip shouted pulling me slightly away and sticking her tongue out at Draven when he growled at her.

"Tough titties Royal Man, this Tootie is mine for the next hour!" And she was right, it did take her another hour to open all her weird and wonderful presents. Some of which included a remote controlled tarantula, bacon flavoured candy, Zombie blood shower gel, vibrating bra with attached nipple clamps, new shoes that had little garden gnomes as the heels, a clutch bag like a bloody cleaver and then something called a GO GIRL, which she got very excited about.

"Yey! I can pee on the GO!" She shouted holding up the pink funnel like she was holding the Olympic torch.

I must confess that I was hitting my limit of being felt up by Draven, as it hadn't taken long for him to get back possession of me. But with his hands feeling up my sides and keep dipping higher up the back of my legs I was ready to get on my knees and beg for mercy.

"And this is from me and Zagan." Sophia said handing over hers. Pip continued to do what she did with most of her gifts and that was to shake it by jumping up and down. Then she tore into it and screamed…again, something she did with each gift she received. In fact I don't think I had witnessed someone so thankful no matter what the gift was, just the fact it had been bought for her was getting her excited. I was starting to think someone had a bit of a gift addiction.

"Oh my, a Willy Wonka Penis Factory! This is amazing, look honey, I got one!" She said holding it up and I had to turn my head to the side in case I was seeing it wrong.

"Is that what I think it is?" Draven laughed behind me and Sophia actually blushed before leaning into me and saying,

"Try not to judge me, I promise you it's what she asked for." She was of course referring to the glass bulbous shape attached to a long green pony tail, with electric blue tips to match Pip's hair.

"It's my very own Rainbow pony butt plug! Oh we are going to have so much fun with you riding me with this in later! I'm so glad I packed our horse whip! Thank you, thank you, thank, you!" She said leaving her husband to stand red faced whilst coming over to hug Sophia.

"Thank you Zagan." She added and he held up his hands and took a step back, then pointed at his wife and said,

"It was all her idea!" Making everyone in the room laugh

and Draven even patted him on the back in a 'We are men, we band together' type of way.

"Whatever, I bet you bought Sophia one of these already!" At this Zagan cried out as Draven's pat on the back turned into his gripping his shoulder in comment to hearing about his sister.

"That would be a big no, no!" Sophia said and then turned round and smacked her brother,

"Don't make me hurt you, now get off my husband!" To which Draven complied. It was all in jest and people seemed to be getting a kick out of seeing what they must have referred to as the 'Royal Family' acting so relaxed.

"Ok, so now it's our present!" I said turning to take it from Draven's hands and having him wink at me in return. I had no idea what he had bought her from the both of us but after seeing all the other presents I was really hoping it wasn't something lame like a grey chess set or a beige designer scarf.

I handed it over to her and she spent half a second saying,

"Aww" at the bag with the rainbow bow. Then she whipped it out of the bag then held it up in front of her and I gasped in shock. It was the Fraggle Rock T-shirt I had seen ages ago and mentioned to Draven when sat with everyone on the roof top. But the major difference was that he'd had it personalised with the words on the back,

'Toots and Squeak, Friends Forever'

This was the side that was facing me now and the reason I had gasped. The thoughtfulness was overwhelming and to know that he had done this for not only her, one of my best friends, but for me too. It was perfect.

"OH WOW! This is so cool, have you seen this baby pop?" Pip asked Adam and he looked to Draven who nodded at the back.

"Turn it round, love." Adam said and once she did there was utter silence…

This for Pip was unheard of. I couldn't see her face as she had it held up high but when she finally lowered it I could see why she was so silent.

Pip was crying with happiness.

CHAPTER TWENTY-NINE

KEIRA

POWER EXCHANGE

After the emotional outburst from Pip it was obvious to the men that we needed special girl alone time, to which Pip shouted,

"But don't worry, I don't mean like muff diving or anything!" To which Adam just shook his head and the rest were obviously not used to 'Pipisms' as I liked to call them so they turned away to try and look anywhere but at the two of us. I was just glad I didn't catch anyone adjusting their pants.

Sophia, Pip and I all went off to have our 'Girly' moment which consisted of dancing to 'Girls just want to have fun' by Cyndi Lauper, doing disgusting shots and trying not to be the first one to pull a funny face…which I sucked at being the only mortal and of course the sacred ritual of going to the toilet together and borrowing each other's make up whilst talking about men. It was actually very easy to forget my friends were two of the most powerful supernatural beings on the planet and that wasn't just down to who their family connections were.

"So you and the Big Kong still haven't popped the weasel out and given him shelter in a warm bed for the night?" Pip asked me re applying her black eyeliner around her lips and adding blue lipstick to the centre.

"Uh?" I said wondering if I had heard her right or whether it was just the blood shots that had got to me.

"She means sex." Sophia said translating.

"No and I am not going to lie, I really don't know how much longer I can last." They both started laughing and no doubt it was at the desperation in my voice.

"I guess it's not like you've had much opportunity since…"

"Since her crazy dead army springing to life ex-boyfriend who really wanted to get stab happy and destroy the earth kidnapped her?" Pip added looking at Sophia who grinned,

"Yeah him."

"Wow, I thought my ex's were massive crapolias but you took the biscuit with that one!" I had to agree with Pip on that one.

"So tonight's the night eh?" She asked nudging me as we all faced the mirror.

"Yeah, in more ways than one!" Pip added and then Sophia shot her a 'shut up now' look.

"What do you mean?"

"Who me…nothing, I know nothing, I swear on bees." Pip said and for some reason adding the peace sign to the mix.

"Bees?"

"Yeah, do have any idea what those little guys do for the planet? I read this article once that 1/3 of all vegetables and fruits produced are pollinated by the stingy little bastards and… and…did you know that some folk estimate it could be up to 80% of the world's food supply affected by honey bee pollination. Crazy shit I know but this is why we need National Honey Bee Day in our lives and you would have thought that after farming the mini vibros for at least 5000 years that we would have more respect when they sting us, I mean they die anyway but what a way to go...!"

"Vibros?" I asked turning to Sophia our resident Pip expert after our bee history lesson had fizzled out.

"Ok, so this is what I have got from that...Vibros are vibrators, vibrators buzz, therefore bees buzz...if that's not right, then I have nothing." We all laughed and Pip added something neither needed to know,

"I have a bumble bee outfit for Adam and he plays the bee keeper." She added a wink she really didn't need to and I shook my head to try and prevent another mental image invading my mind.

"Right lady bees, let's go wiggle this shit!" Pip shouted walking in front of us doing an exaggerated strut and making her little bum sway. We made our way down a staircase I hadn't been on and as I reached the bottom steps Draven appeared from nowhere and before I could react, he had put his shoulder to my belly and flipped me up like a fireman carries the damsel.

"Whoa! Draven what are you..."

"I am done waiting. My gift to you Mrs Ambrogetti has expired and I am taking her back, Happy Birthday." Draven said before turning from her and I looked up to find her giggling in Adam's arms.

"And she calls Adam a caveman." I muttered only to receive a slap to the bottom.

"Oi!" I said holding my bum and trying to pull my skirt down. But instead he just pretended that he was going to drop me and I screamed in protest.

"Then I suggest you behave." He said and you could tell he

was in one of those playful moods that I was looking forward to ending more serious.

"I hope you're taking me to the bouncy castle." I said playing along and getting another jerk when he tried to fool me into believing he would drop me again.

"Oh I will take you *in* the bouncy castle but not until later, not until I have had my way with you elsewhere." He said and as soon as he turned a corner and found it empty his hand went up my skirt.

"Ahh Draven…no, not …ohh…ohhh." I said as soon as his finger found that sweet spot. My head dropped to his back as I could no longer hold it up.

"You were saying?" He asked when I groaned again.

"Don't stop."

"That's what I thought you said." I would have laughed if I'd had my wits about me but then he inserted a finger and I cried out. I had no clue where we were headed and for all I cared it could have been back to Hell and I wouldn't have cared. As long as we were together and he continued to do what he was doing right now.

He hooked his finger round, angling it just right and then he inserted a second finger and I came undone. I jerked over his shoulder and rode the wave feeling myself falling under with not only the orgasm but also being suspended over his shoulder. I was light headed from both and it added to the intensity. He continued to play me until I was begging for him to stop, not being able to take much more.

I felt the delicious cool night air against the skin on my legs and it felt so good washing over my overheated body. He finally had mercy on me and pulled his hand from under my skirt. The he lifted me off his shoulder and let me travel the length of his body until my feet touched the ground.

I looked up into his dark eyes and whilst keeping my gaze he lifted his fingers to his lips and inhaled a deep breath.

"Oh no, please don't…" I said getting embarrassed but he just gave me one of his trade mark bad boy grins that only managed to get me all worked up again.

"I missed your sweet scent, almost as much as I missed your sweeter taste." He said then sucked his two fingers into his mouth and closed his eyes as he tasted me. Then suddenly he opened his eyes, which were now a deep purple, then pulled his fingers from his mouth, yanked me forward and tipped my head back by pulling on my hair.

"It's just not enough!" And then he crushed his lips to mine for a kiss that was all fire and no sweetness. There was nothing gentle and soft about it. No, it was raw, it was pure and it was overflowing with sexual tension that needed to burst…

And it was the effing hottest kiss I had ever had in my life!

I don't know what happened but something snapped inside each of us and our need to be connected overtook our senses. We tore at each other's clothes like wild animals fighting for dominance and I knew I would never win. Hell, I didn't want to but that didn't mean I didn't want the fight…So I jumped.

He caught me and the force sent him back against a wall which pleased me. He had me held with his hands on my butt cheeks and he squeezed hard making me moan from the bite of pain that seemed to inject even more pleasure into my movements. I ground against him, feeling his erection right against my underwear and suddenly that thin barrier became like a brick wall!

I wanted it gone, I wanted his trousers gone as I didn't want anything between us! So I reached down with my hand and yanked at whatever I could to try and free him. I didn't know how I managed it as my mind was certainly not working at full capacity for such things but as soon as I could wrap my hand around his naked length he groaned.

"Oh yes! By the Gods almighty, yes!" He said letting his head fall back against the stone. He still held me and using my other hand I located the waistband of his trousers and pushed them down enough to free him fully. Then just as music started up from somewhere below us I moved my underwear to one side and at the same time he lifted me higher to then thrust into me.

We both cried out and my back bowed with the length of him connecting with my body. Then he lifted me up again and powered into me over and over again until I was screaming with untamed ecstasy. One of his hands reached up as he held me more securely with just one arm under me for the sole purpose of ripping my corset down and freeing my breasts. Then he took a nipple into his mouth and became ruthless with it. He bit, sucked and then bit harder making me cry out and pray for him never to stop.

His teeth were brutal. Then I felt him take it too far as he pierced my flesh and this was the catalyst for my second orgasm of the night. I felt myself rippling around his length and impossibly I felt him grow harder because of it. He sucked on my tortured breast and I fed him the blood he wanted to taste with nothing short of pride.

After he had sucked his fill of me, he left my abused nipple to latch his lips to my neck so his hand could go back to my behind. This was so he had more leverage to manipulate my body but as I felt the next wave coming I lost my mind. I tensed my legs and used my body to power back over him faster and harder than ever before. Usually Draven ended up doing most of the work, just because of the power his body forced upon me but this time it was different.

Usually with Draven the common quickie was unheard of

and I wasn't even sure if he knew of the meaning but tonight he proved me wrong, because tonight I was strong and powerful…

And it was beautiful.

Because for once I felt in command. Because for once I felt like I held all the power over him. For once I felt like he was powerless against me. And for once he couldn't hold back from bursting with pleasure. So as a result we both came together uncontrollably and quickly in a lost passion even the Gods couldn't have stopped.

It was sexy, it was hot and it was fucking dirty! And we both loved every single second of it!

We both fell to the floor in a tangle of limbs and clothes after our bodies gave up from the force of it. I had never known Draven to lose himself like that and I felt as if I had climbed a mountain, survived a jungle and tamed a bloody lion! And in a way I had done all of those things, because I had brought a King to his knees in the most beautiful way possible!

"Holy Gods" Draven muttered still panting as he still held me close.

"You can say that again."

"Holy Gods." He repeated making me smile. I lay with my head on Draven's chest and again listening to every fast beat of his heart was like receiving a pat on the back by everyone at the finishing line after winning the race.

"Wow." He said after a time and I laughed,

"You know I think that's the most human you have ever sounded." I said looking up at him grinning like a crazy person.

"Well after that performance I think you sucked all the power out of me and rendered me human. Although with the way you moved I think it was definitely more demon than angel that got through." He joked and I pinched him in retaliation.

"Oi! Try and remember who saved your demon ass." I said

making him growl at me and flip me over so I was on my back on the hard floor.

"Oh I remember and don't you worry, we will still be having words about that insane risk of your life you took but right now I am thinking about another way to make you pay for unmanning me and losing my pride in such a disgracefully insubordinate way" He said teasing me and I grinned up at him.

"Oh is that right?" I asked and he snapped his teeth at me once making me jump.

"Oh Keira love, nothing I am about to do to you is considered right, but fucking good...? Oh yes, it most certainly will be."

I shuddered in his arms and now I was the one whose head was falling back against the stone.

Because Draven was most certainly a man of his word.

And he was right...

It was fucking good.

CHAPTER THIRTY

KEIRA

I GIVE YOU MY WINGS

"Is that a giant inflatable twister game, only with paint?" I asked Draven and he laughed. We were both still at the same place Draven had brought me to but at least now I had the chance to look around. Once Draven had punished me in the most perfect way a girl could be tortured and that was with Draven's talented mouth between my legs, I finally came up for air…and the first thing I did was giggle.

"I did have something more romantic planned." He said shrugging his shoulders when I sat up and looked at the beautiful setting he had created. We were on top of the roof and at just the right point to overlook the beautiful central fountain of lovers Perseus and Andromeda. But that wasn't the most beautiful part about it.

Draven had laid down thick white blankets and pillows scattered in a space framed by candles of all sizes and flowers covered the floor until the stone couldn't be seen. A bottle of champagne was sitting in a chilled ice bucket made of clear glass and fresh fruit was piled high, peeled and cut ready for the eating.

"Are those chocolates?" I asked homing in to the good stuff. He laughed and said,

"Couldn't have left them out." Then he picked me up and carried my half naked self over to the most perfect setting for the rest of whatever the night held in store for us both. I looked down at my torn dress and said,

"I think it's ruined, poor Pip."

"She can bill me." He said before grabbing the rest of it and ripping it clean down the middle.

"Draven!" I shouted but he just shut me up very easily... with a kiss. And this time it was very sweet. And it was very soft but it was still just as perfect. We both undressed each other until we lay under the stars naked and nothing had ever felt more right than lying with Draven this way. It felt pure and natural, almost as though we were being blessed by the Gods.

I don't know where that thought came from so I turned to look at him and he grinned back at me as if he felt it too.

"Draven?" I said his name as a question I didn't have the words to.

"You feel it don't you?" Draven asked and I nodded not understanding exactly what I was feeling but it just felt that in this precise moment in time we needed to be like this because it was expected of us...

Because the time had come.

"What's happening?" I asked but then he pushed his body weight into me until I was under him and then he whispered,

"Just let it happen."

He kissed me and for long moments we just let ourselves become lost in the moment. He ran his fingertips down my side and I felt the sparks ignite my blood. I reached up with both my hands and ran my fingers through his hair, holding it back so it wouldn't fall forward.

"I want to see you." I told him and he closed his eyes for a second taking my words into his heart and holding them there.

"Do you know how much I love you?" I asked him and he looked back at me with such heat, I felt it warm me from the inside out.

"Keira you went to Hell and back…trust me, I know how much you love me." On hearing this I cried. I took my bottom lip in between my teeth and let my emotions fall down my cheeks. He leant down, placed his forehead to mine and whispered,

"It is an unbreakable strength in your love for me Keira and until this day I never knew it had strength enough to match my own."

"Oh Dominic!" I said and sobbed into his neck as he held me naked in his arms and then just as I said the three words out loud he thrust into me. So these words were at this very moment immortalised in a memory we would never forget. Because these words were said after all we had been through and survived.

And they were the only ones that mattered and the only ones that held enough strength to beat back fallen Gods, to defeat armies against us. To discover those who betrayed us but most importantly, words backed up by selfless acts of love and sacrifice that were strong enough to bring the other back to life.

"I love you Keira, by the Gods I love you!" Draven said as held me close and brought me even closer to that blissful place, cementing me there with his arms around me and himself buried deep at my core.

We came undone and passed out together.

When I finally came to I was surprised to find I was the first to wake. I don't know how long we had been asleep but at some point Draven must have woken long enough to cover us. I was thankful for it as there was a definite chill in the air. I could still hear music in the distance as the party continued but from the look of the sky it wouldn't be that long until sunrise.

I was glad in a way as it gave me chance to look at Draven and take in every detail. His beautiful skin was back and once more had that healthy glow to it that not long ago had been pasty white. His dark hair fell around his face like a man deep in sleep and I smoothed it back making him stir.

"Are you staring at me again, love?" He asked me still with his eyes closed.

"Big head much?" I teased back pulling the covers up to cover my breasts.

"I rather prefer them on show and ready for my personal use." He said opening one eye and I giggled after failing miserably at trying to growl.

"And here I was thinking you couldn't get any more adorable than with that little red nose."

"Ha ha, laugh it up Mr Darcy, I had to improvise." At this Draven threw his head back and laughed like I had never heard before. It was almost uncontrollable and I couldn't help but join in although I had no clue as to what he found so funny.

"Are you laughing at me?" I asked for the second time and again I had to wait for him to try and control himself.

"Oh my lovely girl, I don't think if I lived for another thousand years I would ever get that image out of my head."

"What do you mean?" And again I had to wait as this brought on another round of laughter.

"The sight of you with that ridiculous wig on, a biker jacket and a red nose with a giant penis held high and ready to use as a weapon is not how I imagined seeing you again for the first time after I woke, but I can't say I was disappointed…amused yes but not disappointed, especially given your reaction to seeing me again." He was of course referring to me dropping everything and running into his arms in my obviously desperate act to be there.

I guess that was certainly an image that would stay with you but it would stay with me for very different reasons. Oh the times I thought about bashing Aurora around the head with something…ok so a giant penis piñata wasn't the iron spiked mace I had always envisioned but as I had told Draven, I had to improvise.

"Do you know how angry I was at you when I woke?" Draven asked me and my shoulders tensed knowing the time had come for my official telling off.

"I have an idea. Actually no I take that back and say yes I definitely had a good idea considering I felt the same way about you when you yourself went into Tartarus with the sole purpose to save me." Ha! His face said he hadn't been expecting this part of the argument.

"But Keira you could have…"

"NO! If you want to tell me how stupid a decision it was then that's fine, I might even agree with you considering how things turned out but my decision only affected you and me, not the rest of mankind like your decision did." I said snapping and folding my arms as this would help back up my claim.

"I know you see it like that but I had a plan in place."

"Lucius?" I asked and for a moment pain flashed in his eyes in a purple flicker.

"That was the main part of my plan, yes."

"Then it was lucky you had me to back up the part you didn't expect would happen because like it or not Draven we are a team and that means trusting the other to do what is right when the shit hits the fan! I refused to let you die just as you refused to do the same." I said and for once instead of looking angry he just looked thoughtful, as if it was finally sinking in.

"We are a team." He repeated and I was shocked as I had been all ready with another 'team' speech.

"And I did trust you, along with those around me when they told me they had found you and were bringing you back. Do you know how hard it was not to snap her neck when hearing her lies? I think if I hadn't read your letter first and then been assured of your survival then I would have. But I trusted you and you were right, we needed to know what she was up to."

"Uh…I…" I struggled for words and was so shocked I wanted to take a page out of Jared's book and say, 'Ok who are you and what have you done with Draven?'

"Did your demon get some anger management whilst on its forced holiday?" I asked and once again Draven burst out laughing.

"Do you want to ask him?" He teased by winking at me with blood red fire in his eyes.

"Uh…I think I will pass."

"The truth of it is that after waking I was ready to storm the gates of Hell beating back beasts I met there and demanding you be brought to me unharmed. Then I would have called forth my own legions and brought a war to all the princes of Hell, including my own father if need be." Draven said all this tensing his muscles and clenching his fists, so I picked one up and placed it in my lap and began prying open his hand so I could entwine my fingers with his. I was surprised at how quickly this worked.

"But then Vincent told me how well you handled yourself in my place. He told me how proud I would have been to see the strength in your decision and how everyone looked up to you.

But more importantly he made me realise I had no right to take that away from you. He explained that I represented a balance but not for mortal mankind. And that you were a mortal that had just as much right to free will than any other and if you chose to save me with that will, well then I had no right to stop you... and he was right." I think my shock was more than clear on my face because he laughed once and then tapped my chin as my jaw had dropped.

"See, there is hope for you yet." He joked and this time when he winked at me it was all Draven, dark eyed and dreamy.

"So we are good?" I asked thinking this conversation would have gone a hell of a lot differently when we first met. He nodded and said,

"We are but I intend on making it better." I frowned not understanding where he was going with this, so I groaned,

"I knew there was a catch." To which he chuckled.

"Come, stand with me and let's meet the new day together." He said standing up and wrapping one of the sheets around his waist. I did as I was asked and wrapped my own cover around me and I had to giggle as we looked ready for a toga party.

"We'd better not let Pip see us like this or we will be wearing this at her next party." I joked. I walked over to where Draven had his hand held out for me and stepped over the candles that long ago became extinguished. We stepped up to the balustrades that were spaced by massive stone urns and I took in the beautiful view of dawn rising.

The sky was a rich midnight blue colour casting the land in dark shadow and a faint glow came from the horizon. There were clouds in the sky that were darker in colour and played with the upcoming light. I leant forward and rested my arms on the stone wall and Draven did the same.

"I never thought I would find you." He said suddenly

looking out to the view ahead as if he was almost talking to himself.

"I often looked out at this view when I was here and many others all around the world but no matter the difference in landscape I would always wonder the same thing." I bit my lip before forcing the question through my quivering lips,

"What did you wonder?" He finally turned to look at me and said,

"I always wondered if that day would be the day I finally found you."

"Oh Draven." I whispered putting a hand to my mouth as I listened to the most important words I would ever hear.

"I did so when I woke after finding out you were destined for me and I walked to my window back when my view was the rolling sands of Persia and went as far as the eye could see. I did what I did now and met that new day wondering how long I would have to wait. And even after I lost you I still met the day the same way and now here we are…"

"Here we are." I agreed looking back out to the sun starting to cast its colour to the day.

"I never realised what it would mean, even back then I had no clue what it would mean to be in love. I was so arrogant to such things, thinking you would be just another person to obey me…" He laughed at himself at the thought, before continuing,

"How wrong I was."

"You certainly were, I bet you wouldn't have believed anyone if they had told you what it would really be like, having a wilful Northerner on your hands to deal with."

"No, you're right, I wouldn't have believed them, but I want you to know Keira, that I wouldn't have it any other way. I don't want just another subject to obey me and agree with what they feel is wrong. I never fully understood it until I read your letter. The last thing you actually said to me, about how our souls are entwined, our hearts combined and our minds are one team that work together fuelled by our love for each other..." He said quoting back what I actually said to him in my letter.

"I want you to know I feel the same way. I finally get it. I made a mistake letting you go and thinking that would keep you safe. Because now I realise that together we can face anything and my father was right, if I had spent that time fighting for us instead of against us then none of this would have happened."

"Draven don't...don't torture yourself over what happened back then." I said knowing I was now singing a very different tune than what I did back then. If only I had known this was the way he felt back when I was torturing myself would it have helped? I wasn't sure if it would have made that hurt any less bitter.

"I should have listened to the old bastard for he knew. He recognised the strength it took me for walking away, something he himself had no choice but to do with my own mother but it was I that didn't want to fully recognise what it meant..."

"Recognise what...?" I asked when he paused to look back at the rising sun.

"The strength of love from a mortal. The strength it took you in looking for me the first time and then saving me the second. But now I understand. Now there will be no fighting it anymore and I promise you this...I won't let you down again... and I...I...Ok, so now the time has come." He looked around as if he was stumbling for the right words to say. As if he was trying not to mess something up and suddenly I had never seen Draven looking so uncertain.

Then my heart stopped.

Because Dominic Draven got down on one knee.

"Oh God!" I whispered and he smiled up at me. Then he took a deep breath, one I couldn't yet take from fear of waking

up and he said the most perfect words I had secretly dreamed of hearing since that first day I ever met him…

"Catherine Keiran Williams, I brought you here tonight with the sole purpose of saying goodbye to all the yesterday's spent apart and now welcoming a new forever of days together. For I promise to never let you fall. I promise to trust in you as I ask that you place your trust in me. And all I ask in return is that you believe these words of love and know that I will never let you go again…I will fight for you until the end of days and beyond." He said then took my shaking hand in his and the tears streaming down my face dripped on to my skin like extra proof this was actually happening.

Then he turned over my hand, opened it up and placed a small box there. I still couldn't move to even open it myself and Draven knew this so he helped me. He flipped the lid and I gasped and cried even harder at seeing the beauty that lay cushioned there. It was a beauty that mirrored the stunning sky of the new day and I felt my heart swell…

Then he finally said the words and coloured my world perfect,

"Catherine you own my heart, body, soul and mind. Now I give you all I have left…

I give you my wings…

Will you marry me?"

CHAPTER THIRTY-ONE

KEIRA

SURPRISE!

A fter I had burst into uncontrollable sobs of happiness Draven took me in his arms and held me for the longest time. He turned me to watch the rest of the sun coming up, filling the sky with purple blues and peach pinks in the clouds that floated slowly by. Then just over the rolling green hills were the fire oranges bleeding into yellow. It was the most perfect sunrise I had ever seen but to be honest it could have been raining a thunderstorm and it would have remained perfect.

"Can I take the crying as a yes?" Draven said after a time and I laughed.

"You can take that as a Hell yes!" I said making him growl playfully at my humour.

"What do you expect, I have been to Hell and back twice now which means at least ten years of Hell jokes."

"In that case, I take it back, let's just be friends yeah?"

"How about Hell no! You're mine now Big King Man!" I said mimicking what Pip had called him and then threw my arms up around his neck for a kiss. It started out slow and soft but before long the sheets had fallen and we were quickly strengthening our union with more than words.

I threw my head back against the makeshift bed and cried out for the third time, too lost in my own euphoria to take notice of Draven's own release. It had started off by him lifting me onto the ledge and soon my fear of heights only added to the intensity of our lovemaking. I had protested only for a moment until he whispered,

"Trust me." And then he entered me finding me wet and ready to take him hard. And hard was what he gave me until I screamed the first time and then sweet was how he took me for the second. By the third I was physically spent but mentally he wouldn't allow me to give up until he got what he wanted,

"I want another one, come for me Keira. Come for me my wife to be." As soon as he asked this of me I obeyed without control.

I didn't remember us moving from the ledge but I can say I was happy not to be still there and have to come round from my lust drunken way to find I was still facing the long drop down.

Draven lay down next to me and rested his arm across my body to pull me tighter to his side. Then he started to play with a random curl in my hair that lay loose by my waist. He wrapped it round and round his finger before letting it spring free and he continued to do this until our heart rates slowed.

"Well I guess the quickie days didn't last long." I said as a joke and felt him laugh next to me.

"That is what happens when I allow a Vixen to take control, one orgasm for both of us."

"Yeah, but what an orgasm." I said with a wink that I knew wasn't half as sexy as when he did it.

"Agreed." He said then kissed my shoulder making me shudder, one he mistook for being cold. So he sat up and grabbed one of the fallen sheets and pulled it over the both of us. I saw him grab something else more important than any sheet or even being warm because the next to come was a sight I had wanted to see for what felt like the longest time.

The ring.

"May I?" He asked me and I sat up, pulled the sheet to my chin and gave him my hand for the second time of the day.

"Vena Amoris." He said as he slipped the ring on my third finger on my left hand.

"What does that mean?" I asked thinking whatever it meant it sounded beautiful.

"A tradition that started over thousands of years ago and now one of my favourites. It was a Greek and Roman belief that a vein from the third finger on the left hand ran directly to the heart. This vein was known as the 'Vena Amoris' also known as the vein of love."

"Draven it's stunning." I said looking down at the most exquisite ring I had ever seen and now I knew what he had meant by giving me his wings. The ring was a pair of wings that twisted round the finger and came to the front to hold its centre piece.

"It's a flawless natural Purple Sapphire, one I searched for with only one sole purpose, for when I met you. I had it set in my wings the day I told you I loved you for the first time." This brought a lump to my throat.

"You have had it all this time?" He nodded and then touched it, turning it round on my finger to show me all the smaller diamonds embedded in the dark wings and the more I looked the more I realised, he was right, they were his wings. They had been made to look the same and the detail was incredible. It looked as if you could almost see each individual feather and the way they were lighter at the centre and darker towards the ends.

"I'm speechless." I lifted my hand and let the light catch the main stone that was one of the deepest purples I had ever seen. I had loved my necklace and I knew now why he had given it to me, obviously knowing it would one day match this. Something else I would be wearing every day but this ring represented something more than just a wedding or a marriage, no, it would now be representing *strength in love.*

<hr />

After this we stayed up on the rooftop until my stomach started to protest. A few pieces of fruit and some bubbly which Draven brought back to chilled wasn't enough and what I really needed was something like a big greasy cheeseburger and chips. I almost suggested Burger King again but then giggled to myself after remembering what happened last time.

Once we had made it back to Draven's room we both showered together, which ended up taking longer due to obvious reasons and I was thankful to see a bag had been packed for me. After seeing it was going to be another unusually hot day for British weather I put on a pair of stonewash denim shorts and a light grey t-shirt that had flowers on the front in the shape of a skull. I thought it looked very hippy summer meets rock and when added with some cute dark grey cowboy boots I found in there I thought Bill would approve the gesture.

I was just plaiting my hair to one side letting most of it dry naturally when we were invaded.

"AHHHH! TELL ME, TELL ME, TELL ME!" Pip shouted

and it looked like we were still on Pip repeat from last night. Sophia laughed but then said,

"Oh sod it!" And then did the same thing as Pip and ran in from the doorway to jump on the bed I was sat on. I fell back laughing as they jumped around me and I covered my hand over my head to protect myself. Then Draven walked from the bathroom where he had been shaving and came out wearing only his jeans with a white towel around his neck.

If I hadn't just had another two orgasms and was feeling a bit abused down there I might had been tempted to kick the girls out and had at him again.

"What's going on out here...oh..." He said seeing the bed full of women and now looking scared.

"OH my Goggle Box! Look at her ring! HE ASKED HER!" Pip shouted and Sophia shrieked along with Pip and then jumped off the bed into her brother's arms. He caught her with a 'humpf' sound and she kissed him on his cheek and said,

"Congratulations dear Brother." His face went soft and he picked his sister higher up to kiss her forehead before setting her down on her feet, then said,

"It was long overdue" causing another lump in my throat to form. I kept finding myself catching the ring on my hand and trying not to get emotional at the sight. Could this all really be happening, were we really engaged? Oh God that meant I was going to be...

"Mrs Keira Draven! Oh wow, this means you are going to have to start calling Draven Dominic or you will just end up calling yourself Draven and that will be confusing and that would be weird...would that be weird?" Pip said plucking my thoughts from my mind and giving it a crazier spin.

"I think it's time I left you ladies alone." Draven said...or is it Dominic said? Either way you could tell he wanted to save himself, so he came over to me and kissed me gently on the lips before saying,

"I will be back shortly but I have arranged for food to be brought up to you." At this I felt like kissing him again but when I felt my hand being pulled to the side so Pip could see my ring more closely, Draven knew it was definitely time for him to leave.

"Oh wow, it's amazeballtastic on you."

"Not the exact word I would use but I must agree with her, it fits you beautifully." Sophia said coming back over to the bed and sitting down. I pulled myself up until my back was against the headboard and said,

"So you guys both knew what he had planned?"

"Uh maybe."

"Totally" The two answers came together with Pip's being the only truthful reply because she couldn't lie for a vintage Carebear. Of course it became even more apparent when Sophia shot her a look.

"I have to ask but only 'cause I fear for your life, is that outfit as flammable as it looks?" I asked looking at the gold and shiniest material I had ever seen.

"Oh do you like it, it's one of my birthday presents, my C3PO onesie, complete with sound effects." Then she pressed the button and a robotic voice said, 'We're doomed!' and again with 'I suggest a new strategy, Artoo: let the Wookie win'. Sophia just rolled her eyes and I started giggling and only stopped when she said,

"I never understand why they don't put the button to activate these things over your nipples…makes much more sense if you ask me."

"Yeah but wouldn't that mean if you got cold it would just be going off all the time and the last thing you want is your breasts shouting, 'we're doomed', especially when your husband wants some fun alone time with the girls." This came from Sophia and we all burst out laughing.

"Yeah but then they really would be fun bags!" Pip shouted and it just kept us going until my belly ached not just from hunger.

"Ooh, right on cue! I changed the order you will be happy to know." Pip shouted jumping up and Sophia and I both groaned knowing the Gods only knew what it could be. Pip snatched the tray off the girl after giving her a thankyou pat and then bounced back to us.

"Dada! Cheeseburgers and Fries!"

"Oh my God, Pip I could kiss you." Which was precisely what I did, only as I was holding her to me, we all heard,

'Sir, it's very possible this asteroid is not stable.' And once again we fell about laughing.

Once I had stuffed myself silly and polished off two cheeseburgers with all the trimmings I did what Sophia suggested and changed into a loose fitting summer dress. One that didn't have a tight waistband like the shorts did and therefore have the added flesh coloured bike tyre around the top.

The dress was a navy cross over V neck that was pulled in at the waist but tied at the side with a white ribbon that wrapped around my body a few times. Sophia was also wearing a dress but hers was a long maxi dress that tied around her neck after twisting to cover her smaller breasts. It was a striking rust colour with a scattering of cream flowers at the bottom of the wispy skirt.

Other than the lovely Pip it looked like we were going to attend a garden tea party as we descended the stairs. Draven hadn't come back up but he had someone check on us three times to see if we were ready to leave.

Adam came in and after offering his congratulations, the same as Vincent and Zagan had done before him, he informed us we would be ready to leave within the hour as plans were in place. I asked what plans but he just blushed and had his wife to deal with so he was saved from answering me. And let's face it a small shiny Star Wars character jumping on you from behind was somewhat distracting for conversation.

I had asked her when we had been eating cheeseburgers about Adam's costume where Sophia and I both commented about it being quite tame. She just smirked and then said,

"Well you only say that because one..." She held up one finger that was painted like a Stormtrooper and carried on,

"Nobody saw what he was wearing underneath and two..." This time she held up a Wookie and said,

"You didn't see his Lightsabre, it was made of rainbow candy and by the end of the night there was nothing left...if you know what I mean... gives a whole new meaning to twister pops." She said waggling her eyebrows at us, ones that were still dyed green from last night. My reaction to this was completely different to Sophia's as I just went bug eyed as again Pip didn't fail to attack me with her skills in mental image scarring. Whereas Sophia just shook her head and lowered her forehead into her hand.

"You know sometimes Pip you just don't need to paint such a graphic picture." I said pulling her to me by her shoulders and giving her a sideways hug.

"I know right, I should really just start filming it all and then that would be Christmas sorted!" Then she blew me a kiss and took another massive bite of her burger.

Which was why Sophia had leant into me when walking downstairs and said,

"If we both get DVDs from her we are kicking her out of the gang and not letting her back in until she's burned every copy."

"Deal." I agreed and with her skipping down the steps in front of us, which I didn't know how you accomplished that without falling on your ass, she said,

"I heard that!" And then saw her husband waiting for her and jumped on him.

"Hey Hubba Bubba, I totally have a cool idea for gifts this Chrimbo…how do you feel about taking me Camera shopping later...? Hey Toots, where's the best place to buy a camera around this United Kingdom?" I laughed and then shouted back,

"A shop called Iceland!" Which she wouldn't find out until she went there but it was in fact a shop that sold only frozen food.

"Good call." Sophia whispered obviously knowing this and the wink I received from Adam also told me we weren't the only ones.

It was clear everyone was ready to go as the cars were pulling up ready to pick us up just outside the house.

"There she is." Draven said coming up behind me and whisking me off my feet. The feeling of being in Draven's arms again had me sucking in a deep breath and praying for the next time we could be alone. His low growl in my ear told me he knew what I was thinking.

"Soon Love, soon."

"Right peepshows, this is where I leave you… I know, I know, don't cry for me Argentina!" Pip said coming over and pulling us all in for a hug one by one but me and Draven got one combined.

"Oh you guys! Congrats and shit…Toots I will catch you later for the Wedding planning/ Hen Do we will be having…

don't worry, I am planning the Hen Do...wink, wink, chin, chin, elbow, elbow."

"Oh God." I muttered making everyone laugh and Pip ignored me and shouted one last time as she descended the steps,

"Toodles Pips!" Which I gathered meant goodbye in Pip speak. She and Adam got into a chauffeur driven car but not after I heard her telling the driver in the van behind to be careful as he's carrying important cargo, which I assumed was all of her birthday gifts.

Draven waited for the car to turn around until motioning for what must have been ours to come forward. I had to say after everything we had been through I was more than looking forward to going home. I had missed Afterlife, to what I considered as my second home and the people there my family. I needed to get that back, now that I'd had a taste of it in the past few weeks. But more than that, I needed my time with Draven to make up for what we had lost.

It almost felt like it had in the beginning, where we couldn't stand to be apart from each other. Although I don't think we ever managed to hit that point where that phase wore off, not considering we actually hadn't been together long before... well, let's just call it a breakup and be done with it. Thinking back on it all I could barely believe we were now at this point and it was only hours earlier when he had asked me to marry him.

Well one thing was for certain and that was my life definitely wasn't boring. And neither now would RJ's I thought with sadness. She had already left with Vincent not long ago. Everyone thought it best if Vincent was the one to explain things to her about their kind, as she woke this morning under the impression she had been given drugs at some kind of rave. I had explained things to her last night the best I could but I think half of it she hadn't taken in on account of being hurt about the way Seth left her.

Hurt can do that to a person and make it difficult to be reasoned with and I knew this better than most. But I had to admit, hearing things from Vincent might not actually have been the best choice considering RJ was partial to a handsome man. And facing facts, concentrating on important information wasn't her strong suit if it came from a sexy man, no matter how calm and cool his demeanour. But saying this I had never seen her so devastated about a guy before, so maybe she had really fallen for Seth. I mean it wasn't so hard to imagine, even after one day as my own obsession had started pretty damn quick after meeting Draven for the first time.

"Are you ready?" Draven asked me pulling me from my thoughts about my friend.

"Yeah, let's go home." I said making him smile at hearing it. He put his hand on the small of my back and walked me down the steps to the car. I was thankful to see it was a different car than I had arrived here the day before and I could barely believe all that had happen in such a small space of time.

Draven had explained how it wasn't long after I left that everyone did what they needed, which included moving the unconscious Draven and following us here. Pip had been more than thrilled about having her Birthday party at the old Supernatural party house, shouting something about 'it's like bringing back the 80's' which no one other than her husband understood. Draven had actually woken up in the plane journey over and according to Vincent it had been lucky he had the letter to calm him before he destroyed the plane.

By the time they landed Aurora was already back and waiting to spin her lies but didn't realise that Sigurd had already heard word from Jared that Bill had found me and I was safe. So Bill and I both became break out jail birds and he was now reinstated onto Jared's council with the proviso that Jared would be taking responsibility for any other misdemeanours that involved the Cowboy. Of course we all kept quiet about the punks in the Range Rover putting that down more to a public service.

Once in the car I thought about when I had said goodbye to Jared and of course handing over the precious jacket of his that looked as if it had been to the Stone Age and back, it was that old.

"See ya around kitten, try and stay out of trouble won't you but I guess if you don't manage it then I will see you next time…you know my address." He said winking and catching the jacket in one of those mega bad ass cool ways that just had you wishing you could be just as cool one day.

"Oh and I will let you off with the shades." He shouted over his shoulder as he walked to all his people on bikes and I saw Wild Bill, my new saviour, tip his hat to me, before kicking his steampunk bike into action.

"You're quiet?" Draven said as the car started to pull away and I looked back to see the house that was seconds ago full of splendour was now back to being a mere shell that I first saw it as. Draven's laughter made me leave the house behind us and turn to him.

"If Pip was here now she would be calling you a space cadet." This made me chuckle.

"I guess I was just having one of those 'processing all that has happened' moments. It feels like a dream, all of it." Draven lifted up my left hand and kissed my ring then said,

"Considering the outcome I am glad it isn't." And I had to agree with him on that.

"What do you think your family are going to say?" He asked me and I sucked in a sharp breath.

"Oh no, I hadn't even thought about that. I mean, for a start they don't even know we are back together and only really know you now as the guy who broke my heart...sorry about that." I added when I saw him wince.

"It is of my own doing Keira. As deep and regretful of a mistake it is, it is still one I own up to freely, no matter however shameful. I know now how wrong I was but the only saving grace I hold is that I did so out of love, not hurt." I nodded and squeezed his hand before saying,

"I know... *I know.*"

———

"Wake up love." I heard Draven's voice hum in my ear and I moaned at the lovely sound. It was actually his chuckle that followed my moan that brought me round to the land of the living.

I must have fallen asleep at some point and after the night we'd had together I wasn't surprised. In fact after what I had been through in that week I was surprised I hadn't just keeled over into a month long coma. I was cuddled up to Draven with his arm around me and I was just thankful to see there wasn't a drool mark... 'cause nothing said cool like drool!

"Are we at the airport yet?" I said shifting my body so I was sitting up. I clenched my fist a few times to try and get the blood flowing again as it had gone numb.

"We're not going to the airport." He said and I frowned looking round and trying to figure out where we were going.

"Are we going for a meal first or did you want to stay at a hotel for the night?" I asked as we pulled up to a swanky hotel with a glass front. The car stopped and a doorman approached.

"Mr Draven Sir." He said as he opened our door and Draven unfolded from his seat. I felt a little embarrassed considering I had been snoozing not long ago, so I smoothed back my hair only to feel most of it had come undone. I started unravelling it like a woman possessed as I scooted across after Draven. He offered me his hand but saw what I was doing, so grabbed my elbow instead to help steady me.

"You look lovely." He said kissing my cheek and then taking over with my hair by running his fingers through it then called me,

"My Goddess" making me blush. I straightened my dress, glad I was now wearing one at the sight of this place. Draven walked us inside and the concierge asked us to follow him, informing Draven everything was ready as requested. We came to a set of double doors that had a gold plaque informing us it was a business suite of some kind. I turned to Draven just as he opened the doors and asked,

"Are you going to tell me what we are doing here…Mum?!" I shouted and then took in the rest of the room, looked up at Draven and said,

"It's all my family?" To which he laughed and said,

"Surprise Sweetheart."

CHAPTER THIRTY-TWO

KEIRA

FAMILY FUN

I t turned out that Draven had arranged with all my family to have them picked up and brought to this hotel to celebrate our engagement. Draven had already received my father's blessing in asking me to marry him and I had to wonder how in the dickens he had managed such a thing. I hadn't told Draven as I didn't particularly want to rub it in but after he had left me I wasn't in a great place, so let's just say he wasn't exactly on their Christmas list anymore.

"Libby?!" I shouted as she came running towards me and as we embraced I turned us both round so I could look at Draven over her shoulder. He just grinned at me and I watched my parents both welcome him into the family with a hug from my mother and a firm handshake from my father. I then looked over to Frank and found little Ella fast asleep in his arms, so he just gave us all head nods and a beaming grin.

I found out Draven had had my family flown over in another of his private jets and as soon as we were alone I had to ask if he didn't actually have his own bloody airline because how many private jets does one person need. He simply answered 'for occasions like this, clearly.'

After everyone in my family hugged us and offered their heartfelt congratulations we all sat down to have a celebratory dinner in the private suite Draven had booked. I really didn't know how he managed all this but when the rest of my family all walked in it was my time to cry again.

"Sophia, Vincent?!" I asked in utter shock considering I thought they were all on a plane heading back home. This had all been a tall tale told just to throw me off and when I asked after RJ, she too walked in to join the party. Zagan followed introducing himself as Sophia's husband and I could see my family trying not to stare. In fact, it was my grandmother who took a fancy to him and made the poor guy sit down next to her after pinching his bum once or twice.

He shot Sophia a panicked look of pleading for help but she just waved at him making him growl. One of the nicest parts about this was finally being able to properly introduce Sophia to my sister and Frank. They had met before but it was only under the pretence as just friends but there was no doubt we had been much more than that for a long time now.

But then my shock doubled and my world became complete when the last two walked through the door.

"Pip! Adam!" I screamed their names and launched myself at them both feeling overwhelmed with everything that was happening.

"I told you I would catch you later." Pip whispered to me as I hugged her close. I pulled back and looked her up and down shocked by what I found.

"What, you didn't think I could finally meet the folks

dressed as a damn droid did you?" I laughed and saw her white and red rockabilly style dress that matched her head scarf and I knew for Pip this was classed as tame. She walked past me and I laughed when I saw her tights had a sexy pin stripe up the back with the words 'follow me' going up the side.

"I have to thank you. I have never seen my wife so happy before…and she deserves to be happy, like no other I know. She loves you very much." Adam said standing next to me as I watched the gorgeous girl embrace my family as if they were her own and I relished the sight.

"Thank you for sharing her love." He looked down at me, pushed his glasses up his nose and said,

"My pleasure." And then he went after his wife as she called him over ready to introduce him. I smiled at the sight of everyone chatting like old friends having no worries about my family accepting anyone I obviously held a lot of love for, no matter what they looked like. That was the wonderful thing about my family, they never judged you on how you looked but only on your actions and it looked like Draven's actions had been forgiven. I was glad and more than a little relieved. The last thing I had wanted was the 'Talk' from all of my family members.

I looked back to the door as I knew there were other people we were missing, which I found out later Draven thought it best not to overwhelm the humans. I still couldn't help but look back at the door again and wished to see one more body step through those doors…one I knew had already said his goodbye.

And it dawned on me what he'd been talking about when he said 'Let's just say that I would rather miss what I suspect is to come and let's leave it at that.' He had known and he didn't want to stick around to see it. I looked down at the plush carpet and shed a single tear for my friend and wiped it away quickly as Draven approached me from behind. He came over to me and whispered,

"Did you like your surprise?" My reply came in my actions as I turned quickly and threw my arms around his neck and kissed him passionately. Pip started wolf whistling and then everyone started cheering and clapping, getting up from their seats to celebrate our engagement.

It was wonderful.

The rest of the evening was filled with nothing but laughs and love. My family told embarrassing stories about me, like the time I got confused and thought my hamster laid eggs, when actually it had just tried to eat a beanie baby. Draven thought this was 'endearing' but no matter how cute he might have found it, he still laughed his ass off.

Whenever the three Dravens were asked about anything they all answered questions with perfect ease. Vincent was asked what he did and calmly said,

"I am in charge of mergers and acquisitions for the family businesses." To which my mum turned to me and said,

"Ooh fancy. And so handsome too, just like his brother… you must have your hands full with these two?" She asked Sophia and she just smiled and replied,

"I'm lucky to have mastered the art of keeping them in check." This brought back the sight of Sophia punching Draven across the face after what happened at the cabin all that time ago and I smiled.

"She likes to think so, eh Brother?" Draven said and Vincent laughed.

"I must say you all look very different from each other." My mother commented and my father said,

"Yes but look at the girls Joyce, they are very different."

"Dad."

"Dad." We both said at the same time as if proving him wrong and everyone laughed.

"Vincent takes after our mother." Draven said and I coughed nearly choking on my roll.

"Did it go down the wrong way?" Draven said patting my back and I just wheezed out a,

"Yes." And then I looked over to Vincent who gave me a wink and turned back to continue talking to my father.

"Well this young fellow here is my idea of a dreamboat!"

"Nan!"

"Mum!"

"Edna!" All three of us shouted, including my father and I noticed Pip, Sophia and RJ just all start giggling. Zagan looked petrified and my granddad just nudged him and said,

"Don't worry son, her bark is worse than her bite…plus she has false teeth, so you're good." Everyone burst out laughing including Zagan with only my Nan left saying,

"What did that old coot say about me Joyce?"

"Nothing mum." Again this got the whole table laughing and was pretty much how it stayed the rest of the meal. I don't think I even really paid much attention to what food we were having but that I think was definitely the sign of a good time and this was one of the best times of my life so far. Having all those who I cared about finally coming together, something I never thought would have been possible, was like a dream come true. But to know the reason of why we were all together was for our engagement was more than a dream come true, it felt like miracles were something that could actually happen.

Of course it got really fun when Ella woke up. She bounced from Frank's lap and promptly decided everyone was there for her so she needed to entertain her adoring fans. I watched her make her way around the table and approach the none humans with glee. They on the other hand were in nothing short of awe and I could imagine why. Being a Supernatural who had little to do with the rest of the mortals they shared a planet with, meant their interaction with children was closer to nil.

I had witnessed this when seeing Draven with Ella for the first time, so this was going to be interesting. First up in her line of sight was Vincent and with no encouragement she toddled right over to him holding on to his leg for support.

"Ello." She said looking up at him and batting her beautiful big eyes at him. His reaction to her was the same Draven's had been when he first encountered my niece.

"Hello little girl." Vincent said looking down at her and having no idea she wanted to be picked up. So because he wasn't taking the hint she raised her hands up and said,

"Up, up." He lifted his head and looked to Draven for help making him laugh.

"I think that is code for she wants to be picked up, Vince."

"Uh…is it…?" It sounded like he was about to ask 'Is it safe' which would have been very funny but Libby saved him and said,

"Yeah you go right ahead and pick her up, she loves it."

Vincent gave her a little smile and then looked down at Ella as if trying to weigh up the best way of achieving the task. When no one was looking I made a motion with my hands to pick her up under her armpits and this time he smiled fully. Then he did what I suggested and picked up the squirming Ella. He sat her on his lap where she instantly went for his face.

"Chummba cheeks!" She said pushing his cheeks together and everyone laughed.

"Why thank you." He said down at her making his voice sound all funny and she started giggling.

"Bubble Guppies!" She shouted and he frowned saying,

"I'm not sure that's a compliment." Sophia was looking on adoringly and then said,

"Thank you Ella for my brother's new nickname." To which Frank burst out laughing,

"Well Ella's nickname is Houdini given she can break out of anything. I swear the amount of times I have fixed that playpen is more times than I have had hot dinners…"

"And I can believe it with Libby's cooking!" My father said making everyone laugh but the people who had experienced her cooking, oh and Libby herself of course.

"Oi!"

"Sorry darling, you know we love you but you could burn a cup of tea." At this I burst out laughing, thankfully after I had swallowed the wine I had been sipping.

"Mummy carwot" she asked tugging on Vincent's t-shirt.

"Uh…?" Vincent looked almost desperate to give her what she wanted but was clearly at a loss to what it was.

"Here, give her these." Libby said passing over a Tupperware pot. Vincent opened them and she dived right in pulling out carrot sticks as if they were the best thing ever.

"Wanna Carwot?" She asked holding it out under Vincent's nose and she wasn't happy until he took a bite. She continued to feed him along with herself and every time I looked over to Vincent he looked like he had fallen in love.

"She has a thing about sharing food." Libby informed him and Frank laughed, nudging my father and said,

"Yeah, just be thankful it's not ice cream she's eating…we learnt the hard way, didn't we Libs?" I giggled as I remembered Frank using a whole packet of baby wipes to clean the mess up that day.

"Ok, quit hogging the baby, we girls want a turn!" Pip shouted jumping out of her seat as it was clear she couldn't contain her excitement anymore. Ever since Ella had woken up Pip had looked almost desperate to get to Ella and I heard Adam say quietly,

"Give everyone else a turn." But Pip looked ready to explode with excitement.

"If I'd known there was a baby I would have brought gifts!" She said coming over to Vincent who was still holding Ella. Everyone but my family held their breaths not knowing what Pip would do or how Ella would react but in the end we had nothing to worry about...well maybe how we would ever separate the two. Ella took one look at our Pip and went crazy trying to get to her open arms.

"Come to Auntie Pippy you cutie wutie you." She said taking her in her arms and swinging her round so she giggled uncontrollably.

"Wow, you can tell she loves kids, do you guys have any?" Libby asked Adam and he looked longingly at his wife.

"We can't have children." He said softly as Pip was busy pretending they were aeroplanes.

"Oh...oh dear I am sorry." Libby said and it was a real touching moment for everyone around the table. Adam held a smile for his wife and I felt like crying. She had so much love to give it was hard watching the scene in front of us and knowing she would never have that. More than anything in that moment I wanted to give that to my friend and I would have done anything to get it for her.

"Well you're welcome to babysit ours whenever you want, she's clearly found her soul mate." Frank said thoughtfully and right at that moment being one of those guys who knew exactly what to say and Adam's face said it all.

"That is very kind of you."

"Ah it's nothing really, just means we get back our date nights, eh Libs?" He said winking at my sister who was smiling at her husband like she was proud of him. Of course I knew they still had these date nights because I would make sure they went on them but Frank being the great guy he was wanted to make things better for people. He wanted to make people feel like they were the ones doing them the favour rather than the other way around, so it wouldn't feel like charity. It was a beautiful trait of the human nature and one I was also proud to see coming from my family.

"It is certainly a beautiful thing to watch." Draven whispered to me just after Sophia got up and went over to the floor to play with Ella and Pip. You could just hear Sophia telling Ella what a pretty dress she was wearing and Ella was shouting about the strawberries that were all over it.

"It is." I said feeling myself getting choked up at the sight.

"What are we playing?" Sophia asked as Pip had emptied the contents of her purse to find there were more toys in there than grown up stuff.

"How about we play Pirates?" Pip shouted then took her head scarf off and tied it round Ella's little head like a bandana.

"Well in that case I want to play!" Zagan shouted surprising us all by getting up and going over to them all on the floor. I wasn't sure if this wasn't just a ploy to get away from my Nan's wandering hands or not but either way he looked happy on the floor.

"Wow honey, at this rate date night will be twice a week!" Frank said to a smiling Libby who was watching her child boss around the grown-ups. If only she knew the power of those grown-ups and who they really were she would have been even more impressed with her daughter's obvious skills at leadership.

Later in the evening, after I found out Draven had arranged for everyone to stay at the hotel, I was saying goodnight to my slightly tipsy mother.

"He's such a lovely man, such a gentleman." She said hugging me for the fourth time.

"I know mum."

"We couldn't be happier for you both and after he explained about why you two split up, which we completely understand, it's just so great you got back together and you can see he adores you...can't you see that he adores her, Eric?" My mum repeated to my father who was calling one of the elevators. I was still stuck on what exactly Draven had told them when my dad walked over to collect my mother from hanging on me for support.

"Yes you can. Now let's go see this fancy room, Joyce."

"Oh yes let's. Oh the girls will love to see this place, have you got my phone, I must be sure to take pictures for Facebook." I smiled shaking my head and then kissed my father on the cheek.

"He's good for you and your mother is right, we couldn't be happier."

"Thanks dad." I said giving him an extra squeeze, one he pretended took out his back.

"Oh give over Eric, you're not that old yet!" My mother said and then gave him a wink as if to say he was going to get lucky tonight if he played his cards right. I was slightly mortified and moaned about it,

"Uh, hello daughter here remember...line you don't cross waving right here." They laughed and my mum launched herself at my dad and I was thankful when the lift doors opened to take them away before things got to the point I would need therapy. Because as nice as it was to know your parents were still blissfully married, no child, no matter how old, needed to witness the evidence to it of more than first base...ever.

Libby and Frank had already gone up to their room and taken Ella with them much to Pip's dismay. She had actually fallen asleep in Draven's arms after she spotted him and ran to him shouting,

"Uncle Dom Dom." How she knew to start calling him uncle yet was anyone's guess. It was a lovely sight to see and one I was sorry I would never get to see him holding our own child. I pushed those thoughts from my mind not wanting to go there on such a happy occasion.

Over all it had been the most perfect day and one that followed an even more perfect night. Everyone cooed over my ring and my mother inquired about the sentiment over the wings and Draven just said as a matter of fact,

"She makes my heart soar, so I thought it fitting to give her wings." All the women in my family all voiced their thoughts on this sweet statement by shouting 'Aww' all at the same time. My dad just winked at Draven and Frank said,

"Oh you're smooth and trust me, you will go far with marriage with those skills." Then tipped his beer bottle at him in a male salute.

Draven and I were the last ones left and after he said goodnight to his siblings it was our turn to wait for the lift. We stood silent next to each other and I had the biggest smirk on my face. Then I said without looking at him,

"She did it again didn't she?"

"Yes, yes she did." He said and I burst out laughing throwing myself at him as he stepped in the lift. We were of course referring to my grandmother who had just made Draven another one of her victims.

"Well Zagan survived." I said kissing him in between speaking.

"I think for the first time in his Demonic life he will be going to sleep tonight with the total understanding and concept of what nightmares are."

379

"Ha ha!" I said smacking him on the arm in my Nan's defence.

"Well it just means it's a good sign I will end up a horny old lady." I added.

"Oh I have no doubt about the horny part however the old lady bit will never happen." I raised an eyebrow in question and just as the door opened to our penthouse floor he said something that filled me with dread,

"Not after our marriage ritual."

"Uh, our what now?" I asked and one look at his sheepish face and I knew it was bad but after what he said next I knew it was even worse...

"I think we need to talk."

CHAPTER THIRTY-THREE

KEIRA

SMOKE AND MIRRORS

Being back in my room in Libby's house was strange, as if I hadn't been here for ages, when in actual fact it had been just over a week. If I'd have woken up here I could have been fooled enough into thinking it had all been a dream.

I'd had a lot of explaining to do when we got back, especially to Libby, from whom I received the whole 'I knew it!' and 'I told you so' speech. And of course she was right, after Draven was the one to drop me off that day she told me this would happen. Of course I didn't exactly tell her about the whole psycho Alex thing but I did saying that after being stood up for the last time I told him where to go. I would have liked to have said more, that I found out he had a rotting willy from sleeping with too many crack whores but that would have been derogatory to crack whores.

I'd explained, even though it was obvious to all how I wasn't over Draven but Draven's idea of filling in the blanks was to tell people as close to the truth as he could. He explained to my family that he had received a threat due to some sour business dealings and he became terrified that this threat could get to me. So he broke things off with me, not explaining why so that I couldn't argue with his decision. Then he came back into town after the threat had been eliminated in the hopes of winning me back.

My father and Frank had agreed with his decision wholeheartedly, being men themselves and protective ones at that they admitted to him doing the right thing. My sister and mother had almost swooned over the fact he wanted to play knight in shining armour and the sacrifice made for the woman he loved. It sounded like something from a soap opera or some period drama. I was in half a mind to remind them of my running snot, no showers, over eating, greasy hair and red eye days but decided it best they continued to think about the man I was going to marry as a hero.

During the meal the subject of a date came up and before I could say in about a year, due to what I remember of Libby's wedding planning, Draven surprised everyone. He said very casually,

"In a few weeks." I was just glad I wasn't eating at the time as I might have choked on a mini Thai fish cake. I think my sister and mother simultaneously dropped their cutlery. My father and Frank just smiled nudging each other as though Draven was some kind of ancient war lord that didn't mess around and therefore was to be admired by anything with a penis.

"Excuse me?" I said after finally finding my wits and putting them to good use.

THE PENTAGRAM CHILD - PART 2

"I am not waiting." He said firmly and that was that. I had moved closer to him and said we would talk about it later. But when I tried to do this I found myself thrown on the bed and talking about weddings was the last thing I had on my mind. He claimed afterwards it was to prepare me for the wedding night and I had just laughed before promptly falling asleep from exhaustion.

I yawned now thinking about the three other times I had been woken up throughout the night to find Draven entering me. I was now deliciously sore in all the best places and was getting wet again just thinking about it. Although before we had this wild night of sex, which clearly was both of us trying to make up for lost time, we did have one little 'chat' about things to come.

As soon as he said the words 'marriage ritual' in the lift I just knew this was going to be one of those conversations where I was going to be left feeling out of my depth. I had prepared myself for bad and received the worst. I would have loved to have found out it was something similar to throwing the bouquet or having the groom pull off the garter with his teeth but this was something else alright, and it was happening tonight!

I was trying not to think about it. I really was but so far the longest time I had gone without thinking about it was about 15 minutes and that was when I was changing Ella's nappy, then having to chase her around the downstairs half naked just to get another nappy on her really helped.

Tomorrow was my birthday and what needed to happen for the ritual was at one minute past midnight. It was this or we would have to wait until their New Year's Eve party but Draven didn't want to wait that long, as he was a tad impatient. Another thing Draven was impatient for, which was why I was here now, was me moving into Afterlife for good. He had kindly sprung this on me the first night home and I was just commenting on how much I had missed his bed.

He informed me it wasn't *his* bed but *our* bed as I was moving in as soon as I was packed. I had asked the obvious question, 'isn't it too soon?' to which he just laughed and said,

"We are getting married." And this was the end of that conversation as again it was obvious he had more pressing issues on his mind, like the need to take me again pressing against my pyjama bottoms. I asked him if we should discuss this a bit more and he agreed, only his agreement came with his hand dipping into my waistband. Once there he gathered up the evidence of my arousal and used it to rub my sweet spot over and over. I only managed to say how unfair this was until I was moaning and begging for my release.

After it finished I just managed enough energy to say,

"I will pack tomorrow." The last thing I heard was,

"Good girl," before I fell asleep.

Which brought me back to what I was doing now...*packing.*

To be honest I really didn't have that much to pack so it wasn't this part that I had been dreading doing, no it had been telling Libby. I had expected her to try and talk me out of it or at least say that she thought I needed more time. But in actual fact as soon as I sat her and Frank down to talk about it they started laughing.

"Well no offense Kaz but we weren't expecting you to still live here and not with your husband." And I guess when Libby put it like that it did sound pretty stupid. And it's like she said, it wasn't as if I lived far away and besides, this way she got to go behind the scenes of the famous Afterlife.

I had to say I actually got excited about the idea of showing her around, although I think there were certain places I would be leaving off the tour. Can you imagine… 'And to your left is Draven's weapon collection but I assure you he's not an arm's dealer. Then in this next room is Afterlife's very own crypt that leads onto a prison for Heaven and Hell's worst criminals on earth… oh and then on from here is the Temple, where we hold our death sentences, host sacrifices, some annual fights with bad guys, New Year's Eve parties and tonight our very own Supernatural Marriage ritual'. Oh yeah I could see this going down well with my mortal family.

"Do you need a hand?" Libby asked popping her head round the door and seeing me on the floor pulling things from my bottom two drawers to stuff into the suitcases I had when I first arrived here. Wow that time felt like an age ago.

"Wow, it only feels like yesterday that Frank was lugging those bad boys up to your room." Libby said coming in to sit on the bed and watch me. It was strange how similar our minds worked.

"I was just thinking that."

"I bet you never thought you would be packing to move into Afterlife with your future husband when you were on your first day of work there." I laughed at the thought.

"Definitely not."

"I was surprised to see RJ looking a bit glum the other night, considering Dominic had her flown all the way over to England for your surprise engagement." I let my hands drop to my lap and sighed. It was true that RJ had been quiet during the dinner and especially from how Libby was used to seeing her, so the only thing I could say was the truth,

"She's kind of going through a tough time at the moment." And really that was all I could say. I had spoken to her and she had seemed distant but I could tell it wasn't directed at me, just distant in general. I managed to get a moment alone with her and she explained,

"It's weird, like I know I should be all freaking out about everything that happened and then to have Mr Cool Blonde Hottie out there explain even more to me, you would think I would be screaming in a mental institute by now, but it's like, that's the part I am cool with, ya know?" I nodded agreeing with her that yes this was weird.

"But do you wanna know the part I am not cool with, the part that I am *so not* cool with! It's having that asshole just leave me like that after showing me what it was like having someone all protective over me! Having someone nice to me and sweet and caring and then BAM! He turns into every other asshole I have ever met or been interested in!" And this was the root of it. RJ had accepted this other hidden world around her like she was just moving house but one guy she started to really like turns out to be not so great and it was as if the world was ending…and I could certainly relate!

In fact I didn't feel so crazy now knowing I'd had pretty much the same reaction about Draven. That night on the rooftop when I saw Draven's true form for the first time and the part I lost it over was when he told me he was engaged the next day! It was maddening what men could do to you but when I mentioned this to Draven, he just assured me that woman could do the very same thing.

This then brought on a whole new conversation about how hard he found it when he used to torture himself watching me but knowing he couldn't touch me. This was another one of what I like to call 'Draven dense' times when he got it into his head I would be better off without him. Talk about conflicted! The man could win medals, awards and shiny gold naked statues for being conflicted! Which was precisely what I told RJ making her laugh for the first time that day.

I had called her once we got home but I got her voice mail. I tried again and again until Draven told me to just give her time. They had been assured enough that she wouldn't be telling anyone what she knew and her exact words were,

"Uh duh, as if I want to live out my days known as a Wacker Jack, never find a boyfriend, get laid and then have no choice but to be the town's crazy cat lady…no, no, I think we're good." Later, Draven explained that he didn't know why, nor did he trust the fates but they obviously knew of the reason that RJ couldn't be controlled into believing it had all been a dream. Therefore Draven knew better than most not to meddle in these things so had little choice than to have his men watch her from afar just to be safe. I agreed to this, reluctantly but when Draven said it was more for her protection there was little I could argue against.

"So you're definitely getting married that soon then because that mad friend of yours assured me that I would receive the invite soon in the post as she was helping you plan it." This made me laugh as Pip had threatened the same thing to me before we left the Hotel. I also found out that she and Adam would be staying at the mansion as Pip didn't want to miss a thing, including the Hen Do.

The word 'Hen do' and it coming from Pip's mouth made me shiver as I dreaded to think what it would be like and had to remind her there would be mortals present.

Her reply made me cringe,

"No biggy, we will just cross off the warehouse nightclub that big bear bugger Leivic runs."

"It looks like it." I said to Libby and then continued filling up the last bits in the cram packed suitcase.

"Hey, do you remember this?" Libby said finding my old Halloween costume, the one I wore to Afterlife for the battle of the bands.

"Yeah I do."

"No wonder that man snatched you up, especially after seeing how hot you looked in this! Ha, I remember now, you went with Jack didn't you?" I groaned making her laugh.

"That poor guy didn't stand a chance against Draven, bless him. He was nice, is he dating yet?" Her question went unanswered as thoughts and memories assaulted me. A story of how he fell in love with a girl who suddenly disappeared. Then it hit me. A strange thought coming to me out of the blue…

Where had Celina gone?

There had been no mention of her and considering she was on Draven's council I had not seen or heard about her since Draven came back. Actually thinking back the last time I remembered seeing her was at Draven's Villa at Lake Como. I found this so odd that I got up off the floor, leaving my suitcase and told Libby,

"I just remembered something, I will be right back…"

"Look out!" Libby shouted as I backed into a side table and the box I had packed there came crashing down. It was one I had emptied from my desk so only had art supplies in it and a few note pads from college work.

"What's that?" Libby asked as I looked down to one sketch pad that had opened up and pencil drawings littered the floor from where they had been stuffed in there.

"Oh, I remember these." Libby said sadly, going back to a time when she knew I had issues growing up and started seeing things. I blushed and went to take them from her hands as she started to help me pick them up when something caught my eye. About four months ago I had started having nightmares of recurring demons I used to see. It wasn't that many, and at a guess about one a month. But I would wake up calling out for Draven and wouldn't be able to get back to sleep, so picked up the habit of sketching what I saw again.

I hadn't thought about it at the time I was doing it, as when I was in the zone I just kind of let my hands do the talking in the form of pictures. But now, in my hand it all started to make sense...

"Oh my God." I whispered as chills wracked my body and I landed on my knees and turned the picture round before picking it up and seeing the real horror there in black and white.

"What? What is it?"

I was looking at my last dream, the one I had just before Draven had re-entered my life. It was the one I had just before going back to Afterlife at the end of June, so little over a week ago now. I woke up and did what it felt like I had been trained to do. I grabbed my pencils and a pad of paper and started to draw what happened that day back in school.

I had been like a woman possessed, trying to get out every detail before it faded away into that forbidden place in my memory bank, the one that stored stuff away until you were least expecting it. The one that lured you into a false sense of security until unleashing all its power of fear back on to you when your defences were down. But now I knew that it hadn't been doing this that night just to be cruel, no, it had been trying to give me a warning...

One I ignored.

"Son of a Bitch!" I said running over to the bedside light and turning it on to check what I was seeing was real.

"What? Tell me?" Libby pleaded but instead of explaining the impossible I let my mind lead me back to the probable. I let it take me back to poor Benny Rodgers whose terrified face I had captured on the page. I let it take me back to the gruesome sight that was a sadistic chalk white face and black vertical lines cut through evil eyes, ones ready for torture. But it wasn't the obvious horror that shook me to my core and had me struggling to keep hold of the page.

"Kaz! Kazzy! Christ, you're pale as a ghost! Talk to me!"

"It's her!" I said holding up the page and Libby winced at the sight of what I had drawn from my nightmares.

"Jesus, Keira, what on earth?" At this I laughed without humour as things like this weren't produced on earth, no, they just lived here ready and waiting for the right moment to strike, and that moment was now!

"I have to go!" I said folding up the page and stuffing it into my jeans. I stuffed my feet into my converse and hopped around trying to put them on without sitting down. I looked around frantically for my keys and hated that I had no choice but to rush over to Draven and tell him this terrible news on what was going to be classed as our real wedding. But it couldn't be helped. However I did wonder how nobody had noticed but then again with everything that had happened I was sure something like this was easy to hide.

Because the truth was that sometimes you could rarely see what is right in front of you.

"It had been smoke and mirrors this whole time" I said muttering to myself as I scanned the room for my jacket.

"Wait, you're not making any sense! Just tell me why...? What has you so freaked out?" Libby asked as I grabbed a light jacket from where it was hiding, knowing I would need it as there was summer rain outside. I looked at my sister and felt bad that I couldn't tell her the truth. I don't think I had ever wanted to tell someone my secret so badly before than I did right then looking into my sisters worried eyes...but I couldn't.

Because what could I say...That it wasn't the sight of a poor boy wetting himself that had me freaked. Or even the hideous demon that had terrorised him. No, it was none of those things.

Because it was not the obvious I was looking at, it was the unobvious...

It was the teacher.

And that teacher was none other than,

Celina.

CHAPTER THIRTY-FOUR

KEIRA

7 IS THE MAGIC NUMBER

All the way over to Afterlife all I could think about was how this had happened. How had I seen that face so many times before and not recognised it when being face to face with her for the first time?

Before I had left I'd had an idea and I had gathered all my drawings up in a pile and stuffed them into a canvas bag I used for college after dumping all the unwanted stuff on the bed. I had made up some story about the picture reminding me that someone might be stealing at the club and needed to tell Draven. It was a lame and farfetched excuse but what else would Libby think it could be?

I was now thankful I had brought a lot of my old sketches over with me from England when I moved, feeling that I couldn't throw them away but not wanting to leave them at my parents' house either. I had to hunt around for these and go into the desk in my old room to find them, as they had been stuffed under a drawer to hide them. I was just glad Libby hadn't followed me up there to watch me acting crazy and like someone out of a lame detective show.

After I found them I added them to the bag and realised I was running late now as I had promised I would be back at Afterlife half an hour ago to get ready for the 'Marriage Ritual'. I hadn't allowed myself to think too much about tonight as it was easier that way. For me, personally I was just glad we were having a mortal version of a wedding which was the one I was looking forward to the most. This one for me was more like a technicality and Draven knew why. I was just thankful he didn't blame me for thinking that way as he agreed he wasn't looking forward to a certain aspect of it…and that was the one bit I was again trying not to think about.

Even though I was running late I still had to pull over and check for myself if I was going crazy or not. As soon as I stopped, I flicked the overhead light on, undid my seatbelt and raised up my bum to dig the drawing out. I unfolded it and checked it again.

Yes it was now as clear as day that it was Celina.

I placed that one on the seat and dived right in to all the other sketches, hunting through everyone I had on me. There were ones from when I was a kid and my drawing skills weren't as hot. But even in those, I still found some with a lady in the background that could have been her.

Some I had used crayons or coloured pencils to shade her hair red. Others, the ones more detailed as my skills developed, it was clear by her eyes or the shape of her face. Even her style of clothing changed throughout the years but there was no doubt, in the ones I found with a woman in, it was her every time.

There were 77 in total and I counted all of them as just over 140 sketches, which meant she was in just over half of them.

"How have I missed this?" I said out loud shaking my head in disbelief. I picked up one I remembered when I was about 13 and it was one of those times when it had eased off for a while, which made this one particularly bad.

It was whilst riding my bike around the block one day when I saw a guy delivering a package to some old man who lived on our estate. He walked to his door, knocked and as soon as the man answered the poor unsuspecting delivery driver dropped the parcel and was frozen in some kind of weird trance. Anybody else looking on wouldn't have thought much about it, as for those passing by it just looked like the two were simply chatting.

But for me this was not the case. Because what I saw wasn't the sweet old man that Ted across the road waved at or that Shelia who owned the newsagent said good morning to. No, to me he was the face of nightmares and became the first sketch ever to be drawn where I had to learn how to draw insects.

The skin on his jaw had been torn from the bone and gnawed away by thousands of crawling insects of all shapes, sizes and varieties. There was even what I now knew was a massive praying mantis coming out of his raw nose bone.

I had even drawn the energy as a mist that he had been sucking out of the mail guy and I screamed, dropped my bike and ran all the way home. But this wasn't what I was looking at right now, not the demon or the victim. It was of the face of someone I now knew as Celina stood watching in the background and I didn't even remember drawing her. In fact I never did. It was as if my subconscious took over and created the picture my brain projected without even thinking about it.

"Ah!" I jumped at the sound of my mobile phone going off and I fumbled with my jacket pocket forgetting it was in there.

"Hey?" I said when hearing it was Sophia on the other end.

"She's fine..." Sophia whispered to someone else once she heard my voice and then she came back to me and said,

"Uh, I hate to point out the obvious but you know you're getting married in a few hours don't you?" I closed my eyes and let my head fall back onto the headrest. Oh yeah, I knew alright! I had even considered how much weight you could lose in a day of crash dieting? Because there were things a naked body just couldn't hide!

"Oh come on Kaz, it's not going to be that bad and I know there is one part of it that you're definitely going to enjoy." This time I actually groaned.

"I heard that!" Pip shouted down the phone and burst out laughing. I was running late for the 'pamper girl time' they had planned for me, which I knew was code for 'Mortal Doll play time' But to be honest anything that took my mind off what was to come was never a bad thing, so I had said yes thinking it a good idea at the time. But now I wasn't so sure.

The first thing I needed to do was find Draven and tell him what I had discovered. Maybe he would think it would be a better idea to call off the wedding for now until we knew more of what she was up to. Well whatever it was, this plan of hers had been set in motion a long time ago if these pictures were anything to go by.

"Are you on your way?" Sophia asked and I looked to the passenger seat and all my life's demons spread out before me. It was a sobering sight to see along with a sickening one at that.

"Yeah, I will be there soon." I said still not being able to take my eyes off those images. I heard her say she would see me soon then but just before she hung up she asked,

"Are you alright?" I thought for a moment and then answered in the only way I knew how and hearing those same words said from my own lips, that I had not long ago heard from Lucius',

"Yeah... I will be."

Once I had hung up and stuffed all the images back in my bag I drove the rest of the way to Afterlife. I was on autopilot driving there and before I knew it the beautiful building was looming over me. Of course it wasn't open for the public, not tonight, not for the important royal wedding.

"Oh god." I said banging my head on the steering wheel. Now I was here I was torn. I knew what this meant to Draven which was the same as what a mortal version of a wedding would mean to me on the day. Could I really go in there and lay this all out right now, only hours before we were joined before the Gods and the eyes of his people?

Now I wasn't so sure.

For a start I didn't even know the importance of what I had discovered or what it could mean? But even so whatever it may be I was sure it could wait for a day at least. So with this in mind I got out of my truck and by the time I slammed my door I had decided it wasn't more important than giving Draven this night. So I walked away from the car with the bag of haunting discoveries still on the passenger seat, leaving it for yet another day.

Once inside I was bombarded with the whirlwind that was Pip and Sophia. Before I knew what was happening I found myself being pushed through Sophia's fabulous Gothic fairy princess room and swiftly into her bathroom.

"I am starting to feel like this is déjà vu" I said making Sophia laugh as I referred to the first time I let her play dress up with me. But soon I was sinking into her amazing sunken bath and letting my mind relax in the tropical paradise that was Sophia's bathroom, complete with the incredible scent of a rain forest filling my over worked senses. I let my head fall back on the cushioned rim and soon my limbs felt like dead weights. I was glad now I had already showered at Libby's house and spent the time plucking and shaving and scrubbing every inch of skin, so now all I had to do was lie back and enjoy.

I closed my eyes and let the scented bubbles caress my skin like a lover's touch which brought me back to Draven. I let my mind wander back over time and I could almost feel his hands all over me. I took deep breaths and the more I did this the stronger the memories came crashing back to me. So much so I felt my hand dip under the water and snake down my belly until I found my core.

"Ahh." I moaned as I touched myself intimately and my back bowed, pushing my breasts up higher and out of the water. My nipples stood erect thanks to the cool air licking at them and I cried out again.

"Draven?" I whispered his name as a plea for him to come to me as desperation gripped me. I remembered how he had taken me in the bath and my body ached for him to do it again. I needed him with a fever of the likes I had never known. It felt like my skin was burning and it would only cool with his touch. The movement of my hand quickened but nothing would come to completion. I moaned again only this time more in frustration as nothing was happening. It wasn't like I wasn't turned on enough as it felt like my skin would soon split from needing to burst but it was like nothing was enough.

"Ahh!" I shouted opening my eyes in anger at not being able to come and then found myself screaming again for a different reason. Celina's face was slowly coming out of the water with eyes of burning hatred. Slashed eyebrows were cut into her face and black cracks and infection crawled under the skin like ink injected in to her blood. Her eyes that had once been beautiful were now milky white with only a black ring around the iris and a tiny black dot at the centre.

Lips that split like they had been cut with a knife smiled at me as they emerged from the water. Fangs started to grow from all of her teeth until they became a deadly weapon. She was naked and it looked like her body had been ripped apart and then crudely sewn back together with black fish wire. Actually it looked like the Celina I knew had died in some horrible accident and I was now looking at her body after her autopsy.

She started to come closer and I held my hands out in front of me to protect myself when something happened. That power, the one I didn't understand but knew I had buried deep within me, came out unexpectedly and it was like an invisible force that couldn't be stopped. It hit her and forced her backwards, making her fight against it as it tore away the rest of her damaged flesh. She screamed as it ripped into her and started taking her away piece by piece.

"Go back!" I said in anger sitting up and instead of using my hands as protection I turned them so my palms faced her. Then I closed my eyes and felt the power of energy rising up through my legs and my stomach, spinning there round and round as if building up for greater strength before I knew it had hit its limit. My eyes snapped open and I saw the world differently. A shadowed room void of any colour met me and the writhing body of Celina fighting against my power in the water.

Everything slowed down to a point I could have reached out and held one of the droplets in between my thumb and forefinger. A droplet created by the struggling body of death sharing a bath with me. I raised my hand and saw the tiny streams of power coming from it and when I moved it around it created a wave of energy. It was the reverse of what I saw when Demons or Angels fed from humans. It was as though I was using that sucked up energy against them and as soon as the thought entered my mind everything clicked into place.

My eyes homed in on my victim and I felt the injustice of being spied on as a child fuel my rage.

"Leave me alone." I said calmly before releasing the rest of my power and in seconds Celina was no more. Her body evaporated after it imploded in on itself…

And then the screaming started.

"Oh dear, I think I put in too much."

"You think?!" I heard Sophia saying in the distance. I felt myself moving but it almost felt like I was drunk.

"What are we gonna do, sister roo?" Pip asked sounding a bit panicked.

"What we always do…wing it!" Sophia said and I giggled.

"Well that's got to be a good sign…right?" Pip asked and I was sure I heard Sophia growl.

"Get her legs." I wanted to laugh at that as well, as it sounded like this comedy duo were trying to move a dead body and I guess that dead body was me!

"Am I dead?" I asked as I felt myself sliding along a floor.

"Nope, not dead…getting married yes, but definitely not dead." Pip answered and I opened my eyes to see the blurry green hair of Pip as she dragged me by my feet.

"Is this one of your games?" I asked giggling again. Man what was wrong with me…was I drunk?

"Ha, if it is then the next level after getting your behind out the bath is trying to get you dressed!" Sophia answered before suggesting,

"Come on, let's try getting her up."

"Is that wise...I mean don't humans usually go all pukey after you know...?"

"Well she can't get married lying down, I think Dom might notice!" Sophia snapped and Pip laughed,

"Well she does need to lie down for most of it, couldn't they just say their vows like that as well...or better still during the act?"

"Pip, I think the whole object here was to help her relax ready for *that* lying down part, not to comatose her!" Sophia shouted and I felt her raising my arm up and letting it drop to make her point.

"Ok, so she's a bit...loose."

"Pip! Anymore *loose* and she would be dead! And last I heard my brother isn't into necrophilia!" Sophia shouted and I giggled again.

"Eww. Ok, ok, I get your point, but hey, at least she sounds like she's enjoying herself." Sophia just groaned and said,

"Let's get her dry but be careful, you don't want to get her all worked up again."

"Stay away from the girly bits... Gotcha!" I felt them lifting me onto what I gathered was Sophia's bed and tried to move in a way that would help them only I couldn't feel anything happening. I felt them drying me off and I groaned as that heated feeling started back up again.

"Whoa, I didn't touch anything I swear!" Pip shouted dropping the towel. I moaned again and shifted on the bed feeling like a cat that needed to be stroked.

"Oh crikey and butter Nora! She looks like's she going into heat!"

"How much did you give her Winnie?" Sophia demanded and I felt her feeling my forehead.

"Now don't you Winnie me I…"

"Pipper!"

"Ok, ok so the whole bottle." Pip said after her scolding and Sophia bellowed,

"WHAT?!"

"Well I was worried about her, she seemed to be really freaking out about the whole thing and…and…" I opened my eyes and said,

"Don't fight guys, let's all just have a cuddle." I reached out to them and saw Sophia holding Pip back from getting to me.

"She's doesn't want that type of cuddle, Pip."

"Oh dear."

"Don't you mean oh shit?" Sophia corrected and then got up off the bed and declared,

"There's only one thing for it…we need cocktails."

"Holy Shit! What's in this thing?!" I shouted finally sitting up and leaning back against Sophia's kick ass iron bed that was covered in gothic flowers.

"Uh…it's probably best you don't know just drink up and you will be fine." Sophia said patting me on the leg and I closed my eyes and soaked in the feeling of being touched.

"Ooops, my bad." Sophia said taking her hand off me so the feeling disappeared.

"Oh God, what's wrong with me?" I asked feeling so ashamed but literally if one of them wanted to get it on right now and give me my first taste of girl on girl action then I was more than game! No! Damn it, what was wrong with me?!

"Pip what did you do?" I asked and she blushed fuchsia before she started backing away holding up her hands.

"Our little bundle of colour thought it would be a good idea to loosen you up a bit and relax you before tonight but she didn't read the label and put the whole lot in. Therefore you're a bit…"

"Rampant" Pip finished off for Sophia and I closed my eyes and counted to ten…it didn't work.

"Pip I would get up and try to strangle you but I am afraid if I do that I will end up kissing you and try to get into your pants, so I will just skip it and say…what do we do now?"

"I'd say, bottom's up!" Pip said and I took the drink in my hand and downed the lot. Then I started screaming again.

"By the Gods!" Sophia rushed over to me and took the glass from my hand before it shattered I was gripping it so hard. My throat felt as though it was on fire!

"Jesus! What was in that thing?!" I asked in a croaky voice as though I had been kicked in the larynx by a horse.

"Cinnamon." Pip said and I would have laughed if I'd had the functions left to. Then there was a knock at the door and Sophia and Pip both shouted,

"Shit!"

"Shit!" And then for some reason Pip grabbed the covers and threw them over me as if trying to hide a dead body. I mumbled with my head under the covers,

"Is this really necessary?"

"Coming! Just a minute!" Sophia shouted and came over and pulled the covers back off my face and whispered,

"Don't say anything, we will deal with this." And I got slightly concerned because if I didn't know these girls any better, then I would have thought they were about to kidnap me.

Sophia and Pip went over to the door and opened it just enough to put their heads through the crack, then they both said,

"She's nearly ready!"

"She's nearly ready!"

I would have laughed at their antics if their obvious worry wasn't making me panic.

"What are we going to do?!" Pip shouted once the door was closed and Sophia tried to calm her down.

"Ok, just breathe and the let's think a minute." Pip started taking deep breaths and Sophia backed her up onto the bed counting out these breaths as any minute it sounded like she was going to pass out from hyperventilating. She started getting it under control when she fell on the bed next to me and I turned my head to her and said,

"You good?" To which she just nodded.

"Great, now I hate to ask the obvious, considering I can't move and stuff, but shouldn't we be telling Draven and postponing this little soirée?"

"Ooh good word." Pip said and I rolled my eyes.

"No! We will not be postponing anything! Dom left me in charge of this part of the ritual and I won't let him down...now let's get her dressed." This was not what I wanted to hear.

Halfway through the mission impossible of getting my arms and legs to bend into a dress, I know knew the tortured life of a Barbie. Thankfully though the feeling started to come back to my body and movement became something to celebrate. However, the down side to all of this was that the drink Pip had given me, which I found out was my third, had now started to take effect.

So the good news was that I was about to walk into my wedding using my legs but the bad news was I was doing so shit faced drunk and staggering all over the place. Oh and the side effects still included me to be as randy as a goat on Viagra! Sophia and Pip walked me into the Temple and at the sight of

Draven stood there in his masterful looking cloak, my blood started to boil from need.

"It's working." Pip whispered and Sophia nodded smiling at everyone and said through gritted teeth,

"It would work a lot better, Kaz if it didn't look like you were desperate for the toilet." I just giggled and knew she was referring to the fact that just the sight of Draven stood there had me ready to jump on him and squirming with every step.

"Look at it this way, she's not being shy...at least we accomplished that." Pip added and Sophia sighed,

"There is that."

Oh and this was most definitely true. I looked around and saw everyone as I had that day when first finding the Temple. They were all dressed in robes and the difference in colour was all that distinguished them between the levels of importance as all faces were hidden. I thought this was a bit sad and discriminating but hell what did I know, I was drunk after all!

I looked down and vaguely took in my white dress that was made from the floatiest material I had ever seen. In fact it made me look like I was underwater. It was strapped tight across my breasts like a second skin and it was thin and see-through, showing my erect nipples underneath.

"Isn't my dress pretty?" I said picking up my skirt and twirling it round my legs like a little girl.

"Uh, yeah...sure."

"It's lovely." Pip said after Sophia tried to get me to leave my skirt alone. I looked back up to Draven and saw him stood waiting for me to reach him by the altar. He was tilting his head to one side as if he was trying to understand what was going on. I was about to wave when Sophia grabbed my hand instead.

"My brother is so going to kill me."

"Or thank you...have you seen how frisky she is...meow" Pip said just before we approached Draven.

"Hi handsome!" I said not realising how loud I was and finding it echoing around the Temple.

"Keira?" He asked me and I got up on my tip toes, looked up under his hood and said,

"Can we have sex now?"

"Oh God, we're doomed." Pip said at the same time that Sophia groaned.

"Is she drunk?!" Draven demanded and I placed my fingers on his lips, missing the first time and hitting his cheek.

"Ssshh, don't blame them. I drank too much because I'm nervous and they couldn't calm me down. I was scared I wouldn't be good enough for you and that you would think you were making a mistake and well then I drank too much snatching the bottle and downing it and…" I rambled on and on only stopping when Draven put his fingers to my lips this time.

"Ok, Ok, I understand love. Calm down. Let's just get through this together." After he said this I could practically hear Pip and Sophia sigh together in utter relief. I giggled and Draven smiled down at me obviously just glad to see me looking happy, even if it was from being a happy drunk. He then tipped my chin up and said,

"And don't let me hear you saying you think you're not good enough for me again." He growled this and I felt like clawing at his robe and asking him to take me back to his place, which was hilarious considering we were at his place and about to get married.

"Dom, should I start?" Vincent asked over the altar and I looked to see it was actually Draven's brother that was going to be marrying us.

"Oh cool! Hey Vinny boy, I didn't know you were into the whole wedding gig...? Are we paying him a good rate?" I asked Draven who along with his brother threw his head back and their combined laughter echoed around the massive space.

"Yes love, we are." He answered me and I couldn't tell whether or not he was teasing me.

"Are you ready?" I gulped, looked all around me at everyone stood there waiting but then turned back to the only man that I needed to look at to know my answer,

"I am so very ready to be your wife."

CHAPTER THIRTY-FIVE

KEIRA

VOWS

"Under the Holy Moon and on the eve of your Electus' sacred birth, the Gods deem her worthy of your love and blessed your joining when you asked for her hand. Do you Enki, Lord of the Earth, Dominic Draven take Catherine Keiran Williams to be your soul's keeper long beyond your vessel is dust and lost to the sands of time?" Vincent asked loud enough so all could hear.

"Oh that's lovely." I commented making Vincent smirk.

"I do." Draven said also loud enough for everyone to hear.

"Oh good." I said looking up at him and then mouthed the words,

"Thanks honey." Making him beam down at me before he mouthed back,

"You're welcome."

"Our King has accepted our sacred vows and gifted his soul

to another!" Vincent said making all the people in the room shout out an ancient sounding word I had no clue to its meaning and it thundered around the temple.

"Are you ready Keira?" Vincent whispered to me.

"Yeah totally." I whispered back and then shouted,

"I do!" Thinking this was my part of the question to accept. Vincent coughed over his laugh along with everyone else in the room and I looked back to smile at everyone. Draven chuckled and said,

"In a moment sweetheart."

"Under the Holy Moon, you stand before our King that the Gods deem worthy of your love and blessed your joining when he asked for your hand. Do you Electus, the Gods' Chosen One, Catherine Keiran Williams take Enki, Lord of the Earth and the God's chosen King, Dominic Draven to be your soul's keeper long beyond your body is dust and lost to the sands of time?" I smiled the biggest grin I ever felt in my life, to the point I could barely see with the tears in my eyes and said,

"I do. Most definitely!" I shouted this last part making everyone laugh and cheer, then continue shouting out this word I still didn't know when Vincent said,

"Our new Queen has accepted our sacred vows and gifted her soul to another!"

"Can I kiss him yet?" I asked and I heard Pip mutter behind me,

"Oh, she's going to be doing a lot more than that."

"Keira, are you sure you're ready for this?" Draven asked me and it took me back to our first conversation about this. Denial had been my first reaction and then flat out rejection my second. My last had been worry and that one had stayed with me until this point. Well until the point before Tweedle Dee and Tweedle Dum had decided to drug my bath water before getting me wasted on some crazy cocktails...but hey, mission accomplished I was definitely relaxed. Which was why I answered Draven honestly,

"Isn't it obvious, I'm your Electus…I was born ready." He burst out laughing then pulled me to him, yanked back his hood and kissed me for the first time as my husband. The whole room cheered and stamped their feet like war drums were being sounded. But I didn't care, I was already getting lost in Draven's kiss and falling quickly under the night's spell.

He snaked a hand in my hair and pulled me closer for a deeper kiss, one that made instinct take over. One of my legs lifted up, thanks to the split in my skirt and I hooked it over and around the back of his knee, not quite managing to get it any higher due to the height difference.

He growled low then lifted me up so I could hook both my legs around his waist. Then he walked me backwards and lowered me down onto the altar. It was strange, my reaction to seeing the Temple again, to seeing the altar. To seeing all of it after what had happened not long ago but none of it felt weird. If anything what was happening now was wiping all of that horror from existence as though it was rewriting history. All the bad things these grand walls had seen meant nothing in the sight of what was happening now and what was happening now was…

Magic.

Because as soon a Draven put his hands over my body everything else just disappeared, until we became the only two people there. I heard my clothes tear and for once cared little for the dress. He then pushed off his robe revealing his glorious naked body beneath and I gasped at the sight of such power. His wings unfolded and stretched out as the material fell to the floor. We became two naked lovers ready to consummate our marriage in not just the sight of the Gods but also in sight of all of these people.

He came back to me and I raised myself up and pushed myself against him, desperate to feel him inside me. The need was burning me up inside so quickly it was burning the drugs and the alcohol clean from my system and Draven knew this too.

"That's it, come back to me." He said leaning down and kissing my neck, working his lips up to my ear and then following the line of my chin. He ran his nose along the curves of my face, up my cheeks and down the side of my nose before placing his lips once more to mine. I opened my lips and drank him in, feeling the taste of him bursting on my tongue like ambrosia. It was like a battle to see who could get the most and when I moaned in his mouth he tore it from mine to find my neck to bite. Only instead he just held himself at my throat and I turned my head to show my King, my submission.

His wings shuddered as they cast our ready bodies in shadow and he ignited into purple flames.

Then my King roared out his own vow,

"I make you my Queen!" Then he thrust into me at the same time sinking his extended fangs into my neck and sucking the essence out of me. I came instantly and I was still screaming my release as the next one started to build. He pushed into me again and again, touching every nerve and even the ones I didn't know I had. He grabbed both my hands in one hand and forced them back above my head. Then he pulled his lips that were covered in my blood from my neck and started kissing my breasts. His eyes were the deepest colour of purple I had seen on him yet and the hunger in them was almost frightening.

He took in the sight of my breasts covered in my own blood and the strengthening I felt from him inside me told me he very much liked what he saw. He thrust quicker and bent his head to lick up the bloody kisses he had left and then decided licking wasn't enough. I cried out again as he bit into me for a second time and I pushed myself firmer into his greedy mouth.

He lapped me up as if he couldn't get enough of me and the pain of his bite was giving me such a rush I felt drunk from him alone this time. I pushed against his restraining hand trying in vain to rake my nails down his back, touch him, bite him, anything just so I could feel his skin on my fingertips.

"Draven, Draven, Draven." I said his name over and over as a plea for more.

"Tell me my Queen, what do you want?" He growled out the question and I pushed against his hands again.

"You want to feel me." He said rolling his hips and making me cry out as he touched that part inside me that felt like such a weakness it should have been criminal.

"Can you feel me?" He asked torturing me and I growled back, this time pushing against his length and clenching my core around him.

"Ahh!" He groaned and I smiled up at him doing it again.

"Behave or do you wish to unman me in front of my people?" He asked teasing making me try my luck and doing it again.

"Very well, my Queen, have it your way." And then he really let me have it and he held nothing back. He hammered into me and made me come over and over again until I was begging him for his own release. It was as though I had two forces inside of me fighting against each other. The sensitive parts of my womanhood were crying out as they couldn't take any more orgasms and the force and power it took away from me every time I came around his strength inside me. But then I never wanted this to stop as I became addicted to the euphoria like I needed it to live. Almost as if feeling that if he stopped I would fall and shatter into a million pieces…but that one death would have been the sweetest of all ends.

"I can't…" He started to say and I looked up to see him getting lost in the high too.

"I need…By the Gods Woman! I need you to bite me quick, I need to complete the ritual, now…GODS NOW!" Draven said getting panicked as he couldn't hold it off any longer and I loved that I could do that to him. So I said,

"As my King commands." And then I rose up using the last of my strength and I bit into his neck. The second I felt his blood bathe my tongue every muscle in my body tensed and my senses soared the waves of ecstasy as we came together.

Draven collapsed on top of me and barely had enough strength to hold his weight from crushing me and I too had no energy to try and move him. We'd just completed the ritual in front of the Gods and now we were one.

Now we were married and I was…

Mrs Draven.

CHAPTER THIRTY-SIX

KEIRA

BEING A WHOLE NEW WOMAN

I woke up to find myself cuddled up tight to a warm hard body where obviously I had been placed. Draven had his muscled arm around me and was holding me against his side as if he was scared he would wake to find me gone.

I actually woke feeling different but in a good way. As I usually did after we had made love I felt as if my whole body had been rejuvenated, only this time the feeling didn't fade. If anything it just kept getting stronger. I was actually surprised I didn't have a hangover.

The last thing I remembered was Draven picking me up once his strength came back to him and walking out of the Temple with me in his arms. I was just glad he hadn't walked through that part of the prison and the crypt beyond it, because I couldn't have thought of a worse sight to see after just getting married.

I just remember smiling into his chest after he lifted me higher to kiss the top of my head and whisper,

"Finally, my wife."

I fell asleep smiling. Which was exactly how I woke up.

"Finally, my husband." I whispered back to him and kissed the soft sun kissed skin on his chest. I looked up to find Draven was awake and looking at me in awe. It was how I could imagine he sometimes found me looking at him. Questioning myself if he was real and I wasn't in fact dreaming.

"Good morning, my handsome King." I said acting flirtatious.

"No, say it again." I frowned at first not knowing what he meant until it twigged.

"Good morning, *my husband.*" I said correcting my mistake and when he heard it his eyes seeped into purple sapphires the same colour as my ring.

"Good morning, my beautiful wife." He said before placing his finger under my chin and bringing my lips up to his. It was the most glorious way to wake up but then last night's vows sunk in and my cheeks flooded with colour. He started laughing even without me saying anything.

"Do not think of it my lovely wife, it is done."

"Yeah but we had sex in front of everyone!" I shouted shifting up and hearing Draven expel a 'Humf' sound as I elbowed him by accident in my haste getting up.

"Yes we did but this is how it is done. We consummate our union in front of those we love, those we worship and those we respect above and below us. And I must say you did so perfectly and I was surprised to see without holding anything back…"

"Yes but…" I was about to tell him that being under the influence would do that to you when he blew the wind from my doubting sails with his next comment,

"I am very proud of you." To which I melted.

"Oh and before anything else happens, like the day's celebrations coming crashing through the door in the name of Sister and Pip, I have something I want you to have." He shifted up and I made a sad face at not having him in the bed any longer. Then he laughed at me before grabbing the jeans left over the back of one of the chairs.

"I will be right back." He said leaning over to kiss me then quickly put on a pair of jeans and nothing else. I was most happy about the nothing else part, which changed when he said,

"Why don't you get changed so you will be ready by the time I am back?" He then nodded to the door of our dressing room.

"Why, I thought we could just stay in bed all day and celebrate ...*alone.*" I said waggling my eyebrows at him making him laugh shaking his head. He came over to kiss me again and said,

"You are insatiable my darling wife."

"Yes, yes I am." I said only half joking. He walked over to the door and said,

"Oh and wear something warm."

"Why, where are we going?" I asked raising an eyebrow at him.

"It's your birthday, I am taking you out." I smiled at him almost forgetting it was in fact my birthday. He was half way out of the door when I heard his voice again,

"Oh and Keira…"

"Yes?" I asked as he popped his head back round the frame,

"I told you I was giving you my wings." And then he winked at me and was gone.

I had one of the quickest showers after smelling my armpits and knowing there was no way I could get away with it. So I jumped in and out in record time and wrapped a towel round me to go in search of warm clothes for the day. I looked outside the window as I walked past on my way to the dressing room and saw it did in fact look like it wasn't going to be the nice hot summer's day that I had hoped for. It in fact looked like there was another storm on its way.

"Oh well." I said shrugging my shoulders as I walked through to the dressing room behind the tapestry. I was just debating where to go for a sweater or a top and hooded zip up when I walked straight into a giant present nearly knocking it over.

"Aww, Draven." I said thinking it must be from him and that was the real reason he told me to change. I smiled thinking was this what was in store for me today, lots of surprise presents? I thought back to Pip's party and started getting excited at the idea of what people might have bought me. At the time I had no idea mine and Pip's birthdays had been so close but was so glad it was and I had been a part of it, even after the crazy time I had getting there.

The gift was taller than me and covered in velvet purple paper with a huge black bow at the centre, holding it all wrapped together with its longer lengths of ribbon. I felt like a child when I started to rip into it, tugging at the bow and letting it fall to my bare feet.

"Uh…what is…?" I said as the last piece of paper fell and I was left staring at myself. It looked like a weird mirror that was never supposed to be a mirror. Its first purpose in life was obviously built into a place of worship… *a church.*

It was a tall stone arch that was once a window in a holy place and at one time held stained glass in its fixtures. It was divided into two smaller arches with a small pillar separating the two and at the top, nestled into the arch was a circle which was the only piece left to hold any coloured glass. In it was a symbol I had seen many times before but still had no clue as to what it meant…

My birthmark.

All around the frame's edges were the jagged remains of the glass it once held that no doubt long ago held a picture telling people of some holy story. But none of these were what really interested me or for that matter…

Frightened me.

No it wasn't that at all.

It was the face of a girl I knew staring back at me. It was the face of me from another life. Not the one I lived now. Not one I ever recognised living.

But it was me.

The mirror started to liquefy and took on a life of its own distorting my image, the one locked inside it that wasn't the life I knew.

"No…No…NO!" I screamed as hands reached out and took me.

But it was too late.

I was lost and I was captured by…

My own hands.

To be continued…

ABOUT THE AUTHOR

Stephanie Hudson has dreamed of being a writer ever since her obsession with reading books at an early age. What first became a quest to overcome the boundaries set against her in the form of dyslexia has turned into a life's dream. She first started writing in the form of poetry and soon found a taste for horror and romance. Afterlife is her first book in the series of twelve, with the story of Keira and Draven becoming ever more complicated in a world that sets them miles apart.

When not writing, Stephanie enjoys spending time with her loving family and friends, chatting for hours with her biggest fan, her sister Cathy who is utterly obsessed with one gorgeous Dominic Draven. And of course, spending as much time with her supportive partner and personal muse, Blake who is there for her no matter what.

Author's words.

My love and devotion is to all my wonderful fans that keep me going into the wee hours of the night but foremost to my wonderful daughter Ava...who yes, is named after a cool, kick-ass, Demonic bird and my sons, Jack, who is a little hero and Baby Halen, who yes, keeps me up at night but it's okay because he is named after a Guitar legend!

Keep updated with all new release news & more on my website
www.afterlifesaga.com
Never miss out, sign up to the
mailing list at the website.

Also, please feel free to join myself and other Dravenites on my
Facebook group
Afterlife Saga Official Fan
Interact with me and other fans. Can't wait to see you there!

 facebook.com/AfterlifeSaga
 twitter.com/afterlifesaga
 instagram.com/theafterlifesaga

ACKNOWLEDGEMENTS

To my Dravenites,

As always you guys are the first I wish to thank and feel blessed that you are all still taking this amazing journey with me as you have done with Keira in The Quarter Moon. It has been an emotional rollercoaster writing this book, but I know I could not have done it without all the love, support and understanding each and every one of you.

My next thanks go to the people who not only believe in me but make it their mission to push me to into believing in myself. As much hard work as I have put into this book there are also others behind the scenes that do so as well, so that you all can enjoy this story the way I always hoped.

To my Mum who devotes her time to seeing that each and every one of you never discovers just how bad (and sometimes funny) my spelling really is. As let's face it, no one really wants to read about Draven's Demon battling with his 'Angle' side :o)

We all Love you for it Mum!

Also to my sister who gives Afterlife books beautiful life with every front cover she designs, so complaints why we never get Draven naked on the front cover go to…only joking…we love you too! You make Afterlife shine and now thanks to you hundreds of people are saying,

"We Crave the Drave"

To all of my family and friends for not only following me down this mad road but also making it the craziest trip of a lifetime!

I would also like to mention Claire Boyle my wonderful PA, who without a doubt, keeps me sane and constantly smiling through all the chaos which is my life ;) And a loving mention goes to Lisa Jane for always giving me a giggle and scaring me to death with all her count down pictures lol ;)

. And last but not least, to the man that I consider my soul mate. The man who taught me about real love and makes me not only want to be a better person but makes me feel I am too. The amount of support you have given me since we met has been incredible and the greatest feeling was finding out you wanted to spend the rest of your life with me when you asked me to marry you.

All my love to my dear husband and my own personal Draven… Mr Blake Hudson.

ALSO BY STEPHANIE HUDSON

Afterlife Saga

A Brooding King, A Girl running from her past. What happens when the two collide?

Transfusion Saga

What happens when an ordinary human girl comes face to face with the cruel Vampire King who dismissed her seven years ago?

Transfusion - Book 1

Venom of God - Book 2

Blood of Kings - Book 3

Rise of Ashes - Book 4

Map of Sorrows - Book 5

Tree of Souls - Book 6

Kingdoms of Hell – Book 7

Eyes of Crimson - Book 8

Roots of Rage - Book 9

Afterlife Chronicles: (Young Adult Series)

The Glass Dagger – Book 1

The Hells Ring – Book 2

Stephanie Hudson and Blake Hudson

The Devil in Me

OTHER WORKS FROM HUDSON INDIE INK

Lightning Source UK Ltd.
Milton Keynes UK
UKHW010902201022
410800UK00002B/294